He gulped. By all rights, she should despise him. And yet... "Please."

His heart nearly beat out of his chest in anticipation and fear. How could he dare to beg? Her surprise was slowly replaced with a gentle, knowing smile. It was a smile he'd waited his entire life to see on a woman when she looked at him, full of desire and wicked intent.

He refused to touch her. He had to know she wanted this. That she would kiss him of her own volition. Her head moved closer, leaning inch by inch nearer to him. A strand of her hair swung forward to brush teasingly against his cheek.

Suddenly, she softly pressed her lips against his. Marcus was rendered speechless, bursting with the need for more. Her husky, passionate voice melted over him. "I have wanted to do that since I met you."

He's No Prince Charming

He's No Prince Charming

ELLE DANIELS

FOREVER

NEW YORK   BOSTON

Copyright © 2014 by Ellen Blash

Excerpt from *Once Upon a Duke* copyright © 2014 by Ellen Blash

Forever
Hachette Book Group
1290 Avenue of the Americas
New York, NY 10104

www.HachetteBookGroup.com

Printed in the United States of America

First Edition: October 2014
10 9 8 7 6 5 4 3 2 1

OPM

Forever is an imprint of Grand Central Publishing.
The Forever name and logo are trademarks of Hachette Book Group, Inc.

The Hachette Speakers Bureau provides a wide range of authors for speaking events. To find out more, go to www.hachettespeakersbureau.com or call (866) 376-6591.

The publisher is not responsible for websites (or their content) that are not owned by the publisher.

ATTENTION CORPORATIONS AND ORGANIZATIONS:

Most Hachette Book Group books are available at quantity discounts with bulk purchase for educational, business, or sales promotional use. For information, please call or write:

Special Markets Department, Hachette Book Group
1290 Avenue of the Americas, New York, NY 10104
Telephone: 1-800-222-6747 Fax: 1-800-477-5925

To Mom—
You'd stay up late to read me to sleep,
You'd pretend I didn't sneak out of my room to read ahead when I couldn't,
You'd read everything I wrote and save it in a forever box,
You'd drive me to the library three minutes before closing,
You'd take me to midnight book releases, and
You'd stand in line for me when I couldn't,
You gave me the world when you put my first book in my hands.
Without you, I'd never have been able to do this.
Love you.

Acknowledgments

My thanks go back many years to the many people who have made this story what it is today.

To Judith McNaught, who's book *Kingdom of Dreams*, inspired my love of all things romantic. To my high school history teacher, Donna H., who I now swear is some sort of prophet. Years before I even attempted to write my first romance novel, she would read the vignettes of my academic papers (which I was forced to include because essays are just so boring without them) and announce to the class that I would be a romance writer. To my first college professor, Beverly, who introduced me to National Novel Writing Month for extra credit. Who knew I could ever write all those words? And to Lucy M., for being the first outside my family to read my stories and tell me I was good.

Many thanks to the Unicorn Writers' Conference for introducing me to the world of publishing and connecting me with Gina Panettieri of Talcott Notch Literary Services. I liked her the minute I met her. To my wonderful agent, Rachael Dugas, who believed in my manuscript, and provided constant support and invaluable advice.

My eternal gratitude to the amazingly talented people of the Grand Central/Forever Publishing team. In particular, Lauren Plude, for taking a chance on my novel, and Megha Parekh, my editor, who did a truly incredible job bringing this book up to scratch—thank you for all your patience and expert advice!

To my aunts, uncles, and cousins, I have no words to convey how grateful I am for your unwavering support and enthusiasm. I also want to thank Deb, Denise, Hannah, Maura, Kevin, Vicky, Meghan, and the many others who've shared in my excitement.

And last, but not least, a thank-you to my mom for editing the monstrosities that are my first drafts, and to my dad, who actually read the book—out loud—and tried to make it better. And to my brothers, Dan and Jim, my biggest supporters, who will never read a word I write.

He's No Prince Charming

Chapter One

❦

While Beauty smil'd as she took horse;
Yet smil'd thro' many a generous tear,
To find the parting moment near!

—"Beauty and the Beast" by Charles Lamb

He had many names. The *ton* called him the Beast behind his back. To his face they called him my lord. If he could have stomached friends, they would have called him Fleetwood. His sister referred to him as a pain in her arse. He simply called himself Marcus.x

At the moment, everyone would have called him drunk.

And drunk was exactly what he wanted to be. Being drunk meant he felt nothing. It meant he remembered nothing. The blessed golden stuff meant that he could survive another day in his cage. But the relief didn't last long. Even as he stepped along the rain-dampened path, he could feel the pleasant warmth leaving his veins. He could feel the shadows of the past slowly creeping back to the forefront of his mind. Keeping them at bay was too much effort, but facing those memories was the more terrifying of the choices.

The ringing of his champagne-polished Hessians ceased as he halted on the cobblestone sidewalk below. A gas lamp illuminated the darkness. He opened his coat to search his pockets, ignoring the chill hanging in the air.

"Where is that blasted flask?" he mumbled, grasping clumsily through his clothing.

His hands greedily clasped the smooth metal of the container and quickly brought the opened flask to his lips. In minutes, the warmth spread to his limbs and the quiet oblivion, the numbness, returned. His mind fogged, blurring the past and present to a comfortable degree, allowing him to continue his way home unfettered by memories.

He'd taken only half a dozen steps towards his destination before he caught movement out of the corner of his eye. Marcus flinched, turning quickly with his fists raised, his heart beating erratically in his chest. For a moment, he'd thought...

He shook his head at his foolishness, fishing his flask out of his coat again. *Goddamned memories!*

He tipped the mouth of the flask against his lips, the cool surface like a kiss. But before the liquid relief slipped over the edge, he saw movement again. He jolted as if struck, his body spinning around to meet his assailant. The ring of metal on the ground set him jumping backward, his entire body on alert to defend himself from the lash of a knife or the sting of a whip.

Marcus found himself facing nothing but the empty street, the night shadows draping corners in darkness. He glanced down to find that his flask had hit the ground, causing the echoing ring. What had remained of his liquid relief now soaked the front of his overcoat and starched shirt.

His breath came in short gasps, his hand moved to hold his chest in an effort to control himself. He imagined that he looked exactly like the Beast the *ton* painted him— the whites of his eyes gleaming in terror and a wild look about him.

He bent to pick up his flask, but halted when a clatter echoed in the empty streets, followed by the flash of movement he'd seen before. With slightly unsteady hands, Marcus finished his task, debating whether he should investigate. Despite his constant quest for emotional numbness, he couldn't stop the surge of concern that flooded him. What if the movement was a result of someone being hurt? Frowning, he pocketed his flask and moved in the direction of the noise. His steps were unsteady as he walked closer to the wrought iron gates of an imposing house. Something about the house struck him as familiar. Stepping back, Marcus realized it was the back garden at the home of his fiancée, Miss Anne Newport. He tilted his head, listening for the noise. It was soft this time, but it had the distinctive clang of metal against metal.

Marcus edged around the corner of the tall fence and watched in stunned silence as a trio of boys slipped unnoticed from the gardens. A gas lantern swung in the hands of the tallest as he held open a gate for the other two behind him. The trio then hurried down the dark alley, pausing only a moment as the last turned to close the gate. Without warning he looked up. Marcus ducked back behind the corner as quickly as he could, unsure if he'd been discovered. He waited for some sort of alarm to be raised, but when nothing happened, he looked back around the fence. The alley was deserted.

Without thinking about what he was doing, he turned down the alley to follow the miscreants. Even in his current state, he knew nothing good would come from three boys skulking about one of the finer residences in the area at this time of night. His lips twisted in a sneer as he walked; his plan was simply to give them a scare. Lord knew his face could frighten even the stoutest of hearts.

Unconsciously, he ran a hand down his cheek, feeling the bumps and ridges of the scars he would forever bear. A tendril of darkness threatened to invade his thoughts, sending his shaking hands for his flask before he realized he was wearing what he sought. Closing his eyes against the sting of the past, he beat it back as best he could before continuing. If he focused on what he was doing, he might be able to escape it.

Marcus halted at the point in the fence where the trio had emerged. It looked as if the fence was whole, but when he ran his fingers over the rain-slicked bars, he could feel the slight indents of where they had been separated to create a passage. It seemed that the boys were more than simple troublemakers.

In the face of such ingenuity, he should have sought a constable. Whether it was the drink's false courage or his determination to never be cowed, Marcus couldn't say, but he kept going down the alley. He paused at the other end of it to watch the scene unfolding before him. The alley opened onto a street, fully illuminated by the light coming from the lanterns surrounding a waiting coach. The well-sprung vehicle looked as if it was about to embark on a long journey, with luggage packed tight wherever it could fit. Before it stood the three boys. Only...

As Marcus peered closer at them, he discovered something he would have missed had the light not revealed their figures. Two of the three boys were not boys at all. They were actually petite women dressed as men. Curiosity blossomed, his mind running through the possibilities as to why women would risk their reputations in such a way.

He refocused his attention as the shorter of the two women stepped forward to greet the coachman when the man dropped down from the driver's perch. The pair embraced tightly. Marcus dismissed him quickly enough, judging him to be mostly harmless. He was an average man of medium height, his only distinguishing feature an odd mustache that parted in the middle and curled at the ends. The woman, on the other hand, captured his full attention.

How he had mistaken the little sprite for a boy was beyond him. He could only blame the two bottles of very fine whiskey he had consumed. Marcus watched the seductive roll of her lush hips in the form-fitting trousers. His interest instantly piqued as his gaze roamed over the impossibly curvy figure on such a tiny frame. He felt his mouth suddenly go dry as her shirt stretched snugly across her bosom, showing it off in every detail.

How long had it been since he'd had a woman? His sudden lust sent his mind wandering down an avenue he did not wish to explore. He did not like to think about the sad circumstances he'd been reduced to in order to enjoy feminine company. The few times he'd attempted to take a mistress had resulted in rejection, the women claiming they couldn't stomach him. He'd made a habit of paying a small fortune for a whore in the dark.

Just looking at the wee thing illuminated in flickering rays of light made him long for things he could never have. Things that were simply not for him. Ever.

"John! How have you been, old man?"

Her husky voice flowed across the cobbled street and his mind like cool water soothing a burn. It drowned his dark thoughts, dragging him back to the present, something very few people had ever been able to do. Despite his annoyance that this fraud and prowler could affect him in any way, he leaned forward to hear the conversation better.

"I'm doing as well as can be, Miss Danni. The two boys got into a scrape with ol' man Howard the other day. Me wife damned near took off their 'ides."

At this, Miss Danni shook her head with a soft clucking sound. "I do not blame her. Mr. Howard has threatened to send the constable after them."

"They'll be the end of us, I'm sure. Never have little ones yourself, if you know what's best for you."

It was then Miss Danni smiled. It changed her face from simply pretty to stunning. Marcus caught his breath, his hands clenching against the sudden urge to possess her. It was utter madness, but then again, he'd been mad for most of his life.

"Hush, John! Don't let Hu hear you say that." Her murmured chuckle was as smooth as her voice.

"Too late for him, anyway." The amusement in his reply echoed across to Marcus. John glanced over to the other pair, who waited some steps away. Then, glancing skyward, "You picked a wonderful night for this, Miss Danni! The mud will slow us down."

Her muffled laugh reached him as she inspected something on the carriage. "As if I conjured up this weather! Besides, the roads are still passable."

John motioned about him as if the wet streets were all the evidence he needed to be concerned for the party's welfare.

"Don't fret. You're worse than a mother hen," she continued, ignoring his sudden glare. "We have not been seen and no alarm has been raised. You will all be halfway to Gretna before they even realize Anne is gone."

Marcus tried not to feel emotions. They led to memories, but he could not stop the shock that rippled through him at the name. *Anne.* It couldn't be the same. There were plenty of women bearing that name in London. Possibly even a maid in her household. With growing dread, his gut registered the impending doom before his mind would accept it.

His gaze flew to the other girl, standing beside the only real boy—or man—in the group, his burly build suggesting a much more mature age. He was off at one end of the street, lantern held aloft, casting the second girl in a soft glow as she scanned the night. An anxious expression clouded her angelic face, the face he'd looked at so often this past month. She had removed her cap in favor of twisting it in her hands, exposing a long rope of light-colored hair braided in seeming haste, nothing like her traditional coiffures. There was no doubt as to the woman's identity. It was Miss Anne Newport, daughter of one of London's wealthiest merchants. His fiancée. Running away from him.

He wasn't sure what to feel. How could he have been so stupid? He'd known the marriage was contracted for convenience, but he'd begun to believe she might eventually see him in a favorable light. They'd had amicable conversations. He'd been kind, respectful—a gentleman. She'd seemed cooperative, if perhaps a bit hesitant. Apparently he'd been wrong, as the scene before him revealed the truth. Now he was going to suffer embarrassment on top of his crushing defeat, and he couldn't bear to think about the repercussions for his sister.

Miss Danni bent forward to speak an aside with the coachman, her voice barely audible across the distance. "Where is the groom?"

The coachman shook his head, a worried expression crossing his face. Danni gave Anne a considering look before striding to stand beside her. "He knows that tonight is the night, right?"

Her voice shook as she spoke, sounding as if she was trying to convince herself. "Y-yes, I managed to speak with him in private today to confirm the details. He assured me he would be here. George is not one to change his mind at the last minute. 'Tis one of the reasons I fell in love with him."

Love. Marcus choked back the laugh welling in his chest. He felt light-headed with the absurdity of the events he was witnessing. The vague thought that he was becoming hysterical collided with another sobering thought. There was no doubt that this groom was conning Anne, playing on her schoolroom fantasies and paying his three assistants a large sum to help him lay claim to her inheritance. Marcus could all too easily imagine such a thing happening to someone as naive as Anne. He had half a mind to halt this entire affair, but he couldn't make himself move.

Anger snaked through his chest. That Anne would do this to him, that she so hated the idea of an alliance with him she would run away under the cover of night. Even as he stood there, knowing they had not loved each other, knowing the marriage was a mere business arrangement, he thought she could have at least showed him a little consideration. Revenge curled with anger in his gut. His cruel side wanted her to get what she deserved.

The fraud nodded reassuringly, staring down the avenue as she joined the girl and the lantern bearer in their vigil. "I'm sure he'll be here."

Marcus stood waiting as well, his drunken thoughts swirling down a well of emotions. If this George was really a con man, then why was he not claiming his prize? Could it be he'd grown a conscience? Had regrets? A thought struck his befuddled brain. Could it be that George was the intended victim and not Anne?

His shoulder propped up against the damp brick wall, his mind slowly transformed Anne into his little sister. He could see the desperate hope in her green eyes, shining with worry and hopeful anticipation. In his imagination, he envisioned her returning to her room, devastated from being abandoned by her "true love." Or, perhaps even worse, returning to her home, trapped in a miserable marriage for the rest of her life.

His concern won out over his desire for revenge. If it were Caro in Anne's place, he'd hope her soon-to-be-ex-fiancé would have tried to stop this disaster. His lungs constricted with his anger. It wasn't the sharp, blinding rage that he was so used to. It was a deep-seated, writhing storm, threatening to roll into a more malevolent force. He pushed off the brick, his feet seeming ready to fly him into the light, but a quiet shout from where the three "men" stood stopped him. He drew back as a slender figure stumbled out of the darkness. Marcus caught the gleam of glasses reflecting in the lamplight just before the youth fell forward, seeming to trip over nothing.

"Oh, Georgie! Are you all right, my love?"

Anne fell to her knees, trying to assist George up from the ground. He gave her a lopsided grin. "I'm so sorry to be late, Annie, but Mr. Hessler kept me, and I had to stay if I'm to continue to support us. But I came as fast as I could."

As George spoke, his hands cast around for the glasses that had fallen off when he'd tripped. Danni scooped them up a few feet from him and pressed the wire rims into his hand. "There you go, George. Mind your feet now."

"Yes, Miss Green. I'll adapt to these new glasses at some point."

Marcus wasn't paying any attention. Pieces were clicking together in his head. And as he solved the puzzle, his rage shifted from defending Anne back to condemning her to hell. George was a clerk for his solicitor's office. George was the man who'd been sent over to the Newport house to arrange the engagement documents. Mr. Hessler had mentioned him frequently. He'd said the boy had a bright future in law. With Marcus's fury growing at yet another humiliation, he was in the mood to make sure George never reached his potential.

Marcus watched Danni and the lantern-bearer exchange a concerned glance. He'd wager they were worried they wouldn't get paid if George killed himself in some sort of clumsy accident.

The clerk slid the spectacles back onto his nose before accepting a hand up from the ground by Anne and the burly man. Danni was already walking back towards the driver, her short legs taking quick and confident strides. She pulled a bag from her coat pocket and handed it up to John, the jangle of coins clear across the way. "This should take care of the expenses for the trip. Be careful, John."

"Always am, Miss Danni."

He watched as the couple climbed into the coach with Danni holding the door for them. Before they departed, she leaned inside to speak, giving Marcus a delicious view of her derriere. Her voice carried across the street. "Now remember what I said. You are two brothers going on holiday to the north of Scotland until John says it's safe to change into more appropriate clothing. Then you are Mr. and Mrs. Jenner, on a trip to visit your family. Do not deviate from my plans. They've worked before. Is that all understood?"

"Oh, yes! And thank you so much!" Anne's voice practically squealed with excitement from inside the carriage.

"It was no trouble. I expect to hear from you when you return, and do feel free to recommend my little bookshop to your acquaintances. Discreetly, of course."

The reflection of light in glasses reached Marcus as the groom spoke. "We will, Miss Green. And again, Anne and I thank you for all your help."

"Yes, well, off with you now."

She shut the door and tapped it, giving the signal for the coachman to drive. As it moved forward, Danni waved, a watery smile on her face. "I always love happy endings, Hu. Don't you?"

The lantern-bearer answered with a grunt. Marcus thought he caught a roll of her eyes as she turned away from the traveling coach. "Honestly, Hubert Tollman, can you do nothing more than grunt? I think I've only ever heard you speak one full sentence once in the entire two years I've known you."

Silence reigned before a long-suffering sigh escaped the petite woman. "How in the world did a chatterbox like Annabel ever end up with a man like you, Hubert?"

Again there was no response and Marcus watched as they disappeared into the dark of the night. He stayed in place, waiting for the sound of their footsteps to fade into nothingness before he moved from his hiding spot. Once under the dim light where the event had occurred, he faced the way the coach had gone, and then glanced down the avenue where the two figures had disappeared. He wasn't sure what to make of all that he'd witnessed, his emotions were still too raw, but one thing he knew for certain.

He needed a drink.

Chapter Two

❧

"All that my castle own'd was thine,
"My food, my fire, my bed, my wine:
"Thou robb'st my Rose-tress in return,
"For this, base Plunderer, thou shalt mourn!"

—"Beauty and the Beast" by Charles Lamb

Thunder boomed overhead, followed promptly by the sound of shattering glass. Danni lifted her nose over the edge of the society column long enough to watch her friend storm down the stairs. Her carrot red hair stood at odd angles, her white muslin dress drenched down the front with afternoon tea. As she reached the bottom step, she slammed her foot down on the ground, grinding out a roar of frustration from the back of her throat.

Danni was thankful the newspaper hid her mouth. She doubted her dearest friend, Annabel, would appreciate the smile curling her lips. "I find it truly singular that your husband manages to avoid speaking even when he is nearly on his deathbed."

Annabel's brown eyes narrowed with her ire. "Would that be true. The man is the biggest baby I've ever met. Little Simon behaves better when he has a fever. That *man* only has the sniffles!"

"Those are the loudest sniffles I've ever heard. Does he save up his noise quota for them?"

As if to prove her point, thunder rolled through the shop again as Hu, Annabel's husband, sneezed. Annabel stomped her foot in a helpless gesture, her fair skin flushing to match her hair.

"Might I suggest a heavy dose of laudanum?"

"Hu won't take it. I've even tried forcing it down his throat, but that only resulted in an argument."

"Did the argument consist of glares and sullen stares?"

"Would it kill you to have some sympathy for me?"

"Probably," she smirked.

Annabel stormed over to stand before Danni. Without warning, the redhead snatched the paper from her hands and proceeded to stomp it beneath her feet. When the paper was crinkled and torn beyond repair, her friend stopped, her color high and her chest rising and falling rapidly from her fury. Danni folded her hands in her lap, leaning back into her reading chair. "Are you quite done?"

Brown eyes narrowed to pinpoints. "I would be careful if I were you."

Danni couldn't help but grin with unrepentant glee. "Why is that?"

"You never know when one of your dinners might contain poison."

Danni's uproarious laughter was interrupted by the sudden cries of a baby. Her friend's high color faded, replaced by fatigue. "Now Simon's awake."

Sighing, she took pity on Annabel. "Why don't you go take care of the front for a little while? I'll see to Simon and the big baby."

Annabel's warm arms wrapped around her. Her friend smiled with relief. "Thank you. Don't pay Hu's blustering any attention."

"I never do. Now off with you."

Her grateful friend rushed away without a backward glance. *No doubt running before I change my mind.* With a heavy sigh, Danni trudged slowly up the stairs, not looking forward to what awaited her.

She traversed the untidy sitting room, moving along the hall to the small room that belonged to Simon. Leaning over the crib, Danni gathered up the pink cherub, rocking the little one in her arms. The contentment she always felt when holding him washed over her quickly, followed by a sharp ache gripping the region of her heart. She wanted a baby of her own. At four and twenty, she was still young enough, but for years now she had been far too disillusioned with the opposite sex to attach herself to one long enough to procreate. Spending her first and only season surrounded by fortune hunters could do that to a woman.

She longed for her perfect match, her soul mate, a man made just for her, but that seemed a dream for only a few lucky couples. Caring for Simon always brought to mind the match her father wanted to arrange for her. His choice was a rising political star by the name of Michael Rathbourne, the Earl of Hemsworth. He was a perfect gentleman, who always treated her as if she were a princess. Lord Rathbourne was rather dashing, too, with stunning hazel eyes and a dazzling smile. In the past two months, he'd been her escort to balls and operas, earning her more than one envious glance from debutantes and their mothers. According to all, he was the catch of the decade, and she should be thrilled to marry him. She knew he would be a courteous husband and believed she could grow to love him. And, perhaps, with time, that grand passion she dreamed of would be hers as well.

Her father, a member of Parliament, would be thrilled to have the earl's political connection and Danni wanted desperately to please him, to bring back the father he used to be. Perhaps, if she agreed to the match, her father would finally return to being the kind and warm man he had been before her mother's death, not the distant, cold figure she'd grown so accustomed to.

Pushing away the crushing loss that she would no doubt carry for the rest of her life, she consoled herself with the love she felt for this little boy. She ran her finger over Simon's crinkled brow, watching it smooth under her repeat strokes. His puppy brown eyes widened, and his favorite appendage—his big toe—popped into his mouth. She wanted a child just like him to love. And she could have that with the earl. All she had to do was say "yes" to her father. It all seemed so *very* easy, and yet... she hesitated to do so.

I'm such a fool.

With a soft smile and a sigh, she laid the bundle back in his wooden crib and handed him his carved blocks to gnaw. "Simon, I need you to behave for a few moments while I care for the *real* baby, all right?"

The one-year-old paid her no mind, already occupied by the chewable corners of the blocks. Leaving the room, she entered the one across the hall. A sputtered laugh escaped her when she spied Hu. He sat with his back propped up against the headboard, a lethal glare in his eyes, but a hot water pack draped over his head and his shiny red nose ruined the effect. Danni swallowed more laughter. She moved to his bed, rewrapping the layers of quilts around him and ignoring his glittering gaze. "Poor honey bear!"

His frown sharpened fiercely at the one endearment of Annabel's she knew he despised. Danni had no doubt she would be dead if Hu had had the strength for it. Stifling another laugh, she grabbed the bottle of laudanum Dr. Peters had delivered. Hu's jaw tightened at the sight, as if she could overpower him and force it down his throat.

She turned the brown bottle over in her hands, examining the barely touched contents inside. "Annabel needs a rest. She's left you in my *very* capable hands."

Out of the corner of her eye, she thought she saw trepidation cross his face. *Good.* She and Hu both knew she would not put up with his self-pitying theatrics. "My first order of business is to entertain you, since you do not seem to need anything else at the moment. Shall I read the latest finding from the British Archaeological Association? Or perhaps you'd be more interested in Fordyce's *Sermons*? As you know, I'm ever in need of improving my behavior."

Resigned, Hu silently reached for the medicine. Danni handed him the bottle and grinned as he took a swig of the contents. Hu screwed on the cap and returned the bottle to her with a glare before settling deeper into the covers. "That's what I thought. Have a good rest, honey bear."

With that parting shot, Danni sailed out of the room and walked down the stairs. She was about to settle into her chair with the second copy of the paper she always kept on hand. If Annabel didn't get to it in a fit of temper, Simon's curious mouth did. She had just tucked it under her arm to gather a quill and ink when a frazzled Annabel returned to the backroom.

"What are you doing down here? Where are Hu and Simon?"

"Both are fast on their way to sleep."

Annabel's shock that her "boys" were behaving was interrupted by an angry ring from the bell above the front door. Her harried look returned. "I don't know what to do. Several customers have asked for assistance and I can't find anything in the store. Hu knows where all the stock is inventoried, not me."

"So that bell was…" She trailed off.

"Another customer leaving!"

Danni sighed. She didn't know what books they carried either. Hu was the one who usually ran the bookstore and Annabel assisted him with the transactions on occasion. Danni always entered through the back alleys and didn't even order the new books when inventory needed replenishing. She only cared about what happened in the back.

To unsuspecting society, G. Green Books was a reputable establishment on Bond Street, in possession of fine quality reading, but Gretna Green Bookings, the illicit elopement agency for forbidden lovers, was run from the backroom. In exchange for running the front of the store,

Danni allowed Hu and Annabel to live in the rooms above it and paid them handsomely with the profits from the book sales. Often she split the income from Gretna Green Bookings with them as well.

Danni had no need for the money. She was the daughter of James Strafford, Baron Seaton, one of the most influential men in the realm, and Mary Stowe, the wealthiest heiress to ever grace London's elite ballrooms. Not only had they loved her, but they, quite unfashionably, had loved each other. Danni's mission was to give others the chance to have what her own parents were fortunate enough to share: the kind of respect and passion that lasted a lifetime.

The thought of her mother always caused great sadness to overtake her. Mary Strafford died shortly after Danni's failed debut in London society six years ago, leaving Danni alone with her grief-stricken father. Her father had quickly immersed himself in his politics, leaving her unsupervised. Feeling both orphaned and abandoned, Danni had been ecstatic when Annabel turned to her for help to elope with one Hubert Tollman. She'd been so desperately lonely and aching for adventure. The events had given her an idea and soon after her business had been born.

"Go rest. I'll shout if I need you."

"But—"

"You look exhausted, Annabel. I'm sure I'll figure something out."

"Danni—" The redhead tried again.

She ignored her friend and stepped through the door that divided the store. With a resounding slam, she shut it in Annabel's face, effectively cutting off all that was— while not quite illegal—frowned upon.

A woman running a bookstore was bad enough, but if her actual occupation as lady in shining armor who rescued fair damsels from evil suitors was exposed, said lady's reputation would be in tatters and her father's political career would be destroyed. Not to mention the irate mothers and fathers who would cheerfully string her up by her toes for interfering in their fine marriage contracts.

Her poor toes curled in protest at the thought as she glanced around the storefront. Thankfully, it was empty of customers. Praying no one would enter, she went behind the counter to find the quill and ink pot. Unfolding the daily newspaper across the countertop, she studied the listings of engagements and gossip columns, looking for possible clients. It was just good business sense to be in possession of the latest information, since one of these young ladies could come through her door at any minute seeking assistance.

At that very thought, the bell above the door rang. Hoping it was actually one of the possible clients she'd been considering moments before, she folded her paper and she walked from behind the counter with a greeting on her lips.

Her first thought, as the customer appeared from behind one of the bookcases, was that a prior customer had sent a thug to inflict revenge for poor service. Standing before her was a monster out of a fairy tale. The air virtually crackled around him with barely contained violence, an animalistic draw that kept her eyes riveted as if he would lunge at any moment. He towered over her, a giant with mile-long limbs as thick as trees. His square face was littered with the ravages of a hard life. One scar traveled down the left side of his face from his hairline to the underside of his jaw. Another split a fair brow in two, barely missing his eye. The third slashed across his chin, pulling at his full lower lip. He turned the side of his head with the most vicious scar away from her slightly, his overly long white-blond hair shifting across his brow.

Nothing about this man was reassuring. His eyes made her feel like an object of prey. They were bright as emeralds and just as cold. They expressed nothing, held nothing. If eyes were indeed windows to the soul, this man appeared to have none.

It took her a full minute to tear her gaze from his face and glance at the rest of him. She noted the way his buff breeches seemed poured over his muscular legs. His broad frame was perfectly fitted into a dark blue super fine coat with a silver waistcoat. He cut a dashing figure—a lordly figure—if one didn't look at his face. That thought only reassured her that a spurned customer hadn't sent a thug to murder her. They'd sent a fellow lord instead.

Taking a deep breath, Danni dug inside for courage. "How may I help you, sir?"

His lips moved in a cold imitation of a smile. Danni fought back a shiver of fear as she pressed back into the counter. She would not cower.

But she would stay outside his reach.

He looked casually about the room, skimming the shelves overrun with multitudes of novels and heavy tomes. His removed a pliant leather glove from one hand, then the other, and then pierced her with his gaze as she imagined a collector would pierce a bug. "In the end, Danni, I hope to be the one who will be helping you."

Shocked he knew her name, she gasped. "Excuse me, sir?"

Danni was impressed when her voice didn't quake. It was a small accomplishment in the face of such an overwhelming presence.

"You, my darling Miss Green, are going to help me with some rather unpleasant business. In return, I will agree not to expose your little secret."

Oh God, no! Confusion and fear gripped her so tightly she could barely draw breath. He could not possibly know about her business. Perhaps he knew only that she used an alias. She'd thought by using the name Green, she would shield her father from scandal, but it wouldn't take a Bow Street Runner long to discover whose name was on the deed to the building. "What sort of secret could I possibly have, sir? I am a lowly shopkeeper."

"Come now, don't play the fool. I'd thought you at least had a little intelligence. You're much more than a bookseller."

"I *am*?"

His eyes examined her slowly from head to toe. Danni felt as if he could see every inch of her body beneath her petticoats. "Oh, yes. You *are* a shop owner, but what type of shop you run is debatable."

A ball of tension that had formed in Danni's chest dropped and landed heavily in the pit of her stomach. Which would be worse to be exposed? Her name or her business? Her only defense was to *deny, deny, deny*. "If you look around, you can see there are only books here, sir."

"Stop." His voice was quiet thunder, reverberating through the room and down to the tips of her toes. His face was stretched taut as if he were restraining great emotion. "No games."

"A-all right," she stammered, attempting to appease him. "Suppose what you say is true. I have this imaginary, alternate business. What exactly am I supposed to help you with?"

His face relaxed marginally. Instant relief swept through her, but she would be a fool to lower her guard completely. Before she could blink, the man stepped close to her, too close. Danni felt the pulse of his heated skin radiate into the air between them, suddenly warming her. Startled at the sensation, she stepped away, her back pressed tightly up against the counter, his body trapping hers. Her eyes flew up to meet his, their green depths dark and unfathomable.

Slowly, his head lowered until she felt the stirrings of his breath across the rim of her ear. Her breath froze and her body tensed against the onslaught of his masculinity, held immobilized as if under some spell. The scent of fine liquor wafted towards her. She frowned as his rich baritone rumbled over her senses. "You owe me a wife, little one."

Her mouth went dry. *Oh, God help me!* She knew exactly who this man was—Marcus Bradley, Marquis of Fleetwood.

What was it society called him . . . ? The Beast.

And the man she'd deprived of a bride only two nights ago. One of her worst fears had finally come to pass. A disgruntled member of the jilted party had found her out and now demanded revenge.

Owe him a wife? He couldn't be asking her to be his bride, could he? He'd not indicated he knew about her fortune. But if he did, was he here to court her? *In this manner?* No matter what he tried, she would never marry him. To be forever tied to this beast of a man was too much for any woman to bear.

Determined not to be intimidated or to break eye contact, she gathered her courage and placed her hand on the center of his chest to firmly push him away. The contact seared her palm. She fought the urge to curl her fingers into the soft fabric of his lapel. An unidentifiable spark sprung to life in his mesmerizing eyes. Her throat tightened and she turned her head away. In that instant, they both knew she had acquiesced, and he was the victor in their silent battle of wills. "And how am I to repay this supposed debt?"

His head tilted slightly and away, further hiding the grotesque scar along the side of his face. He seemed to hesitate, then drew in a steadying breath.

Confused, her brow furrowed. "Well?"

"I want your help to kidnap an heiress."

Frozen with disbelief, Danni was not sure she'd heard correctly. "Pardon?"

The imposing giant seemed to step back reluctantly, with a grim smile that she judged was as close to a genuine one as he could produce. "Having an attack of morality, fraud? A little late now that you've been discovered, eh?"

"I can assure you I have no idea what you mean, and I do not appreciate such insults, sir."

"They are hardly insults, little one, when it's the truth."

"What truth, exactly, do you speak of?"

His eyes narrowed to jade slits. "Come now. Must you continue this game? I witnessed your little escapade with Anne, and your goals were clear. You help fortune hunters trap young girls barely out of the schoolroom into miserable marriages. I imagine you manage to abscond with a generous portion of their inheritance in the process."

Danni sputtered with shocked outrage. "That is a blatant lie! I only help trapped women escape unwanted marriages so they may marry for love."

He scoffed. "Ah, I see. Anne was trapped with me, a peer of the realm who is able to grant her every whim, but she's *not trapped* with a law clerk sniffing about her skirts for the money attached to her name."

"And you weren't marrying her for her money yourself?"

Something flickered in his eyes, something akin to guilt? "She was to retain control over most of it after our marriage."

Danni's mind raced with possibilities she'd never considered. Afraid she may have made a mistake, Danni had to ask the one question that mattered. "So you love her?"

The marquis's jaw hardened. It was the only answer she needed. It was also the answer that reassured her she'd done the right thing. Miss Anne was better off with George.

Danni crossed her arms and lifted her chin in a stubborn tilt. "Ha! You are exactly the type of man you accuse me of conspiring with. I am merely assisting desperate young girls to avoid the likes of you."

"Well, unfortunately, you now find yourself in the position of assisting the *likes of me* to save your *own* pretty arse. I am still in need of a bride." He leaned forward, too close again, to emphasize his point.

"So you would like to *kidnap* one? You do realize kidnapping is a hanging offense."

His cold demeanor returned with a vengeance, his eyes transforming to ice. "If that's your only concern, then we best not get caught. Especially you."

Danni squeaked, "Me?"

The man nodded, his eyes sliding insolently over her figure before meeting her gaze again. Danni had the sudden, self-conscious feeling that she had been judged and found entirely lacking. She didn't want it to hurt, but damned it did.

She wrapped her arms protectively, and comfortingly, around her waist. Danni managed to gather enough courage to glare at him.

"I'm a nobleman and as such, I have connections that will protect me. If we are caught, you're the only one in real danger of hanging."

"So I'm supposed to risk everything to make you happy?"

"You"—the man's head dipped, his eyes full of dripping condescension—"won't have anything left if you don't."

Danni stood speechless in the face of such a horrid trap.

"What is your answer, Danni? Will you cooperate with my plan or am I going to spend tomorrow afternoon speaking to every father whose daughter has recently eloped?"

To prove his point, he pulled a stack of newspapers from the pocket of his overcoat. The ball in her stomach turned to lead as she stared at the damning evidence. He had no proof, but even a rumor was enough to reveal her secrets, end her business, destroy her plans for marriage to the earl, and completely destroy her father. Could she sacrifice some unfortunate girl's future to this fiend in order to save her own father? In order to save all of her future clients? In order to *save herself*? Which was the lesser evil?

She felt absolute despair as she turned her gaze back to the marquis's unwavering eyes. She should tell him he need not look any further than herself for an heiress, but she was not about to become a martyr. She didn't wish this beast on any member of her sex, especially herself. Mustering every ounce of hatred for him into her voice, she spat, "'Tis little wonder you're known as the Beast."

His features tightened again, his breathing faltered, his eyes flared green flames. His body tensed, and his fists clenched. For a moment she feared she was in physical danger, but then he turned abruptly. "I see that you won't easily make your decision. You have precisely until ten o'clock tomorrow before I begin my social calls."

He slapped the stack of articles onto the counter as he left, and the bell ringing echoed through the silence of the emptied shop. Danni watched his retreating form disappear from sight through the shop windows. Her gaze fell to the pile on the counter.

What was she going to do?

Chapter Three

Her elder Sisters, gay and vain,
View'd her with envy and disdain,
Toss'd up their heads with haughty air;
Dress, Fashion, Pleasure, all their care.

—"Beauty and the Beast" by Charles Lamb

Marcus stared at the solid oak door barring him from his father's office, studying the twists and turns of the wood, wishing he could be anywhere but here. He'd stayed away as long as he could, but his father was as relentless as he was ruthless. He waited, mustering the courage he needed to face the man who had made his life hell since he took his first breath. His mind turned with all the possibilities for his father's summons, but he had not been able to decipher his motive. He lifted his slightly shaking *hand, pressing it to his chest, where the letter calling him home was tucked away in his breast pocket. To his ears, the crinkle of vellum was deafening in the eerie silence, which was only interrupted periodically by the slow tick of the clock and the scurrying footsteps of the servants trying to avoid their master.*

Finally, he could delay no longer. Taking a calming breath, he raised his hand to knock on the door. The sound resonated down the hall as his knuckles brushed the wood. The force of his knock pushed the unlatched door open on its well-oiled hinges. The smell of stale whiskey wafted from the confines of the room, starting a thread of dread in Marcus's stomach. The tension was palpable. Pressing forward, Marcus stepped across the threshold into the dim interior. He wasn't surprised by the melodramatic scene that greeted him. The curtains were drawn tight; their dark color blocked out the light as well as any hope of escape. A fire blazed in the massive marble fireplace, where stone gargoyles guarded the opening as if they were minions of hell come to life, their faces cast in half shadow.

His father's features were exposed in the same shadows, his face fierce and worn from his years of debauchery. The man who had created him was well known to use all means necessary to intimidate his enemy. That included his own son.

"Shut the door." The words rent the air, soft and silver quick. Marcus had no wish for the servants to overhear, so he obeyed his father for the moment. However, he was no longer the little boy who feared

the man before him. He had spent one and twenty years doing whatever he could to appease the half-shadowed monster before him, but that would no longer be the case. He moved dutifully to stand before his father, keeping the desk between them.

"Sit."

Marcus remained standing. He knew all his father's games. And he'd be damned if he was going to march right across the chessboard and into his trap.

He watched his father's temple indent, his jaw hardening at Marcus's silent rebellion. The man stood, trying to intimidate him with his size as he'd done when Marcus was a boy. With satisfaction, Marcus noticed he was now taller than his father by several inches. He also knew the moment his father realized it, too. His eyes flashed with barely restrained rage before narrowing to pinpoints.

"You are to marry this season."

His father's announcement could not have shocked him more. He stood in stunned silence, his mind whirring, trying to understand. Then he saw his father's lips curl back into a knowing, cruel sneer. Damn him! *How could he know of the vow Marcus had made to himself when he was but a boy? On that cold night, as he lay bleeding and crying in the tower room of Fleetwood Manor, his family's seat, he'd sworn never to marry. He'd pledged never to carry on the line that his father treasured so. Treasured above all else, including his own son's welfare. During all those years in hell, Marcus had known he would survive the abuse, the beatings. He'd known because he was the precious heir, the one who would carry the title on into the future. Marcus's greatest revenge would be to refuse to marry, to deny his father the legitimate heir he craved.*

"I will not." He steadily met the eyes that looked so much like his own.

His father nodded with a wicked, spiteful grimace. His next words confirmed Marcus's suspicions. "I thought not. I do not appreciate your defiance, Marcus."

He stood still, his head held high, refusing to succumb to his father's insults.

"Is it because of your ugly mug? Any decently bred girl would faint upon first glance at you," sneered this man who had sired him.

Fists clenching, he resisted the urge to trace the scars running across his face. The wounds his father had put there.

"Not to worry, I have already arranged the match for you. Gel's a bit young, but they can be trained easier then."

Marcus refused to comment on his father's harsh words. He could only thank his stars that he now had the legal power to refuse his demands. "No."

The short fuse of his father's temper burned out, lighting the cannon. The man's fist caught Marcus off guard, sending him reeling back into a glass table. Sharp, agonizing pain burst along his back as he landed in the pile of shattered glass. He gasped, fighting to bring his senses back to order. Dark red blood dripped from his nose, the tang of iron and salt trickled down his throat. I should have been ready. I used to be able to read his drunken rages better.

His father didn't hesitate, but again charged towards him. Even in his old age, still a raging bull. Time seemed to slow as Marcus watched his father's foot approach. Memories of the years of abuse beat his senses, causing him to choke and gasp with anticipated pain. He felt the sting of the whip across his back; he could hear the screams of the little sister he tried so hard to protect. He could taste the salt of his tears. He could see his father's face looming over him—smell the alcohol that stained his breath.

The present returned in an audible rush to his ears. His father's roar bounced off the walls, "You will marry the damned chit and give me an heir! The Marquis of Fleetwood line will live on."

Marcus's mind and body finally responded. He rolled away from the kick and jumped up to his feet, catching his father's fist before it could land another blow. With a swift wrench, Marcus had his father by the throat, crushed backed against the bookshelves. Heart pounding in his ears, Marcus watched as spittle spewed from his father's gasping lips. His mind was blank to everything but revenge. He pressed hard, feeling the spasming esophagus against his palm, his own fury matching his father's.

Marcus stared fiercely into his father's purple face, recognizing their similar features. His gaze was caught and held by the man's green eyes. Mar-

cus could see his own twisted and frenzied features mirrored in them. Shaken, he let go, stepping back, unaware of the soft crunch of broken glass beneath his boots. He'd never come so close...so close to killing anyone before. He stared at his hands, his whole body shaking with what he'd almost done.

"You're worthless! I'm ashamed my title will fall to you!"

Marcus met his father's gaze again and for some strange reason he almost pitied the man. "I will not marry. You may do what you like, but I will never give you a damned heir!"

Marcus turned to leave, his mind and body numb.

"Marcus." He didn't want to stop, but the tone in his father's voice made him turn to face him. The marquis slowly straightened, his hands running over his clothes, ineffectively ironing out the wrinkles. He raised his head and met Marcus's gaze shakily. Marcus was struck by how old and pitiful he suddenly seemed. A foreboding sneer slowly twisted his mouth. "You will regret this, I promise. There is more than one way to get what I want."

Marcus didn't respond. Nothing his father could say or do would change his mind. He stepped over the threshold and out of the marquis's life.

"My lord?"

Marcus awoke with a start. He blinked back the sunlight streaming in through the curtains. Hovering above him was the concern-wrinkled face of his valet. His owlish blue eyes were looking at him with a carefully neutral expression.

"May I fetch you anything?"

Groaning, Marcus sat up, realizing he'd tossed and turned his way out of bed during the night again. The wooden floor had warmed under his heated skin while he slept. Clutching at his throbbing head, he inhaled deeply, catching the lingering rose scent of Miss Green still clinging to him.

It smelled of everything he could never have.

"Damn," he muttered. Marcus welcomed the anger. "Draw a bath."

He could not stand another moment with her scent engulfing him.

Shuddering softly, Marcus's aching eyes drifted shut as his mind conjured Miss Green's face. He'd imbued a glass of courage before meeting the fraud. It had been the only way to voice his thoughts aloud. The only way to make sure he could carry out his plan. He had not, however, counted on his reaction to her.

The moment he'd walked into the bookstore, his gaze had been caught and held by caramel eyes, wide with fear. He'd meant to be pleasant and persuasive, but the emotions that flickered across her oval-shaped face enraged him. For some insane reason, he'd harbored the small hope that she would be different, tough and fearless, even though all evidence pointed to her underhandedness. He'd been wrong. Worse than her reaction to him was his reaction to her—his wondering, lustful thoughts.

Even as he'd baited and insulted her, he'd imagined her lustrous mahogany hair cascading around her. He'd envisioned her full lips bruised with passion, her eyes sparking with love rather than anxiety and fear. It had taken almost all his strength to control himself when her soft palm had pushed against his chest. She'd been seeking her space, but the beast within him had only wanted to close the last inch, gather her close, and never let go. Only recalling how she had ruined his plans stopped him. *One month of precious time. Wasted.*

Marcus rose from his spot on the floor, forcing his stiff body to obey. He wrapped the cool cotton bedsheet about his naked form. Too agitated to remain in one place, he began to pace the room as servants entered and exited to fill a large tub with heated water.

The moment he'd left the infernal bookstore, if one could call it such, he'd gone and drowned himself in fine brandy. Liquor much too expensive for the purpose he used it. The entire time he'd drunk, he had thought of his father. The man he'd hated his entire life. The man he was glad was dead. The man who had gotten him into this mess in the first place.

He still had trouble believing his father could be so dastardly clever. He had found a way to get him married after all. The damned man was well aware of Marcus's love for his sister. It was this weakness, after all, that often caused beatings. Sometime between their confrontation and his death a year ago, his father had contracted a marriage between Caroline and the Duke of Harwood, a man of far worse temper and reputation than even their father. The match had to be finalized, or the breech of contract conditions would beggar the Fleetwood estate. Marcus's only choice was to marry an heiress to secure enough finances to break Caro's betrothal. Then, with the duke's signature, the contract could be declared null and void. He could not allow Caro to suffer a married life that would be far worse than her childhood.

He'd been so close to securing his sister's safety, only to have it snatched away by a tempting fraud and the bespectacled clerk who'd swept his fiancée out from under him. Damn his father's codicil anyway. Damn Anne. And, most fervently, damn Miss Danni Green.

The sound of sloshing and an enraged shout drew Marcus from his reverie. One of his footmen stormed from the room, wearing what appeared to be the hot contents of one of the buckets. He heard Weller's shout of apology before the sound of pouring water resumed. The footman's lethal glare in his valet's direction made it clear that the footman did not accept the older man's regrets.

Marcus ignored the disruption. Chaos surrounded the clumsy valet. The servants should know to keep a wide berth. He shifted the direction of his pacing, his stiff body moving with aching slowness. Groaning, he clasped hands to his aching head as sunlight poured mercilessly through the open curtains, turning on his heel away from the light to collapse onto the chaise. Bitterness rose, constricting his heart, angry at his current state, even though much of it was his own doing. He had been such an imbecile.

Miss Green had made a fool out of him, but so had Miss Anne Newport. He'd been stunned to discover her making off in the night with her lover. When he'd proposed to her after contracting with her father, it had taken some convincing to get her to accept, but he'd thought she cared a little for him. He knew that it had been her father who'd wanted the marriage more than she. After all, the family would gain his title in exchange for her dowry. The arrangement was a business matter, not one of the heart.

How could he have ever believed her excuses of continuing illness that had prevented him from calling on her recently? He should have known something was wrong. If fate hadn't put him in that spot two nights ago, at just the right time, he would never have known about Gretna Green Bookings.

When he'd left Miss Green with his ultimatum, he'd felt an all too familiar tug on his conscience. Not for blackmailing that manipulative woman of course, but for his intended "bride"...essentially, his victim. He didn't want to do this, but what choice did he have? He had to do it...*For Caro.*

"Would you like your customary glass of brandy?"

Marcus glanced up. Weller's head popped into sight, an eager look on his face. "God, yes, Weller. And, please, try not to break anything today."

His valet ignored his directive, promptly tripping over the Persian carpet on his way from the small room to the sideboard. He crashed into the morning tea service, sending it, and himself, to the ground. Despite watching the china fall, Marcus jolted as if struck. His gaze shifted in a panic about the room, his entire body on alert to defend himself. His constricted lungs allowed only breaths in short gasps, his hand pressed to his chest in an effort to control the surge of his heart. He felt ridiculous.

Shattered porcelain clinked together as Weller scrambled to his feet. He gazed tentatively about him to avoid any new hazard. Caroline, his sister, thought Marcus mad to keep such a clumsy man as a valet. Marcus thought it was a miracle the man stayed.

"I've told you on several occasions to simply look about you before taking a step. It would save me a fortune in china."

"I did look. Just not down."

Despite his pain, Marcus grinned ruefully. "Ah. The fatal flaw of your plan."

Weller paused in his trek across the room, his head cocked in thought. "Up also gives me trouble."

Marcus gave the man a hard look, knowing he would regret asking, "Up?"

"Oh, yes. You would not believe how often tree limbs seem to pop into my path."

Marcus cradled his head in his palms, elbows on knees. "Why do I bother to keep you around?"

Weller poured him a generous helping of brandy. "You don't, my lord. I believe you fired me again last night."

"Then what are you still doing here?"

Weller handed him the glass with a small smile. "You wouldn't be able to function if I left, sir."

Marcus cautiously tossed back his drink, watching Weller as he moved towards the bath.

"Were the dreams bad last night, my lord?"

He sobered at the man's inquiry. He never talked about his dreams. Ever. "Yes."

The clipped reply left no room for further discussion. Marcus sank beneath the steaming heat of the tub before the man could press the subject. The dreams that haunted his nights and the shadows that followed him during the day were no one's damned business other than his own.

Heat permeated his muscles, loosening his stiff joints and old scars that had tightened during the night. He felt far older than his thirty-one years. He was tired. Tired of his life, of the burdens he never seemed able to purge. Tired of the constant battle for his sanity. Tired…so very tired.

He slipped his head beneath the surface. He let the soothing lap of water brush against his scarred face before resurfacing. A bar of lightly colored soap appeared before his dripping eyes. He accepted it with a cloth from Weller to suds the bar, but waited in silence for the valet's retreating steps before he began to wash. He did his best to hide the mangled state of his body from his staff, but he had long ago accepted that it was unavoidable at times in such a large household.

He found his mind drifting back to Miss Green. He wondered how someone so fair had become involved in such an underhanded profession. He wondered if perhaps she'd had a reason or if it was merely greed. If he were a gambling man, he would bank on greed. No one simply helped others without expecting something in return. The idea was blatantly ridiculous.

His thoughts were cut short by Weller's return with a warmed towel. Marcus dunked under the surface once more, then stepped from the comforting confines of the tub. He followed the clumsy man, drying himself as he went. Weller approached the armoire to choose his clothing, managing to only bump into an imported Chippendale table before he reached it.

"Are you still determined to carry out your plan, my lord? I'm sure it is not the wisest course to attempt to abduct a bride."

Marcus glared at the man's back. Weller had not ceased this prattle for the last day or so, despite the fact that he should know how fruitless the effort was. His course was set and he would not waver. "It was damned hard to get even Anne to agree to marry me. I was foolish to believe she might have actually developed feelings for me."

"You were not! Most of those fancy bits play a game in order to reel in the biggest prize. At least, that's what I've been told."

Marcus fought a smile as he wrapped a towel around his naked form. His valet was loyal to him, another trait Marcus admired and believed lacking in his other employees. Most of them tread with fear, afraid to anger the Beast. It was isolating and stung, another reminder of his father's legacy.

At Marcus's silence, Weller continued. "What if you're caught in the act? Is kidnapping a bride really worth it?"

He'd spent his entire life protecting his sister from their father. He wouldn't stop now. The man had been dead a year yet he still haunted them.

Marcus blinked against the dark thoughts, banishing his emotions with them. He had failed again to protect his sister, played a fool by his fiancée. He wished he could have known what would happen when Mr. Hessler's clerk had called on the Newport home with the marriage contract. He wished he'd known what his father was going to do before he'd done it.

But there was nothing he could change now. He had to adapt and move on, but he wouldn't face the *ton* again, searching for yet another wife. The whispers. The averted eyes. The fainting women. No, he now had a guaranteed method of obtaining, and keeping, a wife. Thanks to Miss Green.

For his shave, he sat gingerly in a chair much too small for him, making the same mental note he did every morning: use the chair for the night's kindling.

Weller's brush stroked cool cream across his face. He

then advanced with the freshly sharpened razor, pointed directly at his throat. With visions of scalded servants and shattered china, Marcus snatched it from the man before his neck was slit. He made quick work of his thick whiskers, grimacing at the bumpy slide of the blade over scars thick and white with age. The less time spent in front of a mirror the better. At the last slide of his blade, Weller suddenly paused, a wide but wary smile on his face. "I forgot to mention, my lord, that your sister is here."

"Pardon?"

"Lady Caroline is here. Has been since early this morning. Such a beautiful and charming young woman. And her hair—its color and length...quite remarkable."

His heart immediately jumped, catching his throat and beating erratically with a mixture of fear and anger. *No, not now. Not today.*

"Throw her out."

Chapter Four

❦

The merchant told the tale of BEAST;
And loud lamenting, when he ceas'd,

—"Beauty and the Beast" by Charles Lamb

You cannot be serious. She's your sister!"

"And she knows she isn't welcome here."

"My lord, I would never question your reasons—"

"Then don't."

"—but you're endangering the rest of your life for her safety. I don't understand. You two must work together to resolve this problem."

Marcus moved to his sideboard, reaching for another glass of brandy. It was the one thing that managed to get him through the day. The irony that both father and son overindulged was not lost on Marcus, but for him, brandy deadened the nightmares that his father's whiskey had created.

"Seeing her reminds me of things best left forgotten," he whispered.

He swallowed the glassful in the wake of his confession. He held the now empty crystal up to a ray of light making its way through his curtains. Tiny droplets of the golden liquid slid down the side, gathering in a pool at the bottom. Smuggled brandy was the best, meant to be savored and sipped slowly. What a waste.

He picked up the decanter and tossed more into his glass, trying his best to ignore Weller's presence. He couldn't face Caro right now. He'd been able to keep the terms of their father's will hidden from her for the moment, but only as a result of the distance he maintained between them. A distance he intended to maintain until his dying breath. It was selfish of him, he knew, but he was ashamed of how he could react in her presence.

"Just tell her to write me a letter."

Weller remained where he stood, his mouth set in a grim line. "What would happen if you saw her, sir?"

Marcus put down his glass to accept the starched shirt Weller held out to him. "Nothing you'd care to witness again."

The man winced with sympathy before moving over to the dressing table near the armoire. His valet was always the one who smoothed things over when *that* happened. He'd come to depend on the man, something Marcus was not exactly thrilled about. He turned back to the board in order to pour himself another drink. He was quickly working his way into his familiar haze, cultivating the emotional numbness he needed each day to maintain his role in society.

He winced as the sound of cracking glass reached his ear. He spared only a glance over his shoulder to confirm what had been broken now. His hand mirror, one he never touched, had been brushed to the floor by Weller's awkward maneuvers near his dressing table. The glass lay shattered near its silver frame. Sighing, he resumed his morning ablutions.

Weller appeared before him, holding a pair of new cuff links, glancing sheepishly back at the shards on the floor. "Sometimes it helps to face the past, my lord. Leaves more room for the future that way."

Marcus only shook his head. "No. The past is best left buried."

His thoughts started to wander in a direction he had no wish to go. Hastily, he reached for the tumbler to banish them. In his hurry, Marcus missed the way his valet paused in the process of putting the metal links in his shirt and stared at the threshold to the hall, where a figure stood quietly.

"What would you say to your sister if you could, my lord?"

He blinked, the drink starting to slow his wits. "Whatever do you mean?"

Weller held out a maroon waistcoat. Marcus eased it over his wide shoulders.

"If you could say anything to her without suffering the effects of your...condition, what would it be?"

"I already tell her what I wish through letters. She is better off staying in town with her friends, the St. Leons." He was indebted to that family. Caroline had met the youngest sibling, Althea, at finishing school. They'd become fast friends and, as a result, the family often took Caroline home with them for holidays and summers. She fortunately had been absent for most of their father's brutal rampages, something for which he would be eternally grateful, especially after that one particular incident that changed her.

"I doubt she'd want to hear my voice nagging her every day."

"The problem though, dear brother, is that I never had the opportunity to decide that for myself."

Marcus spun around. A feminine version of himself stood by the entry. Caroline, now two and twenty, had indeed grown up in his self-imposed absence. She was dressed in mint green muslin, her pale green eyes intensified by the color. Long white gloves and a dangling handbag completed her. The same white-blond hair that crowned his head was swept up in an elegant half style on hers, its incredible length spilling over her shoulder, reminding him of the Rapunzel fairy tale. She was taller than the average woman, but thankfully not as tall as most Bradleys. She was a vision of all that was prim, proper, and pure in the eyes of the most elite society. Her dress and grace were impeccable. Her slender frame appeared to glide towards him as his heart kicked into recklessly unsteady beats.

The very sight of her perfection reminded him of how desperately he wanted to protect her from another man such as their father. From what he had experienced the night that had left him scarred so long ago. He had desperately tried to keep her away from their father on that fateful night. And now...now he had failed again to keep her from marrying the creature his father had chosen for her. How could he face her when all he did was fail her?

His hands fumbled for his decanter like the clumsy Weller, his eyes never breaking her gaze. Caroline's face turned militant when she noticed the direction of his reach. "How can you spend your days drowning yourself with drink? Is that why we are on the edge of ruin?"

Her startling tirade stayed his hands. The caged memories threatening to consume him paused to catch a breath like beasts startled into frozen fear. His little sister had become a spitfire as well as a woman during his neglect. It was unsettling.

"What are you implying, dearest sister?"

"Implying? I'm asking you outright. Did you or did you not beggar the estate with your vices?"

"The only vice I have is drink." How he hated to admit that to her. "And I have no notion as to what you are referring."

"I don't believe you."

Marcus could no longer delay another drink. The haze he'd been so carefully creating was swiftly evaporating. He grabbed the decanter, moved away from his sister, and turned his back to her. "Ask Weller here. He'll tell you I only love the bottle."

The clumsy man, nonchalantly picking the mirror shards from the floor while eavesdropping with rapt attention, chimed in at the prompt. "'Tis true, my lady."

His sister sniffed in continued disbelief. She brought her reticule up to her line of sight, close to her nose, digging around inside, searching furiously. The search produced a clip of newspaper, which she brandished about in the air. "Then why are the gossips saying you've ruined us with your beastly habits?"

Despite the tremors starting to claim his limbs, Marcus shrugged. "Because I'm the Beast, I suspect."

He blinked as his sister stomped her foot. Golden curls bounced along her hips with her jerking movement. Paper crinkled in her gloved hand as she clenched her fist. A strong woman lay behind her ladylike façade and Marcus found himself glad of it. The *ton* had not wiped her spirit away. He disliked not seeing a trace of the girl she used to be. The one with dirt always on one side of her face. The one with curls sticking out at every angle, eyes glittering with mischief in the rare moments of freedom. She'd once been the light in his darkness, but now her mere presence cast him into shadow.

"Why must you be so difficult?" Her eyes narrowed to pinpoints when he took a healthy swallow. "And stop that!"

How he wanted to, he thought dimly.

The liquor was taking too long to bring back his haze. He would not be able to fight the past without it. He was shaking violently, his limbs almost unable to support him. He could feel the perspiration on his brow, the inside of his skin unbearably hot. His temper would swiftly follow and then it would only be a matter of moments before the paralysis seized him. Hell would quickly envelop him and he'd be trapped for hours in the horrors of his past.

Marcus retrieved his handkerchief from the table laid out with his dressing items. He patted his brow, trying to focus on Caroline's pacing form.

Suddenly, tears filled her eyes. Their glassy emerald surface stared at him accusingly. "I know you don't care about me anymore, Marcus, but I would have thought you'd at least secured a dowry with which to dispose of me. I won't be able to marry now!"

He wanted to reassure her, tell her how much he loved her, but he couldn't form the words. His tongue felt thick.

Weller interrupted the silence that fell as he dumped the broken mirror into the wastebasket. The chime of the shattered pieces hitting the sides and the bottom echoed through the room. A few missed the bucket, landing on the carpet. Weller frowned at the uncooperative pieces before clearing his throat. "Pardon me, my lord, but I suggest you look at the piece of paper Lady Caroline crinkled in her impatience."

He blinked, his gaze drawn to the ball of parchment.

Caroline didn't bother to hand it to him. She smoothed out the inked surface with her gloves. She paced furiously, fire painting her delicate face brilliant red as she recited aloud, " *'This Author has stumbled upon the most delicious on-dit to storm London since Thursday. While standing at the punch bowl in Lady Shelton's ballroom yestereve, considering the merits of a certain teal-colored dress worn by said Lady S, a conversation reached my ear. This Author would never participate in something so uncouth as eavesdropping, but when one shouts, others must be expected to hear. The rumor, my Dearest Reader, is that a certain Lord B, previously engaged to Miss Anne Newport, is in dire straits. Unless he can marry an heiress, his estate will collapse! Dearest Reader, lock your doors and guard your daughters or they may fall prey to a Beast's vicious claws!'* " She stopped to demand of him, "How do you explain this?"

"I can't." *Not without telling her of the engagement.*

"I knew it! You've ruined us. When are the collectors coming? Perhaps I can fix this. I do have some connections, you know…"

Her ramblings continued until Marcus's temper forced him to interrupt. "Caroline! I can't explain because we are not ruined! It is not true."

His sister paused in her steps, disbelief on her features. "Then why are they saying such vile things? I'll never be able to marry until we can prove we are as well endowed as before."

The liquor could not dim the rage that slid along his veins. He knew exactly how this rumor was circulating. And he knew exactly who to blame.

Damn Anne! It wasn't enough to jilt him. She had to have revenge for being pushed into marriage with him. George, the clerk, must have told her everything about the codicil.

The thought of their father's will thrust him over the precipice on which he'd been balancing. His joints locked where he stood, his muscles freezing, as his mind was pulled into the shadowy depths of his soul.

"Just how are we going to fix this, Marcus?"

When her brother didn't answer, Caroline frowned. Halting mid-stride, she peered at her elder brother, who was standing suspiciously still, a vacant look in his eyes.

"Marcus?"

Concerned, she stepped closer. His tall form was motionless, all his muscles tensed. A finger of trepidation raced along her spine. Swallowing against her sudden fear, she inched closer until she was a hair's breadth away. With a weird sense of disembodiment, Caroline watched her trembling hand connect with her brother's burning skin. He didn't move. She felt her lower lip start to quiver, as if she were five again, running from her father's cane.

She nudged Marcus, studying him intently. His eyes hadn't even acknowledged her as she'd come closer. She squeezed his arm harder. His body started to sway. Jumping back, Caro pressed a hand to her mouth to stop her terrified scream. In agonizing slowness, he rocked to and fro until his limbs suddenly gave out. He pitched to the floor, landing inches from the remains of the shattered glass spread about the carpet, and then began seizing. His entire body jerked with spasms. She couldn't stop the scream that tore through her. Tears burned at the corner of her eyes. "Marcus! Weller, help him!"

She attempted to turn his writhing body away from the glass, her breath heaving. She fought to grab his wrists and hold him down, but he was uncontrollable, crashing against her, knocking the air from her lungs. She tasted salt along her lips, her mind dimly registering that she was profusely crying. "Stop this, Marcus!"

A moan tore from him. Caroline fell back, acknowledging her inability to assist him. Warm arms wrapped around her waist, hauling her from the ground and into a solid wall. Without thinking, Caroline locked her arms about the man supporting her.

She was dimly aware of being escorted out of the room, and of others going in. Weller guided Caroline down the hall and into the family's private sitting room. He rang for tea. She wasn't able to do anything but shake until she had a hot cup of tea in her hand. Ignoring the customary plate, she wrapped her hands about the smooth china surface, welcoming the heat as it warmed her icy fingers through her gloves.

A handkerchief appeared before her line of vision like a white flag waving surrender. She accepted the square of cloth, pulling herself together. She had to take charge, make sure her brother was taken care of and not left to roll about the floor. It was the least she could do after what he'd suffered for her growing up. She was about to issue orders to call for a doctor when the valet took a seat on the chaise opposite her. His fair eyes seemed to pierce into her soul, his face grim. Caro stared at the older gentleman, noting the graying of his dark hair and the lines of a hard life bracketing his eyes and mouth.

"You've never witnessed that before, my lady?"

His calm demeanor shocked her. "I most certainly have not! What's wrong with him? Who is assisting him? Has a doctor been called?"

The man's gaze remained unwavering as he spoke. "My name is Michael Weller, my lady. I believe his lordship mentioned me in his letters."

Now that she had pulled herself together, her patience was at an end. She placed the tea on the table. This wasn't the time for it. Her brother needed her. "I have no time for introductions. I must get back to Marcus! When will the doctor arrive?"

Weller remained unmoving. "He won't be coming."

Caro leaped from her chair. "Pardon? He needs medical care immediately!"

She gathered up her skirts, preparing to run for a doctor herself if necessary, when Weller's sharp voice made her freeze. "Sit."

Caroline sat.

"Marcus is being brought to his bed. The staff is caring for him. We know what to do to make him comfortable.

Not to worry, please. If you will let me explain, my lady, I would appreciate it."

"If I don't find your explanation satisfactory, I am fetching a doctor myself."

"As you wish, my lady." The valet's head dipped for a moment before he looked up. Caroline noted for the first time the sadness in his eyes. "Your brother suffers from his memories."

"I don't understand. How can memories cause the episode I just witnessed?"

"His lordship has a difficult time coping with his childhood, my lady. Some days he is better than others, but his memories of that time follow him like his shadow. At times, events trigger them to rise up and engulf him. He will recover with quiet, and rest."

Caroline remained silent, tamping down her own memories as they threatened to surface. She knew her brother had suffered severely while she was safely hidden away with the St. Leons. "Marcus had it much worse than I."

Weller's shoulders lifted. "I know."

"Then he should see a doctor."

The valet's eyes narrowed in displeasure and heat infused his voice as he snapped, "And let him end up in Bedlam? Do you know what they do to their *patients*?"

She didn't, but his tone made her stomach tighten.

"They chain them to the walls and feed them laudanum. Sometimes they'll try untested treatments on them. If they are fortunate, they die. Your brother's status would ensure he wasn't so lucky."

She felt the color bleed from her face. She couldn't let that happen to Marcus. It mirrored too much what their father had done.

"We can't just leave him like that!"

"This does not happen frequently, my lady. And he was much better while he was engaged to Miss Anne. I believe he thought she was coming to accept him, that he could finally live the life of a normal man—have someone love him for himself, and one day have a family. But, then, you know what happened there." The older man paused before adding, "Unfortunately, when he sees something associated with his past, he has these violent attacks." The valet's eyes shifted away from hers. "Today, that something was you."

The heat of shame and guilt swallowed her, mixed with anger. Wasn't it enough that she had to live every day knowing her brother looked like a beast because of her? She now had to live with the knowledge that it wasn't because he didn't care about her that he didn't associate with her. It was because he could not stand the very sight of her without suffering a second time. She felt her eyes burn. Placing her cup down shakily, she pressed Weller's cloth to them, trying to hold back tears.

Her muffled voice creaked weakly. "And here I thought he resented me for all he had to do to protect me. For all the pain he had suffered."

"He could never resent you, my lady. His lordship would even give up his happiness in order to keep you safe."

"But he's already given up so much," she exclaimed.

Weller's gaze drifted upward, in the direction of her brother's bedroom. He began to speak, then hesitated. A resigned sigh escaped him before his attention returned to her. He gave her a sad smile. "It is his choice, my lady."

Anxious energy tightened her hold on the delicate kerchief, the fabric's touch dulled by the soft kid of her gloves. "And what about my choices?"

The valet's wizened features clouded before he cleared his throat. His voice was calm and steady. "You should trust his lordship. After meeting you, I believe I now understand why he would go to such lengths to keep you safe."

"Mr. Weller, what are you—?"

A knock interrupted their conversation. The butler opened the door, and with a bow to her, informed them, "His lordship has settled and is sleeping comfortably."

Tension bled from Caroline at the simple words. She'd been so worried. She relaxed into the couch and closed her eyes momentarily.

"Also," the butler added to Weller, "a letter from G. Green Books has arrived. Shall I place it in his study?"

"I believe he shall want it when he wakes. Place it in his room," Weller replied before turning to her. "I apologize your visit has gone astray, my lady."

"No need." Now that her brother was going to be all right and she had determined her family wasn't ruined as rumored, she should be going. Caro gathered her belongings and headed for the door. "As you suggested, I shall trust Marcus . . . for the time being."

* * *

Marcus slowly opened his eyes. The soft light of dusk flooded into his room and painted it a golden pink. Everything about him hurt. His head throbbed and his muscles were stiff. With agonizing slowness, he worked each muscle loose, flexing them back and forth to regain movement. Halfway through the exercise, Marcus caught sight of a letter on his night table. He lifted his tense and tired arm to retrieve it. Elegant script belonging to a woman littered the front. Tired eyes traced the black ink. Miss Green had responded.

Part of him hoped Miss Green would deny him. If she said no, he could blame her just as he did Anne for his sister's current situation. He could blame everyone but the true person at fault—himself. If only he'd agreed to what his father wanted years ago, he would have saved Caroline.

His stiff, quaking fingers brushed hesitantly over the green wax seal. Just as he hated the fact he drank like his father, but couldn't stop because of his memories, he hated to do this. He didn't want to rob a poor girl of her future, but he would do it because he had to.

Breathing deeply, he broke the seal. The ruffle of unfolding paper broke the silence in the eerily still room. Marcus's heart rose to his throat and his stomach turned as he read the letter's contents. With a shaky moan, he let the open letter fall to his chest, dropping his palms over his eyes in a pathetic effort to block out the world. His emotions weighed heavily upon his chest, crushing the air from his lungs in a wretched sigh. It would seem he had much to do before midnight.

Chapter Five

❧

The more he drank, the less he fear'd.
Now bolder grown, he pac'd along,
(Still hoping he might do no wrong),

—"Beauty and the Beast" by Charles Lamb

$\mathscr{D}$anni ignored the iron step as she dropped out of the carriage. Her fingers slid along the lacquered oak wood of the door. Her mind wandered as she released the small handle, feeling the smooth metal. Its coldness reminded her of the marquis's freezing eyes. Fresh rage choked her and she slammed the door, rocking the coach. Damn him.

Phillip, a tall and lanky man with dark hair and eyes, peered over the edge of the seat to give her a deadly look. The pious young man serving as her personal coachman wasn't very happy with her at the moment anyway. What was the harm in adding a broken door to her list of offenses? She would not have involved him at all except John, the man who normally filled this role, was not back yet from the trip with Anne Newport and George. Grinding her teeth, she cursed the girl to hell. She'd ruined Danni's organized existence, and made Danni the victim of blackmail. She'd never thought helping someone find happiness could cause her so much misery.

Phillip coughed too loudly for it to be natural. When she glared at him, he tilted his nose in the air. "Your father would never forgive me if he knew I was assisting you, Miss Strafford."

"Then don't tell him."

"And running about in men's trousers! What would your mother think?"

Invoking her mother was the wrong thing to do. She took several deep breaths. She'd had enough of his comments. She had threatened to sack him if he didn't cooperate before, and now she was going to make it a reality. Just as soon as this little job was done. She usually didn't mind her servants voicing their opinion, but his constant nagging was too much.

Danni stepped away from the carriage, scouting about, and *enjoying* the way the trousers gave her freedom of movement. This designated meeting place with the marquis was an excellent spot to leave the carriage. The lighting was dim enough to hide their activities from any casual observer, and with several alleyways nearby heading off in multiple directions, it was also perfect for eluding pursuers.

She wished Hu were here. He usually accompanied her. However, she didn't dare involve him or Annabel in this. They would ask too many questions and try to stop her. And if she were caught, they would suffer as accomplices. As for Philip, well, the way he was annoying her tonight, he deserved to suffer. It was best to keep Annabel and Hu ignorant, and safe. This way they could honestly deny any knowledge of the events.

She was lifting the hoof on one of the horses to check the muffling burlap around it when the sound of an approaching carriage made her glance around. An unmarked coach drawn by a team of four turned the corner. The driver slowed the horses as it approached a curb, and its door swung open, revealing long masculine legs. Goliath, in the form of nobility, emerged from the carriage. Using the step, she noted, snorting divisively. The door shut behind him and the carriage moved on with the barest slowing of the matched pairs' trot.

Crossing her arms, she moved into the lighted section of the street. The marquis's boots rang against the stone. At the edge of the illuminated circle, he seemed to hesitate. Danni was in no mood to be pleasant. "Step into the light. I won't talk to a shadow."

A deep growl emanated from the nobleman's vicinity before he strode forward, stopping too close for comfort. He seemed to be daring her to scream in shock.

She didn't.

But Phillip did.

The cold eyes she remembered spared only a flickering glance at the coachman before focusing on her. It was still alarming to see the disfiguring scars, even though she'd seen them at length yesterday. But it wasn't terrifying. Not now, when she wished the man to the four corners of hell.

"I am surprised you came."

Danni glared up at him, ignoring his slightly smug expression. "Yes, and I'm supposed to reply that I did not have much of a choice. Let's stop the polite chitchat. You knew this would be the outcome of your pleasant little visit."

He leaned forward slightly. A quirk formed by a scar in his lip caused his sneer to skew to one side. "I did indeed."

The reek of liquor slammed into her face as he spoke. "You are drunk!"

He sneered at her, eyes glazing. "Not in the least."

She stared in horror. She was about to commit a crime worth hanging for with an accomplice who was three sheets to the wind.

"Shall we?"

He extended his arm in a chivalrous fashion that didn't fool her for a moment. Danni sniffed, tilting up her chin. "No need to pretend that you're actually a gentleman. You forget that I know how you really are."

The marquis's leaf-colored eyes hardened, his jaw turning to stone. With a sharp nod of assent, he dropped his arm.

"You cannot be thinking of going off with *him*?"

She cringed as the squeal from her coachman emerged from the underbelly of the carriage. Apparently he'd taken cover there when the marquis had shown himself. She was beginning to wonder if she shouldn't have hired someone new for the trip. She didn't dare think how Phillip would behave if there were any mishaps along the journey.

She gave an exasperated sigh. "I am, Phillip."

A muffled sound of disgust erupted from the other idiot beside her.

"Who is that prig?"

"That's our driver."

"This is not even remotely funny, Miss Green. Where is that John fellow?"

"I wasn't trying to be humorous. John hasn't returned from your ex-fiancée's trip. She has become a real bother, that girl."

"I could not agree with you more."

Danni glanced at the marquis with more than a little surprise. She caught the man giving her the same look—an uneasy regard—before they both looked away. He scanned the area around them intently; Danni found particular interest in the scuffs on her Hessians. She did not want to start sharing any of the same opinions with a blackmailer.

"Ach! Look at me. My brand-new livery is covered with dust." Phillip's squeaky whine grated her nerves as he emerged from the shadows.

Danni fought the urge to roll her eyes. Exactly what did he expect? The nether regions of a carriage were certainly not the cleanest of places to hide oneself. She tried to remember why she ever employed Phillip in the first place. It certainly wasn't his character references. His up-tilted nose tilted further. "I forbid you to go anywhere with this—this ruffian! If your father—"

"Phillip."

Her tone sharply cut him off. Her coachman glared, but he knew perfectly well what was at stake. So far she'd been able to keep her true identity and her father out of this mess. She intended to keep it that way. Yet another reason to dump Phillip as quickly as possible. The man was sure to let slip things the blackmailing marquis didn't need to know.

"A father? What is a fraud like you doing with one of those?" The marquis's voice dripped with distain. "I wonder at what kind of man raised the likes of you."

Danni turned on her enemy. "I can stand any insults you think I deserve, but don't you ever think to use my family in your slander. Are we understood, my lord?"

The marquis bent forward, closing the precious distance between them. His eyes smirked at her with that alluring blaze of jade, but instead of the fear they inspired earlier, she now felt breathless.

"Unlike most of the *ton*, my dear little one, I understand ties to family very well."

Time seemed to freeze as Danni stood this close to him. How could someone so repulsive in looks and character be so fascinating to her? As their gazes held, seconds too long, emotion flickered across the glossy surface of his jade eyes. Regret? Need? Humanity? It was too quick to identify and was shuttered as quickly as it came—as if he killed the feeling before it could blossom. The moment left her confused and shaken.

Phillip's groan of annoyance penetrated her thoughts. She stepped back, noting with each step exactly how little space had separated them. She shook her head to clear it. This beast was nothing more than a common criminal, soon to be a kidnapper. And certainly *not* human.

"It is already growing late. Shouldn't you be hurrying?"

The marquis nodded in Phillip's direction. "He's right. We cannot waste precious time arguing."

Danni refrained from taking offense. She was not a child to be scolded, especially when he was the one insulting her. Instead, with deliberately slow steps, she returned to the carriage and dug out a small burlap sack she secured over her shoulders. The marquis gave her a curious look before he led her down the alley opposite her traveling coach.

"Who, exactly, are we going to…borrow?" Danni whispered.

"You might as well say it. We're kidnapping someone."

"I'd rather not, thank you."

She impatiently watched the marquis's white-blond mane shift from one side to the other as he walked, waiting for his reply.

"Well?"

"We're *kidnapping* one of the Foley-Foster sisters."

"Oh, dear God! Of all the people you could possibly want to…to borrow!"

"Why, what is wrong with them? I hear the girls are unusual, but they have wealth enough."

"Their father is the bloody Lord High Admiral!" Danni hissed. *Not to mention a man who is close friends with my father.* She swallowed painfully, desperately hoping whichever girl he took did not recognize her from any of her father's social functions.

"I know."

She halted in her tracks, refusing to move another inch. The marquis turned his head to give her a taunting glance. "What? Afraid the admiral can somehow make his ships land-worthy and launch a pursuit?"

"Actually, I was wondering how someone as witless as

you could possibly have uncovered information about my business."

His lashes lowered only slightly, his displeasure clear. He compounded his outrageous behavior by taking out a small silver flask. He unscrewed the cap and took a swallow. "Can we please proceed?"

"We are risking our necks and you are drinking!"

"Think what you may, but continually saying I am drunk is not going to make it so. Now move on."

Despite her lack of hope, Danni tried one last time to stop him from making a terrible mistake with his life. And hers. "There has to be someone else, some *way* else! Don't I have a say in this matter at all?"

The marquis's even steps faltered. The long scar on his face tilted away from her, almost as if he were ashamed. That was impossible, though. It had to be her imagination conjuring up something she wished existed.

He cleared his throat and resumed walking. "I'm the one marrying her."

"And I'm the one helping you...ki...borrow her."

He sneered at her apparent inability to speak the word. "*Kidnap* her, you mean. *You* are the unfortunate reason we are even here. Therefore, *you* must provide me with the resources to get the girl out."

"Well, I have. Can I go now?"

"Don't be ridiculous. She isn't out of the house yet. And you're not leaving me with that dolt of a driver."

Danni almost choked on the fury surging in her veins. She was sure her fair skin must be on fire. "And what exactly do you purpose to do about the admiral? I suppose you think we're simply going to nicely ask him to hand over his daughter."

He leveled her with a lethal look. He radiated that sense of barely leashed power again. "The admiral is returning from a voyage tomorrow. If we expect to have any chance of success, we have to snatch her tonight. Now or never."

Fairly twitching with aggravation and helpless fury, Danni slammed her fist against her thigh. Everything about this horrid affair was out of her control. She had no choice. Do this or she, her father, the earl, and probably Annabel and Hu would be ruined. And what would happen to dear, sweet Simon? She gritted her teeth and groaned. "Let's get this business over with."

The determined click of Danni's boots echoed across the narrow, stone street. Tonight, nothing in the air suggested rain, the sky was crystal clear. The brick walls running along the road lightened in color as the eye traveled up and away from the street filth. Not an alley one would expect in this fashionable part of London.

Danni's heart pounded in helpless terror. She still could not believe she was about to commit a crime. It didn't matter that the moment the marquis and the girl departed on that coach, she planned to awaken everyone in the house. If this man thought she was going to sit by and allow him to ruin some poor girl's future, he had better think again. Her lips slowly tilted up, already savoring the image of stunned disbelief that would appear on his emotionless features as the authorities descended upon him.

"Why are you smiling?"

She snapped herself out of her daydream, meeting the marquis's stern look. "I am most certainly not smiling, my lord." She lifted the straps of her pack to resettle it.

The motion suggested her word was final, but, of course, the Beast was an arrogant nobleman.

"Then what do *you* call it when your mouth curves up at the edges and your eyes glow with mirth?"

"Frowning."

The marquis looked at her as if she were insane. She fully agreed with him. She felt on the verge of hysteria.

"I believe you are one of the oddest people I have ever met, Miss Green."

Something in his tone halted her flippant reply. He was giving her that look again. The one he'd given her in the shop. The man seemed almost a wild animal. His size and face were terrifying, yet there was a hungry vulnerability in him as well. The contrast was something she couldn't even begin to comprehend. It was mesmerizing, and yet it made her extremely uneasy.

She cleared her throat. "At this rate we're never going to...to borrow her."

The tension was broken by his exasperated sigh. In the empty echo of the alley, Danni could hear him mutter, "A thief who can't even speak of her crime."

She bristled, but they had made it to the wall surrounding the admiral's town house. She stood at the bottom of the ten-foot barrier, her head tilted well back. The surface was smooth and in well repair, without easy handholds to climb. It resembled more the walls of a fortress than the wall of a garden estate. She would not have expected anything less from a military man.

"Get us over, Miss Green."

"Pardon?"

"I said, get us over. That's what you're here for."

"Pardon me?" she repeated dumbly.

"You're the expert in elopements. We need to get in."

"I am not a kidnapper, you fool. The women I help elope *want* to leave. I don't have to force them from their homes!"

She gave him another glare for good measure before glancing up the wall again. It was the perfect excuse to halt this madness. "I can't think how we could possibly enter, my lord. It looks like we must give up."

"If you do not take this seriously, Miss Green, there will be unpleasant repercussions."

Danni stared at the man before her, truly wondering if he meant the threat. Something in his grim expression told her she wouldn't like the answer. Who was she fooling? Any man who would stoop low enough to kidnap someone for their money would not let a ten-foot wall stop him.

Sighing, she stepped back, trying to see if a tree was near the wall. "Can you see anything to tie rope to over that wall?"

The marquis backed up, his great height towering above her. It made her feel ridiculously small. He shook his head, "I can see clear to the top of the opposite wall. I do not see anything."

"This is what happens when you target the home of a mistrustful military man. Why couldn't you have just picked one of the wealthy heiresses from the trading class?"

"His social standing will work in my favor."

"Of course. The man can't get the marriage annulled without ruining his family's reputation."

The marquis stared at her, his face blank except for the tightness around his eyes. He almost looked sad. "If that's what you think."

"It is," she huffed. "Now, I haven't the faintest clue as to how we're going to get over that wall."

The marquis looked at her, then his hands, and finally the wall. His face hardened as if he knew she wasn't going to like his idea.

"I'll lift you up."

He was right. "Absolutely not!"

His scars stood out white against his slowly reddening face. "And what is wrong with that idea?"

"It's undignified. If I were in a skirt..."

"But you're not." He snorted, giving her a knowing look.

"I won't do it."

"Yes, you will. It's the only way. If I lift you, you'll easily be able to get over the wall."

Danni looked at his determined face and then at the wall. She wasn't even going to consider it. "No."

A rumble emanated from deep within the marquis's chest. It was the only warning she had before the man launched at her. A roughly padded hand muffled her screech of surprise. An arm the density of iron manacled her own at her waist, holding her tightly against the hard contours of the Beast and snatching her breath from her lungs. She wriggled furiously to escape.

"Stop struggling." He mumbled furiously.

Danni opened her mouth and clamped her teeth down on his palm. He grunted, but his grip didn't loosen. "If you don't stop, I promise you I will throw you head first over that wall. I wonder what you'll land in."

It wasn't hard for her to imagine a bed of thorns awaiting her. With the admiral in charge of security, there was probably something worse awaiting an unsuspecting intruder. She stopped thrashing in his arms but realized immediately she'd made a mistake.

In the chill of the night, the marquis was a stove, and the heat of his body penetrated deeply into her skin. His hot, ragged breath slid along the sensitive skin of her neck, spreading a warmth that weakened her muscles and flooded her veins. Worse, she was sure she felt a tiny tremor flit through the man holding her as well. A gasp of surprise caught in her throat as a low whisper brushed the curve of her ear. "Do I have your cooperation now?"

She felt drugged as she silently nodded her head. The night's gentle breeze carried his spicy scent into her aching lungs and heart. It was all she could do not to melt back into the marquis's warming solidness. Suddenly, he dropped her.

Danni stumbled, trying to catch her balance. The spell Fleetwood had woven was broken. She took a deep gulp of air to cleanse her lungs, ignoring the way her limbs trembled. She rallied her anger to disguise her confusion. "Do not ever, *ever*, lay a hand on me again!"

His eyes stared at her with dark intensity, his body flinching away as if he'd been hit. A wave of unwanted sympathy made Danni regret her words. The emotion made her furious. His cold words broke the pregnant silence. "As soon as you are over that wall, I promise never to touch you again, madam."

Internally, she flinched. She had every right to be angry with him. He'd blackmailed her. He'd insulted her. He'd manhandled her. But something in the look he gave her made her feel the worst sort of brute.

He stepped up to the brick and cupped his hands together. With little choice in the matter, Danni stepped forward. She placed her booted foot in his grasp, her fingers searching vainly for handholds as she was slowly lifted into the air.

Their combined height put Danni within easy reach of the top. She pulled herself up and positioned herself on the edge. Fleetwood was only a few feet below her. She stared down at his head, her eyes tracing the soft curls in his hair, as a sudden thought came to her. "How are you going to get up?"

For the first time since she'd met the man, he smiled. It transformed his features. His white teeth fairly glowed in his shadow-darkened skin and a slight, mesmerizing dimple appeared in the center of his lower lip, the result of his tight scar. His eyes flashed a brilliant green. Danni's throat tightened, enchanted by the sight. Until he answered her question.

"You're going to pull me up, of course."

Chapter Six

❦

With willing hand and ready grace,
Mild Beauty takes the Servant's place;

—"Beauty and the Beast" by Charles Lamb

*Y*ou're jesting." He was nearly twice her size!

"Not in the least."

"You're intoxicated."

"Wrong again."

"How exactly do you propose I do that? You are literally a giant!" she snarled over the wall, careful to keep her voice low.

"Need I remind you, you are the one who does this for a living?"

"It's becoming increasingly obvious I need to retire," she muttered.

"Not until our arrangement is complete."

Danni lapsed into silence as she realized he seriously thought she was going to somehow manage to pull him up. She turned in her seat, surveying the garden below her through the shifting shadows formed by clouds moving across the moon. The garden was surprisingly feminine and decidedly lacking in thorny rose bushes. She could just make out rows upon rows of the bleeding hearts and irises that lined the garden beds, mixed among a variety of many flowering plants. The garden was a well-tended masterpiece. As she scanned the freshly budding greenery, Danni realized why they could not locate a tree before. There were none. It also meant she had nothing to which to tie a rope.

"I really do not see how you're going to get up. Why don't you just wait here and I'll come back with her?" she whispered down to the marquis, a dark form pacing anxiously among gray shadows.

"You mean come back with the authorities?"

"How could you think I'd do such a thing?" she sniffed, pretending offense.

"Do I need to remind you of what I can do to you, Miss Green? I will be back with the constable long before you could even get inside that house. You will be the intruder. I will be the hero witnessing and reporting your break-in."

Grinding her teeth, she glared down into the gloom, his green eyes the only object visible as the moon slid behind a cloud.

"Get me over this wall at once, madam."

She glanced around her again. There really wasn't anything she could use—

Smiling, she rolled over on her stomach and dropped down off the wall.

* * *

Marcus couldn't believe his eyes. One moment the fraud was sitting atop the wall, pretending to be affronted by the idea of kidnapping, and the next moment she'd disappeared. With the way his night was going, he wouldn't be surprised if she had fallen to her death. "Miss Green?"

Silence.

The image of her bent and broken body lying in a bed of thorns sent him reeling. He panicked. "Danni!"

Marcus ran his hands through his hair, fumbling for his old metal friend for a drink. Despite his attempt to remain aloof, he couldn't deny the sudden mix of dread and regret that gripped his chest. It was bad enough he was forced to kidnap, but if he was responsible for someone's death, he was not sure he'd be able to survive. Especially hers. Her caramel eyes would never again spark with indignation or cloud with confusion. She could be dead. Because of him.

He whispered sharply, "Danni! Answer me!"

A snort came from the other side of the wall. Relief swamped him as he leaned against the cool mortar. Until another thought occurred to him. Rage followed quickly. "If you think you're going to raise the alarm, you are even more witless than I originally thought!"

Her voice rose over the wall, dripping with disdain. "And what do you purpose to do to stop me? You're on the other side of a ten-foot wall."

Marcus ground his teeth to the quick. The damned girl was shredding his, at best precarious, patience. "Do not test me, Miss Green."

"You're really not so terrifying when I'm on this side

of the wall. You need me, so I suggest you stop threatening me, *my lord*."

"Damn it. Get me over this wall!"

"Certainly. Whatever you command, my lord."

Marcus whipped around, surprised when her voice was right beside him. He immediately tensed, on guard, his mind drifting back to his childhood. The specter of his father's hand approaching his face tinted his surroundings. A sweat broke over him and he blinked rapidly. It took all his effort not to visibly flinch away from her sudden appearance, revealing his inner turmoil. Danni was leaning against the wall—on his side. His remembered terror was swiftly replaced with fresh fury. "What game are you playing?"

"No game. There is a door around the corner. You can see it only from inside the garden. Rather clever actually."

"You little baggage. You knew the entire time and you were taunting me."

A sarcastic smile curled her lips. "How very astute of you."

Marcus didn't think. He rushed forward, forcing her back against the wall with his presence. He carefully avoided any physical contact, remembering her threats and his unsettling reaction the last time he let that happen. Her eyes went wide with fear, and it was all he could do not to step back with self-hate. His fist curled at his side in frustration. He was no better than his father, bullying this woman into doing what he wished. "Miss Green, you have every right to hate me, but may we continue? We have very little time for your silly sport. Despite your convictions, I take very little pleasure in our current activity."

She sniffed, her eyes narrowing with barely concealed hatred. He wasn't surprised his words did nothing to absolve his character. They certainly did nothing for his conscience.

"This way," she whispered fiercely.

He followed her through the opening. A false brick wall matching the outer one was attached to a wrought iron gate. It seemed the disciplined admiral even engineered a clever escape route out of his fortress.

"You couldn't have mentioned this when you saw it?"

"And miss the opportunity to make you miserable?"

His hands clenched in response, but Marcus was done trying to defend himself. He was tired of her disdain, but nothing would stop it.

They lapsed into silence as they trod across the lawn, doing their best to avoid unnecessary noise. Miss Green glanced at the windows of the spacious home, presumably looking for some clue as to where to enter.

"I assume, madam, that you do not have a plan for this either?"

The look she gave him clearly communicated her thoughts. She would be glad to be rid of him. She shrugged nonchalantly, her brow arched in superiority. "I'll figure it out as I go. It's not as if I knew what to plan for."

He emitted a small, strangled sound, his rage mounting for the third time. Crossing his arms, he stood back, reining in his temper and a retort. There was no time for this. He watched her carefully as she moved around the house, occasionally testing windows. The third one she tried was unlocked. Gently, she opened the pane.

So much for the admiral's fortifications.

Her head disappeared inside the home. Marcus quickly

moved up behind her and peered over her shoulder. The room was dark. It took his eyes a moment to adjust. The window led into a salon. The wall colors seemed light in the darkness, chairs and settees artfully arranged about the fireplace to invite conversation.

"Stand aside. I will lead from here on."

She snorted. "Not a chance." Her shoulder pushed at him, barring his entry. "I can't move until you do."

Grudgingly, he moved back, ignoring the lingering warmth from her touch. Marcus frowned at her. "I am not waiting here."

Miss Green's voice was low and forceful. "You must."

"I will not. How do I know you won't warn everyone?"

Her brows rose, her lower lip clenched in her teeth. "My plan won't work if you come. I need you to stay here to catch the girl."

His eyes widened in surprise. "You're going to throw her out the window?"

Miss Green shrugged, hiding her grimace. "Well, what do you suggest?"

"I'll carry her out."

Danni shook her head. "Absolutely not! You are too big and conspicuous to go about unnoticed by a servant. You'll be caught."

Marcus's eyes hardened even as he smiled. "I thought that was your goal."

He'd outmaneuvered her, but the mulish tilt to her jaw told him she wasn't done. She stepped aside, sweeping an elegant bow towards the window. "Then by all means, my lord, we'll go together."

Damned woman was going to get in his way, but at least he could keep an eye on her. Determination surged through him as he grabbed her sack and disappeared through the window. Marcus knew he was in trouble as he watched Miss Green maneuver one shapely leg over the sill and pull herself through the opening, her trousers tightening nicely along the smooth curve of her bottom. Unwelcomed, he imagined running his palm along that thigh, and higher... She stretched on her toes to pull the window closed.

He let out a shaky breath. He couldn't decide whether to kiss her or kill her, thus saving mankind from the witch. And that idea shouldn't even be in his head. He should have known he would have a problem focusing when he'd lusted after her upon first sight. Those trousers claimed all his attention and called him to take action. *Probably run screaming if I even tried to touch her again.*

Grimacing, he held the sack tightly to his chest to muffle any clanking of the items inside. Of course someone like her wouldn't want to be within five feet of him. Despite his high title, women tended to run in the opposite direction whenever he approached.

The creak of a floorboard drew him from his musings. Miss Green stood in moonlight, her face set with frightened determination. She was clearly tense and unhappy, but looked resigned to cooperating. Grimly, he nodded for her to precede him through the house. Marcus studied his surroundings in the darkness; deep shadows outlined small furniture and the layout of the salon. Moving as quietly as his big frame would allow, he crept through the room and into the hallway, his gaze focused intently on Miss Green. She hesitated at the threshold, scanning all directions while he waited for her in the hall. Marcus, too, held his breath, listening for any telltale sounds of movement. She froze, a questioning look on her face. He shook his head, indicating he'd heard nothing.

They didn't wait another second. They hurried as fast as they could up the stairs and turned to the right, where another staircase lay. The sisters' sleeping arrangements were common knowledge among the *ton*. They had not wanted to be separated from each other when their father moved them all to London. The house had recently undergone a large renovation to allow them to all sleep in the same room. Unfortunately, the only room big enough for the seven of them was the attic.

When they reached the top floor, Miss Green opened the door silently. Beyond the threshold were seven beds lining the wall, each containing a slumbering female. Marcus paused outside the door, watching them sleep with a heavy, pounding heart. What was he doing? Was he crazy? How the hell did he think he could ever pull this off? He was more likely to hang from a noose for this than to see himself married! He inhaled a shaky, ragged breath and gathered his nerve from his trusted friend—the flask.

For Caro.

He'd chosen one of the admiral's daughters for a reason. Yes, the admiral would hate him, but if Marcus could manage this, he would also be his son-in-law. The admiral would have a vested reason in squashing scandal. When it came time to break his sister's marriage contract with the Duke of Harwood, Marcus was confident the admiral would have no choice but to support him.

He caught Miss Green's inquisitive glance in his direction. He stared down at the wooden doorjamb, his feet refusing to advance. It was idiotic to think of this threshold as a barrier, but it was. Once he stepped over it, there could be no going back. *For Caro.* He took another swig of whiskey before watching his foot lift, seemingly disembodied, and then landed with a soft rap against the old wood. He set his shoulders. It was done. Hesitantly, he continued inside.

He glanced around, evaluating the different bed sizes and the shapes under the covers. Three beds were on one side of the room and four on the other. Moonlight streamed in through the window, illuminating the path between them. Marcus felt like a dirty intruder as he slipped down the aisle, stopping beside Miss Green. She seemed to be assessing him as he moved. He prayed she wouldn't see how truly terrified he really was. He could not appear weak. He needed her hatred and fear to ensure her cooperation.

Another glance at her confirmed his prayers went unanswered. Her voice was soft and tentative as she spoke. "We can still turn back."

He hardened his own, his voice a sharp whisper. "I can't."

The stuffy sniff that escaped her banished Marcus's tension. "I will never stop trying."

He glanced to the bed nearest them, observing the tiniest child he had ever seen. She looked no more than three, perhaps four. *This one must be Griselda.* Poor thing. He was going to turn her world upside-down.

Moving on, Marcus crept silently down the aisle, glancing at the four beds clearly belonging to the four youngest of the admiral's seven daughters. Reaching the last, he turned and started down the room examining the three other beds. He halted at the threshold. Danni appeared at his side.

"Which one?" she voiced, virtually silent.

He shrugged his shoulders casually. "Hadn't thought that far."

Enraged disbelief seized her before she repeated, "*Hadn't thought that far.*" She struggled to keep her hiss low. "Of course. Why am I surprised? To a fortune hunter and a kidnapper, why would her personality matter?"

"Shhh. Miss Green—"

"As long as she's rich and comely enough to beget an heir, you're satisfied. Come, my lord, pick one. They all have the same dowry."

"Danni."

She fell silent, but her anger was visible in the rapid rise and fall of her chest. For a moment, Marcus was enthralled. She stood before him looking so beautiful in her fury. He felt an intense longing to be defended by her just as she was defending these strangers. He would have liked to know this woman better if his life had run another course. But it hadn't. He looked like a monster and he officially was one now. He was here, about to risk both their lives, commit the worst of crimes, and ruin an innocent girl's life.

With a nausea-inducing jolt, he realized he was more like his father than he ever cared to admit. With shaking hands, he took a drink to dull the painful thoughts.

Ignoring Miss Green's reproving stare, he glanced back into the bedroom. He knew of the girls' personalities only through *ton* rumor. He believed the one least likely to give him trouble was Ginny, or the Ninny, as society had dubbed her. He silently approached her bedside, Danni at his heels. He glanced at Ginny's dark red mane peaking out the top of the sheets. She would do. He needed only her money. He hoped she wouldn't mind being married to him when he told her he wasn't looking for an heir. Ginny was still young, and he wouldn't care if she had an affair. Marcus thought she could be content with him. Perhaps . . . eventually.

"Her." Even to him, his whisper sounded forced.

Miss Green grabbed her sack from him and dug around inside. She pulled out a small vile and a cotton cloth. They stood on opposite sides of Ginny's bed. "What is that?"

"It's soaked in an herb solution. It will put her to sleep."

"She is asleep."

She rolled her eyes. "And do you suppose she will stay asleep when we move her?"

Marcus had to agree she had a point. Sighing, he pulled down the covers, revealing a pair of wide, terrified blue eyes. Ginny's mouth opened wide to scream. *Damn it.*

He clamped his hand down, halting the sound. Miss Green let out a groan, quickly handing him the now wet cloth. Marcus forced what he hoped was a reassuring smile to his lips as he lifted the cloth to Ginny's face. "I'm sorry, sweetheart."

Her eyes widened even further and she began to tremble. He feared he didn't have the stomach to see this through, but he had to save Caro. Suddenly, Ginny's eyes rolled back in her head and her body went limp before he had even placed the cloth over her mouth and nose.

"What happened?" He panicked. Could he have hurt her unintentionally?

"She must have fainted."

Miss Green looked uncertain and then shrugged. "Do it anyway."

Determination coursed through him as he held the rag to her face for a few moments. Satisfied, he stuffed it in his coat pocket. "Hush, but move quickly!"

She was already packing up her bag as Marcus began to lift Ginny. With a grunt, he pulled the girl up and tossed her over his shoulder. He groaned as he lifted her. He really shouldn't have drunk so much.

"Shhhhh," Danni hissed.

"Ugh, I'll never be able to carry her all the way. I'm afraid I might drop her."

Miss Green gave him a considering look, her eyes skimming over his body. He felt himself warm a little under such close scrutiny. He hated to think she was looking at his face.

"What are we going to do?"

Marcus grunted, his mind already assessing the possibilities. Then his gaze landed on the moonlight. He followed it to the window, and then glanced at the sack in her hand. "You have the rope, right?"

"Never leave home without it."

"I'll lower her out the window."

Miss Green glanced from the small window back to the girl. "I don't know if that is a good idea."

"Nonsense, it's brilliant."

Marcus quickly tied the rope around their victim's chest. He fashioned it into a type of harness, padding it with sheets and a dark-colored shawl found at the end of her bed. Miss Green stepped back, allowing him easy access to the window.

Easing the window open, he carefully positioned the woman on the sill. Danni then stepped closer to help. Their bodies brushed tantalizingly against each other. His skin tightened under his coat. He gulped against the sudden rush of heat throughout his body.

Burying his desire next to his past, he gently slipped Ginny from the window frame. Danni stepped closer and helped him carefully ease the girl out the window. When she slipped out the frame, Marcus released a breath he hadn't realized he'd been holding. Danni's soft grunt echoed his. He was about to step back to take control of the rope and ease Miss Foley-Foster to the ground when the rustling of movement reached his ears. He froze, halting Miss Foley-Foster's progress out the window.

Please, please, let it just be someone turning over in their sleep.

Chapter Seven

What is it *now*?"

Marcus waved away Danni's comment, holding his free hand up to his lips. He waited for her nod before he shifted his gaze about the room. Just as before, six girls remained in their beds. None seemed in a different position and he could not see the flash of gleaming eyes in the hazy moonlit room. Fear gripped him more fiercely than it had in a very long time. His heart pounded against his lungs, making it almost impossible to breathe. His shaking palms heated with sweat. God, he needed a drink.

Danni motioned silently with a questioning tilt to her head. He shook his head. Nothing.

The rope tied to poor Miss Foley-Foster cut into the

flesh of his hands. Ignoring the discomfort, he stepped closer to the edge and braced himself against the window frame. Hand over hand, he inched the girl to the ground, careful not to let her bump against the side of the house. With a soft thud, she landed on the lawn. Marcus turned to Danni, who was staring intently through the gloom at the beds again. He sent her a curious look.

The fear in her face told him all he needed.

Marcus nodded and gestured to the rope.

Danni glanced behind her at the beds one more time before grabbing her sack. Marcus stepped aside to allow her to go first. No bickering this time. She tied her pack on her back and grabbed the rope. Swinging her legs out the window, she eased down as fast as she could maneuver. Marcus stepped close to the sill again, watching her quickly shimmy down. A fission of fear brushed his spine. What if she fell?

He had just begun to envision himself being discovered in this bedroom late at night with one unconscious daughter and the broken body of Miss Green below, when tugs on the rope indicated she had jumped safely to the ground. He could barely see her move to untie Miss Foley-Foster. After another panicked scan around the bedroom to reassure himself all was well, he searched for something to anchor the rope for his own descent. The room housed only one item that would hold his weight. He quickly fastened it around a large wardrobe, knowing it would considerably shorten its length. Easing himself out the window, he slid down the rope, burning his palms in his haste. He couldn't leave Danni alone with their captive longer than necessary. He still couldn't trust what she would do. She was a wild card in a plan full of pitfalls.

Sure enough, when Marcus reached the ground, Danni was beside the woman, trying to wake her. No doubt she planned to slow down their escape. Glaring at her, he struggled to lift the girl's dead weight and lumbered awkwardly towards the hidden gate. Danni followed close on his heels. Now that they were almost home free, they couldn't move fast enough.

Once they were hidden in the darkness of the alley, Marcus slipped Miss Foley-Foster off his shoulder. He straightened his strained back before leaning against the cool wall and heaved a broken breath. He reached for his flask, desperate for the hot flow of liquor in his veins. He focused to steady his trembling hands. He'd done it. He'd actually kidnapped a woman.

He felt like hell.

When Danni managed to regain control over her own nerves, she whispered shakily, hiding her fear with a disdainful glare at the whiskey flask.

"Do you think anyone saw us? I thought one of them might have woken."

"No, but..." Marcus swallowed a burning mouthful of golden courage. "If anyone did, I doubt they'll be a problem."

"What about a description?"

Marcus paused, turning over her words. "Unlikely. What could they say? A monster and a leprechaun stole their sister?"

Danni smirked mournfully as the full impact of her crime hit home. Her gaze shifted the sleeping heap of Miss Foley-Foster.

"You *still* plan to take her to Gretna Green?"

He glanced suspiciously at Danni. Gulping another

mouthful, he said, "The deed is done. Why shouldn't I?"

"I am getting out of here, then. I'll just see you off. Phillip will not protest overmuch."

He smiled at his unwilling partner with condescending fondness. She was a fool if she thought he would allow her to stay in London to raise the alarm. Marcus knew she was bold enough to foolishly march up to the front door of the admiral's house and sound the alarm the minute their carriage turned the corner. No, she was coming with them, one way or another.

His mind turned over the possibilities, trying to identify the best way to force her into compliance. With a frown, he glanced down at Miss Foley-Foster, staggered to his feet, and heaved her into his arms.

The idea came to him just as they entered the light around the traveling carriage. Phillip hopped down from his perch, his eyes bugging at the body Marcus carried. "Oh! Please do not tell me you did what I think you did!"

Danni ignored the driver, opening the door of the carriage. The coachman did not cease, his voice rising in panic. "Miss Danni! I thought you were only jesting when you said you were kidnapping someone!"

"Hush, Phillip! We are only borrowing her for a little bit. There won't be a problem."

The man snorted, sending Marcus dirty glances. "It's *his* doing, isn't it? Women simply have no sense to avoid men's corrupting influence."

Marcus placed Miss Foley-Foster comfortably in the coach before he stepped close to Phillip. He dropped his voice an octave, using everything about him that stirred up fear. "You will cease this prattle this moment, or I shall eat you!"

Phillip turned silent and pale, and shrank back in terror. It never ceased to amaze him that people thought he would do it. The effect was ruined by Danni's ill-timed snort of disbelief. "Oh, yes, Phillip. He'll boil you and add a bit of salt to ensure taste."

He glanced at Phillip's smirking form before turning to Danni, who was wrapping Miss Foley-Foster in a traveling blanket.

"I hope you realize I was trying to defend you, madam."

She barely spared him a glance. "I do not need any assistance when dealing with my employees, my lord. Now enter the carriage, please. You must depart."

Marcus clenched his fists, suppressing his anger. Sticking a hand in his pocket, he found the handkerchief he'd used on Miss Foley-Foster. In the same instant he found relief that it had not been lost during their escapade, he feared there would not be enough sleeping draft left on it to have its proper effect. But it was his only real option at the moment.

He approached her from behind as she tucked Miss Foley-Foster's feet under the blanket. Marcus gripped her body tightly against his, ignoring the scent of roses on her skin, and pressed the cloth roughly over her nose, whispering in her ear, "So sorry, but I can't let you tell anyone until we're far enough away."

Her response was a sharp elbow to his ribs. Marcus grunted, but it was a feeble effort, as the drug had already won. She collapsed back against him. He quickly placed her in the coach, next to Miss Foley-Foster. He staggered back, his mind wild. After a frantic search, he pulled out his flask, draining half its contents. Another crime, against another woman. What was he turning into?

Phillip's weak whimper drew his attention. He was staring at him, frozen into immobility like a rabbit caught in a hunter's trap. He barked at the man, "Gretna Green!"

The servant glanced at his mistress before scrambling up into the driver's seat. Marcus gently placed a lap rug over Danni's legs. He climbed in, shut the door, and took the opposite bench. The carriage lurched forward. Marcus sagged back into place, exhausted. The hardest part was done. Now they just had to make it to the little town in Scotland without getting caught.

Should be easy.

* * *

Griselda, or, as she was affectionately called, Grisly, quickly pushed back her covers and inched her way across her bed. She slipped off the end, her small feet tangling in her sisters' hand-me-down dressing gown. The cold of the floor seeped into her soles as she fought free of the fabric. It didn't help that she was violently trembling. She finally rushed to the window, her braided rope of bright red hair swaying from side to side.

At the high sill, she realized she was too short to see out. Her blue-gray eyes fell on the small bookcase in the corner. Padding back and forth, she piled the books as fast as she could until she could see down through the open window properly. The book stack tilted beneath her, but held. Griselda watched as her elder sister was roughly carried across the garden below towards the hidden gate. Moments later, she heard a fiercely ordered

"Gretna Green!" barked into the night, and the rush of a carriage headed north along the road leading away from her home.

She glared at the vanishing carriage from her window, her infamous temper rising. Grisly could barely think through the red haze. She realized what she had to do. Someone had come and stolen Ginny away. No one was going to take her sister where she didn't want to go.

Determined, she kicked the train of her gown free of her feet before hopping off the stack. She glared at each of her sisters in bed, annoyed they had slept through such a horrid event. Stamping her foot, she drew in a deep breath. She was going to do exactly what the admiral did when he wanted the attention of his gaggle of girls—yell.

"Wake up! Someone's taken Ginny!"

Chapter Eight

❦

A short day's travel from his Cot,
New misadventures were his lot;
Dark grew the air, the wind blew high,
And spoke the gathering tempest nigh;

—"Beauty and the Beast" by Charles Lamb

I hate you!"

The booming voice bounded around inside Danni's head like a cannon shot. Groaning, she moved to cradle her splitting skull, but another hand beat her to it. A cool compress rested gently on her brow, moving slowly back and forth to soothe the pain. Unbidden, a sigh escaped her lips. The pain dulled from the cold.

A second hand came beneath her neck, the rough warmth supporting her as a tin pressed to her bottom lip. The tang of metaled water filled her mouth, coating it in iciness. She shuddered, pressing back into the warm hand, the water traveling down her throat and into the pit of her roiling stomach.

Another shriek of anger made her wince, erasing the soothing effects of the water and compress. Despite the ruckus, the rough fingers at the nape of her neck began to move in small circles over her muscles. Another sigh escaped her, her skin tingling with pleasure at the foreign touch. No one had ever done this for her before. The feeling was heavenly.

"I hate you! I bloody hate you!"

A fresh wave of irritation shot through her. She moaned in anger. Whoever was yelling needed to stop. She attempted to open her eyes, but the morning light was blinding in its intensity. Danni immediately slammed her lids shut, hating feeling sick and weak. Her world rocked roughly back and forth, jostling her and the contents of her stomach.

Tin pressed to her mouth again. She drank greedily, even though her mouth felt like cotton and her tongue seemed too big for her mouth. Turning towards the source of the hands, she rested her head on a corded arm. The contrast of coolness and heated skin sent a peculiar heat rising inside her. Clutching her stomach, she feared she was sicker than she'd thought.

"I will hate you forever!"

Gritting her teeth, Danni tried to rise with her eyes still held tightly shut, but a particularly violent bump threw her back down. Her confused brain registered its first fact. She was in a moving coach. She clutched her stomach as the contents of her stomach sloshed again, trying to swallow down the rising tide and fighting to keep her dignity.

She smacked her lips to generate more moisture to swallow. The cold edge of what she assumed was a canteen pressed again to her mouth.

"I hate your hell-ridden guts!"

A pained grunt sounded above after the exclamation. She thought it was odd someone should keep yelling like that. Her brow knitted as her mind started to work again. The yelling and the roll of a carriage didn't fit with her apparent illness. She should be at home being cared for...

With a rush her memories flooded back to consciousness. The blackmail. The kidnapping. The goddamn window. And the...

Danni sat bolt upright, forgetting her still unsettled state. Her eyes felt gritty and achy against the bright sunshine. She had to squint against it and what she saw made her lips stretch in an upward curl.

Fleetwood was crouching on the floor of the carriage, a wet cloth and flask in hand. His green eyes were weary and intense as they stared her down, daring her not to laugh. Behind him was Miss Ginny Foley-Foster. Her nightgown was hiked scandalously above her knees, her back pressed against the opposite side of the carriage, allowing her to brace her feet on Marcus's back, which she was currently stomping repeatedly against. "I hate you, you plague-infested beast! You drugged me!"

With a long-suffering sigh, Fleetwood handed Danni the flask, his voice worn as he spoke. "You'd better drink this. It helped Miss Foley-Foster recover remarkably well."

Danni bit back her smile, rubbing her aching brow. She couldn't stop herself from asking, "How long ago was that?"

"Two hours."

A short bark of laughter escaped Danni as she swallowed another generous sip of water. She glanced again at Ginny, who was lost in the rage of her temper tantrum, continuously kicking and flailing about. Her fiery hair hung wildly about her, her eyes like raging sapphires set in a blazing red face.

"Go to hell, you hated devil!"

Despite his obvious pain, Fleetwood grimaced sheepishly, giving Danni a playful look. "I think it's safe to assume she hates me."

She stifled another smile. His tired look tugged at some place near her heart. It was unsettling and best forgotten. "It would seem that London's Ninny has a temper."

Fleetwood's response was another grumble. Danni glanced down at the canteen. She took another healthy swallow; the water eased the effects of the drug. Staring down at the water, she let anger slip into her voice as she spoke, unable to resist the dig. "I trust this isn't drugged as well?"

Fleetwood grunted as Miss Foley-Foster landed a particularly good kick. "If it was, I'd be giving it to her."

Danni frowned, surprised at this teasing side of him. She'd seen him only as a bully. He still was, in fact. So why did she want to laugh? Had the shared experience of kidnapping bonded them? Was she as bad as he now? She sniffed at him. *Impossible.*

At the sound, his green eyes darkened and his face shuttered. With perverse pleasure at the sight, she glared intently, rallying her temper. She would not have any soft feelings for him. Not for a man who had now drugged and kidnapped her as well. Before, she was just angry at his manipulation. Now he'd added a physical attack. She glared. "You didn't have to kidnap me, too, *my lord*."

His own gaze narrowed, a disbelieving snort escaping him. "And let you walk up to the house and alert everyone before I could get out of London?"

She crossed her arms. Why couldn't he be lack-witted, the drunken sot! It would make everything so much easier. As she glared, a smug smile emerged on his face. He knew he'd beaten her. She hated him.

"Damn you, Fleetwood."

"Oh! That's a nice word!" They both turned a surprised look to their captive. They hadn't even been aware she had quieted and was raptly listening to them. At their mutual attention, she resumed her tirade. "Damn you! I hate you both!"

Danni glanced back at Fleetwood, who managed to shrug despite the abuse to his back. She watched him wince as a kick landed in the same spot twice. Enough was enough.

"Miss Foley-Foster." Danni tried to talk calmly to her, but the girl ignored her. Sighing, she shouted sharply. "Enough!"

The girl halted for a moment, glancing at her with surprise. The cease-fire was all Fleetwood needed. He spun on his feet and caught the girl's feet in his hands. She squirmed, trying to claw at his face. Her blue eyes were wide with panic. Danni could understand her fear; the poor thing had no idea what was going to happen to her and Fleetwood was a very frightening man.

Striving for patience, she moved to the opposite seat and caught the girl's hands in hers. Miss Foley-Foster's eyes widened and pooled with tears. "No one is going to hurt you, Ginny. May I call you Ginny?"

She nodded silently, obviously too overcome with fear to utter a word. "All right, Ginny. My name is Danielle Green and this is Marcus Bradley, Marquis of Fleetwood."

Ginny glanced incredulously at Fleetwood before looking back at Danni. "If you promise to stop hitting his lordship, we'll let your feet go and he will sit on the opposite side of the carriage from you. How does that sound?"

The fear slowly crept away from Ginny's eyes, only to be replaced by a slight narrowing, the sure sign of a scheming mind. Danni wanted to stand and applaud the girl.

"I'll stop hitting him."

Fleetwood let go and fell back in the opposite seat with relief. The moment Danni loosened her grip, Ginny raised her foot and kicked Fleetwood in the face. He let out a howl of pain and cupped his hands over his bruised nose.

"Now I'm done."

Danni froze in shock. She had sincerely not expected the girl to act quite so quickly. Part of her wanted to cheer, but when she looked at Fleetwood, the more sensible part of her wanted to run for safety. He rose from his seat, letting go of the nose he'd been holding. His eyes blazed with deadly fire as blood trickled from a nostril. His lips peeled back, revealing snapping teeth. A growl rolled from deep within his throat. He appeared a true beast in that moment.

Ginny still lay prone on the seat, frozen in terror. She was no longer spitting with fury. Instead, tears leaked slowly down her face. Danni was terrified, too. But she'd be damned if she let Fleetwood hurt the girl, not after all the trouble they went through to get her. Shoring up her courage, Danni threw herself between them. Ginny caught hold of her and roughly shifted to hide more securely behind her, using Danni as a shield. So much for cheering this girl's gumption, Danni thought wryly, as Ginny's nails painfully pierced skin.

"Get back! I will not let you hurt her."

He paused, his body subtly jerking. If Danni hadn't been watching for a sudden move from him, she'd have missed it. Something akin to hurt flashed in his green depths before a snarl of frustration escaped him. "Move, woman."

Danni shifted position, determined to stand her ground. His hands clenched into fists, his chest and body heaved with barely contained emotions. He radiated animalistic power. Suddenly, his fist unclenched and he caught hold of her. Danni gasped with surprise as his calloused hands encircled her upper arms. He held firm, tight enough that she couldn't wiggle free, but not hurting her.

Without seeming to expend any effort, he lifted her, turned within the tight coach quarters, and tossed her roughly on the seat next to him. Danni was too confused to do anything but remain there. She'd never been manhandled in such a way. She wanted to spout her outrage, but knew that moment had passed. Their gazes met in silence and held for a second too long. His rage was gone. He seemed spent, and did she see regret, even hurt, in his eyes?

Fleetwood turned abruptly towards Ginny. Fear rushed back into her ashen face at the sudden onslaught of his attention. Her eyes widened and freckles darkened against her alarming pallor. He loomed over the girl's quaking form, his voice low with fury. "I will not hurt you."

He brusquely tossed her the shawl Danni had stuck in the coach earlier. Ginny watched him as prey would watch a predator.

He cleared his throat, his anger still present but much more restrained. "Do not kick me again, madam."

Ginny's hands caught hold of the shawl, tugging it tightly about her. Her large eyes scanned Fleetwood, her mind clearly turning over his words.

In the silence, Fleetwood rested back in the coach seat next to Danni, head down, hands clasped between his open knees. He sighed deeply.

"I do not wish to hurt you, Miss Foley-Foster. I know I have no right to ask it of you, but would you please do me the courtesy of not judging me by my appearance."

Danni watched in wonder at the rapid transformation from beast to a seemingly broken man. She was certain Ginny was going to reject him outright, to tell him to go to hell. But she did not.

"It is your behavior, sir, that I am currently judging you by, not your appearance." She paused, her voice taking on a thoughtful note. "But I do understand false masks."

He gave her a long, quiet look, as if deciding whether to believe her words or not. He slowly nodded and settled back in his seat.

Danni sat in stunned disbelief, trying to digest what she'd just witnessed.

She'd never considered that something like a peace treaty might be formed between these two parties. She had been certain that Ginny would remain a furious, hapless victim until the end of this wretched play.

She glanced back and forth between the two—each silently staring out the same window, each wearing expressions of thoughtful repose.

Ginny leaned back against the carriage seat, blue eyes rimmed red with tears and wide with stress. Her red hair tumbled loosely over her shoulder, wild-looking from her attempts to harm Fleetwood. She clutched at her purple and orange shawl as if it were armor. A sharp pain pricked Danni's heart at the girl's pale and exhausted face.

Her gaze flicked to Fleetwood, lingering. Scars marred otherwise handsome features. Lines of weariness crisscrossed his drawn cheeks. His eyes were sunken, defeated, vulnerable.

Why didn't the idea of Fleetwood and Ginny together sit well with her?

"Did I break it?"

Ginny's voice broke Danni's disturbing thoughts. Her gaze was fastened on Fleetwood's nose, which he'd taken a rag to moments before. His set face turned towards hers, a slight shake the only indication that it hadn't been.

The relief with which Ginny sank against the seat was palpable. "I know I should not care since you kidnapped me from my bed, but I've never hurt anyone before."

Fleetwood barely nodded again. Danni was starting to feel a pinch of annoyance at him. The poor girl was trying to talk to him, and after his earlier attempt at reconciliation, he was not being accommodating to her awkward apology.

Ginny drew a strand of long hair between her fingers,

quickly wrapping it about in her nervousness. "What is to become of me? Am I to be held for ransom? Are you after the secrets of the Admiralty? I can assure you I don't know anything about my father's work."

Fleetwood's gaze locked on Ginny's. He tensed, as if expecting a blow, but remained silent. He slowly met Danni's eyes, and then reached quickly for his flask. Danni couldn't wait any longer. The poor girl had a right to know her future.

"He plans to marry you in Gretna, Ginny."

Her eyes widened in shock, darting from Danni to Fleetwood. "Pardon?"

"His lordship is in need of money and you have a very large dowry."

"No! I cannot marry like this!"

Danni shot Fleetwood a lethal scowl at the girl's wail, but he wasn't looking at Ginny or Danni. He was staring out the window, gulping another deep draft from the flask.

"Please," she begged, "do not make me marry you, my lord. Use me as ransom instead. Then you will have the funds you need."

It was then Fleetwood turned towards her. When he spoke, his voice was hardened iron, rusted with bitterness. "I know I am not anyone's ideal husband, but I must marry you, Miss Foley-Foster. I recognize how unfair it is to you, but by marrying you, I will be afforded a protection from your father that mere ransom will not provide. I will promise you this, here and now, however. Once we are married, you are welcome to do as you please and you shall retain a majority of control over your dowry."

Ginny was still, her freckles stark in her face. Her water-filled gaze flicked to Danni before it dropped to her lap. Danni remained riveted, helpless as to what to say and how to help her as a droplet splashed on top of her folded hands.

Fleetwood pressed anxiously forward, his handkerchief in hand. His throat, thick with emotion, deepened his quiet voice. "I know I am not what a girl dreams of when they think of a husband and I know I ask much of you. I shall never do anything you do not wish and I will turn a blind eye to whatever you do. Just help me. *Please*."

Danni felt she was intruding on a private moment, and was embarrassed at being a witness to the vulnerability Fleetwood was displaying. It was unsettling seeing such a strong man plead.

She gulped. She could not ever imagine marrying under these conditions. But then again, she was well aware that many *ton* marriages consisted of husbands and wives maintaining different households once an heir had been produced.

Ginny shook her head, her face paling even further. "Please, my lord? Let me go!"

Fleetwood pulled away, leaving his handkerchief in her grasp. "I am sorry, Miss Foley-Foster. No."

Ginny burst into tears. And in that moment, Danni had never hated a man more.

* * *

It was several hours before the well of tears ran dry. Danni moved over to her, pulling the girl into the comfort of her arms. It was then Danni realized how thin Ginny's nightgown was. She had been clutching the shawl to her because she was freezing. Feeling a bit exasperated that she hadn't noticed, she retrieved her bag from the floor of the carriage and dug around inside. She pulled out one of the dresses she'd packed for the girl's trip.

She looked at the simple day dress suspiciously, as if afraid to take it. "It's better than your nightgown and a good deal warmer as well. Fleetwood and I will look away."

The man was already staring out the window, so Danni stood, hunched in the carriage, giving Ginny her back and creating the semblance of a curtain with the shawl. There was rustling for a moment before Ginny spoke again.

"I'm done."

Danni turned back to see that she had pulled the dress over her nightgown and rewrapped the shawl about her shoulders, creating another barrier between herself and the world. Danni understood the feeling. When her mother died, she'd felt an immeasurable sense of loneliness and icy terror. It had taken everything in her not to hide away in her bed, buried beneath blankets.

"Good. I bet you—"

The carriage jerked to a sudden halt as shouting surrounded them. Danni lost her footing and landed directly in Fleetwood's lap. Solid arms slid around her, cradling her close as the carriage tilted terrifyingly to one side. Horses screamed in fear and Ginny's voice rose up from the floor. The chaos around her dimmed weirdly as she glanced up into Fleetwood's face and saw the stark resolve displayed there. She swallowed against the sudden rush of her blood, and the heat of his arms seeped into her, making her feel safe despite the fear surging through her veins.

"Your money or your life!"

"Damn!"

Ginny's curse broke the spell. Danni blinked at Fleetwood. She scrambled from his arms to meet Ginny's suspicious gaze. Then the door of the coach was nearly torn off its hinges.

A masked figure stood in the doorway. He looked as if he had just stepped through time, a man from a bygone era. His tall, lithe form was clothed in a billowing black shirt loosely tied at the neck with ruffles surrounding both his chest and hands. A rapier rested at his hips. Black trousers hugged his thighs and tucked deep into the tops of black boots. On his head rested a buccaneer's hat, a black plume tucked into its dark green ribbon band. He tossed back his matching green cloak, reaching inside the coach. Danni met his taunting gaze, his eyes covered by a strip of black cloth. "Welcome to Finchley Common, home of all things stolen."

"Highwaymen!"

Ginny's startled voice drew the man's mocking gaze. He bowed as if they were in a crowded ballroom. "Very astute, Blue."

The girl's lips drew back in a snarl, baring her teeth, even though the man drew a gun from behind his back. "Are you going to bite me?"

Fleetwood cut off her reply, drawing the man's attention. "Her feet are much more deadly," he drawled.

The thief blinked, taken aback by the scars on the Beast's face. A swift grimace followed, before he hid it away behind a grin. "I'll keep that in mind while I, the Green Bandit, rob you!"

They blinked. Danni had the sense she was expected

to know who he was. He frowned, his gaze traveling between them. "You've never heard of me, have you?"

They shook their heads. Ginny's face was the picture of confusion as she asked, "If you're green, does that mean you're new to this?"

He seemed stunned for a moment, almost puzzled, then he gritted his teeth, muttering about getting a different name. The highwayman held out his hand once more. No one moved, a potent curtain of tension descending over them. Danni cursed Phillip to hell. Anyone with the slightest bit of sense knew that the Great North Road near Finchley Common was rife with brigands. She was only thankful they had so little worth taking.

With a slow breath Danni realized she needed to take action. Fleetwood couldn't move. He was not in the proper position to launch at the man, nor would he be able to reach him before the other man could fire his pistol. She knew Fleetwood was unarmed. Unless that damned flask could be used as a weapon.

She scrambled up from her position between the seats, making sure to grab her sack and tuck it behind her. Hunched over, she moved closer to the highwayman. He blinked at her in surprise before holding out his hand to her instead. Danni ignored it and peeked beyond him. There was only one other man—a Gypsy by the look of him—standing off to the side in a matching outfit. However, he was too busy pointing his gun at Phillip in the driver's seat to pay any attention to his partner. She flashed a glance in Fleetwood's direction, hoping he would see she had a plan.

"Madam?"

Danni scanned the outside area quickly once more, and

looked back to the thief's face, surprisingly close to hers. She tried to meet his eyes, but they were shaded by the wide brim of his hat. She cleared her throat. "I am trying to disembark, sir."

He nodded, lifting his hand a little to draw attention to his offer of assistance. She made as if to reach for it before swinging the bag to hit his head. He dodged left, and Danni dropped her body against his, shoving him with all her might. He stumbled, pulling Danni out of the carriage with him. A snarl erupted from the coach as Fleetwood exited the door in midair. He landed with an ungracious thud upon the tangle of bodies that were Danni and the highwayman. The sound of fist meeting flesh was muffled by the thunder of a gun and an agonizing scream.

Danni froze in horror as Phillip tumbled from the driver's seat. The highwaymen's horses escaped frantically in a cloud of dust amid snorts of fear and trembling withers. Danni dropped her bag, rushing to aid her fallen servant, while the highwayman who shot him grabbed at the fallen reins. Fleetwood thundered past her, diving for the man.

Danni reached Phillip's side, where he writhed on the ground, dust clinging to his uniform and hair. Tears streamed down his cheeks, and he clutched his leg. With her heart in her throat, she caught hold of his hand over his wound. "Phillip? Oh God, Phillip!"

Regret swamped her as she saw the blood on their hands. "Where are you shot?"

"Oh, it hurts," he moaned, voice thick with pain. "I'm going to die!"

"Let me see."

Danni steeled herself as another moan escaped him. She tried to peel his hand away from the injury, but the highwayman's voice halted her.

"No one move and she'll live," shouted the Green Bandit.

She turned to find Ginny with the man's arm around her neck and a pistol held to her temple. The man's face was bloodied, and despite the mask covering part of his face, he looked crueler than anyone she had ever seen. Once again poor Ginny was fast blanching, her eyes popping like a trapped and frantic mouse. Fleetwood's arms were high in the air as the highwayman's dark-skinned friend staggered to his feet beside him, pistol aimed at his heart.

Danni stood slowly, pleading, "What do you want from us? As you can see we do not have any valuables on our persons."

The Green Bandit's leer passed slowly along her figure, lingering at the snug fit of the pantaloons she had snatched from the barn boy last year. "No, no, I can see that you do not." He chuckled. "I do so appreciate a woman in trousers."

Danni flushed so fiercely her world spun. In the daze she heard another snarl of fury gurgle in Marcus's throat.

"You have caused my friend and me a significant amount of trouble here. We deserve some compensation," he continued.

Dread unfurled in her stomach. "Of what kind, thief?"

His partner sneered. "Perhaps some female compensation."

A nasty growl erupted from Fleetwood, but neither man paid him any heed. The one at the carriage door grinned broadly, glancing down at Ginny. "We shall take Blue, I think."

The partner shook his head. "I'd rather that one there. She's full of fight."

The gunman stared at Danni with considering eyes. She swallowed her fear. She had to go with them, not Ginny. This was her fault, after all. Poor Ginny had been through enough already.

"Take me," she whispered.

Fleetwood let out a roar of helpless anger, but the gunman nodded. She inched forward to switch positions with Ginny when the girl let burst her perfectly timed temper at her captor.

Ginny's heel collided with a solid *thunk* into the gunman's shin. He gasped. His hold loosened but did not release.

Ginny screamed, "How dare you!"

The gunman muffled a painful groan and shook her violently. "Silence."

Ginny gasped in outrage, her legs and arms flailing about dangerously. "My father is the Lord High Admiral! He will see you hang."

A smile slowly crept across the Green Bandit's face. "Is he now? That's quite interestin'. I think I'm fallin' in love."

Danni cursed under her breath as the man laughed triumphantly. "It seems like we have a take after all. Blue here is our jackpot. Everyone knows the admiral actually loves his daughters and will pay a hefty ransom, I am certain. Ha!"

Ginny was hauled back into the carriage with the lead man, still kicking and scratching for freedom. Without a word, his partner scrambled into the driver's seat and snapped the horses into a gallop.

In a swirl of dirt and a jangle of livery, the three vanished around the bend.

Speechless, Danni appraised the stunned Fleetwood, the fast disappearing coach, and finally the injured Phillip.

Incredibly, unbelievably, the two villains had kidnapped their kidnapped bride.

Chapter Nine

Hail, snow, and night-fog join'd their force,
Bewildering rider and his horse.
Dismay'd, perplext, the road they crost,
And in the dubious maze were lost.

—"Beauty and the Beast" by Charles Lamb

Danni watched Fleetwood sprint after the coach, horror on his face. The carriage traveled much too fast to catch on foot. He stopped, leaning forward and out of breath. She continued to stare at the racing coach, dust settling among the dying echoes. They had kidnapped Ginny from them. If it had happened to anyone else, Danni could have appreciated the irony.

Fleetwood shouted, voice raspy with panic and disbelief. "The bastards took Ginny. We need to go after them!"

Heat flooded her veins. "I know," she snapped, "but Phillip has been shot. And we have no horses."

He ignored her, turning in the direction the coach had disappeared, worry scoring his scars stark across his face. Danni took one last glance herself at the dust trail before she dropped to her knees beside Phillip. Her servant was her first priority. His death would be a horrible addition to the disaster unfolding about them. Especially when she'd forced him to accompany them. Practically blackmailed him, in fact. As if traveling through highwaymen country was his fault. Oh, she wished she could appreciate the mockery her life had become.

"You have to let me see your injury," she implored him.

He shook his head in misery and continued to roll in the dust as if it was all too much. Danni reached out a hand to comfort him, shocked when she felt the tremors in his body. A snake of cold fear wrapped about her heart. Fleetwood approached from behind, sweating, breathing heavily, his green eyes filled with worry. He squatted beside her, his once lordly appearance ruined with dirt and more than a few rips in his jacket. He placed his rough hand upon her shoulder.

"Where has he been shot?" His frown deepened his vicious scars.

She shrugged fiercely, attempting to remove his hand. It stayed in place. The heat seeped through the fine lawn of her shirt. It helped calm her despite her annoyance with him.

"Go away. I don't need your help."

Fleetwood held up his hands in mock surrender. She

pretended not to miss the comfort of his hand. Danni glanced at the coachman. "He's shaking so badly. Does that mean he's going into shock?"

A swath of concern fell over his features. Shaking his head, he took off his jacket. The heavy weight of it settled around her shoulders, and his familiar spicy scent enveloped her.

"It's not Phillip who is shaking, Danni."

She removed her hand from Phillip. Sure enough, the tremors were visible: her hand and arm quaked. Taking a deep, steadying breath, she began to examine the driver. "Will he be all right? I shall never forgive myself if anything happens to him."

A soft smile, far gentler than she could have imagined Marcus capable of, tugged at his lips. He caught hold of Phillip's hands and moved them away from the site of his injury. She couldn't look. She turned into Fleetwood's shoulder, afraid to see the damage that was all her fault. Unbidden, her body leaped at the contact. The urge to bury her face there to block out the world nearly overwhelmed her.

Fleetwood tensed. Silence filled the air. Danni gulped back a sob, sure that the silence meant Phillip was beyond help. "It's terrible, isn't it?"

A snort escaped him. She pulled back, outraged on behalf of her employee. "Do not belittle his pain!"

His voice was low, rumbling with annoyance as he spoke. "Look for yourself, Danni."

Gathering her courage, Danni turned to look at the wound. Except there was no wound. Not really. On an angry breath, she glared down at her *ex*-coachman's leg. The pale limb was marred by a small scrape, from which only a small amount of blood dribbled. Minor purple bruising grew in the surrounding flesh. There was no bullet wound.

She gnashed her teeth in fury. "I cannot begin to describe what I am feeling."

Phillip moaned, but his eyes remained sealed shut. "How bad is it? I just know I'm going to die!"

Fleetwood rolled his eyes heavenward. His mouth tightened with exasperation. "You were not even shot, idiot. You must have injured yourself when you leaped from the driver's seat."

"Don't lie to me! I can feel my life slipping away. Oh God, have mercy on my soul!"

The rein on her temper slipped. "Phillip, if you do not stop your theatrics this very moment..."

"I repent all my sins! Except, of course, this most recent one. She made me do it!"

"Ahh!" Beyond words, her emotions exploded from the back of her throat. "I'm done with you! You are fired, Phillip. I am sure you shall be able to annoy a great many people in your unfortunately long future."

One eye unsealed. The slit revealed disbelief. "You would fire a man on his deathbed?"

Danni lunged at the prone man, her patience at an end. Fleetwood caught her around the waist. For once, she could ignore the sensations his touch stirred as he hauled her up and away from her ex-coachman. She squirmed in his grasp until he put her down several yards distant. "I am going to kill him. I promise you that!"

He chuckled, his restraining grasp steady and strong. "I do not doubt you are completely capable, little one, but I'd rather not compound our crimes."

Eyes narrowed as she considered his words. "What did you just call me?"

Fleetwood froze, and then a reluctant smile shifted across his face. "Little one?"

"Don't call me that. I am not a child."

He chuckled. "Now that I know that, I fear I shall never stop, *little one*."

"I said don't call me that," Danni grumbled, glaring both at him and over his shoulder at the coachman for good measure. Phillip remained lying in the middle of the road. He had lifted his head to watch them. As soon as she caught his eye, his head dropped and he moaned dramatically, his tongue shooting out the side of his mouth.

"Faker."

Fleetwood threw his head back and laughed.

"This is not amusing," she shouted. "I thought he was *actually* going to die and it would have been all my fault."

He fought for a straight face. "I think we should leave him in the road. If we are lucky, a wild animal will eat him."

"What wild animals? A suddenly carnivorous rabbit?"

"There is always hope," Fleetwood muttered.

Despite herself, Danni grinned. His smile transformed him. He was charming and rather handsome. The marred skin seemed to fade and his eyes darkened, glittering with a fire far from the angry bitterness she had grown accustomed to. His lower lip dented in the middle, creating an unusual dimple, no doubt the result of the scar across his chin. She fought the urge to smooth it with her fingertip.

When he caught her glance at his lips, his smile faded. A wary look cloaked his features. Quickly, he shifted his weight so the cheek with the largest scar was hidden from her. Shame roiled up as she realized what he must be thinking.

"Fleet—"

"We need to catch the coach you lost."

"I lost?" Any feelings of empathy disappeared in a hot flash. "What do you mean, I lost?"

"Exactly what I said. If you had let me handle that situation, we would not be short an heiress and a coach."

"Oh, you horrible man! If my plan was so flawed then why did you go along with it?"

"You didn't give me much of a choice. You practically flew at the brigand."

Danni stomped down the road in the direction of their coach and cargo. "I did not see you formulating any brilliant escape plan. I determined I was the only one capable of orchestrating an attempt at diversion."

Marcus quickly reached her side, his large stride eating up her lead. "As I just said, you did not give me time."

"Where are you going?" Phillip whimpered from behind them.

Danni and Marcus halted. They looked back at Phillip resting on his elbows. Danni glowered. "I thought you were dying."

Instantly, he fell back, writhing on the ground in mock pain. "I am." His hand reached for the sky. "I see the Lord!"

Marcus grunted, looking at Danni. "Where *are* we going?"

Danni hesitated, trying to recall the layout of a map she had studied of the area. "I believe if we simply follow this road, we will run into a town. We may run into them there, or find clues as to their hideout."

He grunted again and kept moving. Seemed he was serious about leaving Phillip. Glancing back at the prone man, she frowned. As much as she wanted to, she couldn't just leave him. She returned to his side and crouched with a sigh. "We shall be back with help."

At his nod, she couldn't resist grousing, "Stay alive until then."

Standing, she spotted a burlap lump in the path—her bag of tricks. She knew among the tools inside lay a spare dress. The memory of the invasive gleam in the bandit's eyes caused revulsion to crawl down her spine. She could wear something proper again.

"The longer you stand there, the further the carriage travels," Marcus snapped.

Her mood plummeted. With one last reassurance to Phillip whimpering on the ground, she grabbed the bag and sprinted ahead, trying to match her pace to Fleetwood's. It was an impossible task. He took a single stride for every two of hers. All she accomplished was making herself pant. "Will you please slow down?"

He didn't. He didn't even speak.

"I take it we're going to keep walking until we reach the coach, then?"

Silence.

Danni jogged ahead. With each stride, her annoyance increased. She darted in front of him to plant herself in his path. He halted, his eyes traveling appraisingly over her body. When he met her gaze, the coldness she was accustomed to had returned. Silently, he stepped around her and continued forward.

Frustrated, she hollered back in disbelief. "You are angry at *me*? You truly cannot blame me for all this! Must

I remind you, you blackmailed me into this horrid escapade? You could not just wait a single day to allow me to plan a safe and quiet elopement."

Danni gasped for air. She had begun to vent and there would be no stopping now. "If we had waited, my regular coachman would have been back from your ex-fiancée's trip and he would have known to avoid this road."

"Never mention that woman again," he snapped.

She paused at his sudden roar. Frozen mid-step, she caught the broken, lined expression that turned his eyes a dark, forest green. He suddenly turned away, clearing his throat roughly. "My apologies."

She gaped. He'd apologized?

He resumed his brisk progress. And his silence. Danni bit her lip, feeling oddly put out. She should be happy he was ignoring her. After all, he was the Beast.

They continued for several more yards before she could no longer remain mute. "Fine. If you do not wish to speak to me, then so be it."

Fleetwood did not acknowledge her comment. Grinding her teeth, Danni jogged to catch up with him again. She'd dealt with stubborn men before. This would be no different.

*　　*　　*

Danni managed to remain quiet for all of three hours. She'd no practice telling time by the sun. Instead, she counted each second as it passed. It was better than leaving her thoughts to drive her mad.

"Fleetwood?" she finally muttered.

Silence.

She gnashed her lip and lifted her feet higher, changing from a steady walk to that of a storming slam, crushing greenery beneath her feet. *Even Hu isn't this stubborn.*

At the thought of her friends, she realized how much she needed them. If Hu had come along, none of this would have happened. And Annabel would have been sympathetic to Danni's troubles. She would hate Fleetwood with her. Having an ally would have been a luxury at the moment. As would a sandwich. Particularly a watercress sandwich.

She clutched her protesting stomach. Determination swept though her. She lifted her knees even higher. Her mission was to make as much irritating noise as possible.

A particularly loud snap jolted up her leg, surprising her. She glanced down at a freshly broken stick mingled with the rich dirt of the decomposing forest floor. Fleetwood had led her into this endless green forest almost a quarter of an hour ago. He had not explained their change of direction. He'd simply veered and expected her to follow. *Arrogant man.*

Danni had considered staying on the North Road, but she was not about to endanger herself for the sake of winning their standoff. They were still too deep in bandit country for her to wander off alone. Her fear for Ginny spiked again. She could not allow herself to imagine what these vile kidnappers were doing to her. Danni's hungry stomach turned sick with helplessness and worry. She had allowed this to happen. In fact, she had been instrumental in creating this entire mess. She had sacrificed a poor innocent to save her own skin. She was viler than the thieves.

Her worry that Marcus and she had been spotted kidnapping Ginny turned to hope that the girl's family must have discovered her missing by now. It meant that not only were she and Fleetwood searching for her, but so was the Admiralty. She was suddenly thankful to be off the Great North Road. The admiral could have rounded the corner and captured them at any moment. Her panic at the thought of a noose around her neck nearly matched her fear for Ginny, and, she admitted, of losing Fleetwood in these damned woods. She was not particularly willing to test the theory he would double back to search for her.

So when a particularly ill-tempered branch decided to swing from Fleetwood's grasp and hit her in the face, she'd had enough.

"Where the *hell* are you leading us?"

Her enraged tone raised no response from her companion. As much as she enjoyed staring at his admittedly well-sculpted back, she wanted answers. She also wanted to hear another human voice. If she enjoyed this kind of strained silence, she could have remained with her father at their home on King Street and never opened Gretna Green Bookings.

Thoughts of her father brought thoughts about her fiancé. Well, almost fiancé, assuming the Earl of Hemsworth didn't believe her absence meant she was refusing his offer. She swore to herself, if she managed to return Ginny safely to her family without exposing her life to complete scandal, she would meet with the lord and her father to formally accept the marriage arrangement. She'd have a wonderful life as a countess and Danni was confident she and the earl would grow to love each other very much. It would be the fairy tale ending she'd always wanted.

Vaguely, she wondered if her father was worried about her. She dearly loved and respected him, but he was so involved in his work at Parliament, at times she wondered if he even remembered she existed. But she knew Hemsworth would be. He was a kind and considerate man, and she knew he cared for her.

Surrendering to the silence and her troubled thoughts, she trudged onward. The lush greenery, so rare in London, glimmered quite spectacularly in the sunbeams streaming through the canopy. It reminded her a little of the way Fleetwood's eyes looked when he smiled at her back at the clearing. Danni scoffed at herself. *What fanciful thoughts to have about* him*!* Hadn't she just been dreaming about her future life with her fiancé?

The longer she walked, the more furious she became. This was really all Marcus's fault. He had manipulated her and then blamed her for his own misdeeds. What right did he have to make her miserable as well? He should be working with her, seeing to her needs rather than dragging her through the rough woods and then, on top of it all, completely ignoring her.

She couldn't let him win and she certainly didn't intend to let his stubbornness reign while they tried to find Ginny. An idea mulled in her mind. She'd make him have a part in the discussion. Grinning devilishly, a definite spring developed in her step.

"Oh dear, I believe we are in trouble. You don't know where we are going, do you?"

When he didn't respond, Danni prattled on with an even wider smile, getting into the spirit of things. "I see how baffled you are, my lord. Not to worry! I'm sure we can determine where you've misplaced us."

Fleetwood's shoulders shifted slightly, the only sign he listened.

"Where should we start? My father always said one should study your surroundings. We may find a clue if we do just that!" Danni paused, exaggeratedly looking about her. "We are surrounded by a great many trees. And plants. I think we can safely assume our current position is a forest. You *do* know what a forest is?"

He still wasn't speaking, but by the condescending look he sent her way, she had his attention. "Oh dear! Don't tell me you don't know what a tree is, either?"

A snort escaped the hulking giant before her. His sight remained fixed ahead of him. Dismissing her.

A headache from clenching her teeth stabbed through her skull. She opened her mouth to emit her next mocking tirade, only to swallow a mouthful of leaves and twigs from a sapling branch. Sputtering, she toppled to her bottom. She blinked away her surprise to see Marcus's smirking face quickly swing forward again.

"Oh. You . . . you beast! You did that on purpose!"

"And what exactly did I do?"

"You snapped that tree branch into my face!"

He turned and glanced down at her. His expression was a perfect example of befuddlement. "What's a tree branch?"

Danni gaped. Not even a muscle twitched on his face as he continued. "And this plant you speak of? Is it edible?"

She pulled up her sleeves as she dragged herself to her feet. She glared daggers at him. "Only if you're a rabbit!"

Furious, Danni launched at him.

Laughing, he caught her around the middle, drawing

her tight into his reverberating chest. Danni muffled a gasp. The sound thrummed through her, to the very tips of her fingers. Hard planes engulfed her small frame and big palms splayed over her body. Like a spark to tinder, her blood ignited with heat, pooling between her thighs.

And then he tickled her.

Eyes bulging, she gave a muffled screech at the familiar tingling sensation. Laughter rippled around them until tears blurred the forest solid green. "Stop! Please."

Immediately, he was gone. Danni gasped at the shocking loss of contact. Cold air ripped at her skin and she wrapped her arms protectively about her. She turned, finding him right behind her. Clutching at her sides, she watched with a deep sense of sadness as Fleetwood's—no, *Marcus's*—boyish and utterly heart-wrenching expression of happiness melted away, replaced with his usual stern countenance.

"Sorry," he whispered, his eyes a soft, mint green, resting on her stinging cheek. His hand lifted, catching a strand of her hair between his fingers. Comforting warmth hovered tantalizingly above her skin as he looped the dark hair about his finger. "I meant to hold the branch, but it slipped."

Danni watched the lock of hair slip slowly from his grasp before his fingers brushed gently over the welt forming from the branch. She felt breathless and her stomach churned in odd, uncomfortable flips. Swallowing hard, she searched his eyes.

She couldn't believe she'd first thought they were cold. The green depths exposed every thought passing through his mind. And when he whispered "Forgive me?," she knew he was referring to much more than the branch.

But she couldn't.

Sniffing, she continued her game with forced cheer. "This is so much worse than I originally thought! Perhaps I should explain what a plant is. I think a tree branch is much too difficult for you."

Sadness flickered over his scarred face before it shuttered closed. Her heart actually ached inside her chest. Silence descended between them again as they resumed walking. It was strained and utterly unbreakable.

How did one even go about forgiving someone for the situation he'd forced her into? Perhaps if she understood his circumstances a bit more? All she'd really seen evidence of was an apparent, and pressing, need for funds. Not the reason why.

She'd assumed since he drank, he enjoyed other vices such as gambling and had ruined his estate. It happened to many aristocrats and they often turned to borrowing against their titles to maintain the lifestyle they were accustomed to. Or marrying wealthy young girls.

And then there was that article published in Miss Lavina Lux's gossip column before they left, but that could have been spread by a bitter Anne Newport. After all, rumor was really just that—rumor.

Maybe if she asked, he'd tell her a fantastic excuse that would absolve him and she could help him, without forcing Ginny into marriage? Preparing her thoughts to do just that, Danni suddenly slammed into something solid. Lost in her own world, she'd missed that Marcus had stopped again. She stepped right into his back before being knocked to her bottom for a second time. Her hands gripped dead leaves and moss in frustration. "Did I ever tell you how much the ground and I dislike each other?"

The large man hesitantly half turned towards her. His eyes were shadowed, dark pools. "Did you hear that?"

Danni blinked, tilting her head and straining for a sound that didn't belong. After a moment, she shook her head.

He grunted, his emotions vanishing behind his typical stern and distant expression. His head turned away, shading the worst scarring. His hastily taunting words banished her curiosity about how he had received the terrible marks. "Of course *you* wouldn't hear anything."

She glared as he ran a hand through his curling locks. Danni had to squelch the urge to do the same. To feel the soft silk of his whitish hair, to feel the stubbly points of the curl's end. She could not help but feel it would soothe her as well.

Tightening her fists, she fixed her attention on the forest floor. She had a soon-to-be fiancé and a happily ever after waiting for her at home. She would not jeopardize it for a flight of fancy, or some silly infatuation, or whatever this—this feeling was. She needed to be returned home with Ginny as soon as possible and leave this beast in its natural habitat. It would be safer for Ginny, but much more so for her. The longer she stayed, the greater her fascination with this complicated man.

They had to retrieve their victim. And she needed Marcus to do that. Trying to lighten the mood, she asked, "Does this mean you're speaking to me again?"

A heavy silence descended. His eyes narrowed and his face became chiseled ice. He had adopted another veil. Straining under the weight of it, she averted her eyes.

The familiar pop of dead leaves underfoot alerted her as Marcus resumed his trek through the brush. Danni remained momentarily frozen. Was he going to abandon her after all this?

He paused, turning the unscarred side of his face in her direction. His green eyes blazed with emotion, the shadow hidden, but not gone.

"I have yet to decide."

He continued walking, clearly expecting her to follow. She blinked at the arrogant response to her question. Gritting her teeth, she hurried to his side, railing, "I cannot believe you! I have been blackmailed. I have been drugged. I have been held at gunpoint. Not to mention trekking through this godforsaken forest for hours without an ounce of food, all at your behest. And you do not think I am worthy of a conversation?"

Silence.

"Perfect. Simply perfect! Now I only need it to snow in May and my life will be complete."

Another three hours later. Yes, she counted every second again. Danni struggled to be grateful for small favors. It didn't snow in May.

It rained.

Chapter Ten

🜂

When glimmering through the vapours drear,
A taper shew'd a dwelling near.
And guess our Merchant's glad surprise,
When a rich palace seem'd to rise

—"Beauty and the Beast" by Charles Lamb

Marcus huddled deeper in his jacket as he tried to avoid as much of the rain as possible. It was a useless endeavor. He was already soaked through. Shuddering against the creeping chill in his bones, he glanced back.

Several feet behind him, Danni's body scrunched even smaller against the cold. He stopped walking. She drew closer, each step echoed by the squelching sound of soggy leather boots. Marcus could see the expression on her face much clearer. She was furious.

Despite her indignation, he couldn't stop the urge to

smile, certain she had no idea what she looked like. Her lovely locks of mahogany hung about her in limp tangles, the ends still caught up in the braid she'd started with last night. The rainwater dripped down her forehead and caught in dark lashes. A small patch of soil had stuck to her cheek when she'd launched at him earlier. With the rain, dirt now streamed down her pale cheeks in brown rivulets. For lack of a better description, she looked like a half-drowned rat.

She was beautiful.

"Why are we stopping?" Her teeth chattered together, the sound audible in the silent forest.

One glance at her thin, rain-soaked garb staggered him. Clad in clothing much more appropriate for a mild London evening, the light fabrics of her trousers and shirt were plastered to her skin from the harsh weather. The billowing linen was rendered nearly see-through, outlining every luscious curve. Her pants stuck to her legs, showing her curves off in stark relief. Heat warmed him inside out, his body aching with urges better suppressed.

His gentlemanly conscience suffered a pang. She had on fewer layers than he and her small body had much less bulk for insulation. Before he could change his mind, he shucked his jacket, peeling the layer off as if virtual skin. Instantly, he felt the chill in his bones deepen as a cold wind ripped through the wet canopy. Sometimes being a gentleman was a pain in the arse.

Fighting to speak through his clenched teeth, he held out the coat. "Take it."

She eyed him with suspicion, her arms uncurled as she reached for the wool. He wasn't certain what warmth the soaked coat would offer, but it made him feel slightly bet-

ter. Her death by lung inflammation would end a rather
spectacular venture into crime with a flourish. He'd never
thought he'd fail so utterly.

The moment she uncrossed her arms, Marcus's mouth
went dry.

"This does not change anything. I am still angry at
you," she muttered miserably.

He didn't listen, couldn't. The wet linen perfectly outlined her breasts. His hungry gaze fastened on a tight, pink
nipple clearly visible through the shirt. He swallowed the
urge to touch her, his fingers curled in response. The budded tip seemed to call to him. Ached for him to warm
it with his mouth—to lavish attention on its cold tip. His
blood burned. With a shudder he dropped his gaze.

Misinterpreting the reason for his shiver, Danni looked
at his dark navy jacket, clearly torn. "Perhaps you should
keep it."

Her face said she'd rather eat a shoe than give it back.

Lips tightening, he pressed it back towards her. He
needed her to wear it now. The wet wool would hide her
tempting breasts and temper some of his lust. The image,
however, was forever engraved in his memory.

She settled the extra layer about her shoulders. He
stood near enough to smell the soft scent of roses her
movement stirred.

His nails bit into his palms. Being near her like this
maddened him. He'd thought he suffered from insanity
before, but this...it was hell not being able to touch a
woman so beautiful, so near. With great effort he turned
his thoughts to survival. He needed to find shelter. And a
fire with which they could wait out the storm.

He turned away without a word. He did not trust himself to speak. An aggravated noise came from the back of Danni's throat, before the squelching and squeak of her boots began again. This time Marcus did smile.

"You truly are insufferable. It's not as if I do not deal with silent men on a regular basis. My father hardly ever talks to me—barely recognizes I'm even alive—since my mother died, and Hu has said all of ten words in the entire two years I've known him. But *they* at least find some way to communicate! You do not even look at me when I speak."

A pang echoed through his chest as she let slip the information about her family. Perhaps that was why she became a fraud? To gain her father's attention? The urge to tease her, to wipe away thoughts of her father, overwhelmed him. "If I look at you while you speak, I might run into a... what did you call it? A tree branch?"

"Oh! Oh, I think I hate you."

He hid a smile. "I shall never recover, madam."

A particularly loud squelch-squeak echoed through the trees. Marcus could only guess she'd tried to stomp her foot.

"And I hate these boots, too!"

Grinning, he scanned the tree line, looking for a place they might weather the rain in. Danni fell silent, the only sound from her the constant squelch-squeak of her boots.

"Fleetwood?"

He tilted his head to show he was listening.

A heavy sigh, one as if the weight of the world were on it, came from behind him. "I purpose a truce."

He stopped mid-stride, pivoting on his heel. His surprise was evident in his voice. "A truce? As in we stop fighting with each other?"

Her brow lowered; the overly large coat made her look like a child playing dress up. "Yes. What other kind is there?"

He opened his mouth, but her hand flashed into the air, halting his comment. Or rather the sleeve of his jacket shot into the air. He assumed she still had an arm inside it.

"It will be to our mutual benefit. If we are constantly bickering, I cannot imagine our search for Ginny will be fruitful."

He had to admit that she had a point.

He began to listen to her terms of truce. Something about manhandling, something else about...Marcus stopped listening. Facing her had given him a new perspective of the surrounding forest. Off to one side, a small building—if one could call the dilapidated heap a building—peaked through a pair of towering oaks.

"...and so do you agree to my proposal?"

Marcus ignored her. He caught hold of Danni's jacket-covered hand and dragged her in the direction of the cabin.

"I beg your pardon! I think I mentioned in the terms of our treaty that I was *not* to be manhandled."

He snorted. The desire for shelter and a fire was much more important to him than some hare-brained treaty. The underbrush slapped against them as he pushed through it, until they stood facing the front of the lodge.

It was not as bad as it had seemed from far away. Nature was reclaiming the wooden building, vines climbed and twisted up all sides. But beneath the greenery, the worn structure looked sturdy. And the roof was intact. The door hung on one rusted hinge. It would create a draft, but it was much better than outdoors.

Danni's protests died when she spied the building. She let out a gurgle of pleasure, clapping her hands together. "Brilliant, Fleetwood!"

He didn't exactly think he could take credit for a pre-existing building, but he was not about to argue if it put a smile on her face.

He ducked through the doorway after Danni. The luxurious inside startled him. He would not be surprised to learn the cabin had been someone's illicit nest. The once expensive furnishings were threadbare and weather stained. A well-worn chair caught the steady drip of the leaky roof.

They needed warmth, badly, so he approached the hearth directly. Fumbling among the crumbling bricks and ashes, he found a flint. The small stack of kindling would not be enough. With a sinking stomach, he knew they would never find dried tinder outside.

Across the small room he spotted a narrow bed. Brushing off the dead leaves, he pulled the bed linens from the old, straw mattress. The sheets were passable. He tossed one to Danni, who watched him through wide, silent eyes.

"Take off your clothes." Marcus could feel his face heat but did his best to ignore it.

Danni's outraged cry made her opinion apparent. "I most certainly will not. 'Tis bad enough I have to share these small quarters with you. There is no privacy and if people found out I had..." She paled, her eyes narrowed with rage. "I absolutely will not!"

He tried not to envision Danni clad only in a bedsheet. Sharing the same room. He gritted his teeth. "Fine. You want to catch a fever and die? Then continue wearing your soaked clothes."

Her gaze condemned him to hell. "Turn around and I'll wear the dress in my pack."

The pressure on his teeth increased. "I shall do you one better."

Marcus left the building. He did not stop at her shocked gasp, nor did he go far. He trekked around the edge of the small cabin, searching for firewood, or anything else of use. He located an old wooden bowl. How it had come to be deposited on the small porch was a mystery he did not bother to consider. Gratefully, he held it up to the pouring rain, and gulped several refills before feeling quenched. Returning to the building with the bowl, he remained outside in the rain. Determined to give her all the time she needed.

It wasn't a painless exercise. He unwillingly strained to hear even the smallest rustle of fabric. His imagination took him to places he'd never go. Grasping the bowl tighter, he imagined how her cool skin would feel in his warm hands. His questing fingers warming her as he explored the full curves of her body, the rain beating down outside around them. Even with the deep chill, hot blood managed to reach his groin. A frustrated groan escaped him. This constant state of desire was growing unbearable.

"Are you decent yet?"

She snapped a retort. "If one applies the word loosely."

He shook water from his head as he ducked into the cabin. His breath caught at the sight of her. She'd opted to wear a dry shift, wrapping the thicker bed covering about her. The yards of fabric were artfully draped about her, covering as much of her as possible. Her hair hung in thick strands—freed and finger-combed of its loose braid. Only the small patch of dirt on her face marred the appearance that she had just stepped from a steaming bath.

"The dress is damp. It would have gotten even worse if I wore it now," she muttered, turning away.

The arousal he'd been fighting returned with full force. Blinking against it, he averted his gaze, offering her the bowl. "Have a drink, then you may wish to wash your face."

Her hands shot directly to her cheeks, a look of female panic budding on her face. "What?"

Unable to stop a small smile splitting his lips, he placed the bowl on the chair to catch rainwater. To think she was self-conscious about her appearance in front of *him*. "A bit of dirt. It's from your attempted attack on me."

She shot him a venomous glare as he collected a sheet. "According to the peace treaty, the initiating party of said treaty has the right to attack without retaliation in any form, including words."

That captured his attention. He spun, staring at her with disbelief buried in his half smile. "You cannot be serious."

Her arms crossed, her face carved of stone. "Perfectly."

"It's blatantly ridiculous. I refuse to agree to your treaty."

"You already have."

Marcus's brow lowered. He suspected he was going to have to kill her. Very soon.

"You agreed when you took my hand. It was a bit of an unorthodox handshake to seal the deal, but it still counts."

"Like hell it does!"

"Ah. I shall have to add Rule Number Seven: No crude

words or behavior shall be uttered or undertaken in the presence of the peace treaty's initiate."

"*Hell*." He smirked. "You sound like a *bloody* politician!"

Her face paled and he wondered if he'd pushed her too far. "I apol—"

"Rule Number Thirteen: The agreer of the peace treaty shall make no inferences nor insulting assumptions based on the actions of said truce's initiator."

He batted his eyelids. The audacity of her! She walked around the soaked chair, her bedsheet trailing behind her. She carried herself as if she were in the most fashionable ballroom in London, in the very best gown. Not naked beneath linen and a blanket. In a cabin. In the middle of Nowhere, England. She tossed her head, her nostrils flaring with displeasure. "Shall I add another amendment?"

"This is complete nonsense," he accused.

A devilish gleam entered her caramel gaze, darkening it. "Attempts at an amicable relationship are nonsense?"

A blurt of laughter burst from him. He smiled softly, unfamiliar tenderness stealing through him.

Her face scrunched, her arched brows knitting with mock aggravation. "I am not attempting to be amusing."

He laughed again, and her cheeks brightened with fury. She grit her teeth with frustration. "You would force a saint to murder."

He smirked. Two could play this game. "Rule Number Fourteen: The initiate of truce shall not slander any and all deity figures for the purposes of insulting the signer of said truce."

Her lips parted, stunned. Then she suddenly broke into

a smile. Her eyes softened, gleaming with lighthearted humor. The wide grin changed her face, sending a jolt through his heart. He'd made her smile. He, the man who didn't deserve any civility, had made her smile.

Her eyes shifted to the sheet in his hand. "If I am not allowed to take a chill, then neither are you."

His enjoyment vanished, replaced by a familiar anxiety. Undressing in front of Danni was not going to happen. He did not show others his body, not ever. The few who had seen it, Weller included, recoiled. If the debutantes thought his face frightening, they would die of horror at his naked form.

Her opinion should not matter to him. She was merely a tool with which to accomplish an unpleasant task. But as he stared at her challenging face, he knew her thoughts did matter, deeply. Had mattered from the very beginning. He did not want to be a surly, ill-reputable beast in her estimation. Despite the fact that he was exactly that. And now a criminal, as well.

"The sheet will absorb most of the water. And once I build a fire, the heat will take care of the rest," he evaded.

Swiftly, her anger returned. He recognized the reaction was one of concern. "I do not need you getting sick, Fleetwood. I promise you I make a terrible nurse."

"I shall be fine. I have a stronger constitution than you, little one."

She snorted. Ignoring her, he dried himself, as she muttered, "Of all the arrogant, male statements to make."

Throwing the soggy sheet to an abandoned corner of the room, he moved towards a broken stool, seeking wood for a fire. Leaning it back on its rear legs, he exposed the upper two to the air. With a swift kick, he broke one of the legs free. A loud bang sounded against the floor. A shriek escaped Danni. Marcus reacted instantly.

He dived at her, bringing them both crashing to the ground. He cradled her in his arms, protecting her from the worst of any potential impact, his gaze flitting frantically about the room. He couldn't catch his breath as he positioned himself on top of her, forming a human shield. It was a position he had not been forced to use in years. Not since Caro had been safely removed from their father's house.

"Fleetwood?"

The corners were dark. Nothing moved. From his past he knew that didn't mean danger wasn't lurking.

"Fleetwood!"

His gaze landed on the upturned wooden bowl. The collected water stained the wooden floor and frayed, Persian carpet. Next to it lay the leg he'd broken off the stool to use as firewood.

"Marcus!"

Dimly, he registered pressure against his chest. He glanced down, eyes colliding with Danni's. Her expression held surprise and a bit of fear. He realized what he'd done and, infuriatingly, shame crept up to heat his face. If she had not thought him a monster before, she must now.

He dropped his head, searching for an excuse for his behavior. He avoided crowds and public places for this reason. He never knew what he would react to.

The longer Marcus remained above her, the more his fear receded and the more he became aware of her soft body beneath his. Their legs tangled together among the bedsheet, their hips fitted together perfectly, her breasts cushioned his chest. Her breathing matched his in a deep, calm rhythm. The warmth of her body mingled with his, smooth skin and scents combined into a heady mix that hazed his thinking. He muzzled his face deep into the heat of her neck, lingering in the contentment he found there, suddenly, utterly incapable of raising his head. He dreaded the disgust he would find in her eyes.

A moment's stillness from her encouraged him to peek up, careful to hide the worst of his marred face. He could see Danni's confusion slowly recede. Her cheeks turned the dull red he loved, her eyes softened. Soft, small hands came to rest on his shoulders, palms heating his skin. She shifted beneath him, brushing her thigh against his groin. He couldn't breathe, his heart pounding in his ears. "Do not move, little one."

Her brow knit. "Why?"

With supreme effort, he reined in his raging emotions. He breathed deeply into her neck again, lips barely grazing her sensitive skin. A race of shivers cascaded down his back. "You're ruining my already shaky control."

"Oh." Pink lips parted in surprise. Then her hands caressed his shoulders, rubbing in a circular pattern. "We are safe. No need to worry." She shushed, and then whispered, "Does this help?"

Absolutely not.

His lust roared to life. His skin tingled and tightened at her touch. He could barely breathe. Her body cradled him perfectly. "Er, a little."

Marcus felt her smile, and imagined how it would have lit her caramel eyes. Her hands moved steadily lower. In that heartbeat, he wished he could read her thoughts.

"Marcus?" Her voice was soft, thick, husky. He savored the way she said his given name. Longed to hear it on her lips every day.

"Hmm?" He reluctantly lifted his head.

Her features were gentle and flushed. Softly, she said, "You are quite heavy. Can you remove yourself now? Please."

Shame returned with a vengeance. He rolled to the side and avoided looking directly at her. Running a hand through his hair, he wished desperately for a drink—he'd never craved one more.

He was an utter fool. Not only had he crushed her to the floor because of his damned nerves, he'd actually thought—for a moment...

Shaking his head to clear it of ludicrous fantasies, he rose to his feet, and Danni quickly followed. He tried to hide his face, but her head tilted to follow him, her gaze curious and considering. He despised such close scrutiny.

He used the first excuse that leaped to mind. "My apologies. I...I don't know...I thought the roof may have been collapsing, or that the floor gave way." He cleared his throat, avoiding her gaze, "I thought you were in danger and...I just wanted you...safe."

Tension hung in the air. From the corner of his eye, he saw Danni slowly nod and move a bit farther away. "I'm fine. I was surprised by the wood breaking."

"I see," he murmured.

Swallowing the knot in his throat, he collected the chair leg from the floor to fuel the fire and resumed his task. It wasn't until the first sparks grew to small flames that Danni finally spoke. Her voice was even. Almost too calm. He'd thought she would rant and rave, insisting an immediate return to civilization. Instead, she carried on as if nothing had happened. "Next time, warn someone you're going to break a chair. It startled me."

Marcus was far too stunned to respond. She'd swept his inexcusable and inexplicable behavior away, as if with a flick of her delicate wrist.

He worked intently to build the fire to a rage inside the cluttered hearth, then settled back against the bricks surrounding the fireplace. Warmth spread across his back, drying his clothes. He rested his head against the wall in exhaustion, stress from the disaster he had created causing a pounding in his skull and his vision to blur. He tried to crush the bubbling memories of his father's condemnation and failed. How his father would revel in this dismal failure.

His past crashed upon him. He began to tremble violently, limbs weakening and most assuredly unable to support him. Perspiration broke across his brow and his skin felt unbearably tight and hot. Hell was approaching, clawing at the back of his mind.

The rustle of drapery, accompanied by the soft patter of naked feet, marked Danni's arrival by his side. Closing his eyes at the dizziness, he focused on the heat seeping through his body. He must be strong. He could not let Danni witness the pitiful creature he would devolve into. Her worried whisper echoed in the flickering darkness of the fire.

"Do you think they have…hurt…Ginny?"

Guilt clenched his gut. "No, of course not. She is worth more ransom if she is unharmed."

But they both knew it to be untrue. The admiral would pay any price to have her back, in any condition. Marcus would swear he could hear his father's taunting laugher from hell.

"I hope Philip has been helped, or he located shelter."

Marcus smiled weakly in her direction. She was far too kind to worry about that man. "You are exhausted, little one. Don't waste your worry on the likes of him. His type always finds a way. There is nothing to be done to help either of them 'til morning. Sleep now so we'll have energy for tomorrow."

Despite his words, guilt tore into the fragile control he grasped. Phillip's well-being was his responsibility as well.

Unaware of his turmoil, she nodded reluctantly, bedding down a few feet away before the fire. In the silence, he listened to her breath deepen and slow. He watched her as she fell asleep. Mahogany tresses splayed out around her, bathed in the soft, golden glow of the fire. His stomach curled with envy at the rich reds and golds weaving along her arms and shoulders, longing to wrap it through his fingers instead. His hands clenched and his throat tightened. The silken caress of the single strand he'd touched in the forest was forever engraved upon his mind. Sadness engulfed him. She was everything he dreamed of, yet would never have.

He could just make out the reddened shadow on her cheek from the slap of that tree branch. He hadn't lied to her. The branch had slipped, but he couldn't resist teasing her when it had. A soft smile tugged at the corners of his mouth at her remembered outrage.

Again, he swept his gaze over her deliciously curved frame, noting how her head rested on one arm and her knee rose to her chest beneath the blanket. If only...if only he met her under different circumstances. If only his father had not written that codicil. His father...his father still controlled him, even after all these years. Ironically, in his attempt to escape his father—dead a year now—he had completely ruined his own life, Ginny's, Danni's, and perhaps Phillip's. And he'd also failed to save Caro.

Staring into the flames, his fist tightened, and he was afraid he'd become engulfed by the endless black pit of dark images lurking beneath the surface of his life. He ran a hand through his hair. Sleep eluded him and his stomach ached with hunger, but what he really wanted was a drink—brandy, whiskey, *anything*. Something to slide with quiet fire down his throat and unfurl in his belly. Something warming and numbing. Deadening.

The world shifted again.

Damn.

He was losing the fight. Hell would soon envelop him and he'd be trapped for hours in the horrors of his past. How he wished Weller were here. He'd know what to do. How to hide this weakness from Danni.

Groaning softly, his eyes shuttered closed and his mind swallowed him whole.

*   *   *

A strange whimpering jolted Danni from her sleep. She blinked several times to clear her eyes while scanning the growing shadows in fear. Had some sort of animal been attracted by their dying fire?

Seeing nothing, she turned over, nearer the fire. Her eyes were closed, but her ears remained alert. She heard only the continuous chime of rain outside on the forest canopy. And against the leaky roof above them. The soothing pattern lulled her back to the cusp of sleep.

Another whimper. This one closely followed by a low, keening moan of pain.

Danni sat up. The keening came again. Surprised, she turned towards Marcus to wake him. What use was a large man like him if he did not beat away the beasties?

A cry unlike anything she'd ever heard erupted, bounding about the room. Danni shrank back as a trill of fear raised the hair on the back of her neck. Gathering her courage, she reached towards him. The shape she thought was Marcus shifted. He writhed on the ornate rug. Another pained sound quickly followed. She gasped when she realized it was no animal making those inhuman sounds.

Gurgling with panic and unsure what to do, she scrambled to the pile of wood before the fire. Stoking the embers into an inferno, she sought to examine Marcus better. His lids rippled with the rapid movement of his eyes, his face was gaunt and beaded with sweat. His body seized with violent trembling. With a stunned sob, she sneaked past his flailing limbs.

"You'd better be faking, Marcus Bradley." She pressed her hand to his sticky forehead.

He was burning.

Chapter Eleven

🍂

As zephyr light, from magic sleep,
Soon as the sun began to peep,
Sprang BEAUTY; and now took her way

—"Beauty and the Beast" by Charles Lamb

Marcus?" Her voice wavered. "I wasn't lying when I told you I'm a terrible nurse."

Moving closer, she attempted to shake him awake. "Marcus! Do not make me read Fordyce's *Sermons* to you."

She'd not expected him to wake up. Truly. Well, maybe a little.

Danni bit her lip, not sure what to do. He should have changed his wet clothing when she had suggested it. But no, he had to be stubborn, and now a fever had a firm grip on him. She'd helped Annabel when Hu contracted a cold, but she'd never cared for someone truly ill. She did not even have her own experience with doctors to draw on, having never been sick enough to require one. She'd thought she'd been fortunate to have an excellent constitution. Until now.

"What would Annabel do?" she muttered, casting about frantically. Her eyes landed on the threadbare sheet. "Right. A compress."

Snatching up the damp sheet, she found a frayed end and tore. The soaked fabric held tightly and ripped only with great effort. She threw the one strip she managed to separate into the broken bowl and left it slightly outside the leaning door to catch water. Returning to Marcus, she threw her thick covering over him, ignoring a sudden chill and the naked feeling of her shift. However, Marcus was far too sick to notice and needed it much, much more.

What next?

Whenever Hu fell ill, Annabel made him stay in a heated room. Danni couldn't stop the draft, but she could keep the fire roaring. She searched for more wood. Without Marcus's strength to break furniture she had few options. He'd broken a large pile of furniture already for the fire, but Danni feared it would run out. Already, the fire could use another log.

She considered searching for more outside, but she had only her shift, and with the rain still slamming against the roof, it was doubtful she would find dry wood and was more likely to make herself sick as well. Desperate, her gaze fell on the bed. The sound of Marcus's increasing tremors launched her into action.

Feeling the mattress, hope burst within her. The long strands of straw poked her skin when she squeezed it. With a tug, the mattress from the ornate bed fell to the floor. She scanned the seam, looking for an opening to widen and release the straw. Her search resulted in nothing. She could rip it with her teeth, but the idea was revolting. She hadn't a clue where the mattress had been. The thought of it near her mouth... Ick.

Another wail, higher than the last, drew her attention. Marcus lay curled in a ball, his chin tucked into his chest as he trembled violently.

Danni bit down on the mattress.

She ground the thin thread between her teeth. Her mouth hurt and the fabric tasted terrible, leaving her mouth filled with gritty cotton. It was so horrible she paused. Why was she trying so hard to save the man who had made her a criminal?

She could not lie. She knew exactly why she wanted to save him. She cast her gaze in his direction. Her heart ached for him. She believed he was a good man. A man with flaws and an unknown, dark past that still clung tight to him. He drove her crazy, but she had to admit to herself that she liked it. He made her feel alive— noticed. After so many years of benign neglect from her father, she craved attention. Wasn't that really the reason she was planning to accept the Earl of Hemsworth's marriage offer?

But Marcus was different. She wanted to know—no, needed to know—what drove this man.

Danni pulled at a loosened thread in the mattress cover. It ripped with a gratifying sound. She worked the hole bigger, until her fist could fit inside and pull a handful of crisp straw free. With determined triumph, she pulled the mattress closer to the fire and tossed several handfuls into the flames. The fire flared before quickly burning the golden threads black. It wouldn't last, but if she could alternate between wood and straw, it might hold out until the rain stopped.

Going back to the door, she retrieved the bowl. The fabric was soaked through and cool water had collected at the bottom. Perfect. Dropping at his side, she pulled the blanket tighter around Marcus's writhing form and grasped his hand to reassure him he was not alone. His lips moved, shaping soundless words. She leaned closer with the hope he'd tell her everything would be fine.

"...Caroline. Must save..." She drew back in shock. Who was Caroline? A lover? Could she arrange for them to be together so he could give up on Ginny? Her throat tightened at the image of Marcus with another woman. What was wrong with her? She was engaged! Well... almost.

Frantically, she tried to put a face to the name from her social circles in the *ton*. She ignored the rush of relief when she remembered Marcus had an estranged sister by that name. If her memory was correct, she resided with the old and rather eccentric St. Leon family. But what was this about saving her? From what? Frustrated she didn't have the answers, she leaned in to listen again.

"...No," he whimpered, clutching tightly at her hand, "Please, Father...not the whip. Please..."

Danni fell back on her heels. What on earth was he seeing in his fevered state? His agonized whisper...that heart-wrenching, eye-burning tone...

Deep breaths. You are getting much too worked up. He's sick and you've never done this before. Deep, calming breaths.

She grabbed one of the wet cloths from the bowl,

wrung it out, and placed it on his head. With another, she lightly washed his face and neck, hoping to cool him down. His hand suddenly closed on a fistful of her shift. Danni's gaze shot to his face. His green eyes were glazed with fever, the whites lined with red. Her Marcus wasn't there.

Cold, stark fear welled in her throat. Was Marcus simply rambling from a fevered mind? Or was this some other sort of sickness of the mind? Had she just glimpsed into the past of the Beast? Despite the awful possibilities that his rants were true, she wanted to know more. The Marcus she knew exasperated her and made her laugh. The world saw a sharp, defensive, and angry version of the Marquis of Fleetwood. This Marcus was vulnerable, terrified, and broken.

She placed her hand over his again, attempting to calm him with her presence. His heated, trembling flesh seared her. It felt hotter than anything the fire next to her could produce. He needed a doctor, but Danni did not know where to find one.

"I'm right here, Marcus." His grasping hand released the fabric of her shift and threaded with hers, holding to her like a lifeline.

His voice was soft and hoarse as he spoke. "Little one."

Her heart flipped. She hated the condescending manner he typically used when he spoke that name, and yet suddenly she found it reassuring. He knew she was there for him. She squeezed his hand before adding straw to the fire.

A violent tremor traveled up his hand. His eyes closed halfway, another groan forced from his lips. "Don't leave me, little one."

She gulped, her eyes strangely watering as she breathed, "Never."

And she meant it.

Fiery, soul-burning determination she'd never felt before stole over her. She didn't know much about this man, but one thing was for sure—she was going to make sure he knew life wasn't meant to be lived lost in those shadows of the past.

Crawling closer, she rested his head in her lap. Giving in to temptation and seeking to calm him, her hands stroked the silkiness of his hair. Another whimper escaped him, but he uncurled his body. Biting her lip, she brushed a curl from his forehead, unable to resist the lure to glide her fingers along the length of its loop. His body relaxed and his breathing slowed.

She slipped her fingers lightly down his brow, smoothing the lines of pain. Despite the heat climbing her cheeks from embarrassment, another heat simmered low in her tummy.

She'd felt that same sensation briefly when Marcus had pinned her to the floor. Her surprise at his sudden reaction was quickly overwhelmed by the heaviness of him upon her, his body pressing hers deep into the carpet. Every contour of his hard body had besieged her senses. She had flushed under his gaze; her body ached to have his hands where his eyes explored. His first instinct had been to protect her. That knowledge eased any fear she might have had at his sudden possession of her.

Without thinking, her fingers glided along the scar marring his left brow. She hesitated, wondering if she really should be touching the marred skin. He hid the scars from her if she looked at him too long, as if her examination was a precursor to disgust. Even in Marcus's current state, she feared he would rise up in self-hate at her touch.

She decided to brave his wrath. He fascinated her. She wanted to know everything about him, including what had caused his scars. Had he gotten them in a fight? Or perhaps it was some childhood mishap?

She followed the surprisingly smooth scar at his eye and shifted to the largest one on the right side of his face. Her hand filled with softness. In his sleep, Marcus turned his face into her palm. His whiskers rasped against her skin while the heat of his breath skirted across her wrist. Her heart fluttered, and the heat in her tummy spread lower, burned warmer.

Danni's gaze drifted to the longest scar—it angled up from his chin and stopped right before hitting his full, lower lip. Without thinking, her finger followed her gaze. She held her breath as the tip skimmed across his lower lip. The memory of his dimpled smile made her pause. She did not feel the dimple in his kiss along her neck. Would she feel it if she were kissed on the lips by him? She knew the answers to these questions. The Beast's intensity would overwhelm and control her. His vulnerability would break her defenses.

Her face heated with such shameful thoughts. She knew she should stop touching him in this way. She should not be thinking of a sick man—more important, a kidnapper—as a passionate lover. She breathed in shallow, silent breaths, fearful he would waken and catch her taking such liberties with his person. Her free hand pressed against the pounding heat growing in her core. The other caught on his stubbled jaw. The rough texture sent a jolt through her arm and straight through her body. Her teeth bit harder on her lip to smother a gasp.

The fire cracked as a log fell, breaking the spell. Danni quickly but gently placed Marcus's head back on the floor to add another log to the fire. She threw on an extra handful of straw. She paced restlessly in front of the flames, taking deep gulps of air. She needed to clear her head.

The man may possess a gentleness he kept well hidden, but she could not forget that he had coldly orchestrated the kidnapping of an innocent girl, whom he still planned to force into marriage in order to gain access to a fortune, for whatever reason. He thought her a cheat and a pest, herself a fortune hunter in her own way, bilking young heiresses by assisting them to elope against their parents' wishes. Her soft feelings for him amounted to nothing when compared to those cold realities.

Rubbing her face fiercely, she tried to physically erase her thoughts. The two of them were allies only until they recovered Ginny. The moment she was back in their possession, the truce would be broken. His intentions would not change and hers would not either. She and Ginny were going back to London, both with their reputations and fortunes still intact.

Crawling back to the mattress on the floor, she faced the flames, watching them dance their shadowed play. Being so close to him made her lose sight of what was truly important. She shut her eyes the moment Marcus started thrashing again. Incoherent pleas for mercy and help started soon after. She covered her ears, trying to block out the sounds. She wanted to ignore them, to let him suffer as a beast should, but her eyes opened of their own accord, colliding with his reddened ones across the way. *Leave him be, leave him be....*

But, in the end, she stood, moving back across the fire. Fortifying herself against any soft feelings and justifying her actions as common human compassion, she sat beside him and held his clammy hand. As he calmed, she found herself lying next to him, making sure the cooling cloth was in place. Her head rested on his outstretched arm and her eyes slowly drifted shut.

* * *

Sunlight slipped across his lids, creating a haze of yellows and reds. The sound of England's morning birds filled his ears with their happy songs. A cool breeze freshened by yesterday's rain filled the room.

A beautiful morning.

And Marcus felt like hell.

But thank God it was over. He had survived the night, as he had hundreds of times before.

But he needed a drink. Badly.

Everything hurt. His clenching muscles, his bones, even his teeth. Groaning, he shifted closer to the source of heat at his side and wrapped his arms about it. He filled his lungs, expecting the scent of fresh rain drying in the sun, but the familiar scent of roses brought his gritty eyes bursting open.

Wrapped in his arms was Danni. Her body curled into him, her face buried in the crook of his neck, her soft breath slipping over his skin and sending shivers through his spine. He didn't know how she'd started on the other side of the fire and ended up in his arms, but she couldn't stay there. She'd be furious if she woke up next to him like this.

Glancing around, he noticed several things out of place. The straw mattress was torn open near the fire, half its contents now missing. The wood he'd piled near the fire was gone, the stack now ashes in the hearth, and the broken bowl they'd used for drinking water now contained a damp rag. He also noticed the blanket and thick bedcover had been draped over both of them.

What had Danni witnessed last night? He groaned with regret, rolling to his back to wring his hair. She had seen him at his worst. Ugly face, ugly behavior, and now she'd seen his ugly soul.

Marcus needed some distance. Ignoring the pain that seemed to crack his skull, he removed his arm from her scantily clad waist and attempted to lift her head from the other. A soft mewl of protest escaped her lips. Fearing he'd wake her, he lowered her head back. Danni shifted, snuggling closer still. The weight of her body pressed against his groin. He hissed against the pleasure coursing through him. How long had it been since he'd slept with a woman? No, when was the last time he'd awoken to one beside him?

Never.

He stiffened as bitter memories rushed forth. A breathy sigh escaped Danni, drawing his mind from the past. Her face was pale and the dark lashes caressed her cheek, which seemed to glow in the sun's rays. Her exhaled breath rushed through the small gap in her lips, creating a soft snore. He smiled. Unbelievably, she looked as if being next to him was exactly where she wanted to be.

He wondered how she'd ended up here, in his arms. Could she have wished to comfort him? Obviously she had attempted to care for him. What secrets had he exposed? What had convinced her to stay with him in that state, rather than run through the night for help? She was a miracle indeed.

An unfamiliar feeling of tenderness washed over him. Biting back a moan from the stiffness in his movements, he dared to brush a length of hair from her jaw, enjoying the softness of her skin. She sleepily pressed her hips against his, and a slow simmer seeped through the depths of his abdomen. He gritted his teeth, determined to remain the gentleman. Sharing this moment with Danni was more than he ever thought possible. He would not push his luck.

Her hips shifted again, rubbing against his length. His instinct to return the movement roared. Desires he'd forgotten existed screamed to life. The physical aches in his joints and muscles were defeated by the agonizing need for her body.

His hand settled at her waist, his fingers pressed her lower, pulling her pliant body impossibly closer. Her head angled sleepily towards him as if sensing his intent. The beast inside him screamed to take her, but the gentleman he was fought back.

At Danni's sigh of contentment, the beast won. He'd take only one kiss. Just one. He deserved as much for having to put up with her. His eyes slipped closed. His mind surged with the countless faces of women who'd rejected him, and he envisioned Danni's horror if he woke her. But he could not stop himself. Fantasies of Danni writhing in passion beneath him flooded his mind. His imagination traced the outline of her ribs, felt her mouth moving hotly over him.

Another mewl passed her lips. Just a kiss. Just one and he'd never touch her again. Dipping his head, he brushed his mouth over hers. The first contact stunned him. His lips tingled with the smooth, soft sensation. His tongue slipped over them, savoring their warmth, pressing against them, deepening his kiss, tenderly. He drew away, knowing he must be content with that one stolen touch.

Suddenly, Danni's caramel eyes snapped open, searing into his. He froze, millimeters from her face. He'd been caught. *Bloody hell.* Marcus braced himself for the screams, the curses, even—God forbid—the fainting. But he should have known better. This was *Danni.* She never did the expected.

"Marcus...," she breathed, the air caressing his still tingling lips. For the barest moment she peered into his eyes, frozen with indecision, and then her gaze moved to stare at his lower lip, and with a curious hesitance she gently lifted her head and fused their mouths together. Shocked, he held still, his mind blank.

She was kissing him. *Him.*

Blood pounded in his ears as his mouth merged roughly with hers. Her arms linked around his neck, frantically fisting in his shirt, pulling him closer. Marcus didn't have the strength to pull away, nor did he want to. With stunned disbelief, he cupped her neck, lacing his fingers through the tresses there, and held her head in place, terrified she would break free and run in terror at any second.

She continued to fascinate him the more time he spent

with her. She was a puzzle he would gladly spend a lifetime trying to solve. She valued a marriage filled with love over the kind of status marriage that was so common in their times. She earned her living through trade, but often reminded him of a gentlewoman bred by the *ton*. Never afraid to share her opinion and outrage, she was vexing and downright stubborn. She also made him laugh and was a balm for his past. To her, he wasn't the Beast, but a simple human being. He could not believe his luck at having found her.

A sigh of pleasure slipped between them. He deepened the kiss, lost in Danni's sweetness. His tongue rasped over her mouth, smoothing the little wrinkles of her lips before dipping inside. The scent of roses filled his head, maddening him with desire. He ran his hands over her supple curves. She was made for pleasure, for sinking deep inside. The thought nearly undid him.

His hand dipped lower, kneading her bottom as she massaged his shoulders and stole her fingers through his curls, her nails gently biting into his scalp. He groaned and slid his mouth down her neck, over her collarbone, lavishing the sensitive skin. In his mind, an image emerged, of Danni soaked to the skin and stunning in the rain. His hand sought and seized her full breast through the thin fabric in which she was wrapped.

Danni stilled beneath him, breaking the kiss with a gasp of surprise. Had he gone too far? Quickly, Marcus rolled away, forcing space between them. His body raged with the need to continue. He panted, struggling to bring himself under control.

He sat up to find Danni staring at him with wide eyes, fingers pressed to her lips. Her thin shift gathered tantalizingly around her shapely legs, one strap hanging off her shoulder, revealing the tempting swell of her bosom. Her mass of hair hung wildly about her, gently curling around her shoulders. Flushed cheeks and the rapid rise and fall of her bosom made him clench his fists. He dared not breathe. Waiting...almost pleading...for her to tell him that everything was all right so that he could kiss her again.

"Why did you kiss me?" she whispered through her fingers.

The statement confused him. Why wouldn't he? She was beautiful, vivacious, and caring. But why would she kiss him, a horrid beast inside and out?

"That should be my question."

Her golden brown eyes clouded with so many flickering emotions he couldn't name them. "I don't know." Her voice was soft, distant, and full of distress, "I-I can't, Marcus. I can't do this."

The heartbreaking rejection in her voice cut him deeply. "Danni, I—"

He shifted to make himself comfortable, fighting exhaustion, weakness, and confusion. His headache returned with a pounding rage. He had no idea what to say, could find no words to express his desire for her without insulting her. She had seemed willing, but how could she really be attracted to a man like him?

Bitterly, he wondered if she'd kissed him out of pity. He always ended the fool. Marcus needed to stop deluding himself into thinking others could possibly care for him. Bitter memories flooded back. If only he'd had a different father, one who'd actually loved him and had not left him scarred, would she still reject him?

In his anger, he lashed out. Asking the one question that started it all. "You're the one who woke up and kissed me. Why? Why did you kiss me?"

Why? The question echoed in her mind as she ran from the shelter. *Why?*

She had no idea.

Her skin stung from the slap of the short underbrush and wet tree limbs, but still she ran. Her lungs ached for air. The rain-soaked greenery drenched her shift, grabbing at her bare feet and tripping her. Danni stumbled over a branch, stubbing her naked toe. Biting back a cry, she kept going.

No, that was a lie. She knew exactly why she'd kissed him. When she'd opened her eyes after feeling that soft, hesitant brush of contact, she'd been able to focus only on those beguiling green eyes. In the instant before she reached for him, his soul had been laid bare.

And what a beautiful one it was.

Her heart had ached with the longing and tenderness displayed in those depths. She'd felt heavy with emotion and relaxed from the gentle warmth swathing her. She had forgotten about her promise to find Ginny and return posthaste to her father, her future fiancé, and her future life among proper society. Everything had felt so incredibly right in that single moment, she'd acted on instinct. Nothing but Marcus had mattered to her, just for that moment.

At the first contact, she'd felt a spark—like static electricity—along the seam of her lips. Then softness maddened the nerves, drowning her in the scent of cool rainwater clinging to his skin. Delicious heat pooled at her core, tensing her thighs and curling her toes. His fingers danced over the thin lawn of her chemise, sending shivers through her. His lower lip brushed hers and she could feel the subtle indent, immediately loving the friction the difference caused. It was tantalizing and uniquely him. Blood roared in her ears, drowning out all reason. She had never experienced such a sense of overwhelming pleasure.

She'd never dreamed she could feel so strongly. She'd heard the acts of love between a man and a woman could be joyful, but she'd imagined it wouldn't be more than...pleasant. This passion was all fire and need. She'd certainly never felt anything like that in the company of the Earl of Hemsworth during their short courtship.

Danni slowed her frantic run, trying to steady her emotions. Fingers pressed to her swollen lips. They were warm and plump, and still tingled from Marcus's kiss. Everything about her still thrummed, the imprints of Marcus's palms were burned into her skin forever. If Marcus had not surprised her by touching her breasts, she shuddered to think how long she may have been willingly drugged by his gentle ministrations. He was utterly maddening.

Danni recognized Marcus was much more than a bitter, devilish, fortune hunter. From his fevered murmurings last night, she knew something was driving him to commit heinous deeds, and perhaps if she understood those forces, she could excuse his actions, but it still changed nothing. He was a haunted man, angry and defensive. He was not someone she could, should, become involved with. Not husband material at all. Especially in light of the careful plans her father and the earl had arranged for her future. Rationally, she agreed theirs was the best course for her. Emotionally, she had never been so confused.

She had to regain her focus on the goal of getting Ginny safely back to her family. Unmarried. Then Danni would go home, accept the Earl of Hemsworth's proposal, and finally make her father happy again. He had been so sad since her mother's death. She remembered his vibrant smiles and rapt attention to his family back then, and she knew her compliance to his wishes would do much to close the distance that had grown between them.

What had just happened with Marcus could not change anything.

But she knew, in reality, it had changed *everything*.

Tears of frustration stung her eyes. Marcus's crushed, bitter expression haunted her every step forward. How could she face him? He was hurt, and rightfully so. She was embarrassed by her behavior and furious with herself. Hadn't she decided to steer clear of him just before falling asleep?

A sapling drew a hiss of pain as it struck against her bare leg, clutching tightly to the damp shift. Her naked feet landed particularly hard on a rock, the sting a sharp contrast from Marcus's gentle, heated touch. She groaned in irritation. Would everything serve as a comparison to him? She's been so frantic to escape, she'd left behind her clothing and sack. She was being foolish, she'd have to go back. To face him.

Crashing underbrush startled Danni to attention. It could be anything, but it was most likely Marcus. Panic spiked inside her chest, emotions roiled. She wasn't ready. She couldn't face him yet. Releasing a burst of speed, she dashed through the brush, trying to outrun him. She just needed a little more time to gather her thoughts. But she could hear him getting closer. His long legs had the advantage.

Danni broke through the forest, stumbling as she ran. Her feet flew out from under her when she stepped into a slick of mud. Shifting in the air to protect herself, she tumbled down a hidden decline. She landed hard on compacted dirt, her body rolling and finally halting with her limbs spread out before her. A groan slipped through her clamped lips, suddenly aware that the woods had become momentarily silent. Clutching the back of her head, which had thunked solidly to the ground, she sat up, her body scraped and aching all over. Even the palms of her hands stung. A muffled shout sounding suspiciously like her name echoed from the woods. Gingerly she turned to look, afraid she would be able to see Marcus approaching. Disoriented, she slowly realized she sat in the middle of a narrow road. Unsteadily climbing to her feet, blinking at the muddy ground, she stumbled into a run again.

The pound of hooves shaking the ground made her pause.

She lifted her head, only to freeze in terror. Baring down on her was the largest horse she'd ever seen. Its rider pushed the animal hard and fast around the bend, its broad chest covered in sheen. They approached at an alarming rate, apparently unaware of her. The horse let out a squeal of alarm as it drew closer, but impending doom made her limbs immobile. She wanted to move, everything in her screamed to move, but she couldn't. At the last minute, the rider finally noticed her person blocking the road. He yelled something inaudible over the pounding in her ears.

She was going to die.

Something hard slammed into her side, knocking her to the ground again. Arms caged her as they rolled, absorbing most of the shock. She heard grunts of pain over the hysterical beating of her heart. They stopped, arms and legs tangled together, amid the brambles growing wild along the side of the lane. She rapidly blinked her eyes and scrambled to her feet, disengaging from her savior in a panicked flurry. The rider was rapidly disappearing into the distance. The man didn't even slow to see if she had survived.

She crumbled weakly to the ground, panting in relief. She had braced for pain that had never come. Danni turned her head to see Marcus still lying on his back in the brambles. His hand covered his eyes, and his chest was heaving with exertion as well. He snapped, "Don't you ever do that again!"

She sniffed. "It is not as if I planned to be trampled today!"

He lifted his head, pinning her with his fierce green gaze. "Is that why you ran from me? You couldn't miss your appointment with your maker?"

Rolling her eyes skyward, trying to ignore the worry etched in his emerald eyes, she rose unsteadily to her feet. With shaking hands she quickly adjusted her thin clothing. Fighting for calm, she bit out, "Stop being so childish, Marcus. I did not intend for this to happen."

His gaze narrowed at her shaking voice, before he stood as well. He glanced in the direction the rider had headed before crossing the road. In moments he reappeared with her clothing neatly bundled, her short boots dangling from one hand. She gazed at them longingly before snatching the pile and retreating into the forest.

She stayed carefully hidden behind a wide-trunked tree, and gratefully peeled the soaked and filthy shift from her body. She discarded her trousers, still damp and smelling unpleasantly of mildew. The shirt was freezing to the touch. There was no way she was putting those on again. She'd be sick within the hour. Sifting through her pack, she withdrew the extra day dress. It would be uncomfortable without the proper undergarments, but leagues better than her old clothes. A good deal more proper as well.

As swiftly as she could, she pulled on the dress. The short boots gave her a bit of trouble, the leather stiff and inflexible, but they were her only shoes. After all was done, she still felt miserable and shaky, but properly covered. She was also thankful to be alive. When she reemerged, Marcus acknowledged her sheepish thank you with a contemplative, "We should follow him. This road is bound to lead to a house or an inn."

Danni pushed away her rioting emotions. She needed to function again. She could worry and analyze later. "Or perhaps the highwaymen's camp."

With a swift nod, he set off at a punishing rate. Danni exhaustedly tried to keep pace, her damaged feet screaming in the tight boots. She was determined not to snap at him to slow down, no matter how tempting it was. She needed to keep communication with him cordial if she was to save Ginny.

The road was easier to travel than the forest, and the lack of traffic allowed them to cover distance quickly.

Eventually, Marcus's strides shortened to a more accommodating length, but they didn't speak or meet each other's gaze.

Which was exactly what she wanted. So, of course, she had to open her mouth.

"Thank you. For saving me, and for bringing the clothes."

Marcus's shoulders stiffened. He glanced her way before simply acknowledging her words with a grunt. "We're even now. In exchange for helping me last night."

Danni hesitated, not wanting to remind either of them of that intimacy, but it would be remiss if she didn't ask. "You seem much better. How is your fever?"

"I'll be fine," he muttered, barely audible.

"Are you certain?" she murmured, concerned and hesitant to let the subject drop. She felt like he was hiding something from her again. "You were violently trembling and burning up. Perhaps you should rest more before we—"

"I said, I'm fine," he barked, and strode ahead.

Danni jerked in surprise before scrambling after him. Painful silence resumed. She hated it. It was filled with confusing emotions and unspoken thoughts. She wanted to know what motivated him. She wanted to know more of the past he had partially exposed in his fevered delirium. She wanted to know why he felt he had to save his sister. If it was a good reason, she could even forgive him for the bewildering ways he treated her, and for the blackmail, but she could not forgive him for Ginny. Ginny's future was probably destroyed now—for who would marry a woman who'd spent days in the company of brigands?—and the blame for that landed directly on his shoulders.

And he *was* at fault for the intimacy earlier this morning. He had started the entire affair. She certainly was not sorry for kissing him back. Nothing, no matter how wrong, had ever felt so good. Being in his arms and feeling his hands upon her had been astonishing. She was beginning to understand what drove Annabel to turn her back on her family and London society to choose a life with Hu. That level of passion was the greatest of temptations. Hopefully, she could eventually achieve that with the Earl of Hemsworth, a kind, compassionate, and uncomplicated member of society. She'd just have to work at it and surely that spark would ignite.

"I propose we forget about everything and simply focus on finding Ginny. What say you?"

Danni's head whipped about, meeting Marcus's wary smile. Her breath caught in her throat, her heartbeat ratcheting higher. His smile, although unsure, was a welcomed olive branch. She breathed a sigh of relief, pretending she was as collected as he, and smiled in return.

"Agreed."

The scuffle of their boots on the damp earth was the only sound for several heartbeats. Cautiously, Marcus broached conversation. "Do you really help people elope with their 'true' loves?"

Danni blinked at him in surprise. He looked straight ahead, but she sensed her answer was important to him. Teasing, she smiled. "If you mean to ask if you are the first fortune hunter I have ever assisted, then the answer is yes."

He looked at her sharply. His head tilted as he studied her to see if she was teasing. His face broke into a small smile. "Explain to me how your business usually works, then."

Danni debated whether she should lie to him, or if she could risk entrusting him with information best kept to herself. She didn't want him to think her a fraud. She hoped she might make him see how important love is to marriage. Nothing mattered more. Perhaps if she approached this correctly, she could make him understand why Ginny had to be returned home. Without a husband.

"Usually, I am approached by the intended, and often unwilling, bride," she began haltingly. "She'll ask for our aid in whisking her and her true love to an elopement at Gretna Green before the wedding to their arranged husband takes place. When the couple returns happily married, they tell their friends and often refer other unhappily engaged women to me."

He nodded. "In other words: Women gossip. Men do not."

She knitted her brow, offended for her gender. "Would you like me to carry on or not?"

He waved his hand, gesturing her to proceed.

"You are ever so gracious, my lord."

"'Tis a heavy burden I must bear, Miss Green."

She snorted, but refrained from commenting. Instead, she continued. "At Gretna Green Bookings, we strive for 'Happily Ever After.' We plan the entire elopement for the bride and ensure the couple reaches their destination in ease and comfort."

His scarred brow shot up. "Ha! Is this your idea of a perfect elopement? The last I checked, Miss Green, sleeping in a rundown cabin and walking for miles is not easy. And definitely not comfortable."

"Yes, well. *You* gave me no time to plan. With most of my elopements I have at least two weeks to make arrangements. I have never improvised such a venture before."

"You have failed miserably at it, I would say."

She shot him another glare. "Do I need to cite Rule Number Thirteen about slander again?"

"Anything but that. You have single-handedly convinced me with your treaty never to take my seat in Parliament."

Danni kicked a rock and pretended not to be pleased when it hit the heel of his boot. Marcus turned a suspicious glance on her and frowned. Danni innocently examined the flora about her.

It was his turn to snort. "So how exactly does one break into your line of work?"

"I didn't deliberately start. It simply happened." He nodded but didn't respond, so Danni continued, careful to avoid titles. "My friend came to me one day, distraught that her father had arranged her marriage to a much older man. She would be forced to marry him, even though she loved another. I was crushed for her but helpless to influence the situation. A few nights later, a man approached me. I had only seen him about. I'd never had a conversation with him certainly. He told me he was the one my friend loved. They had been arranging to elope later that week, but my friend's father had found out and thwarted their plans. He was devastated."

Danni fell silent, remembering that night and how very upset the characteristically quiet Hu had been.

"And?"

Danni glanced up, finding that they had stopped in the middle of the road. Marcus's attention was riveted on her as she spoke. "The man had been in her father's employ. He sacked him and locked Annabel in her room. The groom then asked for my help. I couldn't say no. I love Annabel, and I wanted her happiness more than anything, so I arranged it, including bribing several people to help me sneak Annabel from her house. I saw them safely out of London and a week later they returned happily married."

"But why did you continue?"

"You must understand. Before my mother died, they had a marriage one could only dream about. Every day, they said 'I love you' to each other. But more than that, you could *feel* the love they had for each other. When I realized how few couples actually get a chance to have that, I decided to do whatever I could to help." Danni tilted her head to meet his eyes with defiance. "That is the reason I am so strongly opposed to your plans for Ginny. You cannot force her to marry you, Marcus. She will be miserable and she deserves a chance at love!"

He considered reflectively before starting off down the road again, evidently unaffected by her ardent speech. Several minutes passed before Marcus spoke again. "You mentioned your mother died."

Danni looked up from carefully watching her steps, crushed she had been unable to reach him. "Oh." Danni blinked with confusion at his statement before a crush of profound sadness overwhelmed her. "She passed away six years ago. Actually, shortly before Annabel needed my help." She paused. "Perhaps I eagerly helped Annabel and the others because it gives me purpose. In some way, I feel closer to my mother. She would have probably even helped me with Gretna Green Bookings, she loved love so much."

Marcus nodded, then quietly, from a rough, thick throat, said, "It must be very nice to have such a happy home."

She frowned, glancing at him from beneath her lashes. The rigid way he held himself did not invite inquiry, but the simple statement gave much away. Marcus had just deepened the mystery about him. One she now realized she had to solve. It was the key to Ginny's freedom. Maybe if she shared more, he would be willing to share his reasoning?

"It *was* wonderful."

He paused, brow furrowed with confusion. "Was?"

Danni gulped. She never talked about her relationship with her father. Not to anyone, even Annabel. However, if this could help Ginny in any way, she would do it. "When my mother passed away, it crushed my father. He retreated into himself and has virtually ignored my existence since. He isn't unkind, just...not there."

"And exactly how does he feel about your clandestine activities?"

She hesitated, worried she would expose too much. "As I said, he is a very busy man."

"Just not busy with you."

"He loves me," she muttered defensively, "and wants me to be happy, like he and my mother were. I just haven't been lucky enough to find the right partner yet. He and my mother knew each other since their childhood, and, almost just as long, that they were meant for each other." She paused, looking him directly in the eye. "Despite all that, I am certain he would never want me forced into a loveless marriage, as you are forcing Ginny."

Annoyance flashed across his features. He grunted a

reply, widening his strides. Danni gritted her teeth, matching his pace. She wasn't done yet. She hoped to clear up more than one problem. "My father has actually chosen someone for me to marry."

Marcus faltered in his steps, his head whipping about. Surprise was written all over his face. "The woman who wants 'true love' for everyone would agree to an arranged marriage?"

"Ironic, isn't it?" Danni felt her lips twitch in a weary smile. It *was* rather amusing. "I have not yet accepted, but I will. He's a good man, and I believe I can come to love him. And the match will make my father very happy."

"And that's why you ran," he stated, his face shuttering again. Danni looked at the ground. She disliked that such warm eyes could turn so cold.

"Yes," she whispered. "I'm sorry. I should never have kissed you. It was wrong of me. It will never happen again."

He quickened his pace, lengthening the distance between them again, and Danni let him.

After several moments of silence, during which Marcus remained sullen and silent, Danni's regret for her behavior turned to anger at his condemnation. He had *blackmailed* her into becoming his accomplice. He had *kidnapped* a girl from her own bed. He planned to *force her into marriage*, and finally he had *initiated their kiss* back at the cabin. And he had the unmitigated gall to be affronted when she suffered a moral lapse?

Seeming without warning, they rounded a bend in the road and found themselves in the courtyard of a small inn. They stopped short in surprise.

It was a small building, looking a bit worse for wear.

Shingles on the roof were cracked or missing and the paint flecked away in spots. A gaggle of chickens flitted about, pecking at the ground. As they hesitated to approach, the small sign proclaiming it the Jacket Inn broke off one of its hinges and drooped lopsidedly.

She exchanged a look with Marcus as the urgent need for food, drink, and a soak in a hot bath possessed her. Decision made, she single-mindedly strode towards the door.

Marcus watched as Danni sped ahead of him. He let her go, his mind churning with what she'd just told him. Deep down he'd known the truth all along. He'd stopped viewing her as a fraud almost the moment he'd seen her go over the wall into the admiral's garden. She was determined, bright, and loyal. Not many people would have done what she did for a friend, and what she now did for complete strangers.

Marcus kicked the dirt as he realized he envied her. She had friends who cared. Someone who *wanted* to marry her and a childhood filled with loving memories and fine role models.

The weight of his crimes settled like an albatross on his shoulders. How many people would he destroy in order to help Caroline? He watched Danni disappear into the inn. How much was he willing to sacrifice?

Impatience with himself flared his temper. He didn't understand the attachment he had developed for her, nor the sharp pain that came at the news of her impending engagement. She may have responded sweetly and passionately to his kiss, but she'd made it clear she didn't want him.

Dear God, she'd *run* away.

He was a presence only to be tolerated. It would be war again once they retrieved Ginny and he forced them back on the path to Gretna Green, Scotland. And the marriage had to occur. Caro's well-being was at stake. He needed to accept himself for what he truly was: a beast, a fortune hunter, a blackmailer, and a kidnapper. He had a mission to accomplish and he could not allow Danni's attacks on his conscience to distract him.

As much as he wanted Danni, she didn't have the fortune he needed, and she was meant for another—a man who was whole and who could give her the love and marriage she wanted above all. She *deserved* to have both. He could offer her neither. He was far too broken. He gulped, clenching his fists. He was far too like the abomination that sired him to make her, or anyone for that matter, happy.

Cursing his life for the millionth time, he followed her into the building.

Chapter Twelve

❦

*"Your outward form is scarcely seen
"Since I arriv'd, so kind you've been."*

—"Beauty and the Beast" by Charles Lamb

The moment Marcus stepped into the inn, the mass of humanity overwhelmed him. The odor of unwashed bodies, old liquor, and stale air assaulted him, sending him reeling. He staggered back to the wall as he tried to catch his breath, hoping for a glimpse of Danni through the crowd.

As people pressed closer, a cold sweat broke over him. His breath shuddered and his chest pounded as his hands dug into the wooden wall behind him. The solid feel of the building grounded him in the present but he knew, deep down, it was a losing battle. He did not like crowds. He needed to be in a quiet, controlled environment, where unexpected noises didn't bring back memories of a violent father, and horrified stares didn't haunt him. There were too many people here, far too many possibilities he could react badly, and far too few escape routes.

Eyes stared openly at him, fixated on his scars. He gulped air, feeling as if everything was closing in on him. He never had this problem in the open. Here, he couldn't move with the mass of people bumping elbow to elbow.

Fighting for control, he grabbed an abandoned mug of ale. He lifted the metal cup to his mouth with a shaky hand. The acidic tang of the liquor's aroma filled his lungs, turning his stomach. He recoiled. Although his mouth watered to taste the sweetness of the beer, he felt sick at the thought of swallowing it. He had craved the relief of liquor for two days now. It allowed him to push down recollections best not relived. He needed to numb the pain, but now, not being able to drink it...his chest constricted.

He tossed the mug on a nearby table, not caring where it landed. Despite the turmoil, he had been better in the forest. He'd suffered from only that one incident in Danni's presence and she'd dismissed it as a common ailment. But this crowd undid him. Groaning, he turned his back and pressed his forehead into the hard wood of the wall.

He must leave at once. But the thought of Danni alone in the tavern full of unruly, drunken men kept his feet firmly in place. The moment he saw to her safety, he'd find a way to escape and let the insanity of his wretched past consume him.

Gritting his teeth, Marcus pushed off the wall and

scanned the room again. An Amazon of a woman with black silver-streaked hair caught his eye. She had an air of authority about her. The men listened when she spoke. Was she the innkeeper's wife or the actual innkeeper? Either way, she could get him a room and locate Danni. He took several shaky steps before being forced to steady himself on a nearby table as a fresh wave of pain laced his skull.

Danni suddenly appeared by his side, shifting slightly behind him as if to hide.

"What's amiss?" he muttered.

"I feel silly... but I am not properly dressed."

Marcus's grip tightened on the table, not sure what her problem was. She'd replaced her trousers and shirt with a dress back at the road.

He needed but a few minutes for this conversation and then he could leave. Just a few more minutes.

"And..."

"This dress is filthy and thin." Marcus glanced down to see that the skirt was soiled six inches deep in mud and, without the usual petticoats beneath, it hid very little of her figure. "Here... we're back in civilization, albeit a rough one. I feel exposed and... wrong," she finished, crossing her arms protectively about her.

The edges of his vision dulled, but finally Marcus understood her concern. He looked past her, where men leered with lustful smirks. He snarled, his protective instinct surging. He forced himself to stand tall, eyeing them with lethal intent. His fierce visage sent them scrambling, averting their heads, hasty to avoid contact.

Danni glanced back as well, frowning as the men feigned disinterest. Marcus, smugly satisfied he'd marked his territory, wanted to stay near Danni but he knew he was unable. His breathing hitched. "Sorry, little one."

He shucked his jacket once more, and draped it across her shoulders, blocking her body to mid-thigh from sight. She smiled sheepishly, gratefully slipping her arms through the oversized sleeves.

"Oh," she breathed. "Thank you. All our provisions, along with a full change of clothes, were stored in the carriage." She folded her arms to hold the coat close. "I was able to convince that intimidating woman over there that we were separated from our traveling party by bandits and that you are ill."

He nodded. All he wanted was his room and Danni in a safe place.

"I am also your sister for the evening."

"My sister?"

She nodded, frowning. "Lady Danielle Bradley, at your service."

The shadows receded momentarily, replaced by renewed interest. The sound of her name joined with his stirred him, but not in a brotherly manner. Quite the opposite. Instead, with a jolt, he envisioned them married, sharing a bed every night.

Danni caught his arm. He glanced towards her. "Marcus, are you feeling ill again?"

He took a steadying breath. He was exhausted from the fever, but this was another matter entirely. "I need to lie down."

"Go on up. The innkeeper, Ursula, gave you the first room at the top of the stairs. She said a bath and a tray would be brought to you."

Relief flooded his face, and bracing himself, he

straightened, forcing his limbs to cooperate. Her concerned features tightened. "Do you need my help?"

"No!" He didn't mean to snap at her, but he was desperate to escape this place. He needed privacy to let down his guard without humiliation. He took another step and realized she wasn't going to follow. "You plan to remain?"

She nodded. "This is a good opportunity to see if anyone else has been robbed by those men. Someone may know where the thieves camp, or have heard news of Ginny."

He began to protest, but she continued. "Go on. I'm assured I will be safe. Ursula promised me no one will get any ideas into their sod-filled, sheep-bleatin' heads." Her lips twitched. "Her words, not mine."

Wry humor twisted his face as he hesitated a moment longer. The urge to protect her almost made him brave the gathering storm. Almost. Instead, he whispered, "Come with me a moment."

He pulled her a few steps down the hall, well concealed from spying eyes, and while Danni looked on in befuddlement, he reached inside his Hessian and withdrew a small bag of coins. At her surprised expression he muttered, "Do you believe I would embark on this trip to Gretna without a purse?"

She greedily grabbed an extra coin from his palm. "Frankly, yes, I did. Ha! I believe there is hope for you yet, sir." Her grin broadened. "I will treat myself to pie with my plate, thank you."

A drunken sot turned into the hallway, lurching from wall to wall. Danni skipped off into the tavern, secreting the coins into the folds of his massive jacket. The drunk stumbled into him, took one look at his face, and rushed off, muttering curses under his breath. Blood pounded in Marcus's ears and his lungs tightened. He sprinted to the stairs. Once behind his locked door, he slumped against it. Both relief and fear swamped his body. Blackness swept through him. His last thought: he was glad Danni would not see his seizure.

* * *

Danni glanced back after Marcus's rapidly retreating form. When she'd first approached him, she hadn't noticed anything wrong. She'd been preoccupied by the salacious looks following her progress through the room. Then she'd noticed the sweat beading on his brow and his pale face. His eyes dark and wide. His caged behavior deeply troubled her.

Her booted foot tapped out her thoughts. Danni wondered exactly what he was trying to hide. He would not welcome her intrusion. He was a private man. Heaven forbid he would tell her why he needed Ginny's dowry so badly, let alone the cause of his skittishness.

Shaking her head, Danni focused on the task at hand. They needed information on this Green Bandit, and she was the only one available to find it. Thin dress or no, a room full of liquor-loosened tongues was not an opportunity to be wasted. She may even discover the status of any potential pursuit by the admiral. After ordering a plate of food to be delivered to her room, she seated herself at the nearest table, right next to a slight man deep in his cups.

He grinned, his eyes skimming over her. "'Ow pretty you be lookin', lass."

An uncomfortable laugh escaped. "Why...er, thank you, sir." At his continued speculative gaze, she put a note of firmness in her voice. "I hoped you'd like to talk."

His head tilted, contemplating something before he sighed. "Angus Butcher. I make me home in the village a stone's throw up the road."

"It's a pleasure to meet you, sir. I am Lady Danielle Bradley."

He smiled, showing a mouthful of teeth rare in a laborer. "You be passin' through, ma'am?"

"Yes, my brother and I have become separated from our companions."

Angus nodded. "Hope you be stayin' for the festival in the village. Tomorrow we be celebrating our village's foundin'. Our lordy gives us a 'alf day off."

Danni fought a smile upon hearing his sarcasm. Several men at the table adopted similar attitudes. The popular opinion seemed that of tolerance, but not fondness. It was more than she could say for many of the men she knew of that currently held titles.

Angus lifted his mug and peeked inside. By the muttered "damn," she presumed it was empty. Waving for a maid, she ordered another mug of ale for everyone at the table. Angus eyed her with mock suspicion. "You ain't be trying to soften me up?"

Her head shook vigorously, burying her discomfort. *For Ginny.* "Never! I am simply buying my new friends a drink."

Grunting, he tossed back the contents of his new mug the moment the maid arrived, gulping deeply.

Shifting uncomfortably in her chair and attempting to keep anxiety from her voice, she asked, "I don't suppose you know if any of our friends came this way? Two men and a pretty redheaded woman?"

He blinked, clearly waiting for her to continue. "Two lads and a young, redheaded gel? No, no one matchin' that description been seen 'ere. I would 'ave heard 'bout it."

She was disappointed. With the mention of a festival so close by, she'd been sure they would be in the area. What self-respecting highwayman would miss the occasion to rob so many travelers?

Another man sat down next to Angus, drawing his attention away. Danni sat quietly, debating her next move, when their conversation caught her ear.

"Did you 'ear the Green Bandit and his crew struck again over in Auburndale?"

"My"—Angus chuckled into his mug—"that be thrice just this week. Bold lads, I say."

"Must be good pickings. Surely they be at camping near the fairgrounds by now, laying low, celebrating their success."

Danni's heart pounded with excitement. She could barely wait to tell Marcus. However, she moved to another table and repeated the process, trying to avoid suspicion. She was careful not to ask too many about her "friends," mindful of any possible pursuers. If people remembered her, and she was sure they would, she couldn't have them spouting what they'd discussed. She hoped the ale they were drinking so freely would help to blur their memory to the facts.

She quizzed three more men, trying each time to determine the exact location of the camp without ever truly asking, but each conversation ended with disappointment. People only seemed willing to discuss the festival. She admitted defeat, the lure of the hot bath awaiting her too much to resist. As she passed close to the stairs, a man seated at the bar drew her gaze. There was something very familiar about him. He was slumped in his seat, gulping from a steaming mug. Other emptied ones lined up haphazardly across the table. He ate so ravenously, the meal laid out before him disappeared as she watched. Her stomach clenched, reminding her of the meal that should be waiting in her room by now.

Curiosity getting the better of her, Danni approached the bar. She dared not approach him directly. His familiarity could only spell trouble. Instead, she caught the innkeeper's eye. The Amazon followed her progress to the end of the bar. Leaning over the scarred, stained countertop, she nodded to the man. "Will you tell me about him?"

Ursula eyed her speculatively, her lips tight. Understanding, Danni surveyed the barroom as if nothing was happening. She knew how to bribe; she'd done it several times before.

"Perhaps an extra few pounds appear on our final account in the morning. What say you about the man then?"

Onyx eyes narrowed. "Make it five and I'll tell you why he's here."

Danni smiled. She didn't really care how much it took, as long as Marcus had enough funds. It wasn't her money. "Done."

Absently cleaning a mug with a new rag, the dark-haired woman whispered, "'E's a scout sent by the Admiralty. Apparently, the man be searchin' for three persons—a man and two women, one with dark red hair. 'E won't say who they be, or why they are bein' searched for. One can only assume they be fugitives." Ursula paused, her eyes glancing back to Danni in open curiosity. "Almost thought it were you and yer brother, but I ain't seein' a red'ead."

It took everything in her power to mask her shock. The innkeeper examined her reaction far too closely for comfort. Seeking to avert suspicion, Danni smiled with what she hoped was innocence. "No, no other woman with us. Just my brother and me. The Admiralty, you say? Interesting. I remember now that he was the horseman who passed us on the road. Nearly ran me down. Almost killed me, but spent not a moment to see if I was injured."

She forced a smile, quelling her inner panic. *It couldn't be…the admiral would have needed time to get this far! And how would he know about Marcus and me?*

Ursula hurrumphed, returning to her cleaning.

"I'll be in my room. Thank you for everything, Miss Ursula."

Another grunt followed in her wake. The moment she was out of sight on the stairs, Danni bolted, taking them two at a time, intent on warning Marcus of impending danger. She ran down the small section of hall, halting at the plain wooden door. The first one at the top of the stairs.

Danni didn't hesitate. She burst through the door.

* * *

Marcus sighed as he sank into the bath water. His tense muscles absorbed the heat, melting away the strain of his past. He tilted his head back, eyes drifting shut. The only thing missing, he thought, was a glass of brandy.

But there was nothing that would induce him to wade through that mass of humanity again in order to secure one. He'd resolved never to leave this room until the blasted festival was over. He already tired of hearing of it from the lads hauling hot water to the sitting bath. And he'd learned more than he wanted about one sot's relationship with a buxom girl named Mary.

His thoughts slowed, his mind heavy with exhaustion. He had not rested well the previous night. He didn't remember much, but he'd been aware of Danni tending to him, and his unquenchable desire for liquor to deaden his memories.

At the thought of Danni, her gentle touch and her heated kiss, he groaned. Everything he'd been trying to forget flooded back to him, tightening his body with need. *Damn.*

He submerged beneath the steaming water and rubbed soap through his hair. Surfacing, he ran a hand through his curls, wiping the strands from his eyes and clearing away the excess water with the other. It did no good. He couldn't clear the sounds of Danni's soft sighs from his mind or forget the warmth of her body intimately against his. She was driving him to insanity. And he did not have that much further to go as it was.

With closed eyes, he let his mind wander to what could have been if she hadn't rejected him and run away. If he hadn't repulsed her.

In his mind's eye, he imagined the weight of Danni's breast resting in his hand, its soft fullness pressing against his calloused palm. He imagined kneading her beaded nipple, enticing a soft gasp from her sweet lips. He'd dip his head, plunder her mouth, taste roses and sweet honey.

He imagined tracing each curve and dip of her smooth, creamy skin, savoring every touch.

And in response, she would clutch his curls, pulling his mouth closer, her body arching towards his. Marcus would tug her closer, impatient. His heart stuttered as he pictured gazing into her passion-drugged eyes. They would blaze gold with an emotion he'd never seen before. A soft smile would spread her lush lips and she would whisper, "I love you."

Marcus leaned back in the tub. A short bark of black laughter escaped him. The very idea he *wanted* her love, the very idea she even could love him...it was absurd.

He stepped out of the tub, shaking the water from his body. He welcomed the cool air's slap across his heated skin. The sound of pounding footsteps in the hall drew his attention. He shook his head at the locals' antics. One would think the people below had never had a day of festivities in their lives. Without another thought, Marcus reached for the drying cloth folded neatly on the chair beside him.

Suddenly, the door to his room burst in on its hinges. Marcus froze, his mind racing to the past, when nights of terrible pain would start with so similar an action. For several seconds, he became the boy again—cowering in his bed as his father's heavy steps collided with the door.

Heart pounding, he realized Danni stood riveted at the threshold, her eyes wide with astonishment. The cloth hung forgotten in his hand as he stared back, his entire body revealed to her. Neither uttered a word. The swift tingle of goose bumps rising on his skin spurred him to act. He had nary a stitch on and a young, unmarried woman, be her respectable or not, currently gawked at him.

Clearing his throat, he colored and dropped his eyes to the task of tucking the cloth tightly about his waist. He fought the urge to cover himself. Marcus wanted Danni to see him. Unreasonably, he felt the inexplicable need to make her understand exactly what she had rejected when she'd run from their kiss in the forest. He wanted her to understand everything about him, and in a way, frighten her away. He didn't want ludicrous fantasies of her love.

Out of the corner of his eye he watched Danni's cheeks redden that wonderfully unattractive shade. Her gaze flitted across the room, clearly trying to avoid looking at him. Her uncertainty gave him the confidence to straighten and bare the full brunt of her scrutiny even as he braced himself for her embarrassed retreat or fainting scream. Few saw this, his deepest and most well-hidden secret.

Raising his scarred brow, he asked, "And what prompted you to interrupt my bath, Miss Green?"

The fading red returned in a rush. It was clear that if a hole had opened in the floor, she would have cheerily jumped in it. "I came here to warn you."

"Warn me? And what is this warning?"

"It's terrible, Marcus! We've…" her words faded as her eyes drifted down the length of his torso.

He held his breath, her impending reaction bringing a bad taste to his mouth. Her eyes predictably widened with shock. He shifted his attention to a point over her shoulder, wishing to avoid any participation in the incident. He winced in anticipation of the gasp of disgust. Instead, his muscles jumped under the warm stroke of her hand as she stepped closer, tracing over a particularly brutal scar across his stomach. He flinched back instinctively. Danni stepped away, her eyes still wide. She cradled the hand that touched him as if it burned.

He grimaced and moved around the tub, putting it between them. He couldn't seem to catch his breath. No one had ever touched him. Touched *them*. They were his private marks of pain. He felt raw, exposed in a way he never thought possible. Her eyes were glassy as she continued to examine him. He followed her gaze, knowing which particular scar she looked at by the way her eyes changed in size.

When she finally spoke her words came out unbearably soft. "What happened to you?"

He turned away, giving her the smoothest side of his face. Taking even, deep breaths, he cleared his mind. "It is not open for discussion."

Danni stepped close, forcing herself into the path of his vision, her face full of sympathy. He stepped away, determined to keep his distance. Instinctively, the beast in him knew she would only cause him more pain in the end.

He sent her a sharp look of warning. He didn't want her pity or her concern. He wanted to forget. He wanted to be treated as a regular human being. He turned his equally abused back to her, ignoring her sharp intake of breath. Pulling a freshly laundered shirt over his head, he effectively hid away the image he had deliberately presented to her. His voice was gruff, thick with emotion, when he spoke. "Some do not have the privilege of a happy life, Miss Green."

There was silence as he looped the buttons near his neck closed. *Good. She's gone.* His shoulders relaxed.

"Well, I came to tell you we may have been discovered."

Marcus stiffened again. Why hadn't she left? She should have fled when given the chance. Should have bolted as if chased by the demons of hell. How had his plan backfired?

Standing in his shirt and drying cloth, he faced her. "Discovered?"

"You remember the horseman who almost ran me down?"

His fist clenched as he nodded. He would enjoy killing him for what he'd almost done. "He's a scout for the admiral. And he's downstairs!"

He struggled to remain calm, his mind reeling more from her lack of reaction than from her news. "A scout means nothing. He's simply searching for a sign of her. Since we don't have Ginny with us, we'll be safe."

She shook her head. "No. Marcus, we must have been seen that night."

His stomach sank. Couldn't any of his plans go right? "By whom?"

"I do not know, I…Perhaps one of the sisters? Or even…" Her fists clenched, her eyes narrowing with distaste. "Phillip?"

He scowled. He would not put betrayal above the man. They'd even left him on the side of the road for the admiral to pick up.

"That's why they have a description of us!"

"But how would they even know to head north? Wouldn't they have thoroughly searched London first?"

Danni scowled. "One of the girls *must* have seen us, and reported us immediately. It's the only reason they would have been able to catch up so quickly. And if they located Phillip, he would only confirm they are on the right track."

"Phillip would have told them that we no longer have her."

"Ursula said the scout's looking for a man and two women, one with red hair."

"Then he is a forward scout. He probably hasn't heard about the escapade with the Green Bandit yet."

She ignored his logic. "The admiral and Phillip cannot be far behind. What should we do?"

Sinking to the bed, he rested his head in his hands, his mind turning. With drinks flowing freely, he doubted any of the inn's occupants would report them, a supposed brother and sister, as potential fugitives. Marcus was not inclined to flee the inn unless danger was imminent. They were in desperate need of food and rest. Most likely they would already have been arrested if the scout suspected them at all.

What he truly could not fathom was Danni's presence here in his room. She should have run. Should have fainted, or at the very least shrieked. Instead, she stood before him, speaking to him as if nothing were amiss. As if he were any normal human. Not a beast. Merely a man. He didn't understand.

"Marcus? I don't know what we should do," she repeated.

Swallowing against the rising torrent of emotions, he asked, "Is the scout still here?"

"He's seated at the bar having a meal. From the looks of it, he means to stay the night."

"Was he drinking?"

Danni pulled her lower lip between her teeth. The action sent a stab of desire through him. "Absolutely. He downed two mugs of ale in just the few moments I was present."

"Then I don't see why we shouldn't stay here for the night. He'll sleep well past dawn. We will leave at first light." He paused, thinking things through. "Tomorrow we can go into the village and try to get more information on these bandits' whereabouts."

She spoke as she walked to the open door. "I overheard that they have a camp in the forest near the village fairgrounds. I'll see if I can quietly arrange for mounts. It will certainly be quicker and easier searching for Ginny."

At the threshold, she paused, looking back at him. The murderous fire suddenly blazing in her eyes stunned him. "And Marcus, I would cheerily hang beside you should you decide to kill the man who gave you those scars."

Her hand reached back to grab the door and pulled it closed.

With the click of the latch, Marcus fell in love.

Chapter Thirteen

> "We only wish'd a few new clothes;
> "BEAUTY, forsooth, must have her ROSE!"
> —"Beauty and the Beast" by Charles Lamb

*M*arcus hesitated outside the Modern Modiste, breathing deeply of the crisp dawn air. He had no idea what the bloody hell he was doing here so early in the morning. He just knew he'd spent the entire night tossing and turning, his mind determined to do something nice for Danni—the irritating woman he'd insanely and quite irrationally fallen in love with. Although he knew he could never have her, he wanted her to be happy and as comfortable as possible. To that end, he hoped she would accept the only gift he could think of—a proper dress. So he'd awoken before the roosters and made the trek to the small village down the road from the inn on foot.

Palms sweaty, he took another breath and pushed open the door. A bell tinkered above him. Immediately, his senses were filled with an array of colored fabrics and the soft, slightly musty smell of linens, lace, velvets, and brocade. Scanning the store's contents, he felt his heart quicken. Display upon display of fabric samples and ready-made garments on feminine forms filled the tiny space. Each gown was unique and designed upon the current fashions populating a London ballroom—or so he had to assume, since Marcus had finally realized the biggest flaw in his plan.

He knew next to nothing of fashion, and even less about women's. He could not remember the last time he had entered a ballroom. He hated the crowds, the stares, the gossip. He cared no more for society than it for him. So why he thought he could purchase a dress for Danni boggled his mind.

He was a bleeding idiot.

As he spun his heel to make a quick escape, a warm, gentle voice caused him to freeze in place.

"Hello. How can I help you this morning, my lord?"

Again facing the inside of the store, Marcus found himself inches from a tall, middle-aged woman. A blinding and completely unexpected smile made him blink. She was certainly a beauty in her day. Graying blond tresses swept up in an elegant motif of fresh white daisies. A perfectly tailored, high-collared russet dress covered her from neck to toe. Wise brown eyes glittered from a dainty, aristocratic face. She gazed at him with quiet acceptance, neither repulsed nor frightened by his appearance. Even the most skillful at covering their reaction to his scars had a momentary lapse, and quickly recovered their politeness. This woman emitted a soothing, motherly air, something he'd only ever experienced from his own mother—a woman he barely remembered.

"My lord?" she inquired, a polite expression of curiosity sweeping across her features. "May I help you with something?"

Anxiety swept over him again. He clenched his heated palms and swallowed against the lump in his throat. He felt more like a callow youth now than he had when he actually was one. "I-I am looking for a dress."

A kind smile brightened her features. "As you can see, we have several of those. Perhaps you can be more specific?"

"It's for a woman."

"I should hope so." She chuckled.

Heat crept into his face. He felt ridiculous.

"Could you tell me what type of woman she is?"

Marcus opened his mouth and then shut it again. What type of woman was Danni? His eyes narrowed as he remembered their trip. He growled, saying in a rush, "Absolutely infuriating, stubborn, self-righteous, manipulative...determined." Adopting a softer tone, he whispered, "Strong, bright, funny, caring to a fault, and—" Feeling suddenly embarrassed, he coughed into his hand and looked away.

"And?" the woman prompted, a secret smile on her face.

Marcus cleared his throat again, feeling the color come back to his face. He mumbled, "And the most beautiful woman I've ever known."

"Ah." The seamstress whispered with a knowing look. "She's *that* woman."

He blinked, surprised he had actually spoken the words. "What do you mean by 'that woman'?"

"Your true love."

Marcus shifted on his feet, focusing on a point above her head. He may have admitted as much to himself, but he was definitely not ready to say it aloud, to anyone, not Danni, and especially not this stranger. He still couldn't believe he was even behaving like such a besotted fool.

Another chuckle came from the woman. He realized her willowy frame stopped just below his chin, of a similar height to Caroline. The thought of his sister made his stomach turn. He knew he was being foolish. He had to manipulate Ginny into marrying him for her money. And Danni was destined to marry a man she could stand beside proudly, and whom her father approved of. She deserved that kind of happiness—a happiness that would be nonexistent with a man like him—who hid from staring crowds and jumped at loud noises.

And even this image of the future could be mere fantasy if they were caught. He knew he'd spend the rest of his life rotting in a prison cell, or, if he was lucky, be spared by the hangman's noose. Such thoughts made him all that more determined to find her the perfect dress. Something she may someday remember him by with fondness.

"Shall we see if we can't find what you are looking for?"

The modiste wandered deeper into the store. Marcus hesitated to follow. Should he really be doing this? He had no idea what kind of dress Danni would like. Or even if it would fit her. Perhaps he should have just brought her here later in the day.

"Marcus?"

His gaze shot towards the woman. Her serene gaze and reassuring smile beckoned him forward. As if under some sort of spell, he followed her to a small corner of the room filled with ready-made dresses.

She gestured to one mannequin featuring a yellow-gold dress with bows and fancy sashes. "Perhaps she would like this?"

Marcus tried to picture Danni in the monstrosity.

He rapidly shook his head. "Absolutely not."

"I see. Then perhaps this one?"

The seamstress pointed to another dress a bit farther back from the bunch. It was a creation of deep scarlet velvet with black lace trim. He didn't think it was absolutely horrible, but it was definitely too dark for Danni.

Again, he shook his head.

"Hmm." She paused, crossing her arms and elegantly tapping her chin with her index finger. Marcus shifted on his feet, feeling uncomfortable again. Perhaps she had nothing. Perhaps he wouldn't be able to find something Danni would like. Perhaps he'd have to go to a new store and do this all over again.

He paled at the thought.

"Aha!" she suddenly exclaimed. Startled, he felt his heart rate shift for a reason other than anxiety. Taking deep, calming breaths, he fought to focus on something in the present as the modiste disappeared behind the counter. Taking advantage of the private moment, he closed his eyes.

Calming thoughts, he told himself.

Unbidden, an image of Danni filled his mind. He focused on her warm, caramel gaze. The soft touch of her palm brushing his scarred chest. The subtle, addicting smell of roses that enveloped her. He felt his muscles un-clench. His heart rate slowed and a peace like he'd never known before slipped over him.

"I believe this will be perfect, Marcus," the seamstress whispered.

The gentle voice startled him. Opening his eyes, he found the woman right before him again. He frowned; something about her unsettled him. Before he could put his finger on it, a dress was presented directly in his face. He blinked to focus and then felt his stomach drop.

"This one," he breathed, already imagining it draping Danni.

"I thought so," the woman crowed with triumph. "Shall I include the under layers, and perhaps something more casual, as well?"

"Please," he answered, still unable to remove his eyes from the dress.

"Wonderful." And in a flash, she disappeared again, reappearing moments later with a carefully wrapped package.

"Will you apply the bill to..."

"No need. Think of it as a gift."

"But—"

"I hope you finally find happiness, Marcus."

He opened his mouth, confused at her wording, but she vanished behind the counter again. His mouth closed with a click. What an odd woman, he thought as he quietly ex-ited the shop.

It wasn't until he was halfway back to the inn when he realized something even stranger.

She'd called him Marcus, and yet he'd never given his name.

* * *

The early rays of morning streamed in the small window. The wooden room didn't have much to recommend it in daylight. The walls were a simple whitewash on the top half, darkly stained on the bottom. The colors blended with the creaky floors below.

The beds were terrible as well, only straw with a spattering of feathers. If she had been anything like Annabel, she would have pitched a fit and refused to stay. She had always been the most pragmatic of the pair. Since they were young girls, she had been the anchor Annabel needed and Annabel had been her source of fun with her flare for dramatics and her nose for mischief. What she would not give to have her here now.

Danni waited impatiently, seated on the edge of the equally creaky bed, drawing her legs to her chest. She was clad in a cleaned and pressed dress. Her aged boots were polished and on her feet. Her hair had been combed and braided nearly an hour ago. Her breakfast tray in the corner lay emptied. Ready to leave, but not wishing to go.

Sleep had not come easy, nor had it been restful. Every time her eyes drifted closed, the sight of Marcus's naked body appeared in her mind, the pink-white scars slashed deeply across his skin. Standing proudly, he dared her to be something other than a simpering London miss, to accept him as he was, without pity or scorn.

Color stained her cheeks as she thought about the incident in his room. She'd been so worried about the scout, it had never occurred to her to knock. She'd seen... well, everything. She wasn't completely clueless when it came to the male body. Her mother had told her more than most and Annabel answered any questions she had.

She'd thought Marcus a large man, but seeing his nude body overwhelmed her. He towered above her, the essence of masculinity, nothing more than sinew and muscle. She'd been fascinated by the way his body rippled and flexed as he'd moved. Inundated with the full force of him, she didn't at first notice the latticework of scars covering his flesh.

He'd known the instant she'd seen them. He'd straightened, his face turned cold and militant, daring her to turn away or squirm with disgust. She could understand why he expected such a reaction. She had no problem imagining others of her social class doing exactly that, but it hurt he thought so little of her. And it angered her. She'd known him for only a short period of time, but Danni knew there was much more to him than his appearance. Didn't he know by now she would not be repulsed by him?

He wasn't evil or unkind. Despite the fact that they were engaging in crimes that required a cold heart, she knew he did not have one. His angry and defensive exterior was a hard shell, but brittle and easily cracked. She knew under it lay crushing pain and distrust. Now she knew why.

Simply rushing to rescue Ginny was an indicator of his true character. If he really only cared about her fortune, he would have turned back to London and picked a new girl to steal from her bed. He never raised a hand to Ginny, even after she kicked and punched him mercilessly.

And then there had been his kiss. He'd been gentle as he'd claimed her, passion slowly simmering to the surface with his brief contact. No one who could make her feel so cherished could be that horrible. She prided herself on being a good judge of character. It was part of her business to determine whether those she helped elope truly cared for each other.

She deeply believed he was a gentle giant with a compelling reason for his actions. One she was going to discover today at all costs. Danni would not take another step further until she understood what the bloody hell was going on.

Her head fell to the tops of her knees as she sighed. What kind of person could inflict those kinds of wounds on another? The scars were old, faded, and white. They had been inflicted on him many, many years ago. As a child?

That Marcus had been hurt so grievously made her furious. Her eyes burned as she thought of the pain he must have endured. He must have lived in terror of another impending beating for most of his life. How could anyone's soul be untouched by such horrors?

She remembered the trembling fear in his hands. And the way he startled violently at unexpected noises. She'd noticed how his mind could be with her and then suddenly drift away, shadowed by invisible memories. It all made sense now.

Marcus must constantly revisit the past memories of when he received those scars. The terror he experienced, and still must battle, would be overwhelming. And then to be saddled with a physical reminder each time he looked upon himself…whenever he undressed, looked in mirrors, or saw fear and disgust in the eyes of people around him…

She swallowed the lump in her throat. Her father had told her stories of men who returned from war, so shaken by their experiences there that they were forever haunted. He worked in Parliament to pass legislation to provide aid to those men's families. Many of those men ended up in Bedlam, their minds too unstable for the civilized world.

Danni glanced at the door. How had Marcus managed? She could barely contemplate his life without feeling hopeless despair.

A soft tap echoed against her door. Sighing, she buried her thoughts and pulled the door ajar. Marcus, fully dressed, stood on the other side, his face full of challenge. "That is how you properly request entry into a room, Miss Green."

She flushed, grimacing. She'd resolved during her endless hours of wakefulness to apologize to him. But looking at his wary features, she did not know what to say. She knew offering her condolences would be wrong. He was proud and would not welcome her pity. Did she just continue on as if nothing had happened? As if she didn't care about him? Because Danni could no longer pretend she didn't.

He took the choice away from her by thrusting a package into her hands. The brown paper crinkled in her grasp. She fingered the thin, white twine holding it together. "What is this?"

"A package."

Her suspicious stare caused his face to melt into a teasing smile.

"What is it really?" she demanded.

He cleared his throat, suddenly uncomfortable. "A gift."

Danni's eyes widened, her hands automatically pressing it back. "I cannot accept this."

He stared at her in hurt disbelief. "Why the hell not?"

"A lady should not accept gifts from gentlemen."

His features twisted. His arms bulged as they crossed his barrel chest. "Well, I'm no gentleman."

Her hands tightened around the malleable bundle. She hesitated.

His face softened suddenly. "At least do me the kindness of opening it before you give it back."

Nibbling her lip, her curiosity won out. She tore into the paper, revealing a hint of rose-colored cloth. In wonderment, she pulled the wrapping free, revealing the prettiest dress she'd ever seen. The soft muslin slipped through her fingers, falling elegantly. The skirt was decorated with delicately embroidered roses of the deepest red. Under the bust was a white satin ribbon, the sleeves and neckline bordered with lace. It was simply beautiful.

Stunned at his thoughtfulness, warmth washed over her. Even through his struggle with his own demons, he'd listened to her complaints regarding her attire, and taken it upon himself to make her feel better. She glanced from the dress to his watchful gaze, blinking back tears.

He cared for her. For the first time in several years, she felt special. She'd forgotten the power a gift could bestow. Annabel and Hu pegged her as independent and practical, and as much as she loved them, their gifts reflected that. Her father was too busy to even notice her, even though she tried to make him happy. Not even her future fiancé had given her a token of his affection.

The gathering pools in her eyes threatened to spill. She clutched the dress to her, surprised by the force of emotions that ripped through her. A virtual stranger, someone by all rights she should hate, had given her a gift. A rose-colored dress.

Panic struck his face. "You're crying. You hate it."

He reached to take the dress back. Despite proper dictates, Danni found she could not give it up. "No!"

He froze.

"I love it. Truly. I-It's ... Thank you so much." Without thinking, she wrapped her arms about his waist, the dress caught between them. On impact, his spicy fragrance, the scent uniquely his, filled her lungs. A rush of happiness bubbled in her heart.

Slowly, hesitantly, solid arms lifted and wrapped about her, engulfing her in his strength. Instinctively, her head fell to his chest. The steady, rapid rhythm of his heart brought a gentle heat to her face. She'd never felt this close to someone before. "Thank you," she whispered softly into his chest.

Abruptly, he drew back, red staining his high cheekbones, clearly ill at ease. "Yes, well." He glanced towards the ceiling, clearing his throat before looking at her again. "Shall I meet you downstairs once you've changed?"

Danni nodded speechlessly, wiping her wet face and disappearing back to her room.

She stared at the folded gown. Another reason to believe this man was not the monster he presented to the world. He cared. He listened. He understood.

So much for confronting him about his compelling reasons for kidnapping Ginny. So much for not moving forward another step without an explanation for his actions. She was trapped. She trusted him. She knew eventually he would tell her, just as he had exposed his soul when he exposed his body to her. Answers to her questions would come when he was ready to tell her.

Quickly taking off the thin canvas shift, she slid into the proper undergarments she found nestled below the dress. For the first time in days, she felt appropriately dressed. Her relief was palpable. No more gawking eyes or shocked stares. As much as she wished to, she couldn't bring herself to wear the rose creation. It was too beautiful for the muddy countryside. Danni wanted to save it for a special occasion. Instead, she opted for the simple blue dress folded beneath it.

Rewrapping the rose dress as if it were the finest china and tucking it in her trusty pack, she stepped out into the hall. It was a short walk to the bottom floor. Already men and women were arriving in droves, drink flowing freely. At their approach, the Amazon behind the bar spotted Danni and smiled in welcome.

"Good morning, Ursula. Busy already?" Danni tilted her head to indicate the men already surrounding the keg.

"Oh, aye! Always is this time of year. What can I be gettin' for you and his lordship, little lady?"

"We arranged for a pair of horses last night."

She grinned. "Of course. I'll tell the lad you're ready."

Danni turned to scan the room, ever conscious of the scout. She didn't see him, but that didn't mean he wasn't about. "Marcus?"

She caught hold of his forearm. He flicked a hesitant gaze towards her at the contact. Danni refused to let go, afraid he might see it as the rejection she was sure he expected. "The horses should be ready."

His split brow rose, his gaze lingering on her grip against his sleeve, before his face shuttered and hardened.

Nodding, he gently removed her hand from his arm, his fingers lingering for a split second, and headed towards the exit. Her fists clenched. He'd been so wonderful and now he was acting as if she'd done something wrong. She'd thought they'd come to some sort of understanding, a friendship of sorts. Why else would he make such a beautiful and thoughtful gesture by gifting her that dress?

She went after him. Once outside the courtyard, she found him at the mouth of the stables, already mounting a solidly built chestnut. The mare tossed her head as he settled in the saddle, the spirited animal tugging anxiously against the reins.

Danni picked up her pace, waving off assistance, and lifted herself into the sidesaddle with ease. As soon as she was seated, she ran her hand down the neck of her shining black gelding. It snorted lazily, stomped the ground, and rolled its docile brown eyes as if imploring her to allow it rest. Out of the corner of her eye, she caught Marcus smiling softly to himself.

Of course he would commandeer the animal that would actually be fun to ride.

Accepting the reins of the horse from the stable hand, she shot Marcus an overly sweet smile. "You get the mare for half our journey, and then we must switch."

His smile widened, erasing Danni's anger with its charm. "Not a chance."

With that parting shot, he pressed his heels into the horse's underbelly. The mare took off, heedless of the increasing crowd in the yard. Swearing under her breath, she chased after him, knowing full well her little horse would never overtake him.

They spoke little since leaving the inn, but it was an

easy, uncomplicated silence. They carefully circled back through the forest several times to ensure they were not being followed, and reached the outskirts of the fairgrounds in less than an hour. Marcus dismounted, Danni quickly following behind.

"I believe we should explore the village." He spoke softly, "We may be able to find a clue as to Ginny's location or the bandits' campsite."

She nodded, watching as he moved casually among the wares. Mimicking his actions, she eavesdropped on shoppers' conversations. Glorious fabrics, linens, and ribbons brightened the atmosphere like colorful flags. Jewelry of all colors and gems glittered in the morning sun. In her old life, she would have had the time and the funds to enjoy the festive day, feasting and spending recklessly. Today, nerves raw, she impatiently marked wasted time, time that Ginny waited for rescue, and exposed them to potential discovery by the admiral's scouts lurking about.

If only she could shake the information she needed from these people.

When she met Marcus at the next stand, he said, "I'll be back shortly. Look around a bit, and keep your ears and eyes open." Tossing her the reins unceremoniously, he disappeared into the crowd, which quickly separated as people caught sight of his face.

She glared at his retreating back. Dragging the horses out of the flow of the crowd, she waited by a stall selling meat pies. She had eaten the last morsel of her second pie, when a creeping fear that Marcus may have been captured churned the food into a swirling pit in her gut. When he eventually returned, carrying another tightly wrapped package under his arm, his eyes seemed to smile when their gazes met, and Danni sighed with relief.

Unable to resist teasing, she held out her hand towards it. "For me?"

He snorted. "No."

"Fine! I see. You raise my hopes only to dash them."

"I wouldn't wish to spoil you, little one."

She smiled softly, enjoying their light banter. Danni was secretly glad he hadn't actually bought her a gift. She simply could not accept another one. "That implies more will be coming."

He laughed. "Possibly, if you do not try my patience too much."

She tilted her head in an exaggerated examination of the parcel. "What is it then?"

"Food."

"Oh." She tried to hide her disappointment. She'd been hoping the contents were more interesting, "But I just ate meat pies."

"You will be more pleased with my purchase later today when your belly aches. Have you found anything to lead us to Ginny?"

"No. And you?"

He frowned. "Apparently, this village seems to admire the bandits in the area rather than condemn them. The Green Bandit is a local legend. According to one of the stall owners, they like to camp to the north of here, but no one wishes to share more. Perhaps later, when the ale has flowed, they will be more forthcoming, but I am loath to wait. This crowd is thickening by the minute. Let's head north and see if we can pick up signs of travel."

Danni nodded in agreement, noticing for the first time

his sweaty brow and slightly trembling hands. She rudely licked her lips and fingers to finish her pie with haste, taking a sip of her watered wine. His frown told her he'd found some fault with her again. Sighing, she said, "What have I done now?"

When he didn't answer, she realized his eyes were riveted on her fingers as she licked the juices of the pie. Her heart responded to the heat blazing in their depths. Immediately, the ghostly memory of his lips brushing hers caused her to swallow awkwardly. Her pie hung forgotten in her hand as her mind conjured droplets dripping from his water-soaked hair across his corded neck.

Marcus's hand reached out. Drowning in his eyes, she leaned into it. Her heart leaped and her skin tightened with the anticipation of his touch. She wanted nothing more than to feel the heat of his body against hers again. To wrap her palms in his rich white-blond hair. To trace the dimple in his lip with her tongue.

His breath fanned her face as he spoke, sweeping a quiver through her thighs. "Danni."

Impossibly, the world seemed to spin.

Then an elbow collided with her back. She fell forward, dropping her pie. Marcus caught her with a ragged growl. The perpetrator and his companions laughed as they taunted, "The inn's down the road!"

Danni's face burned. She'd been trained from birth in proper behavior, the earl was waiting for her, and Ginny desperately needed rescue. What had come over her since this man had entered her shop?

Scrambling from Marcus's embrace, she noticed the crowd's knowing smirks, glares of disapproval, and stares of shock. She turned to Marcus, searching for a face free of judgment. She met stone. Too late, Danni realized that pulling away must have seemed a rejection to him. He turned and strode with determination towards the outskirts of the fair.

Panicked, she grabbed the horses' reins and yanked on them to follow. She hurried after him through the crowd. Perhaps it was for the best if he were angry with her. They had no possibility of a future together. They needed to focus on poor Ginny.

"Marcus, shorten your strides."

He stopped, but when she reached his side, she realized he hadn't stopped for her. He quickly sidestepped around a nearby corner, pulling her roughly with him. He stared back intently at a man bartering a shawl at one of the several seamstress stalls.

"Do you recognize anything about that shawl?"

It was dark purple in color with a design bordering its edges in a burnt orange. She didn't need to get closer to know exactly what that design was. It would be vines of laurel leaves.

"It's Ginny's. And that's the highwayman I fought with." Danni stared at the Green Bandit's Gypsy companion. "The one who wanted me over Ginny."

"Exactly. Let's follow him."

She couldn't believe their luck. Ginny could not be far. And, Danni thought sadly, if the scout was near, she would have no trouble getting Ginny to safety.

But what would happen to Marcus?

Danni studied his intent face. If Ginny told her father about him, he would surely suffer severely, if he was not hanged outright. She could not bear that.

"Damn!"

Marcus's angry curse died in the air as the man slipped away through the stalls. They pushed hurriedly through the streets after him, but the press of fairgoers engulfed them. They broke out of the crowd to find themselves at a small clearing edged by deep woods on all sides. Marcus raced fruitlessly along the edge of the fair, looking for tracks leading from the clearing into the forest. But who was to say he had even left the fairgrounds yet? They split up and searched again, until they had to admit they had lost him.

Danni stood staring out across the fields to the woods. Ginny was being held captive somewhere out there. As she gazed into the hidden green depths of the foliage, she felt a surge of hollow guilt: She shouldn't be so happy she didn't have to choose between either of them just yet.

Chapter Fourteen

❦

Such wants and wishes now appear'd,
To make them larger BEAUTY fear'd;
Yet lest her silence might produce
From jealous Sisters more abuse,

—"Beauty and the Beast" by Charles Lamb

Instead of escaping the village and all possible danger, they decided to return to the inn.

Danni had a difficult time arguing with Marcus's logic. Searching the woods would be dangerous and most likely fruitless. They could become lost and be attacked by the bandits again. Darkness would approach early, they could become trapped and spend an uncomfortable night in the forest. Besides, it was entirely likely the highwaymen wouldn't move on from the village until the festival was over. The gathering of people would be the perfect oppor-

tunity for them to lift purses and rob travelers on the road
to and from the village.

Marcus and Danni would return to the fair tomorrow,
better prepared to track them to their lair and to recapture
Ginny. In addition, since they had yet to see the admiral's
scout, it was quite possible he had left the area. They had
safely stayed at the inn the night before and, he argued,
another quiet night there was most likely a good bet. So,
despite the possibility of sharing a roof with potential enemies, they went back to their rooms.

They arrived back at the inn as the sun sank low in
the sky. The Jacket seemed a very popular place. Loud
noise echoed with the fading light, and lanterns cast a soft
glow as they were lit. The stable hands ran to and fro,
on errands for patrons inside the inn. A boy approached
to take their reins and walk their horses to the barn. As
she dismounted, she began to remark upon Marcus's lack
of sharing skills of a certain high-spirited horse but the
scowl he wore as he looked towards the ruckus could only
be described as murderous. She judged it best to remain
silent as they entered the inn.

The moment she pulled back the door, she was greeted
by a slew of humanity. The crowd inside was louder and
denser than even the night before. People competed to be
heard over their neighbors and shouts of raucous laughter
echoed from one corner near a large keg. The smells of
sweat and spilled ale poured through the doorway, pushing her backward as if by a physical onslaught. The noise
was deafening. She held back a moment to steady herself,
bracing to enter the fray. Then she noticed Marcus lag-
ging behind, deep lines of tension about his mouth. He
hovered just outside the door, scanning the room with an

ashen face. His breath came in short, shallow gasps. His hands shook slightly as he reached for the wall as if he were dizzy.

Coming back to the inn was obviously not the best decision. If only she could go back in time. They would have continued to search the woods for Ginny. With any luck they would have already rescued her and be readying to depart for Gretna Green. She groaned. But if they had found Ginny, she would be overcome with the task of extricating Ginny from Marcus's plans. Nothing in her life could ever be simple.

Marcus visibly swayed. She hesitantly touched him.

"Are you all right? We can leave here if you would like."

His look of annoyance gave her some measure of relief. She could read him now. He was directing his fear of the crowd onto her in the form of anger. She could work with that. She dropped her hand in disgust.

"You do realize I am getting tired of always being glared at and scolded."

His eyes only narrowed further, but the terrified look was slowly fading as his anger was restored. The visible transformation actually made her smile.

His lips curled back in a snarled response.

"Fine." She huffed. "Continue acting like a child. I am going to find a different entry. I have no wish to brush up against strangers in there."

She wasn't sure if he was going to follow, but Danni slammed the door shut and strode in the direction of the stables. The tension in her shoulders eased when she heard gravel crunch behind her. She resisted the urge to glance back at him smugly, her smile broadening. He was doing exactly as she wished. She wasn't sure why she hadn't tried this tactic sooner. Her sense of judgment had been seriously skewed ever since he had walked into her shop.

She practically skipped up to the young boy in the stables. He turned a surprised gaze to her, widening quickly when his glance flicked to the space behind her. Marcus, she assumed. A stab of emotion cut her heart. He was just a man.

"How can I 'elp ye, milady?" he asked with a nervous edge.

"I hoped you could possibly direct us to another entrance of the inn? It's frightfully crowded and I'd rather not be forced to deal with a drunken mob."

"'Course! If ye go 'round the back, ye can enter the common room by the kitchens."

"Thank you." She offered him another quick smile before hurrying in the direction the boy had pointed. The crunch of gravel continued behind her until she reached the door near a small herb garden.

Suddenly, Marcus was in front of her, his body blocking her way. She stepped back, crossing her arms in defiance. He glowered down at her for several moments before speaking. His voice was low and full of warning. "I know what you are doing and I do not appreciate it, Miss Green."

Her heart sank. She'd thought she could help him cope without wounding his pride. She dropped her arms by her side, lifting her shoulders in bewilderment. "I haven't a clue as to what you mean. Please step aside."

"Haven't a clue? Do not insult me. You know of my distaste for crowds."

"It isn't hard to fathom. Your eyes were wild and your hands were trembling. The other night, you could not escape the tavern room fast enough."

"Let me make this very clear." He fairly growled. "I do not want or need your help. I've managed before you and I will manage after you, once I am on my way to Gretna."

Danni stepped back as if he had struck her. So that was that. She shouldn't be surprised. She yanked her spine straight, her jaw tilted with determination. He was set upon this crazed scheme. He would force a terrified girl into an unwanted marriage. And he planned to never see her again.

She knew beneath that gruff exterior was the heart and mind of a caring, compassionate man, but he was still a beast. He was still going to force Ginny to marry him for her money. The mere idea was almost a physical pain streaking through her chest. Tears burned at the back of her eyes. His gaze was shuttered and his face still as stone. It was that barrier again. "Why do you need her fortune, Marcus? Are you really as destitute as the gossip columns report?"

He mirrored her stance, his eyes unreadable, but worse, unfeeling. He wasn't going to answer. She feared he never would. Well, then, she could worry about him no longer. In the beginning, she had gone along only with the intention of raising the alarm the moment Marcus was out of London. Then, in the woods, she feared for him as well as for Ginny. But now she no longer cared. If he carried through on his threat to expose her to the *ton*, so be it. From now on, her sole concern was Ginny.

"If you consider 'managing' your problem by drowning everything with liquor, then feel free to enter the inn by the front entrance. There is plenty of it available to you in the tavern. I am entering this way. Please move."

He stood in place, dumbstruck.

Blinking back more tears, she hissed through her teeth. "Marcus Bradley, if you do not move out of my way this very instant, I will not be responsible for my actions."

A smirk split his lips as he measured her up and down. She could see he considered her threat futile. She saw her lack of worth in his eyes, and tried to hold in her tears. She couldn't believe he would belittle her honest effort to help him. She'd been so wrong about him. So very, very wrong.

Anger spurred her to retaliate. Gritting her teeth, she swung back her leg and let her foot fly. A satisfying crack resulted as her boot connected solidly with his shin. He let out a grunt, grabbed his leg, and shifted out of the way. She didn't know if he was more surprised or hurt. She didn't care. Danni pushed past before he could recover, slamming the door to block him out. Ginny was not the only female who could kick.

A harried kitchen servant scurried to her side, clucking about eccentric females before ushering her out of the crazed space and into a back hallway. At the end lay the staircase to the second floor. A few feet away, festivities roared from the common room. She marked her place at the end of the bar, clear of the servants' path. Ursula, the innkeeper, stood at the end of the counter talking with someone just out of sight.

Steeling herself against the rush, she pushed through the crowd. A man stepped up to grab her arm—the look on his face told her he didn't want to simply talk. Danni shifted out of the way, narrowly avoiding a collision with a tray before finally coming to a stop next to the Amazon. She gave her a surprised look. "Lady Bradley! I didn't expect ye back. 'As somethin' gone amiss?"

Shaking her head, she ignored the man at the bar with Ursula and addressed the owner. "My brother is not well enough yet to travel. Would our rooms still be available for tonight?"

Ursula was already nodding, waving the issue away. "'Course! 'Ave the same ones!"

"Thank you, Miss Ursula."

"Pardon me, milady. Must clear the floor for the dancin'."

Danni leaned against the countertop, waiting for a serving girl to move so she could head to the stairs. A discordant note of a fiddle floated across the common room.

"Care for a dance?"

Danni met the gaze of the man Ursula had been talking to. He had a friendly smile and didn't appear overly drunk. She found she did not want to return to her room to wallow in her thoughts.

She knew this was not a smart thing to do. There was much at stake. She scanned the crowd for the admiral's scout. The room was jammed full of villagers, so loud and boisterous she would never be spotted unless she was directly beside him. She thought of Ginny and regret flushed through her. How badly she wanted to right the mess she had helped to create. Then Marcus's grim face flashed through her mind and anger washed away regret. What did it matter what he would think? He'd made it plain that for him, she was just a means to an end.

The man encouraged her with a charming smile and

reached for her arm. Danni surrendered. It was time to forget all and enjoy herself for a moment.

Accepting his hand, she was drawn to the center of the dance floor. The final discordant tuning of the instruments evolved into the first strums of a quadrille. The dancers scrambled into position, laughter erupting as people bumped into one another. The man was already on the turn with her by the time the others had fallen into place. Danni weaved in and out of the lines, the music an unexpected pleasure in this run-down establishment. 'Twas no wonder it was popular.

The next steps of the dance drew them together. Danni realized her dance partner was much more impaired than she had originally thought. His face was flushed and his hands skirted her body. More than once she quickly removed one that skimmed too far down her back or far too high on her chest. His charming smile turned threateningly wicked. Danni wasn't amused, and turned towards the crush to make an escape.

The man suddenly grasped her close, leaning deeply against her, his lips brushing the rim of her ear. Her skin crawled with discomfort, and she unwillingly recalled the shiver of excitement that Marcus stirred in her. Hurt and pain crushed her heart again as the stranger staggered heavily into her. "Ye right pretty, milady."

Some may have been flattered. She was anything but. "Sir, it's best if we sit, I think."

He pulled back, his clouded eyes clearing slightly. "No. Another dance, instead."

"I think one is enough. Please release me this instant."

His eyes narrowed. His hands dropped low, too low, against her back, pulling her close against the full length of his body. Alcohol-stained breath wafted unpleasantly against her face when he buried his face in her neck. She wanted away. Now.

Danni tried to pull free, but his grip tightened. Her heart beat faster. The unpleasant situation was fast becoming out of her control.

Then an angry roar erupted behind them, and the man was abruptly pulled off her. Marcus stood before her, holding the shorter man by his throat, feet dangling in the air. Shocked, Danni pulled viciously on Marcus's arm. "Stop it, Marcus!"

He looked terrible. His brow was beaded with sweat and his grip on the gasping man trembled violently. He managed to look directly at her and Danni saw the incredible rage inside him. She stepped back, letting him go. For the first time, she was truly terrified of what Marcus could be capable of.

He shook her dance partner. "Stay away from her!"

He chokingly assented, head bobbing as best he could against the pressure of Marcus's huge palm. Marcus released him to crumble on the floor. Danni moved to assure herself he would recover, but the giant dragged her towards the door. She did not fight him. Instead, she glanced back, relieved to see bystanders help the drunkard stagger to his feet.

Marcus spun her about, clutching her closer than propriety allowed. He breathed erratically as his eyes shifted about, searching for an exit. He barely spoke. "Come."

Did she have a choice?

Latching onto her arm, he dragged her up the staircase to the floor of rooms. He pulled up short in the hallway outside his door.

"You should never have allowed that man a dance."

She knew that, but he had no stake in what she did or did not do. "I may dance with whomever I choose, Marcus."

His face twisted, turning uglier than she'd ever seen it. "He almost kissed you!"

Danni opened her mouth to retort, but clamped it shut with an audible click. Why should she defend herself? It was not as if she'd encouraged that man.

"What kind of woman are you? Did you want him to kiss you, Danni? Did you like having a man like him maul you? What about your fiancé? What about m—?"

His mouth snapped shut, and his glower deepened, shadowed with pain.

"What do you mean, a man like him?" she managed past her thick throat, ignoring the mention of the earl.

He bared his teeth, turning his eyes away. "Whole and fair of face."

She drew back in shock. He really thought her so shallow? Did he truly think she would preach true love, and risk everything to assist those who sought that happiness, but still care only for physical appearances?

She snapped back, "You are an ass!"

"Your fiancé must be a dandy, then. I'd rather be an ass than a dandy."

Danni tugged her arm to free it from his grasp. Fighting tears of helplessness, she said the first thing she knew would hurt him. "No, not a dandy, but he is a whole man, not the mere shadow of one!"

He blinked, his eyes stark with pain. It was as if her voice had literally struck him, killing some inner part. He dropped her arm, his shoulders sinking. Danni instantly regretted her words, but it was too late to take them back. A hot tear streaked her cheek.

She almost didn't hear him whisper, "You are right, Miss Green. I could never be a good man for you, or for anyone."

He stepped away, the weight of his defeat drowning out all else surrounding her. Danni winced as his door slammed closed.

Danni remained frozen in place for several moments, trying to catch hold of her emotions. A sob broke free. Gasping, she pushed herself down the rest of the hall to her room.

What had she done?

Chapter Fifteen

❦

"Ah! tremble not; your will is law;
"One question answer'd, I withdraw—
"Am I not hideous to your eyes?"

—"Beauty and the Beast" by Charles Lamb

𝒟anni sat on her bed, examining the same wall that had started her day. She decided white was a hideous and depressing color. Devoid of life, empty. She ran a sleeve across her cheeks, drying her tears, and then began readying herself for bed. Stripping down to her shift, she methodically folded her dress, brushed her boots free of the day's dirt, and braided her hair. The temptation to crawl under her blankets and draw herself into a ball overwhelmed her. She'd never felt so alone.

She had to take care of things herself. She did not need anyone. Really.

Sighing, she tucked herself into bed, curling her legs closer to her body. She wished she could turn back the clock and change the outcome of the day. It had been so wonderful when Marcus gave her that beautiful dress. And she thought he was about to kiss her there in the village—she'd *wanted* him to, even with her soon-to-be fiancé's image hovering at the edge of her thoughts.

And she'd had the best of intentions when she found the back entry to the inn. She'd wanted to help him. Then that vile man attempted to kiss her and Marcus's pride had gotten in the way. It seemed everything she did, he misunderstood. She shut her eyes against her tears.

Her exhausting day had reminded her exactly where her priorities lay. Her brain knew she should be focusing only on retrieving and returning Ginny, but damned if she couldn't seem to remember that when Marcus was around. He ran hot, showing her things that made her mad with wanting, and then cold, as if he could barely stand her presence. She pressed her eyes into her knees in confusion.

Most of all, Danni couldn't believe what she said to him. She knew about his struggles, and knew her words would cut him deeply. He struggled with so many inner demons. She had no experiences that she could use to help him. She needed to apologize....

She closed her eyes to sleep, willing the day to end, but blessed oblivion remained elusive. Tossing and turning, she finally lay on her back, until she decided she hated the brown on the ceiling as well. If she only knew what she was going to say the next time she saw Marcus, she wouldn't feel so anxious.

A hollow knock at her door startled her upright. She

frowned at the wooden barrier, uncertain if she should answer it. She had deserted all sense of propriety on this trip, but unbolting the door while a mass of drunken men feasted below was foolish. Any one of them could easily have stumbled to her room.

Another, louder knock echoed. It was followed by a familiar growl, announcing the identity of her visitor. She debated whether she was ready to talk to him. And she'd not yet decided what to say to him.

Sighing, Danni wrapped the blanket around her shift and approached the door. Had she not just been debating the best course of action to reopen lines of communication? If she rejected him now, she may never get another chance.

Lifting the latch, she pulled inward. Marcus leaned against the door frame, face carefully blank. Immediately, Danni realized something was wrong. Sweat spotted his forehead, his fists were clenched at his sides, and his body was unnaturally rigid. His tanned skin was an ashen color, making his scars stark and bleak.

"May I enter?" he bit out.

She stepped aside, worry about his condition erasing all her previous thoughts.

For half a second, she contemplated leaving the door open. But the last thing they needed was a patron to overhear their conversation. She turned as the door latched in place, finding herself inches from Marcus's chest. He looked down at her from sunken eyes. The pupils were large and almost obliterated his beautiful green eyes. He looked as upset as she. Without thinking, Danni lifted her hand to his face, wishing to soothe him. His tired eyes widened; he caught her hand, holding it away from his face. "Don't."

She nodded, inexplicably hurt. His drained eyes drifted shut as a visible shudder racked his body. Heat radiated out of him in waves as he inched achingly close until he stopped, a hair's breadth from full contact.

She longed to close the distance, to feel the familiar rush when he touched her. The thought of his hands running over her, pressing her closely, sent heat surging to her weak legs. She shuddered against the thickening haze clouding her thoughts, mesmerized by the sadness in his eyes.

"I'm so sorry." His voice was choked with emotion. "I should not have said those things. I didn't mean them."

A rush of moisture blurred her vision. He seemed lost and alone, unsure how to accept anything other than the obvious cruelty he suffered. Her heart clutched with pain.

"I cannot be whole for you, little one. Not like your fiancé."

She hated herself even more for her angry, thoughtless words. If she could only take them back. "Shh, Marcus. I did not mean those things either. I was angry."

He didn't seem to hear her, his mind drifting to a place she could not follow. He closed the space between them. His hands fell to her waist, resting gently on the soft curve of her hips.

Danni stiffened, surprised.

"Please. Let me..." He shuddered. "Let me hold you for just a moment. It—it was too much for me down there."

She bit back a gasp, shocked he would admit such a thing. It simply proved how emotionally overwrought he was.

At her nod, his eyes lazily drifted half shut. With agonizing slowness, he closed the gap between them, treating her as if she were the most fragile of glass. Marcus's head dropped to the crook of her neck, nuzzling her ear. His warm breath swept her sensitive skin. A throb matching his rhythmic breathing began low, deep in her body, tightening with each exhale. She held still, afraid to break the spell he had created with his touch. Afraid to frighten him away. He was trusting her, and she would not disappoint him this time.

When he spoke again, his voice was soft by her ear, laced with pain. "I am envious of you, Danni."

She blinked in surprise and whispered, "How so?"

"You have such happy memories of your childhood. Of your mother and father, and their love for each other. Of how they loved and cared for you. I have none of that."

Her breath caught, her chest tight with sympathy.

"My mother was a beautiful woman. Every time she would come see me, I would think how graceful she was. When she held me, I'd feel so calm and safe. Whatever troubles I had that day would wash away." He paused, his voice full of fondness. "She smelled of chamomile."

He shuddered and Danni felt her heart would burst with the sorrow that radiated from him. Biting hard on her lip, she tasted the metal tang of blood. The urge to hold him close was strong, but she wanted to hear him speak. The answers to her questions and doubts were a breath away. She wanted badly to understand this complex man. One arm, unbidden, closed tightly across his back, soothing, encouraging.

"My father was a brutal man. He could be very cruel to her. She would vanish periodically in an effort to get away from him. The times she was away, my father drank and grew more violent and because I was her son... he took everything out on me, Danni." His swallow was audible as he continued, "When he decided my mother had been gone for too long, he'd go fetch her, sometimes literally dragging her back. The last time she was brought home, I was nine and Caro was born. I-I know she loved us. She cared for and protected us from him. But she left again shortly after, leaving Caro and me, and never came back. My father he was so angry, Danni. Always so very angry... I... Sometimes, Danni, I am almost certain he would have killed her."

Danni stifled a gasp, determined to say nothing, do nothing, in fear he'd stop sharing.

He took a deep breath. "I fear I am just like him. I do not think I was ever meant to be a normal man. I've always struggled with the black inside, consuming me a little bit more every year. One day, I fear I may completely disappear. Sometimes, memories of him consume me. I cannot function. I live in fear that my soul will no longer exist and I truly will become the Beast everyone believes me to be."

Danni remembered his episode in the cabin. "Is this what happened to you in the woods?"

He trembled harder, nodding. "I am already so much like my father. He would have had no qualms about kidnapping Ginny the way I did."

Unable to bear it any longer, she wrapped her other arm about his bowed neck, pressing against him, seeking to give him the comfort he craved. The grip at her waist tightened and his big body sagged into her.

"You are *not* like him, Marcus. It is obvious you take no pleasure in this. Why can't you return her?" She held her breath for an answer, pleading with the heavens for the one she wanted to hear.

"I wish I could."

She stiffened in his hold, desperately tamping down on the urge to rail at him. Instead of demanding, she kept her tone gentle. "Why?"

Danni felt his shoulders tense. The grip on her hips tightened briefly before it abandoned her completely. He moved just a few steps away, breathing ragged, hands trembling. His absence sent a chill racing across her heated skin. She swallowed against a hollow emptiness growing in her heart, fists clenched by her sides.

His shoulders rose and fell in quick succession. Alarmed, she took a hesitant step forward. "Marcus?"

"Sometime before he died, he"—Marcus bit out savagely, the fury in his voice making her cringe—"he arranged a marriage between my sister and the Duke of Harwood."

Danni gasped, her hand instinctively covering her mouth. Everyone knew of the Duke's reputation, but only very few actually knew him. He had lived out of the country for several years now, after his father had died under very suspicious circumstances.

"Wasn't he the leading suspect in the murder of his father?" She gasped.

Marcus nodded, anger hardening his voice. "I cannot allow my sister to marry that man. But to break the contract, I have to secure more money. My father's vices drained the estate long before I gained control of the finances. It's a slow process, but I'm regaining some semblance of security. However, it's just enough to cover the break of promise stipulation. There would be no extra to support my tenants and Caro would have no dowry for a future marriage. I can't let that happen, Danni!"

"Oh my God," she breathed, stumbling back, realizing this was the source of his nightmares in the woods. "How could a father do such a thing to his child?"

Bitter laughter rent the quiet of the room. "Oh, that is my fault as well."

Confusion brought her close again. She longed to reach out to him, to soothe the painful rigidness of his spine, but she sensed he would not welcome her touch at the moment.

"What do you mean? Your fault?"

"Several years before his death, my father called me to his office. He commanded me to marry, but I refused." His fist thumped ruthlessly on the nearby wall, making Danni jump. Anger rolled off him in waves. "I didn't want to marry, to trap some poor girl with someone like myself. And I swear the only thing that kept him from killing me during his tirades was the fact that he wanted an heir to carry on his line. If I died, so would the Fleetwood line. I vowed to never marry, to never father children, so he would lose that satisfaction."

Danni ignored the unexpected pain in her chest at that confession. He never wanted to be a father?

Marcus smirked sarcastically. "We argued and I left. He said he would make me pay, and he knew I cared for Caro above all else. Knew I'd do anything for her. The betrothal to Harwood was his way to force me into marriage." He suddenly spun on his heel, facing her again. Danni felt her eyes widen at the desperation twisting his face. "I hate that he's winning, little one."

"But he's dead, Marcus."

"Ha! Not to me, nor to Caro. He lives on, forever, in us." He stepped closer, seeming to seek her absolution. "I will never force myself on Ginny. She can have children with whomever she wishes and I will never say a word otherwise. I simply need her money to break the betrothal, and her father's power to fight Harwood in court, if necessary."

Danni felt sick. Everything clicked into place. She now understood why she was here, why Marcus had chosen Ginny. "What do you mean he kept you alive, Marcus? I understand he was unforgivably cruel, but would he really seek to kill his own children?"

Marcus fell silent. The color that had returned with his anger bled from his face again. Hesitantly, she took another step forward, pleading softly, "What did your father do, Marcus?"

"He..." His hands fisted, and his gaze fixed behind her.

The image of his scarred body stepping from the tub flashed before her. Biting her lip, she took another half step closer, clutching at the blankets hanging forgotten in her hands. "He caused your scars?"

His voice seemed dead as he spoke about—reported—the past. "The last time my mother came back and Caroline was born, my father got drunk, exceedingly drunk. That night, I was in my bed, hiding, and my parents were arguing. His words...they were the drunken ramblings of a crazy man, Danni. He was screaming that Caroline wasn't his child, despite the fact she shares the family white-blond hair and green eyes. I think he hated her."

His soft timbre paused as he drew another breath. "They were so loud. My mother...she was hysterical, pleading with my father to leave Caro alone, swearing Caro was his daughter. I could not hear all that was said, but my father snapped. A sound like thunder drowned her cries. Later, I learned he'd put his fist through a table."

Danni bit harder on her lip, trying hard to be silent as tears slipped down her cheeks.

"My father had always been violent. I learned at a very young age to avoid contact with him. I became the most obedient and respectful of children. It was born out of fear of him. But that night…my mother threatened to leave him again. Then his footsteps were on the stairs, approaching. The house fairly shook with his screams to my mother—he would not allow her bastard to live under his roof. He headed towards the nursery. To Caro. I knew his tone of voice well. Knew what he'd try to do."

He refused to look at her. Danni closed the distance, tentatively touching him. Her hands moved over his back, trying to soothe him the way she would Simon when he cried. It was all she could think to do.

"I couldn't let him hurt Caro. She was so small. So fragile. The only good thing in my dark world. She would smile every time she saw me. She didn't know how I cowered like an animal from my father." His throat thickened. "I loved her so much, and she, me. I was determined to protect her…she made me brave."

Tears fell from her eyes as he continued to recount his tale. Her heart broke piece by piece for the little boy trapped in hell.

"I ran as fast as I could, arriving in her room before my father. She was still asleep, a tiny thumb in her mouth." He paused, as if gathering himself to tell the rest of the story. "I grabbed Caro and hid her in the linen closet across the hall. When my father came in the room, he was furious he could not find her. He struck me, throwing me into a corner of the room. Pain so intense I could see colors exploded in my skull. Before I had a chance to rise, he'd grabbed my shirt. I was so close to him I could almost taste the stink of liquor on his person. My mother came flying into the room, screaming. She beat at his back, trying to stop him. He threw her out and locked the door. He hit me again, roaring with rage. Demanding to know where I put Caro."

Her heart raced. She no longer wanted to hear the rest. She knew what was going to happen, what he was going to say. But she couldn't stop the tide of emotion swirling through her. The anger she'd felt for him had slowly changed over the last few days to tenderness and confusion. And for that reason, she could not halt a story she knew he'd likely never told anyone before. She knew above all else that he must never feel she was repulsed by him or his past. The rejection would likely kill him.

"He took out the knife he always carried in his boot. He'd threatened me with it before. He told me he'd cut me if I did not give Caro up. I refused, afraid then and still convinced now that he would have killed her."

He swayed, crossing his arms tightly across his chest. Danni realized he was reliving the horror as he told her. She wrapped her arms about his waist, hoping to soothe them both. "The more I defied him, the more insane he became. He caught my face, wrapping his arm around my neck to hold me still. I struggled against him. I fought as hard as I could. But he was so much bigger. So much stronger. I cried as the metal touched my face. It dug so deep, hurt so much...but I could not yell. If I had, Caro would have cried and he would have found her."

Danni shook her head, tears freely falling down her face. She clutched at his back as he continued to look away from her. "Sometimes I wonder if he would have stopped had I told him. Sometimes, I wonder how my life would be if I had not gotten out of bed that night."

"Marcus..."

Broken eyes laying bare all his pain clashed with hers. "Maybe I would be a whole man. Maybe you could have loved me."

Her chest burned. Could he really care for her? He'd had so much pain in his life, it was little wonder he hesitated to care for anyone, let alone her. He needed to shield himself.

Ignoring all her misgivings, she acted on the need that rocked her entire being. She wanted to make him happy, to make him realize how wonderful he was. Without breaking her gaze from his moss-colored eyes, she pulled him closer, molding her body to his. She refused to let him regret his sacrifice because of her. "Marcus, if you hadn't tried to help Caro, you wouldn't be the kind, compassionate man you are today."

Wonder filled his eyes as he stared down at her. His hand reached out hesitantly to stroke the hair at her temple, twisting a strand about his long, blunt finger. "Do you know how beautiful you are?"

Danni's eyes widened as his hand cupped her jaw, his thumb feather-light across her bottom lip.

"So very, very beautiful," he muttered.

Unbidden, her eyes drifted shut, and without thinking, her tongue darted out, swirling across the pad of his thumb. The ridges in his skin felt foreign on her mouth as she tasted salt and... *him.* Her nipples tightened, straining against her shirt, reaching for his warmth. She ran her palms across his body, soothing and reassuring the hesitant beast.

Marcus drew a shallow breath. His body held taut as she explored him, his fear of rejection palpable. Pressing closer, she ran her hands over his waist, feeling the leanness of his hips. His arms came round her, joining her to him, fingers threading through her hair, cupping the base of her neck. Her forehead pressed against the center of his chest, she relished the way his warmth seemed to fill her from the inside out. With her lips and the tip of her tongue, she tasted the sweetness of his muscles along his collar, and felt at his shuddering response. She palmed the hard plain of his chest, inhaling deeply of his slightly spicy scent.

His grip tightened. She felt the press of his lips against the top of her head before his hand caught her chin, drawing her gaze level with his. "Look at me."

She obeyed.

His haunted eyes blazed with internal fire, but his face filled with sorrow. "This is all for naught. I'm not the prince of your dreams. I am ugly, surly, and disreputable, prone to periods of deepest despair and anger. I'm not meant for you, the fairest of all."

He grinned sadly.

With a sinking stomach, thoughts of the earl waiting for her acceptance and her father's certain disappointment swamped her. She should stop this, she needed to agree with Marcus, and allow him to leave, but the words would not come.

Danni doubted she would ever have moments like this—moments of such intense and deep connection—with the Earl of Hemsworth. She would have a good life with him, a carefully planned and very secure life, but the trials that truly united a woman to a man would not surface. Danni knew she and Marcus would be forever changed, forever bonded—in more than a physical way. And as she stared up at his ravaged features, she realized she couldn't leave him tonight with another rejection. She hated that Marcus may believe she did not want him. Because she did. Desperately.

So she whispered, "No."

Marcus stiffened as if she'd struck him. She refused to let him retreat. Not after all she'd learned about his past. He needed her as much as she wanted him. She held firm to his wrists, allowing him no quarter to run.

"No," she said with more force, "I will not pretend that you are something you aren't. I have never met anyone with more courage and strength. You are beautiful inside and out."

He snorted in disbelief. "You, little one, are daft as well as blind. I'm hideous."

She smiled. "You are perfect."

And then she kissed him.

He froze under her kiss, unresponsive long enough for Danni to fear he would reject her. Then he seemed to make sense of her words. His soft lips moved over hers, deepening the kiss. Delicious sparks tightened her throat. Fabric rustled as the sheet fell to the floor and her free arms encompassed him. Large, rough hands caressed her body, leaving not an inch untouched. She shivered. His hands moved down her ribs, brushing the sides of her breasts, cupping the roundness of her bottom. She became aware of his hardness, brushing her belly, causing her fingers to dig into his shoulders in surprise.

Marcus overwhelmed her senses. He seemed a man possessed—as if afraid she would stop him at any moment. However, Danni was so lost in the swirl of emotion he stirred inside her, she couldn't have formed the words to stop him even had she wanted.

She moaned, her head tilting back as his mouth shifted, trailing hot, open-mouthed kisses along her collarbone. Gasping at the intensity of her emotions, Marcus returned and invaded, rasping along her tongue. She drank hungrily of his kisses, the taste drugging her with longing, filling her with him.

Closing her eyes, she imagined his hands exploring her naked body, feeling the rippling of her shift, the barrier gone, and his skin against hers.

Marcus nipped at her earlobe, her toes curling in response. His voice ragged with desire, whispering, pulling back once more. "I want you, but we cannot do this." He sounded pained as he added, "I care too much about your future. And your future right now is promised to another."

With a soft gasp, Danni was lifted off her feet. Marcus turned them around, striding towards the straw bed. Her hands threaded through his thick curls as his lips trailed gentle, almost desperate kisses over her face.

"Marcus," she breathed, as he gently laid her across the bed. He stood back to leave, but Danni caught his wrist. Plucking up her courage, she met him straight in the eye. "I want this. I want you. Just this once. Regardless of what happens in the future, I want to have this memory. So don't stop. Don't leave me . . . please."

Emerald eyes glittering with an odd mixture of tenderness and pain as he surveyed her face, trailing over her prone body. Suddenly, Danni became aware of just how scantily clad she was without the sheet. Her shift had slipped off one shoulder, exposing the curve to cool air. The hem of the thin garment had ridden up to her thighs. She made to cover herself, but Marcus caught her hands.

"You are beautiful, Danni. Never hide."

Heat rushed to her face and she looked away.

A soft chuckle drew her frown. "Marcus, it's not amusing."

"Yes, it is," he whispered, his knuckles softly skating up her outer thigh. Her breath hitched, flames licking up her skin to her center. Fingertips slipped under the shift, brushing the edge of her bottom. With a groan, he surrendered and climbed onto the bed. His heavy weight tilted the bed precariously. Her hands latched onto his shoulders as he shifted to his knees between her legs. Nerves tightened her grasp. His palms swept over the tops of her thigh. "Marcus..."

"I know, little one. Just a touch. No more." He added with sadness flitting across his features, "It's not my right."

Danni gulped, tamping down words to tell him she wished it were. But for all intents and purposes, she was engaged and she had to remember that, even in this stolen moment of passion.

"However," he whispered secretly in her ear, "I can still do a great deal."

"M-Marcus!" She felt her eyes widen as a calloused finger dipped into her core. Her hands dug into his shoulders as it shifted, sending a jolt of pleasure through her.

A devilish grin she'd never seen before, nor imagined him capable of, flitted over his lips. The odd lip dimple deepened, renewing her desire to kiss it. He leaned over her, pressing a soft kiss to her temple. His gentle smile was both soothing and breathtaking. "Trust me, Danielle."

He'd never used her full name before. Emotions swam through her, drowning her ability for words. She could only nod.

Marcus leaned on one arm, possessive fire blazing in his gaze, trapping hers. One questing hand smoothed the hem of her dress over her hips, the touch like a butterfly's kiss. Cool air licked her heated skin. He continued to lift the fabric up her body, raising her arms above her head. She moaned, her legs tightening about him. He paused, her hands still in her sleeves. He wasn't looking at the shirt. The new position had placed her breasts level with his mouth. Hot breath skated over them, beading the aching tips.

A thrill of anticipation shot through her. As if seeking permission, he hesitantly leaned forward and captured the pink tip between his teeth.

Danni almost screamed.

Her hands twisted in her shirt as he laved the sensitive underside of her breast. She melted with pleasure. Her arms were suddenly freed as the shift disappeared. Danni felt herself falling back against the pillow. Marcus shifted his attention to her other breast, engulfing the sensitive tip in his unbearably warm mouth. Her legs tightened, coming to rest on his hips. They quivered with the foreign, pleasurable touch.

Groaning, Marcus placed a soft kiss on the curve of her

shoulder. She whimpered at the loss of his mouth, even as warmth washed over her from the tender touch.

"Shall I show you something else?" he whispered against the pounding pulse in her neck. Wrapping herself around him, she nodded, marveling at the change in him. Gone was the broken and cold man. In his place was a confident, tender lover.

She found she liked this man much more.

He kissed her greedily again, before drawing a line down her body with his mouth. She could scarce catch her breath as he worshipped her, her skin leaping and burning.

"I want you so much, little one." His murmured endearment warmed her as he wound her tighter and tighter. He kissed her ribs, stomach. The lower he moved towards his goal, the tenser she became.

"Oh." The word escaped her on a breath as he pressed a light kiss to the small patch of skin between her stomach and apex. Gently he spread her thighs, giving her a chance to stop him. Danni held her breath, waiting, wanting to know what he would do next.

A slow smile dimpled his lip as he glanced down at her exposed center. Heat rushed to her face and she had to bury her fingers in the bedsheets to stop herself from hiding. Even then, she squirmed in pleasure. His rough hands massaged the backs of her knees, loosening the muscles. His husky voice seemed hesitant as he whispered, "Do you want me, Danni?"

She gasped as his thumb inched higher, close to where she desperately craved his touch. His ragged breath feathered over her skin, "Do you *desire* me?"

His hand came so close...but moved away. Her eyes

clashed with his. Green pools drowned her, bringing her under his rapidly rising sea. Despite his teasing caresses, she saw how much her answer would mean to him. Danni's chest tightened, ached to banish that look. She mustered her courage, and buried deep every reservation she had. "Yes. Very, very much."

Relief and pleasure brightened his green depths. His eyes drifted shut for a brief second; his palms warmed the length of her thigh. His mesmerizing smile widened a fraction. When he looked at her again, Danni saw the beginnings of a new man.

Her vision blurred. "Marcus..."

"Lovely Danni," he whispered and lowered his head. She tensed, her vision clearing with uncertainty as to what he was about.

And then she felt his mouth on her.

Her shocked gasp ended with a moan. Her hands flew to his head, entwining with the silken curls. Her body tightened as she whimpered with the pure, unadulterated pleasure of it. The roughness of his tongue rasped over her, sending shudders of delight through her. He pushed her legs farther apart, moving deeper inside her.

Danni could hardly take any more.

And just as she thought that, she felt something enter her. Instinctively, she tightened around the invasion, but a pleasant sense of fullness, completeness, flooded her. Gasping, another of Marcus's fingers slipped inside. He lowered his body onto hers, bringing himself as close as possible. Warming her skin and entangling his legs with hers. Her head fell back and her hips arched. He kissed her neck, moaning with deep pleasure.

She wanted more. So much more.

Her body tightened and she held the sheets in a death grip. Danni bit her lip, trying to hold in the scream tightening her throat. Her heart beat faster as he stroked her center. Her hips lifted, straining for something, having no idea what. She burned hotter and brighter, fingers digging into his hair, his mouth again latched to her breast.

Danni rolled her head over the cool pillow against the growing coil in her. Her body lifted and a sob escaped her as wave after wave of pleasure consumed her.

Warm arms pulled her back against a solid chest. Protective warmth and strength washed over her as her erratic breathing slowed. He gathered her close in his arms, wrapping her in a protective cocoon of contentment and strength. The steady thump of Marcus's heart lulled her. Wonderment and tenderness throbbed in time with the lingering pleasure between her legs, as a feather-light kiss pressed against the slowing pulse at her neck. Sighing, she snuggled back into his bulk. His voice, still horse with desire, rumbled over her. "So beautiful, little one."

Rolling in his arms, she rested her head on his collarbone, watching his peaceful face. His lips split with a grin, his eyes still closed. Her heart stuttered at his expression of wonderment. Marcus spoke once more, the word barely audible on his exhale.

"Perfect."

Chapter Sixteen

❦

The Brothers cried, "Let us away,
"We'll perish, or the Monster slay."

—"Beauty and the Beast" by Charles Lamb

I am hideous."

"You're perfect."

He felt his lips tilt in a smile, enjoying the dream. He held Danni in his arms, her eyes shining up at him with all the love and wonder he'd ever fantasized.

He snuggled deeper into the pillow, willing the dream to continue. Holding the small slice of heaven near his heart. His arms tightened, imagining her softness. The murmur of a sigh forced his heart to skip a beat.

Not again!

Marcus dreaded what he'd find. Gulping, he opened his eyes a crack. The bundle in his arms definitely had the right color hair. As her head turned, his stomach balled. It was Danni.

Damn.

He slammed his lids closed again. Childishly willing her away. Peaking through the slits, he glanced down. Still there. And definitely Danni.

Swiftly extricating himself, he rolled to his side in the direction of the window. His eyes snapped shut again, blocking out the light streaming in. And reality.

How could he have allowed what happened last night?

He gulped, cradling his head between his hands as he sat up. How could he have been so stupid? He'd treated her abominably. Of course, she'd be furious with him.

From the corner of his eye, he glanced at Danni, safe and seemingly content in the warm nest of the bed. He focused on a faraway point of the white walls, reliving the events of the night before.

Guilt and shame had spurned him to seek her out last night. He had treated her abominably at the stable. He knew she had meant to help him avoid a stressful situation in the crowded taproom, but once again, his anxiety and defensiveness had blinded him. And to compound his actions, he had, for the first time, been consumed with raging jealousy. After a moment of calm in his own room, he knew she had done nothing to entice that damned drunkard. He'd gone straight to her, determined to do whatever was needed to make amends. He had never expected to spill almost every secret he stored in his dark soul.

Brilliant job, Bradley, bloody brilliant.

He rubbed his hand over his face. After everything

he'd done, after everything he'd said to her, she'd still given him the greatest gift. She'd touched him softly, as if she loved him. She hadn't rejected him or his awful past. Danni had behaved as he'd always wanted a woman to— wanted *his* woman to. To accept him as a normal human being, a man, *a whole man*.

And that was the crux of it. Danni wasn't his and never could be. She would soon belong to another. He didn't deserve her, despite his title. He had no right to take advantage of her good heart. Her father was committed to have her marry another, just as Marcus was committed to resolving his sister's dilemma. He must find an heiress to wed. Last night had changed nothing.

Memories of her flawless skin and passionate moans filled his mind. He was a dishonorable brute to have done this with her. He had nothing to offer. And, most important, he was sure she now believed he had changed his mind about Ginny. But he hadn't. He had no choice. Ginny would be safe with him. He would be kind to her. But he would marry her.

Marcus turned restlessly to gaze at the little ball curled in his side. Danni lay with the scratchy woolen blanket against her pale skin, her hands resting under her cheek. She looked small and fragile. So contrary to her waking self. Unthinking, he reached out and brushed a lock of hair from her face. Another sigh escaped her; her breath skated off his skin.

Shots of lust traveled straight to his groin. A growing dread formed in his gut, tightening his stomach until the back of his throat burned. He'd tasted the forbidden fruit. Could he be stronger than Adam and ignore the temptation Danni presented?

Danni shifted in her sleep, pressing closer to his bare thigh. He gulped, her warmth igniting a simmer beneath his skin.

He was doomed to Dante's nine circles of hell. He would marry Ginny, and dream of Danni his whole life long.

Gingerly, he freed himself from the blanket, crawled over her, and backed away from the bed. The sheet slipped, further exposing her. He hungrily feasted on the tempting swells of her bosom before reining in the surge of lust. Careful not to touch her, Marcus repositioned the coverlet over her. A sickening thought shot through his heart.

What if she'd let him touch her only because she pitied him? He'd said enough last night to invoke anyone's sympathetic feelings. He had been a blubbering mess. Danni wanted to solve everyone's problems. To her, could he have been just another heart to mend?

Glaring out the window, he clenched his fists. No, she wouldn't use herself like that. Still...if she had...it was just another reason he had to say good-bye to her, and soon. He was a broken man, unfit for any woman, and he would be forever.

Once they found Ginny, he'd bring the girl to Gretna and marry her. Then, he'd deposit Danni back home so she could accept her father's match and become a happy wife with a happy ending, just as she'd always dreamed. Happily ever after. The end.

He'd never touch her again. Never think about her again. Never long for her again.

He quickly grabbed his jacket from the corner, not sure how he'd managed to remove it. In his haste, he did not stop to check the hall for passersby before he dashed out, closing the door behind him, and scooting across the hall to his own room.

Already missing her warmth, he groaned. How was he ever going to face her again?

*   *   *

Danni stretched, rolling over to the center of the bed. Cool emptiness met her searching hand. Her brow lowered in confusion. Something was missing. Her body felt deliciously languid and heavy.

Images flashed behind her lids. She sat up, grasping the bedsheet to her chest, her body rushing with heat from both embarrassment and renewed longing.

"Oh my," she whispered, fingers touching her lips and thighs clenched against the warmth in her core. She couldn't believe what she'd done last night. It had been wonderful—maddeningly, mind-numbingly wonderful. And they hadn't even made love. Her fingers pressed tighter to her bruised lips. This lovemaking business was far better than Annabel had ever alluded to.

She swallowed against her desire, her hand brushing the cool sheets again. Where was Marcus? Why had he left her? A groan slipped past her fingers and she curled her knees to her chest.

How could she have allowed what happened last night?

What was she thinking? Of course he would leave. He had exposed so much of his emotions, of his past, and was probably terrified that once again she would reject him. Could he not even trust her after last night?

She moaned. Their current circumstances had not changed. Marcus was intent on marrying Ginny. It was the only solution he could see to save his sister. She could no longer paint him as a reprobate fortune hunter. What he was doing was still morally wrong, but he was driven by desperation to protect the only person he'd ever cared for. She could no longer hate him for that. Danni didn't want to admit it, but in the same circumstances, she might have been driven to kidnap as well.

She knew the simple solution would be to discard the match her father made for her and reveal her identity as an heiress. Her feelings for Marcus were growing each day. He was a wonderful man beneath the harsh exterior. He had treated her with such delicacy and tenderness.

But she hesitated. Her father would be devastated. He had chosen the earl for her with much care. Finding her a loyal and kind husband had been very important to him. How could she tell him that she wanted to refuse a solid, upstanding member of the *ton*, and instead devote her life to a haunted, disfigured marquis from a disreputable family? Her father may have become distant since her mother died, but Danni knew he wanted her to have a loving and stable home. Even Danni was unsure Marcus could offer her those things.

And she so longed for her father to be proud of her and happy again. It had been her hope the match with the earl would improve his outlook since her mother had died. He could embrace his new son-in-law and the future children they would produce. Danni doubted her father would so easily accept Marcus.

And then what about the impact her rejection would

have on the earl? Although the arrangements had not yet been formalized, she knew there was an oral agreement between him and her father. Instead of the heart-leaping excitement she knew other girls experienced at the prospect of marriage, her heart had been torn in two. When her father had first introduced his plan, she'd asked him for a proper courtship so she and the earl could learn about each other, and he had kindly agreed, but everyone in their circle eagerly anticipated the announcement.

She hated to admit the earl chose her because of her father's position in Parliament. He was an ambitious man, and had repeatedly told her during their courtship what a wonderful politician's wife she would be. With his eye firmly fixed on political power and his sterling reputation, she grimaced at the thought of his learning about her elopement agency, not to mention her scandalous behavior these past few days. While she did believe he cared for her, she knew it was more affection than love.

Danni sighed. She had so dreamed of a fairy tale love like that of her parents and the couples she helped elope. She wanted that grand passion, but knew not everyone found it. And lately, in light of her father's wishes, she'd begun to believe she wanted a husband and children more than she needed the grand passion of a fairy tale. Perhaps she would have to settle for a good life, rather than a grand one.

Danni flushed to think of herself sharing the intimacies of marriage with Lord Rathbourne. She was certain the Earl of Hemsworth would not bring such fire to her heart, but she knew he would care for her and treat her with the utmost respect. She could have a happy ever after with him.

One thing she was certain of: her father and the earl would both suffer great embarrassment at her rejection of the betrothal.

She wasn't yet ready to risk it all for Marcus. She did not want to marry him because of money. She couldn't announce her true identity without knowing with certainty that he was as committed to her. She would not risk her relationships with her father and the earl unless she could be sure he loved her just as much. And this situation with Ginny. How could she truly love someone who was capable of hurting Ginny so badly?

And he was so complicated, too. He had a temper when pushed too far. He was so tormented by the past it shadowed his eyes. He was self-conscious and broken in a way Danni wasn't certain could ever be repaired. She feared for Marcus's future if he could not find a way to break free from the memories of his father. His soul was unpredictable and...uncertain.

Last night, she'd seen a glimmer of what he could become if he could accept someone's love. She wanted that for him with all her being.

She could just arrange for Marcus to have the money he needed, if she could manage to convince her father that helping Marcus was a good use of that money. Of course, she would have to do that before she married the earl, as the funds would be transferred to his oversight upon their marriage. Perhaps, if necessary, payments to Caroline and Marcus could be part of the marriage contract. Her heart clenched at the thought. Marcus would be free, and she would not.

Resigned to a life without Marcus, she prepared for the day. They must find Ginny before the rest of this farce could play its final scenes.

Grabbing her belongings, she headed across the hall. Taking a steadying breath, she swung the door open, forcing false cheer into her voice. "Good morning!"

The blond man's head snapped up. Marcus froze in the act of packing, looking at her with surprise and hesitancy. Danni felt her stomach twist and her palms dampen. What was he going to say? What would he do?

His lips tugged into a frown, and he continued stuffing his blanket into a sack. "Do you have something against knocking, Miss Green?"

Danni opened her mouth, only to snap it shut. She swallowed her embarrassment, muttering, "Seems only when it comes to your room."

A snort from the giant narrowed her gaze. He placed an extra shirt in the sack and tossed the bag over his shoulder. His movements were stiff and radiated discomfort. Wonderful, she thought grimly, he has no idea how to behave either.

With a sigh, she braced herself for another round of silent Marcus. "Shall we eat in the village?"

He grunted, brushing past her towards the door. She stopped him with a rough yank on his arm.

"That's it? This is how you will treat me after last night?"

She felt his skin quiver and rise with goose bumps. His features softened when he looked at her.

"I will always long for more, but nothing has changed. I am more determined than ever to find Ginny and bring this tragedy to an end."

He gently pulled his arm free and strode out the door. Danni stiffened at the mix of regret and sadness the brief contact gave her. Pinning his back with a long, reproving glare, she followed.

This was going to be a long day.

*　　*　　*

Danni sought out the stall selling meat pies. She tilted her head to better breathe in the heavenly aroma. Her eyes drifted closed. Her mouth watered in anticipation. She took a bite, savoring the explosion of flavor, and when she opened her eyes, she sighed. She so relished this first moment's peace since she had awoken that morning. Their journey to the village had been completed in strained silence, just as she'd expected. When they'd arrived at the village fair, she and Marcus had separated without speaking.

Danni took another bite of the pie, grateful for a few moments to collect her thoughts. She shifted her pack on her shoulder, feeling the weight of his gift bump her side. She was still reeling from the thoughtfulness of his gift, and how, in her mind, the dress was evidence Marcus could be redeemed. It was a bright spot in an otherwise horrible series of events. Everything else had been a disaster since he'd walked into her bookstore. She really didn't think the situation could get much worse.

And then she met the scout's gaze.

Naked fear shot through her. She had seen him only briefly, but his face was not one she would soon forget. The man was small, only an inch or two taller than she. His sandy hair gleamed in the sun. His face and body were reed thin. Perfect for fast travel. He looked the absolute soldier: purposeful, regimented, and mean.

And he held her fate in his hands.

His light gaze flared with recognition. She'd been discovered.

She ducked among a group of passing women on their way to sell their wares. She scanned the masses of people, searching for Marcus's familiar face. She may not understand her feelings for him, but she certainly wasn't going to leave him behind.

A shout rang out behind her, quickly followed by another. "Stop her!"

She weaved through bodies, ignoring the chaos in her wake. Danni scrambled over a counter, hoping to lose her pursuers, and crouched low among curtains of fabrics. Footsteps pounded past. With her heart in her throat, she lifted her eyes above the wooden counter, watching the scout and several others disappear into the crowd. Other soldiers began a systematic search among the stalls along the narrow fairway. She slowly crept out from under the stall, backing up to a nearby alley between two shops.

She was almost hidden in the darkness when a rough hand caught hold of her arm. Another smothered her scream. She fought viciously for freedom, lashing out wherever she could.

"Shhh. Cease your cursed squirming, little one."

Marcus's grumble made her go limp. She sagged against his solid frame, gaining comforting strength before he turned her around. In her relief, she realized she would always want him near her, holding her and calling her his little one. It was a disturbing thought.

The contact was over all too quickly and her fear spiraled back. "You did not have to grab me in such a way. What have I told you about manhandling me?"

His scornful gaze immediately shifted from her, his eyes narrowing on the path through the stalls. "Who were those men?"

"One of them is the scout, Marcus," she hissed, her hands waving madly. "He recognized me."

A snarl pulled his lips back, stretching his scars into stark relief. "Perhaps we should not have left your coachman to die by rabbit."

She nodded, a wry smile reluctantly tugging at her lips. "You should have let me kill him. The little weasel."

Marcus shot her a half smile. The expression was so at odds with the situation, she scowled at him. "You have quite the bloodthirsty streak in you."

She smirked back. Now was not the time for humor. Fists tightening, she glanced around for escape. "We must leave. Now. Where are the horses?"

"Unfortunately, they are tied up right there," he pointed to a hitching post where one of the scout's men searched through their supplies strapped to the saddles. Danni grasped the bag containing her gown tightly, grateful to still have it in her possession.

Marcus guided them to the back of the alley, then moved in front of Danni to hide her from sight. He also blocked her view as he scanned over the heads of the crowds milling in the street. Ducking, she peered through a space at his side, trying to see if she could spot the scout. Spotting no one, they prepared to brave the thoroughfare.

"We'll continue on foot. Let's head for the forest.

North, where the bandits' camp is supposed to be. Perhaps we can steal both Ginny and some horses from them. There must be tracks from your carriage somewhere out there. No one has found it abandoned yet."

She nodded in agreement. They had little choice. They moved into the open, sticking to the shadows cast by the walls. They skulked along, tension high, neither daring to speak. Marcus led them towards the woods. They would easily lose any pursuers in the dense foliage.

At the edge of the village a shout rang out. Danni ran, panicked. The scout barreled down on them, two large men in his wake. The vision of a noose about her neck flashed before her eyes, spurring her to greater speeds.

She approached the small clearing of grass between the village and the trees. It seemed to stretch and grow in length as the pursuers drew closer. Marcus caught her hand, pulling her off balance and into a stumbling gallop. She worked her short legs as fast as she could, trying to keep up with Marcus's longer ones. He tugged harder on her hand, his voice snapping through panted breaths, "Run faster!"

"I'm trying," she gasped back, feeling her pack slap against her thigh.

In that same moment a gun fired behind them. Danni screamed as a bullet snapped into the earth nearby. Shouts came from another direction. Apparently reinforcements had joined the chase. Another blast from a pistol rang through the air. Marcus stumbled. She grabbed hold of his hand as she surpassed him and entered the safety of the forest. They continued to run deeper and deeper into the dense green, weaving and zigzagging through bramble that seemed to come alive and grab at their feet. They didn't stop until they reached a small moss-covered patch encircled by a haphazard row of large hedges.

Danni collapsed onto the ground, spread-eagled. She stared up at the light streaming through the netting of leaves overhead. Her feet and legs ached from exertion, her lungs were on fire, but she was alive. And free. A patch of pretty blue sky peeking through the canopy was covered by the fluffy white of a cloud. She watched it float by, breathing deeply to control her heart.

She frowned after several minutes. Marcus hadn't spoken a single word. She sat up, saw him sitting against a thicket of hedge branches. He was hunched forward, one boot jutting out and the other bent at his side. His arms were wrapped about his waist. He was unusually still.

Remembering the shot, Danni hurried to her feet. She was at his side in an instant, trying to steady her shaking hands. He protested weakly as she peeled away his arms. Slightly above his left hip was a steadily growing patch of blood.

Chapter Seventeen

❦

And there, alas! he now was found
Extended on the flowery ground.

—"Beauty and the Beast" by Charles Lamb

You've been shot!"

His head tilted back, his eyes opened towards the sky, sucking in his breath. "Yes, good, Miss Green."

Exasperated, Danni hit his arm. "Take this seriously."

"How can one not take a gunshot to his side seriously?"

She grunted. Her brows lowered. "Marcus Bradley. I am going to kill you someday."

"Yes, well, let us ensure I am available for that first."

Blinking back the sudden burn in her eyes, she lifted the edge of his shirt to examine the wound. She sighed with relief. Despite the large amount of blood flowing

from the area, the wound did not look as bad as she'd
imagined. The bullet had skimmed his side, cutting deep,
but it had not lodged in his flesh.

"How is it?"

His strained voice reminded her that, even if the
wound wasn't fatal, it was still causing a good deal of
pain. "You will survive. The bullet only grazed you. The
slash is deep and long. It is bleeding badly."

He grunted, pushing her hands away and replacing his
shirt. He held the fabric hard to his side. "Good." He tilted
his head back again and shut his eyes. "Now leave me."

Danni sat back on her haunches in disbelief. "Leave?"

One closed eye peeked open. "Yes."

"Are you mad?" Her mouth dropped. "We are in the
middle of the woods, in a place I have never been in my
entire life. Where exactly do you propose I go?"

"Across the channel would do nicely."

She sputtered, her anger nearly choking her. "Don't be
ridiculous!"

His face turned mutinous. "Truly, Danielle, leave me.
This is your chance to escape. You can get back to the
village and return home from there. Take the rest of the
money to pay for a horse. If you stay here with me, you
will be caught, ruining your own life and your father's.
I will take my chances with the law. Most important, together the admiral and I will recover Ginny. Please go.
It's for the best."

Danni hesitated. He was willing to sacrifice himself for
her. And he was right. She should leave him.

But...

Her gaze drifted down to the wound he was clutching,
the red stain seeping through his shirt. It needed to be

properly cleaned and dressed. She didn't want him to survive the bullet only to die of infection. She would not desert him.

"Remove your shirt, please."

His eyes shot open in shock.

"I need either your shirt or your jacket. Choose."

He pulled off his jacket obediently, his features tightening with the movement, then let the item drop by his side before collapsing into his previous position. Danni scooped up the jacket and disappeared into the woods. She needed to find water.

Marcus refused to open his eyes to watch Danni walk away. It was the best for both of them. She could move on with her life and marry her fiancé. She could start fresh. It was simply best to push her away now, ending this sooner rather than later.

Perhaps he would simply die here. He would not have to live with his demons anymore. He wouldn't have to live to see Caro marry a monster, or witness another man enjoy Danni's love.

Leaves crackled, followed by the snap of a twig. He opened his eyes, wondering if the admiral's men had found him, and reminding himself that, unfortunately, he truly did want to live. However, it was Danni standing beside him, her face creased with worry. In her hands she cupped a dripping rag.

"You fool. You should be gone!"

"Lift your shirt." Her voice held a note of command he was growing accustomed to. He obediently pulled it up. He could see now that the rag was soaked with water and a small puddle formed in the bottom of her hands. She met his gaze with a tender smile. "This may sting a little."

He ignored the way his heart skipped a beat in relief that she was with him. Grunting in response, he flinched as the cold water cascaded down his side, biting into the wound. He tried to pull away but Danni's hand caught the back of his neck, holding him in place.

The subtle heat of her hand offered surprising comfort. It soothed him and sickened him in the same instant. He had no right to this kindness, not after everything he'd done to her. He'd assumed she'd taken his jacket to keep warm on her journey away from him, but his Weston creation was now in rags being used to clean his side.

Her fingers rubbed softly against the base of his neck. His body instantly tensed, his blood heating. He breathed deeply, still able to detect the faint scent of roses that always clung to her. Despite the cold numbing his side, everything about him was hot, burning. Her voice was close and soft as she tenderly stroked the rag along his skin.

"I do not like to see you in pain, but we don't have the proper liniments to care for the wound. Can I do anything else to ease the ache?"

Kiss me.

His mind shied away from the thought, even as his body clamored for it. He couldn't ask that of her. It was amazing she wasn't currently turning her bloodthirsty little mind on him in a cruel act of revenge. It was truly stunning she could still care about his comfort.

"Danni."

She lifted her head, eyes shining with sadness and sympathy. He didn't mean to say it, but before he knew it the whispered words had escaped.

"Kiss me."

She blinked in surprise. She remained frozen for several agonizing moments. It was the longest hell of his life. His stomach dropped, threatening to rebel in his anxiousness. He couldn't believe he had said it. It was one thing to offer him solace in the heat of such an emotional moment last night. It was quite another to do so in the light of day when they were both thinking rationally. Or at least when she was.

He gulped. By all rights, she should despise him. And yet... "Please."

His heart nearly beat out of his chest in anticipation and fear. How could he dare to beg? Her surprise was slowly replaced with a gentle, knowing smile. It was a smile he'd waited his entire life to see on a woman when she looked at him, full of desire and wicked intent. Her caramel eyes melted to liquid gold, her thick lashes lowered. Danni ceased the gentle washing of his skin and shifted her body nearer.

Marcus's heart beat with a vengeance. His hands itched to capture her to him. But he refused to touch her. He had to know she wanted this. That she would kiss him of her own volition. His body held immobile. His breath stilled. Her head moved closer, leaning inch by inch nearer to him. A strand of her hair swung forward to brush teasingly against his cheek.

Just centimeters from his, her lips stopped their progress and her smile deepened. Her sweet breath caressed his mouth. Marcus stared deeply into her eyes, his body straining against invisible reins while his hands clenched deeply into the rich soil around them. The nagging fear she would retreat held him back.

Suddenly, she softly pressed her lips against his bottom lip, playing at the center. Danni pulled back a little, her smile wider. Marcus was rendered speechless, bursting with the need for more. Her husky, passionate voice melted over him. "I have wanted to do that since I met you."

A shudder racked him as his blood was pounded in his ears. Then in the blink of an eye, her mouth was on his again, smothering his lips with hers.

A determined sigh escaped her at the contact. Marcus's eyes drifted shut. Her wonderful tongue caressed his lip again. He wanted more of her. His hands released the dirt and clutched at Danni's waist. He made to shift her, to pull her closer to his body, but froze as an agonizing pain ripped through his side. He grunted and Danni's arms immediately surrounded him, adjusting her position, so she leaned against his uninjured side, her fingers dancing along his back as he buried his face in her neck. He held her tightly as the burning pain slowly subsided.

Marcus marveled at the way she fit perfectly against him. He'd noticed last night as well. At the thought of his embarrassing emotional display and the liberties he had taken with her, he pulled back. "How can you not hate me?"

His puzzlement was deepened by her genuine look of surprise. "I should hate you?"

"Yes!"

Her brows lowered in confusion. "Why? You pester me beyond reason, but you've done nothing to make me hate you."

"But I blackmailed you. You said yourself that I treated you horribly in the woods. Then last night, I..." He shifted uncomfortably, wincing painfully. "I don't understand how you can even tolerate my presence." He leaned closer, examining her face for the signs of a lie as he continued, "Why did you let me touch you?"

Her eyes brightened and her mouth twisted with puzzlement, then understanding cleared her features. "Do you think I only let you do...*that* because I felt sorry for you? That's why you have been ignoring me again?"

He avoided the anger sparking in her eyes. "Among other reasons."

"You are an impossible man!"

He blinked in disbelief. "Pardon?"

She huffed, a dark frown tugging her generous mouth. "Marcus, I'm extremely confused about what's going on between us, but I can only be honest and state how I feel. First, I understand why you've kidnapped Ginny and while I don't condone your actions, I can forgive you for it."

Disbelief flooded him as she continued. "Second, for some unknown and entirely insane reason, I find you terribly and irresistibly attractive."

He sputtered, trying to comprehend those impossible words. His grip on her tightened.

Could all this actually be true?

"Third, I want to see you safe, and happy."

His heart seemed to have stopped beating. She *cared* about him?

"But, Marcus, I am to be promised to another."

His hands instantly dropped away. He felt as if he'd been slapped. Her words crushed him. He flinched as he felt her fingers thread through his hair.

"I am not sure what name to give these feelings I have for you, Marcus, but I want to help you. Once we recover Ginny, perhaps we can find a solution that won't involve forcing the poor girl into marriage."

He exhaled heavily, barely hearing her. Would the misery that chased him through life never end? He had found a woman capable of accepting him with all his faults, yet she was not free to be with him. And the longer he was in her presence, the more certain he was that she was the only woman for him.

"Someday, you must find a way to move on from your father, Marcus. He's dead, but he still has a tight grip on you. Don't let him have that power."

He grunted, stiffening at the mention of the man. He turned away with the pretense of sitting up, hiding the jagged scar down his face. "Easier said than done."

"Somehow, this will be resolved." Her arms wrapped about him, holding him close.

"You know, I enjoyed myself," she whispered, turning his favorite color: ruddy red. "It was . . . nice."

Nice. That was not exactly how he—or any man for that matter—wished to be described as a lover.

He grunted again, and smirked, trying to lighten his mood. "Never use the word *nice* to describe a man's prowess in bed, little one. It's insulting."

She laughed, releasing him, and resumed cleaning his wound. He sat patiently as she spoke of locating Ginny and heading home.

He remained silent. His view of the situation was not so simple. He had committed a crime, and his only hope for salvation was to find Ginny first, secure the marriage, and pray the admiral would let it stand rather than go through the scandalous process of an annulment.

As much as he loved Danni, and she, unbelievable, apparently cared for him, it did not change his situation. She was penniless, using her little business to support herself.

He needed money—lots of it—to break Caro's engagement. Ginny had that money.

No matter how he felt about Danni, he was going to have to marry Ginny when they got her back.

"Marcus! Look!"

Grunting against the pain in his side, he managed to shuffle across the forest floor to where Danni crouched among the trees. He rested his hand on the middle of her back to peer over her shoulder. Her back tensed to bear the extra weight. He was beginning to worry that he might cause her strain. Standing this morning had nearly outdone them both. Since then, out of necessity, he had used Danni as a crutch.

"What are we looking at?"

Danni extended a finger, pointing to a dark pile of ash. The surrounding leaves had been brushed away and the underbrush was crushed in the shape of bedrolls.

"Ah, a campsite." He groaned stiffly.

"Exactly. And they left a trail to follow"—she pointed to a large pile in the grass before adding—"It won't be a pleasant track, but I've never been more thankful for horses."

He grunted without humor. "How do we know whose trail this is? I don't see any signs of a carriage."

"Would you rather crash about the woods aimlessly, or would you rather hope for the best and follow this trail?"

Marcus knew better than to argue with that mulish look. She straightened, draped his arm across her slim shoulders, and led him down the horses' odorous trail.

He glanced down at their joined bodies, a foreign warmth spreading through him. She had managed to dress his wound using the remaining pieces of his expensive jacket, but he could feel his blood slowly staining the fabric beneath the extra shirt he'd put on. And this from a flesh wound. The bandage would have to do until they found a surgeon. Agonizing pain periodically shot through his chest; he struggled to bear it bravely. How he craved some brandy.

She squeezed him for encouragement, and he moved as fast as he could without tugging on his wound. He vaguely remembered the affection his mother had shown him as a young boy, but it had been a very long time since anyone had cared enough about him to extend kindnesses his way. Receiving them from Danni made them even more precious.

As long as it lasted.

Chapter Eighteen

How much her Sisters felt delight
To know her banish'd from their sight,

* * *

They labour'd hard to force a tear,
And imitate a grief sincere.

—"Beauty and the Beast" by Charles Lamb

The sun beat high overhead when they finally heard the rumble. As they closed in, words became more distinct. Danni could hear the jangle of horse tack as animals shook their heads. The distinctive sound of two men arguing vehemently was followed by the bite of a female voice.

Elation swept through her as she recognized it as Ginny's. "Do you hear me, Bridger Bishop? I *hate* you!"

Marcus shot Danni a look of wry amusement. It seemed they were not the only ones to experience the force of Ginny's wrath.

A deep baritone thundered, "You are a demon! I cannot believe you could fool all of London into thinking you are a ninny."

Echoes of violence crashed through a copse of trees, followed by loud, inventive cursing. Another voice yelled over the pair, "Enough."

Silence followed for several seconds before Ginny screamed, "I bloody hate you, too, Otieno!"

With a silent signal for Marcus to wait, Danni hunched close to the ground, moving as quietly as she could through the low underbrush. She stopped behind a towering oak. In the midst of a clearing was the highwaymen's camp. Danni immediately sought out Ginny. She stood with her back against a large tree, arms outstretched and tied with a length of rope around its trunk. Her hair was in disarray, the mass of dark red threaded with leaves and twigs. Despite her ordeal, Ginny looked rather well composed. Danni was more surprised by the fact the men seemed to have secured a new dress for her since she'd been kidnapped. The woolen gown sagged in all the wrong places and stretched tight in others, but Danni would bet her life Ginny felt much warmer than in the simple day dress she had given her.

She turned her attention to the two highwaymen, evaluating their positions and weaponry. She knew that she and Marcus would have to rely on their wits rather than brawn if they were to succeed in re-kidnapping Ginny. She was half their size and Marcus could barely walk.

She immediately recognized the largest man as the

one they witnessed selling Ginny's shawl at the fair. Danni conceded he could possibly be bigger than Marcus. Even seated, he seemed to tower amid the clearing. He had tan skin and the deep ebony hair common with the Romany. Even his loose clothing with patches of color reminded her of what she'd heard about the nomadic people. His face was drawn and tired, his expression one of supreme strain as he glanced between Ginny and his companion.

The Green Bandit strode about with agitation as he shot Ginny looks of ill-disguised abhorrence. Her chin tilted higher with distain at each pass, further enraging the man. Although his disguise and mask had been discarded, Danni immediately identified him as the gunman she'd tackled when Ginny was taken from them. His dark brown hair flopped in the breeze and an angular face framed brown eyes. Slashing brows a darker shade than his hair were lowered in a fierce scowl. Suddenly, he halted in front of Ginny. He bore down on the girl until he stopped just inches from her face, his voice sharp. "I look forward to the moment I receive your ransom, and I can be free of you."

With a cry of rage, Ginny drew up her leg and landed a lethal knee-blow to his groin. "Here!"

The man collapsed on all fours. Danni winced in sympathy as he promptly emptied his stomach. "Bitch!"

A soft rustle from behind drew Danni's attention from the drama in the clearing. Marcus struggled forward, dragging himself forward by his elbow, his pained gaze riveted on the prone man.

"I warned him about those feet."

Despite the situation, Danni smothered a snicker of

laughter. Marcus moved closer to her, leaning heavily against a tree as the Bandit's companion guided his friend to the edge of the clearing farthest from Ginny. He seated the hobbling man on a stump before sending a scathing look in Ginny's direction. He crouched to speak with his friend intently.

Marcus's face was drawn with pain, but humor sparked in his eyes. "As terrible a pun as it is, I'm grateful she's alive and kicking."

Danni rolled her eyes. "Brilliant. Now wait here while I go get Ginny."

He frowned, catching her before she made to leave. His head bobbed towards the opposite side of the clearing. "I'll get the horses."

Seeing the distance, she immediately shook her head. "You won't make it, not in that condition."

He looked affronted. "Of course I will. I've survived much worse."

Banishing the negative thoughts those words brought, Danni clenched her teeth. "Fine. Meet me at the pathway on the other side of the clearing. But if you're captured, do not expect me to rescue you."

Instead of forcing him to reconsider, his lip dimpled. "Now, Miss Green, you are far too kindhearted to ever leave me at the mercy of those men."

"Don't tempt me!"

The bandits' voices grew into a heated debate, drawing the two from their own discussion. Ginny slumped against the tree, appearing worn and exhausted. Danni knew now was the time to move. Nodding to Marcus, she hustled forward, hunched close to the ground again. Her feet sank into the mossy earth as she carefully avoided

leaves and twigs that would snap under her weight. Clinging close to the bushes, she moved among the forest's
shadows towards the tree to which Ginny was bound. All
the while, Danni watched the two men from the corner of
her eye.

She was almost at Ginny's side when her foot landed
heavily on a large stick. The snap of wood seemed to echo
repeatedly across the entire clearing. She stood motionless, her gaze frozen on the men. The man who had been
kicked still clutched his groin in agony, but the Romany
turned his dark, alert gaze in the direction of the sound.
Their eyes met with a flash of recognition. A slow smile
spread its wings across his face.

Danni was certain she was doomed. He turned his head
towards his companion, no doubt to warn him. He said a
few words, but no alarm was raised. She frowned in confusion. Surely he would try to stop her?

Then he started to whistle. It was a loud and jaunty
tune, its sound amplified by the dense canopy. Her confusion deepened. She was so sure he'd seen her. He *had*
to have seen her. Shaking her head, she continued on, in-
tensely vigilant.

She reached Ginny's tree, hoping she could untie the
ropes at the back. Danni searched the taut braid, traveling
her hand over it, searching for the knot. She soon discovered the restraint was one long length. She leaned
dangerously beyond her hiding place, her eyes following
the length of rope. With a groan, she fell back into the
shadows near the tree. The goddamned men had looped
the ends around Ginny's hands. It meant she would have
to leave cover to untie the girl.

Danni watched attentively as the injured man continued his tirade against Ginny and the grievous injury she had inflicted upon him. The tanned man continued to whistle, his back towards her.

Danni slid out of the shadows. Before she attacked the ropes, she quickly caught hold of Ginny, clamping a hand over her mouth. The girl's eyes widened in surprise, her gaze darting from Danni to the men. Her body sagged against the tree as genuine relief flooded her face. Danni held a finger to her lips, indicating that she remain silent, then, after a hasty nod of agreement from Ginny, she uncovered her mouth. Danni immediately set to work on the knots.

The rope was thick, rough, and prickly—not the kind one wanted against her skin for any length of time. As she moved it, she could already see the burning red rash around Ginny's wrists. One of the rope fibers pricked her thumb, and an audible hiss escaped her. They both froze, turning to look at the men on the log. The only response was an increase in volume of the whistling from the Gypsy. Danni frowned at the man, her suspicions increasing.

There was no time for hesitation. Hurrying, Danni managed to free one of Ginny's hands. A soft sigh of relieved pain slipped through her lips. Danni didn't wait, she moved quickly to the other. Several moments later, the rope dropped to the base of the tree, camouflaging itself among the roots.

Ginny's arms suddenly locked around her neck, her voice barely audible against her ear. "Thank you."

Danni nodded but didn't dare speak. She didn't know how much longer they had for an escape. They moved quietly across the ground as fast as possible. Gleefully returning to their shelter, Danni found Marcus seated on the ground, horse reins draped in his fist, his drawn appearance worsened.

She crouched by his side. His breath was hot with pain. "That was more difficult than I expected."

She snorted, brushing a lock of curl from his forehead. "But now we must move, Marcus."

His green eyes lit with determination. One arm shifted around her neck and he clutched his side with the other. Danni gritted her teeth, straining against his weight. But then suddenly, he wasn't so heavy. She opened her eyes to meet Ginny's blue ones. Her head was ducked under his other arm, evenly distributing the weight. She nodded, and together they hauled him to his feet.

When they approached the horses, one of them tossed its head in agitation, a soft snort echoing through the woods. Danni reassured herself that the bandits were not approaching them. The whistler had stopped his tune, but she noticed the way he kept his companion's gaze from the tree. He was allowing them to escape. But why?

Ginny approached the animal's side, stroking the white stripe between the mare's eyes to comfort her. She quickly wrapped the straps of her pack to its saddle.

"Can you mount?" Danni hissed to Marcus.

His body tensed beneath her hands, but he nodded grimly. He truly had no choice. With Ginny's help, they managed to steady him on the most docile of the horses.

When Danni was certain he was secure, she helped Ginny onto the large bay mare. It was then that she mounted her own, the largest and fiercest looking of them all. He was a sleek stallion, his tan coat brushed to perfection. She stroked the horse with appreciation.

"That's Otieno's most prized possession." At Danni's confused look, Ginny clarified, "The Romany."

She felt a pang of regret she would deprive the man of his horse when he'd helped them escape, even if he was the one who'd insisted she be taken for less than savory activities. "I *almost* feel sorry."

Ginny's grim smile only reinforced her sentiments. "Do not. He stole it from someone else."

"What lovely irony to steal it back from him."

"I could not agree more."

Danni examined the other woman closely. She had noticed how Ginny's gaze shifted in every direction, her mind working, absorbing everything around her. She walked with confidence few would feel after being taken hostage not once, but twice, in short order. Danni also saw the gleam of intelligence in her eyes. The Bandit's comments from earlier floated back to her. *She let London think she was a ninny?*

She could almost laugh. So the *ton* had yet again misnamed one of its members. What Danni wanted to know was why Ginny didn't correct their perception.

They shared a quiet smile, then Danni placed her foot in the stirrup and swung her leg over. Settling in the saddle, she glanced at her companions. Ginny looked eager to be gone and Danni had no objection. Marcus had fallen silent, clutching his hip. He needed proper medical attention and staying in the forest would not provide that.

"The main road and an inn is this way."

Ginny turned purposefully, leading her horse west. As Marcus followed, Danni twisted towards the clearing. She froze when she spied the brigands.

Marcus called to her, his face concerned. "Why are you waiting? We must flee."

Danni waved him off, her eyes riveted on the bandit with ebony hair still talking to his partner.

"What's amiss?"

Finally, she shook her head. "Nothing."

Danni directed her horse's head towards her companions, pressing softly against its sensitive underbelly. As the group burst through the forest, her mind was still in the clearing.

She could have sworn Otieno mouthed "Good riddance" and waved good-bye.

Chapter Nineteen

❦

"Swear not to leave me!" sigh'd the BEAST:
"I swear"—for now her fears were ceas'd,
"And willingly swear,—so now and then

—"Beauty and the Beast" by Charles Lamb

The moon was halfway over the horizon when they reached the next inn. Traveling hard and fast on their stolen horses, they put as much distance as possible between themselves and the robbers. The party remained silent through much of the ride, and Danni periodically caught Ginny peering anxiously behind them. However, her main concern was not their newly recovered captive. It was Marcus.

Face drawn, his eyes were dark with pain and his expression stony. Bleary green focused intently on the point ahead, as if looking elsewhere would cause him to tumble from his saddle.

The ache in her own shoulders burned. She knew it was from the tense, vigilant state she had maintained for many hours, in addition to the strain of carrying Marcus's weight earlier. At any moment she feared hysteria from Ginny, a collapsing marquis, and an attack from the bandits or the admiral. Not to mention other unknown dangers of the road they had yet to encounter. She was both physically and mentally exhausted.

So catching sight of the wooden sign of the Dancing Dragon brought her instant relief. Reining their horses to a stop inside the courtyard, she quickly dismounted. All she needed to do was safely tuck everyone in for the night before she could crumple into sleep.

Ginny hurried to help as Danni approached Marcus's horse. Danni was grateful the girl had not yet confronted them about her captivity or their future plans. She remained silent, observant. Together, the two women supported the injured man as he slid from the horse. A groan escaped him as his arm slipped about her shoulder, pulling her close. His weight shifted, leaning heavily on them. "Sorry I'm so heavy, little one."

She snorted, straining under most of his weight. "It's not as if you can help it."

Ginny's eyes widened when Marcus managed a weak laugh. "No. I suppose I can't."

Their captive gave him an assessing gaze, confirming Danni's suspicions in the forest. She was no ninny, after all.

Danni was the first to greet the innkeeper when he hurried out of the lighted common room. He was a small man, the same height as Danni. "Welcome, ladies and sir.

I'm Mr. Pensly, the owner here. Welcome to the Dancing Dragon!"

He paused, eyes widening as he took in their tattered appearances and Marcus's stark face. Danni scrambled for some sort of explanation, but her fogged mind was slow. Ginny unexpectedly came to the rescue. Her expression blanked and her head listed to the side as she stared owlishly at the innkeeper. "Dragons don't really dance, do they?"

Danni opened her mouth and clicked it shut, at a loss for what to say. Had she really thought Ginny possessed intelligence? She bit back a groan as the innkeeper floundered for a response. He obviously didn't want to offend them, but she could see he was struggling. He decided to laugh uneasily. "Well, I am not certain, ma'am."

Danni grimaced as Marcus suddenly dropped more weight on her. She glanced at his pale countenance. He needed food, water, and a warm bed.

Clearing her throat, Danni diverted the innkeeper's attention to her. He seemed almost relieved. "Sir, this is the Marquis of Fleetwood. He needs attention immediately."

The man seemed to jump at the title, his color lightening a shade. "F-Fleetwood?"

Marcus straightened suddenly, bearing down on the shorter man with a feral smile. She knew he was at the end of his rope. "What my wife means to say is that I have been shot and require a doctor. *Now.*"

Danni stiffened at being called his wife, but did not protest. It would give her access to his room so she could tend to him. Pretending to be his wife was too close to her dreams. But she was far too weary to deal with those thoughts right now.

The man gasped, his hand fluttering to his neck. "Oh, my! Yes, yes. I shall summon the doctor posthaste."

Ginny followed without comment as the innkeeper led them inside the worn, aged inn. Danni pointedly ignored her. She had no answer for the girl's probing looks.

The inn was filled with activity. Boisterous men seated about small round tables laughed and guzzled from large mugs. Anxiety engulfed her when one of the men grabbed a barmaid's behind. What kind of establishment was this? Uncertainty dashed her hopes for safety and rest. She turned red on the barmaid's behalf before hurrying to keep close to the innkeeper. He snapped sharp orders to a young man, who then sprinted off. Danni hoped he was fetching the doctor.

Mr. Pensly frantically motioned for them to follow him to the second level. Ginny led the way, allowing Marcus to brace himself on the rail for the climb. It was a painstaking business. She felt his agony with each step, the wound splitting at each shift of his hip. His face beaded with sweat. Danni panted with the effort of supporting him.

It was much easier for Marcus to shuffle down the flat, wooden surface of the second floor hall. The owner's keys jingled as he fiddled with the set at his waist. Handing a small one to Ginny, he said, "I hope this room will be acceptable to you, miss."

The redhead glanced at Danni, apparently unsure she would be allowed this freedom. Danni did not particularly care where the girl stayed. She had no resources with which to escape, and after this strenuous day, she most likely wanted to bolt the latch and collapse into an endless sleep. Nodding her agreement, Ginny quickly turned the key in the door and disappeared.

They moved farther down the hall. Danni counted three rooms before he stopped and loosened a key from a large ring. He unlocked the door and swung it wide open. A giant sleigh bed took up a majority of the wood-paneled room. The bedding shimmered a beautiful dark blue as the innkeeper lit the candles in the falling darkness. She felt her brows lift in surprise as Marcus's grip tightened about her shoulders.

The proprietor grinned proudly. "This is our newlywed room, my lady."

An audible choking sound escaped her. *Dear God.*

Marcus didn't help. He managed to remain silent, but she could feel him trembling with painful laughter. A wheeze suddenly escaped him and his twisted features deepened. Again, hands fluttered as the innkeeper was spurred into action. "Dr. Grogg should be along shortly. We should get him into bed."

Danni nodded, more than ready to be relieved of her load. By the time they had him seated on the edge of the bed, she was perspiring with exertion.

"We should undress him, my lady. He'd be more comfortable."

Danni froze, glancing at the innkeeper. He could not be serious? His expectant look told her otherwise. But it was something a wife would do for her husband.

She swallowed the squirming in her stomach. She needed to maintain their cover. The challenging rise of Marcus's split brow and the smirk upon his crooked lip dared her to comply. Grumbling, Danni squatted down at his feet and yanked none too kindly on his boots.

The innkeeper cleared his throat. "I shall just fetch some warm water and cloths to clean the wound."

"Mr. Pensly," Marcus groaned. "Please have the doctor check on the other young woman first, when he arrives."

"Of course." He nodded, placing the key on the nightstand before exiting. The man thought they required privacy. She wanted to laugh.

"Thank you for thinking of that," Danni murmured as she managed to pull off Marcus's first boot and stocking.

He grunted as she started on the second. It was then, feeling his eyes on her, and her own gaze wandering about, that she felt her face heat. She couldn't help but stare at his naked foot. It was a massive thing, lightly dusted with blond hair that glinted in the lantern light. She felt a familiar coil grow in her stomach, and her throat grew thick. She had no idea she could find feet attractive.

She was sure she was bright red. A quick glance at Marcus's smug expression confirmed her suspicion. Her frayed patience in danger of snapping, she made quick work of the second boot and stocking. To add insult to injury, Marcus carefully lifted his arms like a child being dressed by his nursemaid. Danni glared, her hands coming to her hips. "It's very ungentlemanly of you to enjoy my discomfort so."

A devilish glint sparked his eyes. "And very unladylike of you to enjoy undressing me so."

"You—" Danni choked, rendered mute as her face heated. Blast it, but it was true.

He chuckled, arching his split brow.

Boldly, she stepped between his legs and roughly pulled his shirt over his head. The minute his hands were free, he caught her hips, dragged her close, and rested his forehead against her stomach. "I cannot tell you how relieved I am that Ginny has been recovered safely."

His voice trailed away. She smiled, soothing and kneading the muscles of his naked shoulders. She knew exactly what he meant. After their long and onerous journey, they'd managed to find and rescue Ginny. An incredible weight had been lifted now that the girl was back in their possession. However, Danni dreaded the oncoming battle. She needed to think of some way to resolve Marcus's problem before he was well enough to move on.

First, she needed rest. "I know. Ginny seems fine, but I'm glad a doctor will be checking on the both of you."

He snorted, his eyes drifting closed. "Making sure the doctor sees Ginny first is the least I can do. This is all my fault and I couldn't bear to think...if she were injured..."

"Everything will work out." Her smile brightened and her heart skipped a beat.

"But how could you possibly know that?"

She attempted to lighten the mood. "I'm all-knowing."

His fingers tightened briefly as he puffed a weak laugh. "If only, Danni. If only..."

He raised his head, allowing her a glimpse of sad and vulnerable eyes before his lips connected with hers. He kissed her with a need so strong, a desire so deep, she was breathless. Her hand stole around his neck, holding tight. Strong, rough palms spanned her ribs, clasping her firmly against his chest. Her thighs tightened from the heat his touch always created there.

Gasping, she pulled away. His mouth did not break contact; instead, his lips traveled in a hot arc down, behind her ear, along her neck, approaching her breast.

"Marcus," she murmured, cupping his head, guiding his journey down...

"I do not think his condition is as dire as you may have thought, Mr. Pensly."

Danni jumped back, aghast at being interrupted, humiliated at being seen. Standing in the doorway, the innkeeper and a man she assumed to be the doctor smothered their amusement.

"Ah, to be young again," the elderly man said as he lifted a dark leather bag onto a nearby chair.

The innkeeper's hands fluttered helplessly about him. "A thousand apologies, my lord, my lady. I did not think…"

A satisfied laugh erupted from Marcus as he pulled his shirt closed, hiding his scarred chest. Despite his self-consciousness, the rotter looked well pleased with himself, while she wanted the floor to swallow her up.

"There is no need to apologize, Mr. Pensly. My bride and I cannot seem to control ourselves."

Danni's face flamed and her fists clenched at her sides. She was going to kill him.

The innkeeper's face cleared, a dreamy smile budding on his face. "Oh, newlyweds! I knew it."

Dr. Grogg gave her a conspiratorial wink. Even Danni's palms burned with the blood rushing through her system. A hole in the floor wouldn't be big enough to hide her, she decided.

Marcus's grin seemed to grow brighter. "I find her the perfect pain relief."

"Understandable." The doctor chuckled good-naturedly. "If I may say so, your lady is very pretty, my lord. Even in such an obviously exhausted state."

Oh, God. I must leave this room. Clearing her throat, she nodded to the kind doctor. "I shall leave you to your examination now, Doctor. I must check on my cousin."

She darted for the door, intent on escape, even if it was only to Ginny's room, but Mr. Pensly, the innkeeper, stood in her path. The doctor waved her to the bedside. "There is no need. Certainly, your husband wishes you to stay."

Marcus's eyes danced devilishly. "Yes, she is such a comfort."

Gritting her teeth, she haltingly stepped to the head of the bed as her *husband* eased himself back for a proper examination. She bent close, whispering in his ear, "Would the bullet have aimed true."

His intense gaze made her heart skip. A slow smile lingered, transforming his face and stealing her breath. How had she ever thought him ugly?

"Darling, as much as I love hearing all the things you wish to do to me as soon as we are alone, now is not the appropriate time. The good doctor is trying to tend to me."

Danni gaped at him. The doctor and the innkeeper gaped at her.

Simply shooting him was too easy for him. She'd need to think of something more torturous. Glaring, she snapped, "I think I may require a separate room this evening, Mr. Pensly."

A dreamy expression floated across his face again. "A lover's quarrel! I simply love lover's quarrels."

She transferred her glare to the short man. All she needed was for Ginny to enter the room and ask some inane question, such as, Is the sky falling?

Dr. Grogg came to her rescue. "Now, now, let us leave the poor lady be. I think we have embarrassed her enough for the evening." He turned his attention back to the wound. "How exactly were you shot, my lord?"

"We were held up by highwaymen. My wife's poor cousin suffered a terrible fright."

It wasn't a bad story. Especially since most of it was true.

The doctor halted a moment and reported, "Ah, yes. At your request, I just examined her. Such a sweet young woman. Some minor rope burns on her wrists, for which I gave her a balm. Also told me she was not... manhandled"—he met the Marcus's eyes knowingly— "by those heathens. They have been particularly bad in this area of late. Something must be done before a death results."

Danni could feel Marcus's relief at the news, and she squeezed his hand to signal she felt the same. She nodded her agreement to the doctor, especially since the Green Bandit and his companion were complete dolts. How they had not yet killed anyone was miraculous.

She peered on as the doctor worked, slightly sick, as he cleaned the filthy, clotted blood from the wound. After pronouncing that Marcus required stitches, he cleaned a needle by the fire and threaded it swiftly. Mr. Pensly arrived with a bottle of brandy, offering it to Marcus so he could dull the pain.

Danni interjected immediately, "He cannot drink it, sir."

The innkeeper rechecked the label on the bottle, clearly confused. "I do not understand. It's our finest! A family recipe."

"I am sure it is an excellent vintage, but I am no longer able to stomach liquor. It makes me quite ill," Marcus explained. Danni, although she'd had her suspicions since he had not touched the stuff since their time in the forest, was relieved to hear it.

Mr. Pensly's eyes widened. "But the pain, my lord!"

Marcus subtly reached for her hand. Danni held tightly as the doctor appraised Marcus's scarred chest. "I am certain this man will be able to handle a few stitches."

It was then the innkeeper glimpsed the scars spattering Marcus's skin. He paled and swayed slightly. Biting back her annoyance, she took his elbow and led him to the door. "Perhaps it is best if you see to your other guests. I am sure Dr. Grogg will update you when he completes the procedure."

He clutched the bottle to his chest. "Yes. That is a brilliant notion."

Danni closed the door behind him, glad to be rid of the pest. She returned to Marcus's side and seated herself on the other side of the bed. His head shifted away from the doctor's preparations, eyes wide with uncharacteristic nervousness. Sweat beaded his brow, his legs trembled. She feared these moments of pain would open a rush of terrible memories for him. He seemed to hesitate before mouthing, "Don't leave me."

Danni's heart skipped. She caught his hand in her grasp again in reassurance. Danni knew she shouldn't respond. She knew it would only cause problems for them later, but she couldn't stop herself. A piece of her would always be his, no matter the resolution.

"Never," she whispered.

His hand squeezed back.

"I'm going to have to pull the skin together. That will be the most difficult part of the procedure," the doctor said, needle in hand, poised to start.

Marcus grunted, a frown already twisting his features. "I know."

It took the doctor ten minutes to stitch the wound, but time moved slowly.

When Dr. Grogg tied off the last of the thread, Marcus visibly relaxed. He had winced, but never once let out a cry of pain, nor showed signs of the past overtaking him. His brow smoothed and relief swept through Danni when she saw his clear, calm eyes.

She disentangled herself to show the doctor to the door. The man stopped in the hallway, his expression troubled. "I do not know exactly what your husband has been through, madam, but remember that the horrors he has seen do not leave a man. He carries them for a lifetime. Be kind and patient with him."

Her chest tightened. "I know, Doctor."

A soft smile played at the serious line of his mouth. "You are a very strong woman, my lady. I wish you and your husband the best. The road ahead will be long." Danni quietly shut the door, hoping Marcus had not overheard. But Marcus's tight features had softened and his chest rose and fell in an even rhythm. He was asleep.

Leaning against the door, Danni took a deep, shuddering breath. She desperately wanted to make everything right and everyone happy, especially Marcus. She could offer herself in marriage to him, bring her fortune to the Fleetwood title, and thereby resolve everyone's problems.

Except her father, her fiancé Lord Rathbourne, and her own hesitations stopped her. Even the doctor, a virtual stranger, had warned her. Life with Marcus would not be the happy fairy tale she'd always dreamed for herself. Was she willing to marry him, knowing she may not have the strength to drive his demons away?

She desperately needed rest. She stared at the large,

empty spot beside Marcus in the bed, hesitating to put them both in tempting circumstances. Exhaustion won out. She collapsed into the soft, silken sheets.

*   *   *

Marcus startled awake. He sat up with shock at the sound of the closing door. The stitches in his side shot hot fire across his torso. Despair tore from his throat before he lay back on the pillow. The physical pain from the small wound brought a deluge of memories, of injuries much worse. He felt himself descending to the pit of hell.

Warmth and softness suddenly enveloped his wrist. He was dimly aware of a cool caress against his cheek as he fought to calm himself. Danni's face emerged at the edge of his vision, twisted with concern. Her voice smoothed his tormented mind. He gasped a deep, relaxing breath, feeling the darkness and panic fade. He nuzzled his face into her soft palm as she stroked his brow. Her presence made his life bearable.

"I'm better."

A smile budded on her lips, twisting his heart. *God, he loved her.*

"I'm sorry the door woke you, Marcus. A maid just delivered a tray."

He nodded his head, spying the food on a nearby table. Delicious smells wafted towards him and tightened his stomach.

"How long was I asleep?"

"It's morning. Here." She offered him a piece of toast with jam. Gingerly, Marcus sat up, accepting the food. He swallowed it in three bites and reached for another.

"Is the wound causing you discomfort?"

He chuckled softly. "I would be worried if it didn't, little one."

She grimaced. "I am concerned about both your welfare and your poor joke."

Marcus smiled up at her. Had he ever smiled so much in his life? How could such a woman want him? Want to *be with* him. Despite all his scars and his haunted past, she cared. She truly cared.

"Did the doctor say anything?"

"Just to rest. I checked on Ginny and she's fine. A night of sleep seems to have restored her, if the number of *I hate you*s I received while checking on her is any indication."

Marcus chuckled, imagining the scene. He took an apple from the tray and consumed it in short order. A contemplative silence fell between them. Soft light illuminated the room and Danni's pensive features. Marcus was certain he knew what was on her mind, but was just as reluctant to bring up the subject as she. He grabbed a boiled egg and downed it in two bites. Finally, a frustrated gust escaped her.

"Damn it," she barked. A heartbeat passed before she faced him, caramel eyes burning wide with accusation. "Even understanding the situation with your sister, I can't let you do this to Ginny, Marcus. I just can't allow it."

His heart plummeted. He knew this was coming. He'd wanted more time to enjoy the fantasy he'd created.

He avoided her gaze and let out a hefty sigh. "But I have no other choice, Danni."

The eggs and fruit in his stomach curdled at the idea of turning over his baby sister to the Duke of Harwood.

He would not condemn her to a lifetime of such misery. "I can't let Caroline marry that man."

Danni began to pace. "I know. I've heard all the rumors about him. To think he may be a murderer... There must be an alternative."

Frustrated, he scrubbed his hands through his curls. "What would you have me do? You're asking me to pick a stranger's well-being over my sister's."

"Have you thought that you are not only asking Ginny and me to live with your choice, but Caroline as well?"

He stiffened. "What?"

Danni came to an abrupt halt, eyes narrowed. "I cannot believe your sister would be happy to learn you forced an innocent woman into marriage in order to save her. I'd be livid."

He looked away. He hated to admit it, but it had never occurred to him to think about Caroline's feelings. He'd known Caroline would be upset with him, especially after she'd confronted him over that gossip column, but he'd been too focused on his own predicament to think of her feelings at all.

A frustrated growl emitted from Danni. "I bet you haven't even told her what's going on."

When he remained silent, he could hear Danni stomping to and fro. She suddenly seized his chin, forcing him to look at her. Startled, he could only blink as she ranted. "Damn it, Marcus! You can be so selfish and stubborn." She released him and took a step back to cross her arms. "This is about your sister, so therefore your sister should be involved in the solution. I know you want to shield her from harm, but she has just as much right—no, even *more* of a right—to make decisions on this matter."

"But it's my fault," he whispered, remembering that day in his father's office.

She stomped in frustration. "I'm tired of you blaming yourself, Marcus. It's no one's fault but your father's. He was a horrible man and I would happily flay him alive if it were still possible."

And there was her bloodthirsty streak again, he thought grimly.

"Your father is dead," she continued bluntly. "Dead, buried, and rotting in hell. I know it's hard, but you need to let everything he did go. It's over now and will never happen again."

He opened his mouth to reply, but snapped it shut when no words would come. Danni could not be right. It would mean everything he'd done for Caro was for nothing. He'd spent so many years isolating himself, he was not in the habit of thinking of others' opinions and feelings.

But now that he stopped to think, he realized his actions, while they might successfully break the contract, would only serve to make everyone involved miserable. Ginny would be trapped in a marriage she didn't want. Caroline would feel guilty for the rest of her life. And he would lose the love of his life. And Danni, how would she feel? Glaring at him for a final time, she picked up the empty food tray and headed to the door.

"Now, I want you to think long and hard about what I said, Marcus. I'm positive we can find a solution to this if we all put our heads together."

Dimly, he nodded as she left.

Even as his mind spun, he couldn't help but feel like a chastised child.

* * *

"Stupid man," Danni muttered, carrying the tray past Ginny's room and down the stairs. She barely acknowledged Mr. Pensly as she placed it on the bar and stormed from the inn. Fresh air would do wonders for her temper.

Coming to a stop in the middle of the courtyard, she kicked the dirt in frustration before putting her hands on her hips and drawing in several lungfuls of air. The country breeze was tinged with the crispness of spring and cool, refreshing rain. Early morning dampness hung in the air, sending a slight chill through her tattered day dress. She glanced at the mud-spattered hem of the blue garment and winced.

A longing to wear Marcus's gift shot through her. She was glad she'd managed to hold on to the sack through yesterday's events. She would have been so disappointed if she had lost it.

Oh, that dress...that night...

"Troubles, my lady?"

Danni started, not having noticed the servant approach. She was older than Danni and seemed out of place in this rough environment. She was elegant as well, her willowy frame full of quiet grace. Graying blond hair was gathered in a tight chignon at the nape of her neck. Inquisitive brown eyes set in an angular face examined Danni.

Danni hesitated to speak, but the woman's motherly demeanor made her comfortable. She kicked the dirt again as she spoke, mindful of the farce they played as guests here.

"My husband is being an arse."

A tinkling laugh filled the courtyard. Danni was surprised by its sophisticated quality.

"I see." She smiled. "What has he done?"

"Behaved like a man."

The woman chuckled deeply, clasping her hands behind her. "But you still love him?"

Danni stiffened. Did she love Marcus? He frustrated her. He was stubborn to a fault and self-consumed.

But he was also gentle with her and listened when she spoke. He demonstrated kindness and could be incredibly caring. He made her feel alive with a single, charming smile and his touch made her burn with desire.

He was a diamond in the rough. She knew he could be everything she ever wanted in a man and a husband, if she was willing to live with and help him fight his demons.

She gulped. Did she love Marcus? Then, with sudden blinding certainty, she whispered, "Yes, I love him."

A dazzling smile shifted across the woman's face. "That's wonderful! Love in a marriage is so rare nowadays."

Danni nodded her agreement. Her gaze shifted back to the inn. She loved him, but she was still hesitant. Could she dishonor her father for him? Could she humiliate the earl, who had been a kind and caring suitor? Could she risk her scandalous behavior damaging both their careers? And she still had to inform Marcus of her true identity. Another barrier. He would be heartbroken. He may even reject her for keeping such a secret. She could very well emerge from this muddle banned from society, ostracized by her family, and without the man she knew she truly loved.

"Is there something else?" the older woman asked,

a frown marring her aristocratic features. Her soothing, comforting, almost motherly tone encouraged Danni to confide her fears.

"What if loving him makes others unhappy?"

The woman blinked before sighing in understanding. "It will be difficult, my dear. But I do not believe those who truly care about you would want you unhappy. You must follow your heart, and trust that those who love you will come to accept your choices. It just may take time."

Her words eased Danni's doubts. She moved towards the Dancing Dragon's entrance. "Thank you. So very much. You have really helped me. I think I'll go check on him now."

"Of course. Please give Marcus my best."

"Sur—" Danni froze, spinning back in confusion. She shouldn't know Marcus's name.

However, any confrontation Danni may have planned was dashed as her quick survey found the courtyard empty. Where could she have gone?

What a mysterious woman.

Shaking her head, she hurried back inside.

Chapter Twenty

❦

Amaz'd she stood,—new wonders grew;
For BEAST now vanish'd from her view;
And, lo! a PRINCE, with every grace
Of figure, fashion, feature, face,

—"Beauty and the Beast" by Charles Lamb

"I'll bring Ginny home tomorrow," Marcus announced the moment Danni entered the room.

She froze in the doorway, blinking at him, completely stunned. He learned that he loved to surprise her.

"W-what?"

He shifted his perch on the bed, somber lines framing his lips. "I said, tomorrow I'll send Ginny home."

Her eyes narrowed, and her voice was skeptical but tinged with hope. "Unmarried?"

He nodded, feeling a burden lift. He knew all was not

fixed. They must return Ginny to her home, and some-how elicit her help to avoid legal consequences. Danni was right. He had already hurt too many pursuing this op-tion, and more were sure to be added to the list. There had to be another way to nullify Caro's betrothal. He was not his father and vowed he would never be.

"Oh, Marcus," Danni cried, launching herself at him. He braced himself for the onslaught, an uncontrollable "ummhp" forced from his lungs. He shifted quickly, pro-tecting his aching side from the weight of her body—the stab of the injury a small price to pay for her embrace. Her warm arms latched around his neck, and her soft body molded to his. A perfect fit.

He trembled, his hold on Danni tightening, as her soft words brushed over the pulse throbbing along his throat. "Thank you, Marcus. Everything will work out, I promise."

He nodded, burying her face deeper into the curve of his neck, the silkiness of her braided hair catching on his stubbled cheek, and breathed deeply of roses. It had fast become his favorite scent.

For the first time in his life, a sense of peace swelled inside him. She made him hope that somehow all this would be resolved happily, and he found himself believ-ing it would be if she said it was possible. He squeezed tighter, pulling her closer to him. If only she could stay here, with him. Forever. He knew she was the one for him. The love of his life.

But, with life's typical cruelty, she was a woman who belonged to another man.

Shutting his eyes against a sting of tears, he drew away.

"Marcus?"

Avoiding her confused gaze in favor of the window, he considered his options. He was back where he had started—no money, no plan, and Caroline engaged to a monster. Now, to the list of his failures, he could add an inability to win the one woman he had allowed himself to love.

Once, he had hoped Caro would be grateful for his intervention, and that Ginny and he could achieve some sort of understanding and be content. Now no one would be happy.

Well, perhaps Ginny, he thought with a smirk.

Marcus stroked his fingers through his hair. "I'm glad Ginny will be free, but I'm right back where I started."

She lifted his chin to look in his eyes. "Not entirely. I'm with you now. We will find a solution together."

"No, Danni, I don't get to keep you."

Uncertainty flickered across her features. He could swear he could actually see her thinking.

Marcus was tired of his dark existence. Of the codicil. Of his memories. His stomach roiled at the thought of Danni with another. He didn't want to let her go. He wanted to wake up beside her every day. He wanted to hear the slightest details of her day, to be her confidant and lover. To possess her completely. He'd waited so long for someone—hoped for someone he could love and trust.

Her features tightened. "But, I don't know. I...I don't love him."

Blood rushed in his ears. She didn't love the man. That meant, if she married him, she wouldn't have the happy ending she fancied. Was she...

He could scarcely keep his hope at bay. "Do you plan to break it off?"

She was hesitant and nervous, rare emotions for her. She was usually confident and full of conviction.

"The arrangement is not yet official. My father asked me to accept, wants me to accept, but I have been delaying. My intended is a kind man, and has been giving me the time I need to think. A marriage to him would not be all I ever dreamed of, but I planned to say yes. Then you kidnapped me, and now..."

He sucked in a breath. He could scarcely believe what he was hearing. Did he have a chance? Could he convince her he was worthy? Could she overlook his surly disposition, his ugly mug, and his tendency to be dragged into the depths of dark nightmares for days on end?

Despite his thoughts, he whispered, "Choose me, little one. More than anything, I want you. I...I'd do anything to make you happy."

A soft smile flitted across her eyes as she leaned into his caress. He couldn't breathe. He could not believe what he read in her gaze.

"Marcus."

He felt light-headed, blood pounding in his ears. "I love you," he dared say. "I love you."

Her eyes widened.

And then fear crashed over him. What would he do if she rejected him? Panicked, he pushed her away and stumbled to his feet, clutching the ache in his side as if to stop the fear in his heart.

She darted into his path, clearly surprised. "Wait! Where are you going?"

"Away," he croaked, trying to step around her.

Amusement tinged her features as she stepped forward, blocking his retreat to the door. "Why would you want to do that?"

His eyes narrowed. "Are you taunting me?"

"Maybe." Soft laughter shook her shoulders. "I never imagined that when a man professed his love to me, he'd then try to run away."

"I just said something rather important, little one. Can you take the situation a little more seriously?"

Marcus crossed his arms, feeling ill. He avoided her eyes, fearing what he would see there. He desperately wanted her reply, but at the same time, he wished he could grasp his words from the air and make them disappear. She might be willing to exchange heated caresses, but he knew from experience that did not necessarily mean affection.

Oh God, why did I speak?

"Marcus." Her hand reached towards his face. Eyes widening, he reeled back, his heart beating rapidly now for a different reason. Danni crowded closer to him, frowning. He stepped back. And again. Determination hardened her jaw. He halted, his back against the wall. He had nowhere to go. He gulped as her hand reached towards his face.

He braced against the touch. Braced for the rejection. Her fingers were cool and soft as they made contact with his cheek. They slowly traced the thin scar that split his brow. Instead of pulling away, she caught a fist of his shirt and brought his head down to her hushed whisper.

"You know, this scar here, the one that stops right before your eye?" she said as she stroked it.

He swallowed and nodded.

"It makes you look adorable."

His eyes widened, stunned.

"It gives you a devilish look I can't resist."

He blinked, unable to believe his ears. She'd lost her mind. He wanted to pull away before he was lost forever. But he couldn't move, could scarcely breathe.

"And this scar here"—she traced the worst one, the longest and deepest; her voice was laced with pain as she spoke—"the one that must have caused you such agony. You always try to hide it from me."

She leaned up on her toes, softly brushing her lips against his ragged skin. He burned at the contact, held in place. "You should be proud to wear it," she whispered, "because you saved your little sister."

His world shifted, spinning. He'd spent his entire life shunned and cursed, called an ugly brute. But this small woman somehow saw him differently. To her, he wasn't a beast, but a hero.

"And this one here?" she whispered, her voice heating his blood. "The one that angles across your chin?"

She traced it, the tip of her finger resting in the center of his lip. She brushed the small circle in the center until his skin throbbed. His nerves jumped, lightning rushing through his body. He strained under her touch, aching with the need to kiss her.

Her gaze fixed on his lower lip, passion darkening her eyes. "This scar is my favorite because it makes this little dimple in your lip when you smile. And your smile. Rare and wonderful."

And then she leaned forward, up on her toes to press her mouth softly against the mark. Hesitantly, he palmed her hips, pulling her flush against him. A wave of need and wanting rumbled deep in his heart.

"I love you," he murmured again, so much more certain than before. He would never want another. He'd find a way, some way, any way, to make her his.

She smiled against his lips, her voice clear and the words unmistakable. "And I love you."

Relief and joy mixed with doubt. He didn't understand how she could possibly care for him, want him, but he would not question it.

"Danni." He grunted. His mouth captured hers, scorching, possessive. He traced her lips with his tongue, teasing and nipping the soft edges. Strong palms cupped her head, holding her close to receive his kiss, deepening, joining them. A gasp escaped, panting filled the air. Her body softened, pliant in his arms, despite the tightening of her nipples against his chest.

Her hands threaded in the curls at the base of his neck, fingers bit gently into his skin, sending jolts of pleasure straight to his groin. His heart pounded with the knowledge that she was willing to give herself to him, to make herself completely his.

Marcus groaned, crushed by the unwelcome thought that she could not be his, not yet. She was taken, and the possibility that, by taking what she offered, he would destroy her chance for a contented and peaceful life halted his hands.

He lifted her, placed her gently on the bed, separated from her warmth, and sat at her side. Feet on the floor. Firmly set in reality.

"Marcus?"

"We shouldn't do this. Even if this other man is not

right for you, you will find someone else. I cannot lay with you now and destroy your chance for a future marriage. I cannot be so selfish. I want you to be happy too much for that."

"But I want this, Marcus. I want you. I want one night where we can pretend nothing outside this room exists. Pretend we can be whole and happy together."

"I—" He shuddered, wanting to give in to her fantasy. "Are you absolutely certain? There will be no going back."

"I know. Please," she whispered. "Please lay with me."

He hesitated for one more moment before finally giving in and reaching for her. Damn her father, her suitor, Caro, Ginny. Damn them all. He would grab this chance, and if this was only for the day, he would be content with that. Danni wanted him, was willing to give herself to him, and he would not reject her.

Kissing her deeply, hands shaking in fear she would stop him at any moment, Marcus fumbled with her stays until bare skin lay exposed. He smoothed his hands inside her dress, along the soft, taut lines of her ribs. Her heart pounded against his palms, echoing in his own.

He brushed aside the opening of her blouse, the soft nubs of her breasts heating his palms. With one warm finger, he traced the trail of her long dark braid over her shoulder and curving between her breasts, continuing along her hip, sweeping low between her legs. Blood rushed to his groin. Leaning forward, he trailed his mouth where the braid lay, stopping at the sensitive underside of her breast.

Delighting in the faint scent of her skin, he shifted to his knees, dipped kisses in the valley of her breasts, swirling his tongue in her belly button. The muscles quivered under his questing mouth. Her uneven breath was music to his ears.

Eager to give Danni her every wish, he pushed the shift past her hips. He kissed the small strip of skin above the fabric, as inch by painful inch the perfect triangle of dark curls was revealed. He groaned, his desire burning him up at the sight.

He had to have her. Shocks of pain from his hip did not stop him. Everything in him urging to take her. He shook with the strength of wanting her. To possess her.

Gritting his teeth, he forced himself to steady. This was for her. This was to show her she hadn't been wrong in choosing him.

With deliberate slowness, he pulled the layers of cloth from her body.

She made no move to cover herself, lying proudly before him this time. His eyes caressed her, every mesmerizing curve, every shadowed place of her body. The heat inside him raged.

"Your hair," he murmured, fingering the plait, slowly loosening the three ropes into a thick veil of glistening brown shadows.

She shook her head, the strands settling around her shoulders. Waves of hair fell around her. They shimmered in the sunlight streaming in from the small window, softly curled from their bindings. He caught a strand, twisted it between his fingers. "So soft."

She smiled at him, her light eyes glowing with tenderness. He swallowed, suddenly overwhelmed by the gift she was giving him. "Danni."

He caught her hips and she shuddered with the contact.

Her hands stroked his sides and ribs. His blood raged higher whenever her caresses approached the length of him. Her body leaned forward, bracing herself against him, nails digging into his shirt, tugging eagerly. "Marcus...I want more."

He glanced up, meeting her darkening gaze. Her eyes were filled with want. For him.

He gulped, realizing she wanted his shirt gone. He pulled back, playing nervously with the hem of his shirt. He suddenly felt like a virginal bride, struggling to control his anxiety. She'd been shocked at the sight of his body before, but what if she was now revolted?

Seeming to sense his concern, Danni pushed onto her elbows. She stayed his hand, her smile warm and accepting. "They will not disturb me, Marcus. They are a sign of your strength."

He looked at her, unable to believe the words. He tugged his shirt over his head, carefully avoiding his injured side, and stripped from his trousers. Marcus gently pushed her back on the bed, positioning himself between her legs. Her light brown eyes flared with desire as he leaned over her, her dark hair spilling across the feather pillows. She was completely exposed for his exploration.

Her eyes flared as he cupped one of her breasts. He marveled at the fit of it in his hand, as if she'd been made to fit him. She gasped when he flicked his thumb across her taut nipple. Her arms were about him, hands moving over his skin, tracing ridges of ruined flesh and pressing hot kisses to the side of his neck. A thrill coursed through him as her tongue laved at his collarbone.

He felt a wicked twist emerge on his lips.

She spotted it, shooting him a skeptical look. "What are you thinking?"

"Something perfectly devilish."

He easily caught her hands between one of his, pinning them above her head. With his free hand, he created a lazy trail with his mouth, her skin leaping and tightening under his ministrations, and enjoyed the breathy gasps that slipped past her swollen lips.

His explorations led him to the mound of one breast. He circled the beaded, dusky tip, fanning hot air over it. She writhed beneath him. Grinning, he caught the tip of her breast in his mouth, sucking and laving her nipple. She arched towards him, her eyes rolling shut with passion. "Marcus."

He craved hearing his name on her lips, the way she always ended it with a breathy sigh, even when she was furious. He switched to her other breast, paying it equal attention before pressing hot, open-mouthed kisses down her belly, longing to touch her, to taste her everywhere.

He moved farther down, easing her legs open. Her body stiffened and he could feel the muscles in her legs tighten, but she didn't snap them shut when he exposed her hidden folds. She smelled heavenly, of woman and heat. He groaned in pleasure.

"Marcus?"

He glanced up at the question in her eyes. With a devilish smile, he kissed her, just like the night back at the Jacket Inn. A sob escaped, her hips rising at the sensation. He caught her, holding her still as he explored. Her fingers slid through his hair, holding him in place, her body thrashing in pleasure. All the while, he pleasured her with his lips, his tongue, his teeth. He went slowly, deliberately taking his leisure. Determined to make this even better than the last time.

Pants filled the room. "Marcus. Please...I...Please..."

He chuckled, changing tempo. Her legs came around him, squeezing as he held her, not content until he'd had his fill. Her sobbing increased. He could feel her body coiling, growing closer to the edge. "Please, Marcus, do not stop!"

But he did.

A whimper of frustration escaped her. "Why did you stop?"

He chuckled at her impatient tone. Eagerly, he settled above her, pressing his mouth deeply against hers, and reveled in the softness of her lips and the hesitant stroke of her tongue against his own. He moaned, his breath catching.

Rocking his hips, he rubbed his length against her slick heat. A pant escaped both of them. She felt so good. He couldn't wait to be inside her. But he hesitated.

"Are you...are you sure, Danni?"

Soft hands caressed his face. He still marveled at her willingness to touch him. "Very sure."

He gulped, nuzzling the crook of her neck. "This may hurt a bit. I'm sorry."

"I know," she whispered, wrapping herself about him.

It was all he needed to hear. As gently as possible, he entered her. Sweat beaded on his brow as his tip was engulfed in her fiery heat. Moving as slowly as possible, he gritted his teeth, allowing her to adjust to the invasion. He felt her tense.

"Marcus," Danni whimpered, her concern sparking his own.

He met her gaze, offering a reassuring smile and slipping his hand through her hair, cupping the back of her head. "Just bear with me, little one. It will get better, promise."

He heard her gulp before nodding with large eyes. Gritting his teeth, he held her gaze as he slowly slid inside. He groaned as her hot sheath pressed tightly around him, threatening to pull him into a lust-filled haze.

A startled squeak escaped as Danni stiffened. His heart tugged at seeing her wince. Keeping his lower half as still as possible, he pressed gentle kisses over her face. "The difficult part is over."

She nodded, her eyes clearing, and he held tight. He sucked in a breath, still surprised by her utter acceptance. And then he slowly moved.

She moaned as he moved gently in and out. Her hands traced over him, her fingers digging into his buttocks, pressing him deeper. A surprising purr rumbled close to his ear, hardening him further. "Marcus, do...not... stop."

He growled as she pulsed around him.

"More," she whimpered, panting.

He filled her to the hilt, thrusting faster, with more power. He gritted his teeth against the pain of his burning side. Marcus's gut tightened as the edge approached. He could feel Danni tightening around him. But he wouldn't let go unless she came with him.

He drew back far enough to look at her. Her hips rocked with him, meeting each thrust, her body arching to accept him. Her half-lidded, passion-hazed eyes fixed on him. She was stunning, more beautiful than any woman he'd ever seen.

And she was his.

With a growl, he lay his body on top of her. Her warmth and softness engulfed him. He prepared for one last thrust.

"You are mine," he rumbled, nipping at her shoulder.

And he thrust home.

She arched off the bed with a shudder, a silent cry of release on her lips. Tenderness filled him, bringing him over the edge. Marcus groaned as he let go deep inside her, lost in the drugging heat of her body wrapped around him.

Panting, heart pounding against his ribs, he fell on top of her, engulfing her in his arms. Her hands trailed lazily over his slick skin, her chest rose and fell rapidly against his. Lifting his head, he smiled at the warmth shining brightly in her gaze. "Are you happy?"

"Mm-hmm. Very much so."

His breathing slowed and he shifted to his side, afraid he would crush her with his weight. Immediately, he mourned the loss of her warmth, so he gathered her close, her back to his chest, and held tightly. "Sleep, little one."

"I love you, Marcus," she said with a contented sigh. Smiling broader than he'd ever done in his life, he nuzzled her neck, breathing deeply of roses. Of passion. Of warmth.

He listened as her breathing evened and she fell into a light sleep. Gazing at her relaxed face, he felt his tattered heart swell and couldn't help whispering the words one last time before sleep claimed him.

"I love you, Danni. Always."

Chapter Twenty-One

❦

"Alas!" said she, with heartfelt sighs,
The daughter rushing to her eyes,
"There's nothing I so much desire,
"As to behold my tender sire."

—"Beauty and the Beast" by Charles Lamb

Danni shifted languidly alongside Marcus. Turning, she snuggled deeper into the curve of his warm, relaxed body. The arm under her head flexed briefly. His hand stroked her hip and she stretched pleasantly.

"Morning, Marcus."

A chuckle echoed through his chest. "Wrong time, little one."

She frowned, lifting her head to gaze out the window. Gauzy curtains at the window glided in the breeze, exposing long shadows slipping into evening.

She shrugged and rolled her eyes. "Fine. Afternoon, Marcus."

"Afternoon, Danni. Did you have a nice nap?"

She smiled and nodded, scooting as close as possible to him. His skin, stretched taut over strong muscles, made her feel treasured and safe.

Danni felt a silly grin split her lips. She was so happy.

If only these moments could continue. She wasn't foolish enough to think their path would be an easy one. There were still so many problems. Marcus needed to return Ginny home. She had to speak with her father and the earl. They needed to avoid criminal prosecution. And, most important, she needed to tell Marcus who she was.

Her stomach pitched and her grin slipped. Now that she was sure she wanted him in her future, surely he would be as excited as she that her fortune could be used to rescue Caro. He had to see how her money was the solution to all their problems, but she feared he might not take the news well. Marcus would be upset with her for keeping secrets from him. She knew he'd understand once she thoroughly explained and he'd had some time to calm down, but she prayed he would not feel betrayed.

Gulping, she traced her fingers along the arm across her hip, tracing a white scar several inches long, hoping to gather courage from his presence. The limb tightened briefly, startling her. Rolling on her side, she watched Marcus shoot her a soft smile before gingerly lifting himself out of bed. Dragging a blanket, he moved about the room to collect clothing, pointedly keeping his naked form as covered as possible.

She frowned. She didn't want him to feel the need to hide. "Marcus..."

He glanced over his shoulder, a charming smile slowly skewing his dimpled lip. "I'm trying, and I promise to continue to try, but being comfortable with you will take some time. Now, hurry. Dress. We have much to accomplish before dark. First, we meet with Ginny."

Danni was acutely self-conscious as his eyes followed her movements from the bed towards her clothes. She could not stop the blush coloring her from head to toe as she reached for her shift.

"Turn around, Marcus. I'm not entirely comfortable with you watching me, either."

"But you are beautiful," he said with a boyish grin. "I don't want to miss a moment."

"Oh, you infuriating man," she exclaimed with no real heat. "Turn about so I can dress. We must have a discussion before Ginny, and I will not do so in a bedsheet."

She had no idea how to broach the subject. She picked up her dress and petticoats and slipped them on, lacing her stays, using the moments to gather her thoughts.

"Marcus, what...what if, completely hypothetically, of course, I had some money available to me that we could use to break Caro's engagement."

Marcus blinked and his face softened. "I don't think your savings would be enough, little one, but thank you for offering."

She cleared her throat, playing with the hem of her sleeve. "Well, what if the sum was quite substantial?"

"What are you saying?" The uncertainty in Marcus's tone made her wince.

Taking a deep breath, she straightened her spine and braced herself. Meeting his confused eyes, she asked, "Marcus, what if I was an heiress?"

"Checkmate."

Ginny smiled as she moved her pawn into place. The stable hand stared at the board in disbelief. Their tiny audience clapped their hands. With a laugh, she jumped up from her seat on an upturned barrel and curtsied as if the king himself were present. How she enjoyed victory.

"I want a rematch!"

She considered the challenge. He'd not been a particularly good opponent, but she was in a rather generous mood. She'd already won several matches today and the sun had yet to reach the horizon. She'd been losing her mind in the small room down the hall from her captors. One could count the knots in the wooden ceiling only so many times before one was destined for an asylum. When she'd thought to leave her room, she'd found her door unguarded and the voices from her captors' room reassured her they were not concerned about her welfare.

They were a rather unusual pair of kidnappers. She'd read stories of torture devices and the horrible conditions prisoners such as herself should expect to endure. Instead she was treated with benign neglect. More like a traveling companion than their captive.

At least they were better than the highwaymen. She rubbed her wrists where they had been chafed raw by rope. Those men had been odious—especially the leader, Bridger Bishop, or, as he was better known, the Green Bandit. He was a rather odd man, a puzzle Ginny would have loved to decipher had she the time. Glancing down at the finished game still laid out on the board, she had to give the brigands a smidgen of credit. They'd known how to play spectacular chess.

Unfortunately, her current opponent was fuming at her

victory. His mouth twisted and he called her a ninny. *It's not as if someone had not called her that before.*

After he calmed down, he gestured towards the board for another round. So she retook her seat on a stool inside the barn, the smell of hay and manure strangely comforting, and nodded for him to reset the game. She propped her chin on her knee. The man had meant to goad her, and now Ginny felt she had to prove a point. Women were a lot smarter than men.

It was a bother to have a brilliant brain. Her father often laughed at her for saying so, but it was true. From what she had observed, men did not want their wives to be smarter than them. They wanted them subservient and obedient to their every whim. It was her very unfortunate luck to possess a superior intellect.

And so, to society, she'd become Ginny the Ninny. It was the only avenue that would allow her to marry someday. And she did want to marry and have children. Sadly, a ninny was attractive to men. An intelligent, educated equal was not.

Ginny snorted.

She moved her first piece, her knight, into position. While the man across from her contemplated his next move, Ginny turned her head in the direction of the inn, wondering what her kidnappers were doing. Probably exchanging doe-eyed glances. One would have to be blind and a fool (and Ginny was neither) not to see how those two felt about each other.

She was curious about Danni, though. How could the woman think Ginny would not recognize her? Their fathers were both members of the House, and she'd seen her at several social engagements over the years. She had been very surprised to hear Danielle Strafford calling herself Miss Green, but Ginny was not about to expose her secret. Women had to stick together.

Sighing, she moved a pawn against the stable hand's bishop. She had her own rather spectacular plan at the moment. The best she'd ever come up with.

It was to do absolutely nothing.

She'd thought to come to the stables and escape on horseback, but it became clear escape was unnecessary. Danni had the money Marcus apparently needed and Ginny knew they both loved each other but were too stubborn to admit it. Soon enough the two would work this problem out, and then they'd all return safely home. In the meantime, she was having quite the adventure.

Easing back against the bench, she castled her king. Silence fell as the game progressed. Ginny focused more on experimenting with strategy than winning. If she didn't, she'd quickly be without an opponent and be back to counting the ceiling knots—on the fast track to Bedlam.

A sudden shout drew attention from the game. Confused looks were exchanged between the group, and one of the servants moved to the barn doors to investigate. Another shout quickly followed, and male voices became increasingly agitated. Ginny's natural curiosity got the best of her. She stood with a nod of concession to her opponent. Upon exiting the barn, she was immediately immobilized by the stunning sight before her.

Mounted men flooded the courtyard. They halted in line, each man bigger than the last. Their faces were set with grim determination, and the setting sun created a halo effect about their heads. Cloaks swirled in the breeze, pulled back to reveal the firepower each man had strapped to his person. Such a sight she'd witnessed only during military exhibitions. A ripple of fear filled her; instinct forced her back in the shadow. They could be here to rob the inn.

One man in the center of the group inched his horse forward, sitting perfectly erect, his gaze fierce. He met the owner of the inn, who hurried from the common rooms to greet them. Her heart swelled with pride and relief as she recognized the man, and she dashed tears of joy from her eyes. No one would ever guess how well the sea legs of the Lord High Admiral adapted to a saddle.

"Papa!" She burst from the shelter of the barn, running towards him. Her father's grim expression crumbled when he saw her. He dismounted, met her halfway, and caught her tightly in his arms, swinging her about dizzily.

"Ginny! Oh, God." His voice shook as he spoke. His grip tightened around her once more before thrusting her at arm's length.

She'd never been happier to see him in her life. She grinned so widely her cheeks ached, drinking in the sight of him as his concerned gaze swept over her. "You haven't been hurt?"

She rapidly shook her head, unable to speak. Her father was not what one expected of a Lord High Admiral. He wasn't much taller than she. His strawberry-blond hair was overly long and a permanent, mischievous twinkle glinted in his eyes. He didn't look as if he had sired seven children, so youthful was his countenance.

"Let me look at you."

She laughed with abandon, unable to believe she could finally go home. "I'm a little bruised from the ride, but none the worse for wear. How did you ever find me?"

A small tear slipped from the corner of his eye. His relief for her safety palpable. "Thank the lord for Grisly. If it had not been for her witnessing your kidnapping, I would have taken much longer to find you. She was able to tell us in what direction you had headed, and provide a good description of your assailants." He took a deep breath, adding, "I was so afraid, Ginny."

She felt her lower lip tremble, realizing how much she had really missed her father. After a moment of emotional silence, the admiral's demeanor transitioned immediately to one of military sternness and command. "Where are they? This man and woman."

"Papa. Wait. I think—" But he wasn't listening to her any longer. He barked a command at his men and strode across the clearing. They swung from their horses in unison, and the stable hands she'd been playing chess with rushed forward, accepting the reins of the massive animals. Within moments, the men had arranged themselves in formation.

Ginny could only watch in horror as her father halted in front of the terrified innkeeper. "You are harboring known fugitives in your establishment. I am the Lord High Admiral, and you *will* allow us entrance."

Her father didn't have to ask twice. The man practically jumped to the side to allow the men to storm the building.

Ginny felt a sense of helplessness as they spread out and searched the premises for Danni and Marcus. Kidnapping was a hanging offense. Despite taking her for devious purposes, she found she could not wish such a fate upon them. They'd rescued her from those highwaymen and for that she owed them a debt of honor. Ginny was certain, too, they would never have gone through with their horrid plan to force her into marriage at Gretna. They were just mixed up about their feelings for each other, and once that was resolved, all was going to be well.

She wanted to call the entire event a misadventure, and head happily, safely home.

But her father would never agree.

It was one of the reasons, after all, why he *was* the Lord High Admiral. He possessed a keen sense of right and wrong, as well as a burning need to see justice triumph. Her father would be enraged when he learned it was his compatriot's daughter who'd stolen her away. And even more so when he learned the marquis planned to marry her against her will.

Ginny was unable to warn her captors of their impending doom, but she would do all she could to help them. One thing her father had taught her—never let a debt go unpaid.

Chapter Twenty-Two

❦

"I charge and warn you to BE GONE!
"And further, on life's penalty,
"Dare not again to visit me."

—"Beauty and the Beast" by Charles Lamb

How could you be an heiress, Danni? You run a fake book shop and live off commissions from elopements."

Danni rapidly shook her head. She wasn't certain how he'd come up with that idea. "I've never taken money from the girls."

Marcus's eyes widened in confusion, but before he could say another word, the door to their chamber crashed inward. Splintering wood flew through the room, and echoes shook the floor beneath their feet. Half a dozen heavily armed men flooded the small space, fanning out around the perimeter. Two headed directly towards them.

Danni was rooted to the spot, unsure what to do. Suddenly, Marcus was before her, his body blocking the attackers' advance. They didn't hesitate at his size, but kept advancing, another leaping into the fray to assist in his downfall.

"Run, Danni!"

Marcus's voice roared as one of them aimed a fist for his face. He caught the punch, twisting the arm behind his opponent's back. A second man aimed for his feet. Danni watched in horror as Marcus's green eyes dimmed, panic and wildness consuming him. She trembled as she watched the man she loved fall back into the abyss of his childhood.

The violence that unfolded shocked her. As the second attacker swerved to buckle Marcus's legs from beneath him, he lifted one leg and slammed his heel against Marcus's knee. Marcus barely tilted under the blow. A loud pop echoed through the room as Marcus snapped the arm of the man he was holding. He screamed and collapsed to the floor. The third oncoming man was quickly cut down, then a fourth.

Danni was paralyzed by the ferocity the men displayed. It seemed each was set on killing Marcus. A fifth man leaped upon Marcus. With each blow landed by the armed men, Marcus became more crazed. He fought back ferociously, but ineffectively, against so many opponents. Danni couldn't bear to watch any more. "Please. Marcus, stop!"

He caught a man by the throat, lifting him off his feet. His frenzied gaze held hers. Her heart broke at his distant expression. She knew in his mind, he was fighting his father.

"Marcus," she forced herself to speak calmly. "Let him go."

Something sparked deep in his eyes, bringing their green depths to light again. "Danni."

He gently lowered the man to his feet, his gaze never leaving hers. All activity seemed to slow. Another member of the squad rounded the edge of the door, halting at Marcus's left. Her gaze locked on the admiral's man as he crouched. His muscles gathered, bulging as he flew directly at Marcus. His shoulder collided with Marcus's hip, landing directly against the wound in his side.

Danni screamed in anticipation of his pain. Her lover's head fell back as an inhuman roar erupted from him. His arms clawed at the air in self-defense as he slowly sank to his knees. In that moment, she didn't care whether he was human or beast, she was not afraid. She knew he would never hurt her, rather, she knew that he would die trying to defend her. Danni tried to catch him, to hold him, but two men seized her arms.

Suddenly, a short, forceful man burst into the room framed by a swirling riding coat. His face was chiseled iron as he calmly strode up to Marcus. His men moved in to seize the incapacitated man.

He snarled. "So you are the cur who took my daughter. From under my own roof, no less!"

Ginny's father lifted a hand to strike him sharply across his face. Danni struggled against her own captors, trying to stop any additional harm to Marcus. "Stop! You don't understand."

The admiral's seething gaze landed on her. His mouth opened, his eyes widening in his stunned shock. "Miss Strafford?"

She grimaced. Marcus's head pivoted towards her, his features dazed.

"Please, sir, don't hurt him. We will cooperate with you now."

"Danielle, what in God's name are you doing here?"

She grimaced, looking down in shame. "It's a long story, sir."

Marcus stared with confused disbelief as the admiral riddled her with rambling questions, "Long story? Why are you not in London with your father? I heard you had become betrothed to Hemsworth! How did you ever become involved in this?"

At Danni's shuttered gaze, the man backtracked. "Right, of course, Seaton doesn't know what you are up to, does he?"

The admiral barked an order to his second in command. "Bring that young man here. Now!"

Danni's heart lurched. He couldn't be here. It was impossible. But sure enough, the thin frame and pious face of her ex-coachman appeared in the doorway to their room a moment later.

"Phillip!"

She shared a stunned look with Marcus. Danni was glad he had been found and cared for, but... what exactly would he have to say? He was a blathering idiot.

"Ah, yes, Phillip. Come. Clarify again what's going on here, lad." The admiral waved him in.

The dark-haired coachman glanced at Marcus and then smirked. The powerless, whimpering dandy was gone. Phillip was about to get his retribution for Marcus's earlier intimidation. She dreaded his version of events.

"Until recently, I was in the employ of Miss Strafford,

daughter of the Baron Seaton." She heard Marcus's sharp gasp and felt his eyes burning into her back, but Danni kept her eyes fixed on Phillip, silently pleading with him to keep his mouth shut. "She was blackmailed by this... ruffian, the Marquis of Fleetwood, to help him kidnap Miss Foley-Foster."

The admiral's eyes narrowed dangerously in Danni's direction. "Is this true?"

Danni wanted to argue, to defend Marcus somehow, but it was nothing but the truth. She slumped in her captive's grip and stared shamefully at the floor. She would not condemn Marcus. "He never hurt either of us."

The admiral scoffed. "What happened next, young man?"

Danni could only shake her head, knowing the next chapter in their story would only make matters worse for them. Phillip, however, did not hesitate to fill in the commander. "When we left London, our coach was set upon by highwaymen. The leader called himself the Green Bandit. He and his associate stole Miss Foley-Foster to hold her for ransom. That's when I was shot! All because of this...this monster."

Rage purpled the admiral's face. He was out for blood. Marcus's blood.

"You let my child fall into the hands of those filthy criminals?"

Every man in the room flinched at the note in the admiral's voice.

Danni struggled to free herself, trying to draw attention from Marcus. She hoped she could keep him alive. "She's fine. He risked his life to save her from them and brought her here. He had her examined by a doctor, even before himself, even though he was suffering from a gun-shot wound."

The admiral ignored her. He turned to Phillip. "Do you know for what purpose this beast took my daughter in the first place?"

"He plotted to marry her. He directed me to bring them to Gretna Green."

He turned on Marcus, fury fairly dripping from him. "You planned to *force her into marriage*?"

Danni cringed. "He meant her no harm, I promise!"

The admiral swung towards her. "You will remain silent. We will speak privately about your role in this matter later, Miss Strafford."

She turned her gaze to Marcus. Emerald flickered with a swath of emotion—shock, vulnerability, and resignation. The last hurt most of all. He'd given up.

Marcus finally spoke, his voice very soft. "I do not know this Miss Strafford you are speaking of, Admiral. I know this woman as Miss Green."

Danni felt sick.

The admiral looked from Marcus to Danni; some of the rage dimmed and was replaced by grim satisfaction. "You did well to hide your identity, Danielle. If he was after money, he very may well have forced you."

Marcus's face paled and his gaze dropped to the ground. She caught the glimmer of pain so deep it hurt. He thought she didn't trust him. Danni felt her heart break. "I'm so sorry I didn't tell you sooner, Marcus. I was afraid you'd force me to marry you instead. But that was before..."

She bit her lip, silencing her next words in front of so many strange men.

He didn't respond, not even a twitch to acknowledge he'd heard her. Desperate, Danni turned to the admiral, pleading. "Let him go, please, I beg you."

"Let him go? Danielle, you've lost your mind. This man is a criminal. If not for your coachman, I may never have found you and Ginny."

She bit back a hiss of hatred for Phillip, the whimpering dolt. "Marcus was only doing what he had to! He's in desperate need of money to help his sister. You would stop at nothing to help your family. Right before me is the evidence of that. And Marcus had planned to return her safely today. "

The admiral glanced at the men he'd brought with him before his gaze hardened. "Do not be so foolish, Miss Strafford. He is playing with you. Tugging all the right heartstrings to bend you to his will. He has taken advantage of your gentle nature."

She shook her head, denying the accusation that Marcus had deceived her. Blackmailed, kidnapped, yes, but never deceived her. The bleak emotions on Marcus's face when he'd confessed everything and when he'd demonstrated his love for her had been real.

She willed Marcus to defend himself, to say *something*. Instead, he remained on his knees between his captors, silent, his eyes focused on the dark-paneled floor.

"Why didn't you tell me?" Marcus finally croaked, his voice thick with agony.

She opened her mouth to fully explain herself, but the admiral cut her off. "Obviously, she could not stand to be forced into such a marriage, either. What respectable woman would?"

The blond giant held still, a slight tensing in his muscles the only indication he'd heard.

Tears filled her vision. Desperately, she wanted to wrap him in her arms and reassure him she loved him. She tugged at her captors' grip, but they held firm.

"Marcus, that may have been true, at one time. But not now."

"I will see you hang, Fleetwood," the admiral intoned like a death knell.

"No! I will never let you hurt him."

The admiral's gaze flicked to her guards and then towards the door in a silent command. The men steered her away. Danni dug the heels of her boots into the wood, trying to stop them. "Let me go! I won't let you do this."

She fought wildly against them. Her legs kicked about. One man grunted when her elbow connected with his side. His grip loosened momentarily and it was all Danni needed to yank free. She pushed her way past the admiral, taking a position between him and Marcus. "I will not let you do this. He's a good man."

The admiral shook his head as Marcus spoke to her. "Move, Miss Strafford. We both knew this day would come."

"But Marcus—"

"Be gone."

Danni cried at the soft, broken words that came from Marcus. He couldn't give up. She wouldn't let him.

Her guards seized her, dragging her from the room. She managed to hold the door frame long enough to catch one last glimpse of the man she loved.

The admiral viciously smacked Marcus with the butt

of his gun, and her beast fell silently to the floor, without having moved a muscle to defend himself.

* * *

The sun had set long ago, and the streets of London had settled into a sort of quiet busyness, so unlike the daylight hours. In sharp contrast, anxiety and fear crackled like lightning inside Danni as the admiral's carriage slowed to the curb outside her home on King Street.

Before the vehicle came to a full stop, Danni bounded out, skirts gathered about her knees. She raced up the steps of her home, briefly waving back to Ginny. The girl had been so kind to her, doing everything in her power to console her, and promising to intervene on Marcus's behalf with her father. But nothing could change the fact that she'd destroyed Marcus. The way he'd looked at her, utterly emotionless. He'd surrendered. She could see his failure and despair written in every fiber of his being. Now that he was in jail, facing the noose, he would never be able to set his sister free from Harwood. And he'd also given up on them. Idiotic man probably thought she'd never truly love him and would be better without him.

But Danni would not give up. She had one last resource available to her.

Fumbling with the knocker, the door swung inward. Danni didn't wait to hand her coat to the butler, but pushed past him, racing to her father's study. At this time of evening, he would be seated in his wingback chair, studying his notes from Session.

The double doors flew open under her palms, banging

against the walls in her haste. Her father sat up in his chair, his surprise turning to worried relief.

"Danni! Where on earth have you been? I've had Runners looking for you everywhere."

She stopped in the middle of the room, shocked. "You noticed?"

Her father, well known for staring down his toughest political opponents, turned bright red with shame. "Of course I did. You have been gone for almost a week! I know I have not been the best of fathers since your mother died, Danni, but I do worry about your well-being."

Until that moment, Danni hadn't realized how much she'd missed her father. This small, simple revelation sent her over the brink into hysteria. She'd been so determined to solve every problem on her own, so focused on getting Marcus free, she'd not stopped to think. Now, as the weight of the week overwhelmed her, she broke. Launching herself into her father's embrace, she clutched at his shoulders. Her body shook with uncontrollable sobs. "Oh, Papa! I don't know what to do."

His hand patted the back of her head awkwardly in an effort to soothe her. The tenderness and worry in his tone only caused her to cry harder. "Whatever it is, I'm sure we can fix it."

"No, Papa. I..."

"Darling, tell me what it is and I'll be the judge."

Danni pulled back, absorbing his sorrowful gaze before the answer broke from her. "The man I love is sentenced to die!"

Confusion swamped his features. "What are you talking about, Danielle?"

Fighting to steady her heaving chest so she could form words, Danni launched into an account of everything that had happened—from how she'd first opened Gretna Green Bookings, to Marcus's blackmail and her role in Ginny's abduction, and, finally, to her "rescue." When she was done, her pale father collapsed back into his high-backed chair. "Oh, God."

Unwilling to give him an inch, afraid of how he might react to Marcus, she quickly followed, dropping to her knees by the armrest. Seizing his hand, she pleaded, "Please understand, Papa. I know he's done terrible things, but he was desperate. He didn't take Ginny and me for self-gain, but for self-sacrifice."

Her father's eyes looked stormy, his expression clearly conflicted. "Danielle, let me process one thing at a time."

She gnawed her bottom lip to keep silent.

"Let me see if I understand this correctly. After your mother..." He cleared his throat and shifted in the velvet-upholstered chair. Inwardly, Danni winced, realizing how hard it was for him to admit her mother had passed away, even after all this time.

"Six years ago, you started a business," he tried again, skipping over her mother entirely.

"Yes."

"And this business of yours, while pretending to be a bookstore, is actually a place where couples can arrange an elopement."

She nodded, letting her father work his way through his thoughts.

"By *God*, Danielle! Do you have any idea what you've been doing?" His voice rose, louder than she'd heard it in years. It was actually near a shout. "Not only could it *ruin* you so thoroughly you could be shunned by the *country*, but you could get me tossed out on my ear from Parliament. Do you have any idea how many of the common people depend upon the work I do in the government? And there is the earl. This scandal could *destroy* him. And the others...oh, God, the fathers!"

He stood abruptly and began pacing the room. She had never witnessed him in such a panic.

Danni grasped at his arm, seeking to calm him. "I *do* know how bad this could become, which is why I've kept my real identity hidden."

"That obviously wasn't enough if that...that *monster* was able to take advantage of you! Not to mention the admiral and his men now know about you." He paused and then started towards the study door. "I must go meet with him. See what damage I can repair."

Danni rose to her feet, ignoring everything but the icy hot rage flooding her body. "He is *not* a monster! He is a man and the one I *love*!"

Her father turned to her, his face filled with righteous anger and rampant worry. "You love him? He blackmailed you! He *used* you, Danielle. What's to say he won't again?"

Danni bit her tongue. He was worried about her, and the ramifications for their futures. She knew that, but she resented it. How dare he start to care about her again, *now*, after all these years? What gave him the right to speak to her as if she were still a child, who didn't know her own mind and the consequences of her actions?

Gathering her courage, she met her father square in the eye, refusing to waver, to prove to him that she was no longer the little girl he'd left behind when his wife died.

"If he is using me, then it is my mistake to make. All I ask is your help to secure his release. Then, if he'll still have me, I want to marry him."

Her father's eyes widened in shock. His mouth opened, as if to speak, before it snapped shut with an audible click.

A sudden knock on the door shattered the tension between them. Both heads turned to the door as the butler pushed it open and bowed. He announced, "His lordship, the Earl of Hemsworth, has arrived, my lord."

Her father nodded silently, and the moment the door closed, her father sagged back into the chair. His crushed, defeated demeanor was startling. He looked so much older. And so very tired.

"I forgot the earl was coming." He sighed, pinching the bridge of his nose. "He has been asking for news of you every day."

Danni pushed away the guilt she felt at the statement. Checking for news of her after she'd disappeared was very like him. She doubted he'd have spread gossip about her, either, and would be forever thankful for his discretion. She understood the rules of the *ton*, and even though she distained many of them, it would be difficult to maintain her family's current status within society if it became known she'd vanished without a chaperone. People would assume the worst. Ironically, in this instance, they would be right.

"Go meet with him, Danielle. I need a moment to gather my thoughts."

Obediently, she rose and headed to the drawing room where the earl would be waiting. Her mind was awhirl with thoughts of Marcus and her father, but right now, she had another task—explaining all this to the Earl of Hemsworth. She knew it would be difficult. Not only did he seem to genuinely care for her, but their names had been linked with the intention of marriage for months. He'd be humiliated and didn't deserve that.

But, more important, he didn't deserve a wife who would never love him, and who would compare him to another for the rest of their days. They'd both be miserable.

Opening the door of the drawing room revealed said man pacing restlessly before the bay window. He abruptly turned towards her and froze. Even obviously agitated, Michael Rathbourne, Earl of Hemsworth, was an extremely attractive man. His honey-brown hair was cropped short on the sides and artfully windswept atop his head. His finely cut clothes framed a tall, lean figure. Warm hazel eyes radiated kindness to friends and ruthlessness to foes. He was self-confident, successful, and ambitious—he knew exactly what he wanted out of life and was determined to achieve it.

Many women would have fainted at the thought of him in their parlor. And over the course of his courtship, Danni was well aware of more than one debutante's hateful glances in her direction for "snagging" the earl. He was the *ton*'s angel, revered by men and fawned over by women.

He did absolutely nothing for her.

All she could think about was how he compared to Marcus. How Hemsworth's eyes were much too brown. How his hair was too dark and straight. How his physique was too lithe and his face too smooth, too *perfect*. His confidence bordered on arrogance, and his strict adherence to propriety was exhausting.

God, how could she have ever contemplated marrying this man? She'd be bored to tears within the first week of their marriage.

"Miss Strafford!" His exclamation was followed with a shocking display of affection. Lord Rathbourne, ever the gentleman, *touched* her. Of course, it was only to grab her shoulders and give her a comforting squeeze, but the man hadn't so much as kissed her cheek during their courtship. "I'm so glad you're all right. Where have you been? Your father and I have been worried sick."

Danni offered him a hesitant smile. How the bloody hell did one end a courtship? She'd heard the younger girls discuss the issue all the time, but she suddenly couldn't remember any of it. Especially when faced with such obvious relief at her well-being.

Mustering up her courage, she replied weakly, "I'm sorry. My time away wasn't planned."

"Of course. You're much too sensible."

She bit back a snort. Sensible? Even Danni could admit that wasn't one of her virtues. "Thank you, my lord."

"I told you to call me Michael. Now that you're back and once we've made sure you are unharmed, we can see about moving this engagement along. There is a big vote in Session next week and I need Seaton's support."

Danni clenched her fist. She knew he didn't mean to be callous. He was simply confirming to her what their union had been about—political ambition.

She would thank fate every day that she'd met Marcus. He'd shown her what real love was, and now she would never be able to settle for anything less.

"Lord Rathbourne," she spoke more firmly. His brows rose in surprise at the tone. She'd always presented herself as meek and biddable in the past. She was certain this new facet of her personality would send him into shock.

Stepping back from his gentle hold, she met his warm eyes, trying to push away the guilt that consumed her. "I regret to inform you that I will no longer be able to agree to the arrangement made by you and my father."

"P-Pardon?"

"I will not marry you."

His eyes widened and his gloved hands hung limply at his side. Confusion colored his features as he exclaimed, "But why? I thought..."

Managing a soft smile for his benefit, she whispered, "I thought so, too. You are a good man, Lord Rathbourne, and any woman would be lucky to be your wife; however, I cannot."

He half turned away from her, running his hand through his hair. A lock fell across the frown creasing his forehead. Turning to face her again, hurt clear in his gaze, he asked, "Would you care to explain this sudden change of heart? I really do care for you, Danielle. Did I do something wrong?"

God, she felt as if she'd kicked a puppy. How come he'd chosen now, of all times, to use her Christian name for the first time? Still, he was right. She owed him nothing less than the truth. So she said the words that she hoped would explain everything.

"I fell in love."

The man straightened, as if shocked. His hazel gaze assessed her, looking for the validity of her statement. And then he did something that made her wish she could love him, because he so clearly deserved it.

His eyes softened and a small smile tilted the corner of

his lips, revealing a dimpled cheek. "Well, I'll be damned. Congratulations, Danielle."

Her heart broke in a new place. He was *such* a good man.

Just then, the door of the drawing room opened, revealing a harried-looking baron. He glanced between the two of them and groaned. "What are you doing, Danielle?"

"I have broken off with the earl. It's the only right thing to do."

"But the vote—!"

"I must assure you that nothing has changed on that front, Seaton," the earl said, looking a bit forlorn. "We'll speak about the vote at a later date. Obviously, you and Danielle have much to discuss."

Turning to Danni, he gave a smart bow. "I'm glad you are back, safe and sound. Perhaps you will tell me exactly what happened at another time, when cooler heads can prevail."

She smiled. "I will. Thank you for understanding."

He bowed to her father, but then hesitated at the threshold. Looking back over his shoulder, he gave her a sad smile. "He's a lucky man."

All was quiet until the front door clicked shut, signaling the earl's departure from the house. Then she turned on her heel to escape her father's anger and confusion. She'd just managed to brush past him in the doorway before he caught her arm.

"I don't understand. You've never behaved like this before."

"Yes, I have," she snapped, suddenly feeling exhausted. It was too much. Everything that had happened over the past week was finally taking its toll. She didn't want to tiptoe around her father anymore. She didn't want to feel so anxious about upsetting him, or worried she'd say something to remind him of her mother. It was about time he realized there was more to living than breathing.

Filling her lungs, she let it all out. "The only reason I agreed to consider the earl in the first place was to make you happy again."

"What are you talking about?"

She scoffed. "You've withdrawn completely, burying yourself in politics. While you grieved for Mother, I was still here grieving, too. I've watched you, Papa. You never smile anymore, you never tell me the latest absurdity from Session, you never say 'Good night, I'll see you in the morning' or 'Love you, poppet' anymore. You haven't been yourself in a very long time, and I wanted to fix that. Desperately. Foolishly, I believed marrying Lord Rathbourne would restore your old self."

Danni panted, trying to catch her breath after relieving herself of her pent-up frustration at her father. It was terrifying and liberating at the same time. "Thankfully, I realized our marriage wouldn't make anyone happy, not truly. One lesson I learned this week is that one person cannot sacrifice themselves to make another happy. It doesn't work. Too many are hurt in the process. We can only do what is best for ourselves, and hope others will understand and eventually accept our decisions because they love us."

He stared at her for several moments, clearly unsure what to say.

"That is what I need from you, Papa," she continued. "I need you to understand that my marriage to the earl was not going to make any of us happy. But you can help me marry the man I have chosen for myself. You have to trust that I have chosen someone who I want and who I believe will make me happy, and from that, maybe you can reclaim some happiness, too."

Gritting her teeth, she turned on her heel again, marching towards the stairs to her room. She would try to sleep and then, when she woke up, she would exhaust herself trying to save Marcus.

"Danielle!" her father called behind her. "What do you think you're doing?"

"I'm going to rest for tonight, and then I am going to save Marcus, Papa. With or without your help."

Chapter Twenty-Three

❦

There, on the lawn, as if to die,
She saw poor BEAST extended lie,
Reproaching with his latest breath
BEAUTY's ingratitude in death.

—"Beauty and the Beast" by Charles Lamb

The dungeon door shuddered under Marcus's boot. He gritted his teeth against the vibrations; his foot had long since gone numb. The shouting of the guards had stopped. They were waiting for him to tire out. He slammed it again, fighting rising panic. He hated dungeons, prisons, and enclosed spaces. With one last shuddering thud, Marcus fell back against the wall. His heart hammered as he fought for calm. Dark shadows of his childhood terrors danced wickedly before his eyes.

He growled, trying to remain calm. He slid down the

wall, heavy helplessness settling over his shoulders. Dampness seeped through his worn shirt, stealing away any body warmth he had. Marcus rested his chained wrists on the tops of his knees. He dug his boots into the dirt and straw, trying not to inhale the rancid air. The prison cell was larger than he would expect for someone scheduled for the noose. It was a luxury compared to the dungeons at Fleetwood Manor. He knew from personal experience.

His hands tightened, the irons on his wrists cutting his flesh.

Danni.

Her smiling face flashed before him. The image of her calmed his chaotic memories, and replaced them with crushing sadness. She'd lied to him. She had never really trusted him. And as much as it hurt, as much as he felt betrayed, he knew he deserved it. After all, he hadn't given her a reason to divulge such information without fear he'd use it against her. Not until the very end. Not until he'd realized their love meant far more than money.

He stomped his numb foot into the ground, trying to awaken it. He knew his discomfort would only increase the longer he remained in this hellhole. Just as he knew the pain constricting his chest would never ease. His eyelids dropped to shut out his surroundings. He'd been a fool to believe he could escape the consequences of kidnapping Ginny. A foolish, rash decision made in desperate moments by a man so steeped in brandy and nightmares he could barely reason.

How could he be angry with Danni for not offering herself as a sacrificial lamb on the altar of his lunacy?

And then there was Caroline.

Now his sister would be alone in the world, all of her family gone. Facing marriage to Harwood, she would be left without a male relation to fight the codicil for her. He could only hope her friends, the St. Leons, would watch over her.

Bitterness welled up in the back of his throat, washing his mouth with acidic self-loathing. He was such a *bloody* idiot.

His bowed head rested in his cold hands. The silence surrounding him crawled with real and imagined creatures. Marcus wondered how long he had. He didn't believe his title would spare him from the gallows. The admiral was determined to see him hang. This would be the end for him. He just wanted it as soon as possible.

Danni's face flitted through his memory again. This one filled with pained caramel eyes. She regretted not telling him, even if she was justified. He knew she cared about him, although he did not think she loved him as much as he did her. He was certain being with him for so long and in such a stressful situation must have impaired her judgment. No one could ever love a beast like him.

They were better off ending this way. She could marry her fiancé, whom she could have complete trust in. And Marcus would most likely hang.

If he was honest with himself, the prospect of death didn't terrify him. Death would be a release from his constant torment. Neither his father's torture nor Danni's soft touches and heated sighs would ever haunt him again. No, the afterlife didn't scare him, but how he would get there did.

He shook his head of the grim thoughts. He'd sworn to

be better, to try harder to escape his dark thoughts. The scurry of something in the dark caught his eye. He shuddered. He hated rats. With a grim smile, he wondered if carnivorous rabbits might dine on the plagued species.

The jingling clink of keys drew his attention. Turning his head in the direction of the large wooden door, he waited, curious if perhaps he might have a cell mate. The soft glow of fire peeped through the small, bar-lined square in the door as two sets of footsteps drew closer. They stopped outside his carved door. Rattling keys echoed off the stone walls as the jailer sought the right one. There was a slight scrape of metal meeting metal before the lock clinked open and the door swung in.

A tall man, rounded with age, stepped in. His hair was speckled with shades of gray and his face was lined with fatigue. His gaze swept about the room, taking in the deplorable conditions, before focusing on him. The brown gaze dissected him, sharp and unrelenting. Marcus felt himself straighten under the scrutiny. He stood, hoping his full height and fearful countenance would intimidate his visitor. Was he about to learn his fate?

The silence stretched and uncertainty set in. Surely he did not come just to gawk at the infamous Beast finally put in his cage.

"So you're the man who captured my daughter's heart."

Marcus jerked at his visitor's words. Taken aback, he closely searched his visitor's face. The resemblance was there. The shadow of Danni's jawline was present in the determined jut of his chin. Her eyes crinkled at the corners in the same manner as this old man's. The same small ears.

He looked away. "With all due respect, sir, I believe you must be mistaken."

Danni's father arched a brow in skepticism. Marcus averted his scarred left side further, his chains rattling. He could feel the baron give him another once-over. "You are not exactly the man I imagined for my daughter, Fleetwood."

A grim smile lifted the corners of Marcus's mouth. "I'd wager no parent imagines his daughter with me."

The man grunted his agreement. He leaned back against the open doorway, waving the guard away. Arms crossed over his chest, he said, "Danni has explained your predicament to me. Your father was a despicable man. However, I cannot say I approve of your behavior as well."

Marcus shifted uneasily, irons clinking. The Baron of Seaton was well known for his radical liberal politics. Peers and commoners alike viewed him with a mixture of suspicion and awe.

"I did what I thought I had to. Although Danni was very vocal as she pointed out the errors of my ways."

The baron chuckled, scratching the back of his neck. "Yes, well, she has always had a way with words."

It was Marcus's turn to grunt. The baron glanced down at his feet before he stared fiercely into Marcus's eyes. "Do you love my daughter, Fleetwood?"

Marcus gulped, looking away. He fought a tide of self-loathing and hate. He ached with missing her. With wanting her. With loving her. But he did not deserve her.

A sigh came from the door. He turned to meet the older man's strained expression. "I have muddled up."

Marcus was surprised at Lord Strafford's statement.

Danni's father frowned. "I was so immersed in my grief for my wife—God rest her soul—that I neglected my lovely daughter." His voice wavered, almost imploring Marcus to understand. "Danni's season was cut short by my Mary's death. Consumption." He gulped audibly. "I must admit now that her death, in essence, left Danni without both parents."

Marcus nodded. He'd heard some of this story from Danni on the road. A shuddering breath wracked the man in front of him. Marcus could hear the pain of his wife's passing still in his voice, even years later. Marcus could empathize. He did not know what he would do if something happened to Danni. He may never see her again, but knowing she was safe with her family eased some of the ache in his chest.

Seaton continued, his throat thick and voice strained. "For a long time after Mary's death, I could not bring myself to care about anything. The one person who'd made my life feel worth living had been taken from me and I couldn't understand why. I spent hours buried in my work, trying to forget. And Danni…The girl looks so much like Mary. A spitting image. It was so hard…so hard to see Danni's face and not think of my wife."

"Danni should have given you purpose. Not your politics."

"I know that now." He ran a hand down his face. His shoulders slumped. "Today, I finally remembered I had a daughter, and at the same time, I realized how much of life I let pass by while missing my wife. How much joy I failed to see. When I finally *saw* her, I found a grown woman in the place of my little girl. She'd managed to create a new family with her friends. I saw someone who'd successfully survived the loss of both her parents, one from death and one from neglect. And I also saw my little girl in desperate need, crying and begging me for help to save a man who'd dragged her into criminal activity."

Marcus cringed at his condemnation and leaned against the wall, unsettled.

"Tell her to forget me. I am to die for my crimes. She should find someone else to marry and move on with her life."

"Would that it were only that simple."

Marcus grunted in agreement.

The baron continued, "Realizing that I've missed a large piece of my life while consumed with pain, I feel I must offer some advice—do not make the same mistake I did."

Marcus's chains rattled as he swiped his hand through his dirty curls. His heartbeat quickened, his heart suddenly leapt with hope. Would Danni's father offer wisdom if Marcus were to hang in a few days? Could it be possible this man was here to assist him?

Seaton hesitated. "I know you have spent a lot of time with Danni. Unchaperoned."

Marcus fought to keep the heat in his cheeks at bay and averted his eyes. *That* territory was not something he wished to explore with him. *With anyone.*

Her father sighed. "I can't say I'm thrilled to be giving up the match between Hemsworth and Danni, but because Danni professes a sincere love for you, I'm willing to give you a chance to prove your worth."

Marcus stiffened, budding hope and anxiety warring within him. Marcus shook his head, confused. Shouldn't he be telling him to stay away from his daughter? Shouldn't he be saying she deserves better? And how could he prove his worth against the Earl of Hemsworth? The bloody angel of the ton *versus* him? The absurdity of such a comparison made him snort.

The man chuckled. "It does seem like you have little chance, my boy, but Danni chose you, so there *must* be something in you I can like."

Marcus kept his face straight at the insult and name. He wasn't anyone's boy.

Seaton glanced down at Marcus's wrists and grimaced at the irons around them. "Remind me to put forth a bill for better prison conditions."

Marcus shifted his weight, still unsure exactly what was going on. "Why did you come here, exactly?"

The baron seemed genuinely surprised. "Thought you'd have worked that out by now. This little chat is the price you had to pay for all the trouble I went through to secure your release."

Marcus froze. He could not have heard that right. "I beg your pardon?"

"I said you are free. Never thought to see it in all my days, Fleetwood."

His brow knit in confusion. *He was free?* The admiral wanted him dead.

The man continued, disbelief smoothing his features. "There I was in the admiral's home, practically begging on my knees for your freedom. It is the only thing Danni has ever requested of me, and I was fairly certain I wasn't going to succeed. But then all seven of his daughters filed into the room, led by Ginny." He paused, flashing Marcus a wry smile. "My friend is a national hero. He has bravely faced down some of our most vicious enemies on the high seas, but he could not withstand the will of those girls." He snorted and smiled. "Amazing. No one in Parliament would ever believe me."

"Ginny and her sisters *helped* me?"

Seaton visibly relaxed and broke into a grin. "It was rather glorious. If Ginny was a man, she'd be our next prime minister. She told her father, in no uncertain terms, that you were to be released. Ginny claimed it was all a grand adventure and to seek punishment would only create unnecessary pain and damage to all involved."

Marcus was sure he was hearing incorrectly. The isolation of this cell had clearly affected his mind. "My friend did not want to let you go, but when faced with all seven of his children united in their determination, it appears he is unable to say no."

"Incredible," Marcus murmured, stunned. Never in his wildest dreams would he have imagined the girl he'd kidnapped would come to his rescue.

She really was a ninny.

"I am truly free?"

Seaton nodded, tossing something in the air. Marcus caught it, the chill of metal in his hands. He opened his fist to see the iron key resting on his palm.

"Thank you," he breathed, relief mixed with incredulity clogging his throat.

The man frowned. "I'm only the messenger."

He made to leave, but paused, glancing back. "I don't like you, not one bit, but for Danielle, I'm willing to give you a chance."

With that the man exited the room, leaving Marcus clutching at the key to his chains, dumbstruck.

Chapter Twenty-Four

❦

BEAUTY delighted gave her hand,
And bade the PRINCE her fate command;
The PRINCE now led through rooms of state,
Where BEAUTY's family await,

—"Beauty and the Beast" by Charles Lamb

One week later...

The door opened, quickly followed by the slide of the curtains and light streaming into the darkened room.

Danni winced.

"I've had enough of this, Danielle Mary Strafford."

She groaned, rolling in her bed away from the sunlight. "Go away."

"You have been lying in bed, sulking, since you've returned from your little trip. I'm fed up with it. Even a sick Hu is not this bad."

Danni picked up her pillow and placed it over her head, trying to drown out the sound of Annabel's ranting. Ever since she'd returned from her kidnapping escapade, the woman and her father hadn't let her out of their sight. Her father had even hired a maid to trail after her wherever she went and she was forbidden to enter a carriage ever again unless accompanied by him, Annabel, or Hu. After so many years of doing as she pleased, it was incredibly frustrating.

Her father had even sold her business. Well, not sold per se. He'd given the bookshop to Annabel and Hu as a belated wedding gift, explicitly barring Danni from the backroom and any dealings with Gretna Green Bookings.

Her eyes narrowed in the dark. As soon as she could find the motivation to leave her room, she'd develop a plan to get it back. Annabel and Hu wouldn't mind. They knew how much the business meant to her. Especially now that she had nothing else.

Her balled fist flew to her mouth to hold in the sob. She was miserable. Once he was free, she'd hoped he'd come to her. Hoped he'd call so she would have a chance to speak with him again, reassure him he was exactly what she wanted in a man. In a husband.

When he didn't come, she'd hoped for a letter. Something acknowledging the gift she, her father, and Ginny had sent him and Caro, and whether he had accepted it or not. The moment her solicitor's office had opened, she and her father had gone to her man of affairs. Against his frantic council, she'd drafted a bank note for a majority of the fortune from her mother's estate and sent it to

Marcus's town house. She knew it wouldn't make up for deceiving him, but she hoped it would help to save Caro, thereby easing his mind.

But nothing arrived. Not him, nor a letter, nor anyone associated with him.

She'd checked every day, and even the money had not yet been transferred. It was as if he had just vanished.

"Stupid man," she growled into her pillow.

Danni sighed. She just missed him. Ached to be near him, to be held by him.

"Ow!" Danni sat up on her bed, clutching her stinging arm. The smack of Annabel's newspaper still echoed through the room.

She glared at her longtime friend as Annabel straightened, placing the rolled-up newspaper beneath her arm.

"You are a vicious snipe!"

"Now that you're up," Annabel replied, smirking, red hair still wild and brown eyes bright, "I have news."

A determined smile washed away her humor. Danni had a feeling she wasn't going to like what she had to say. "We are attending the Hornweatherby Ball tonight."

She was right.

Slumping back on her bed, Danni repositioned her pillow. "Go home, Annabel. I don't want anything to do with anyone."

A huff, followed by stomping feet approaching the head of her bed. Annabel yanked the pillow from Danni's grasp and threw it across the room. It smacked against the wall with a satisfying thump.

Danni gaped at the redhead, speechless.

"I am not going to allow you to spend the rest of your life wallowing in misery."

Danni scowled. "Seems to be a family trait. Now go away."

"Nope," Annabel announced, her voice so bright it grated on Danni's ears. "I am going to get you dressed and out of this house, even if it kills me."

Unbidden, Danni's eyes watered. "I don't want to leave. What if he comes while I'm out? I'll miss him."

Annabel's face softened with sympathy. Heedless of her pristine, baby blue morning dress, she climbed into bed next to her. A comforting arm snaked over her shoulders. Danni fought the urge to give in to her tears for the hundredth time. It was utterly ridiculous how much she'd cried over the last few days when she hadn't shed a tear in years. Perhaps she was making up for lost time.

"I know how terribly heartbroken you are, Danni. You feel like nothing is ever going to be right again, that you'll end up without the man of your dreams and be alone for the rest of your life."

Danni nodded, swatting at stray tears. Annabel did understand, except the love of *her* life had married her.

Drawing her knees to her chest, she rested her chin on them. "Hu wanted to marry you. Marcus doesn't want me."

"Oh, Danni." Annabel sighed.

"I just want what you and Hu have, what my parents had. You glow every time you look at each other. A perfect love."

Humor pinched Annabel's lips to a thin line. "Glow? Perfect? What world are you living in?"

Danni glared at her friend. "I'm talking about the perfect marriage. You love each other so much and you're always so happy."

Her redheaded friend snorted. "Are you forgetting all the times Hu and I fight? The man drives me insane. And I'm almost certain the same happened with your parents. You probably just don't remember. Your head has always been in the clouds when it came to love, Danni."

"Excuse me?"

"Love and marriage are work. Hu and I were very fortunate to have married for love, but it's not easy. He's stubborn and constantly wants to do things his way when I want to do them my way. He hates the city and I love it. He loves books and I've never willingly opened one in my life."

Danni was stunned. "But you're both so happy."

"Of course. Happiness is not a magical state that comes hand in hand with love and never ends. We have rules. We never go to sleep angry with each other and we always start the day with a reminder of how much we love each other." She paused, her face becoming serious. "I've heard a lot about Fleetwood from you and your father. While I think I'd like him, I also think he'll never be completely free from the horrors he's lived through. With time and the right support, he can probably live with them, perhaps they will even fade, but it will be the commitment of love that will see him through. Hard work and commitment to each other makes a marriage last, Danni. Love makes it stronger. Happiness is only a result of the joy you have of building a life together."

Danni stared blankly at her friend, her mind in a whirl. She'd never thought of marriage from that angle before. She knew she loved Marcus and wanted to make it work, but she'd had some reservations. Hearing Annabel's thoughts erased the final doubts she might have had.

Shaking her head with a rueful smile, she nudged her friend with her shoulder. "How did you get so wise?"

Annabel laughed, sliding off the bed. "I actually picked up one of those books Hu's been pestering me to read."

Her friend moved to the bell pull near her armoire.

"Do I really have to go to this ball?" Danni whined.

"Yes. Your father even managed to convince me to go to the ball with you. That only proves how much you need to get out."

Danni winced. Her father's negotiating skills were second to none. Since her elopement, Annabel was adamant in her avoidance of society where matrons openly shunned her for marrying beneath her station.

Tugging the rope to call for a dressing maid, her friend began to rummage about in her closet. "I have nothing suitable anymore. Let me borrow something?"

Danni shrugged, plucking at her sheets, still searching for an excuse to beg off.

"Oh, Danni, I've never seen this before."

Danni knew exactly which dress Annabel was about to pull from the rack. She was off her bed in a blink, carefully removing the pink muslin dress from her friend's grasp.

Instantly, tears pricked her eyes. "Marcus gave me this."

"Really?" Annabel blinked in surprise. "I've never known a man to go dress shopping for a woman."

A soft smile slipped across her lips as she traced one scarlet, embroidered rose. "I complained how uncomfortable I felt without proper clothes. I only needed a large shawl, or a cloak to cover me. He went out early the next day and bought this. Isn't it wonderfully sweet?"

Annabel sighed, eyes wispy. "If only Hu were that romantic. The most I've gotten was a ribbon I begged just
ages for."

Danni laughed, tracing the delicate white lace under
the bust and bordering the neckline. She remembered
how embarrassed he was at her profuse gratitude. She
gulped, her eyes stinging. She missed him. So much.

"You should wear it tonight."

"What?" Danni asked, startled. "I couldn't. It reminds
me so much of him."

Annabel pushed the dress towards her with a secret
smile. "Wear it. It may bring you luck."

Staring at the dress, Danni slowly nodded. Maybe she
would feel closer to him.

Suddenly, the door opened and her maid hustled in.
Soon, a flurry of cloth and happy chatter erupted in
Danni's room. Perhaps tonight wouldn't be so horrible.

* * *

"Did you hear about the dairy heiress?"

"Yes!" exclaimed a woman waving an ornate fan. "She
ran off with a Frenchman from Hamburg."

"I heard she was carrying his child!"

Danni rolled her eyes. Hamburg was in Germany, not
France.

She had forgotten how much she truly hated society. It
had seemed such a grand time a few years ago, attending
balls and flirting with eligible bachelors. But she now saw
it all as so silly and frivolous.

She shot a lethal look in her father's direction across
the ballroom. He was standing with a group of his friends

from Parliament, pretending he wasn't watching her like a hawk. Gritting her teeth, Danni counted to ten. She'd been doing it quite often lately. Either when she was angry or when she thought about *him*.

She blinked rapidly as Annabel tugged at her arm. She was more than thankful her friend was accompanying her tonight. Her company made the ball tolerable. Danni could not have faced this alone. Already she'd had to avoid several offers to dance and escape to a secluded corner to avoid suitors.

"Helloooo? Is anyone in there?"

Danni blinked, pulling back from the hand being waved in her face. "What?"

"Finally! I've been calling your name for an age." Annabel's face was the picture of annoyance.

She arched her brow. "Most assuredly not true."

"Well, I have. And now that I have your attention, look over there."

Danni scanned the heads, trying to see through the various turbans and plumes. "What am I looking for?"

"Damn." Annabel cursed with unladylike fierceness. They ignored the outraged gasp from a group of fluttering matrons behind them. Serves them right for eavesdropping. "I can't see him anymore. Where'd he go?"

"See who?"

Annabel simply smiled. Danni would not have minded her friend's secretiveness if it were not for the devilish glint in her brown eyes. Annabel caught her hand and dragged her around the edge of the room. They ignored dancers and throngs of debutantes, weaving through tiny spaces that opened in the crush.

Annabel stopped short behind a potted palm positioned at the doors leading onto a balcony. If Danni hadn't been paying attention, she would have crashed into her and sent the palm rolling to the floor. Her friend's arm pushed her back into the shadows of the foliage. Danni frowned as Annabel leaned forward, her head cocked to the side.

"What are we doing?"

"Shh!" Her friend waved her to silence.

Sighing, she lowered her voice to a whisper. "What the devil are you doing?"

"Spying."

Danni opened her mouth to respond, but thought better of it. Clamping it shut, she leaned forward to listen through the leaves as well.

An unfamiliar female voice reached them. "I thought you'd sworn never to attend a ball again after what that Newport girl did to you. Did your time behind bars change your outlook?"

"Cease the prattle, Caroline."

Danni stiffened. He was not supposed to be here. He hated attending these events. Suddenly, her friend's insistence and her father's manipulations made sense. They'd planned for their paths to cross. Her stomach flipped into an angry knot. He had not contacted her in days, even after she had pleaded for his release from jail and donated her fortune to aiding his sister. He could not call on her at home, yet he could attend a ball? Fury shot through her.

But she also needed to see him like she needed air to breathe.

"I thought it was him. He would be hard put to blend in with a crowd," Annabel whispered, her face dancing with mischievous glee.

Danni's heart sank. Oh no.

Before Danni could escape, Annabel grabbed her arm and pushed her onto the balcony.

She froze as Marcus and his companion swirled in her direction. She fought the urge to blush. "H-hello, Marcus."

He looked well, although faint purple bruises shadowed his jaw. He seemed to have recovered from most of his injuries. Her eyes skimmed over him, following the exceptional cut of his hunter green jacket and the fit of his silver striped waistcoat. Her gaze dipped to his trousers, heating briefly before she looked at his face. She felt the familiar tug of pride as she looked at him. His strength amazed her.

He stood tall, his shoulders back. His demeanor oozed his scorn of being in this place. To anyone else, he appeared arrogant, aggressive, and frightening. But she could see through his armor now, and knew only sheer will and determination kept him there. To anyone else, he appeared hard and cruel, his eyes shuttered, but she could see the uncertainty in his posture. To anyone else, he appeared a hideous beast, his scars making him difficult to look upon, but she knew the scars were integral parts of his being. To her, he was the most handsome man she'd ever seen. And she'd missed him so very much.

He gave her the same perusal. His eyes widened. Self-consciously, she fiddled with her lace gloves, feeling his gaze touch about the lace and embroidered roses of the pink dress and linger on her most intimate places. She hoped his heart beat harder, as was hers. She hoped his breath caught in his throat, just like hers. But most of all, she hoped he'd missed her, too.

Marcus cleared his throat, tilting his face to hide his

scar as he always did when he was uncomfortable. "You look...," his hands clenched by his sides and his bright gaze snapped to hers. "You look lovely, Miss Strafford."

Her stomach fluttered. She disliked his formal tone, but at least he'd spoken to her.

"Thank you. You look rather dashing yourself."

Green eyes widened before he turned his head again. She could see his bravado. Suddenly her anger was gone. She knew why he had not come to her. A soft smile tugged at her lips. Such a silly man.

A throat delicately cleared. Danni shifted her gaze from Marcus to his companion, who was clearly his sister, Caroline. They looked so alike. A tall, willowy frame clad in a fashionable pale peach gown. Elegantly coiffed white-blond hair framed her face, a long braided strand escaping over her shoulder and down her body. Danni had never seen such long hair.

Caroline's pale green gaze flitted between them. Her brow knit with confusion. "Marcus, please make introductions."

He shifted restlessly. Looking everywhere but at her, he mumbled, "Lady Caroline Bradley, may I present Miss Danielle Strafford, daughter of the Baron of Seaton."

Danni dipped her head in a curtsy. "It's a pleasure to meet you."

"Likewise. How do you know my thick-headed brother?"

Danni briefly met Marcus's gaze, uncertain about how much he had shared.

She decided to keep it simple. "We recently met during a trip to the countryside."

"Oh." Caroline sounded perplexed for a moment, before her head snapped rapidly between them. "Oh! You're from the Gretna Green place."

"Yes, oh," Marcus grumbled, resuming his study of the balcony.

Danni stared intently at Marcus, willing him to look at her. She tamped down her frustration at his evasion.

"I'd best be going," Caroline suddenly announced.

Danni nodded, refusing to shift her gaze. If Marcus could stare at a balcony all evening, she could do the same to him. Her eyes would remain glued to his face.

Several heartbeats passed before Marcus sighed.

Danni crossed her arms. "Why haven't you contacted me, Marcus? I've been waiting all week. If my father had not told me you were released, I'd still be panicking, trying to find a way to free you."

He stiffened, his expression hardening. But did she see a flash of sadness there?

"I really can't say."

She ground her teeth. Could he still be upset about her deception? He must understand why she'd done that. "Fine," she snapped, her anger returning in a rush. "Did you receive my gift?"

He scoffed. "Are you referring to that promissory note you forwarded to me?"

"So you did receive it! The funds have not been transferred. Why haven't you used it?"

His profile darkened dangerously and immediately she knew his pride was wounded. She'd feared that might result when she'd sent it, but she had also believed he had to understand she intended only to help him, and Caro. "It was the only solution I could think of after... after that night at the Jacket Inn."

His fists curled, whitening his knuckles. "Do you really think I'd take your handouts? Especially of that size. What did you do, empty your coffers?"

"Only on my mother's side."

Green eyes widened in the shadows. His head turned slightly towards her in surprise, but he quickly looked away again. She was beginning to lose her temper with this foolishness.

"You are truly worth that much?"

She shrugged. "Actually, much, much more."

"That's obscene."

"I agree." She bit her lip, pleading for the courage to say what she needed to. To convince him to accept her help, even if he never wanted to see her again after that. "Is there any way you would keep it? For Caro? As a loan, perhaps?"

He held still for a moment, his face set in stone.

She plunged ahead, hoping he'd listen. "If you can't accept the money from me, then think of it as a loan from my father. We will draw up the legal documents with terms of repayment. It's for Caro, not for you. Would that be acceptable to you?"

His head turned further away, until all she could see were the shells of his ears and the nape of his neck. Why wouldn't he look at her? Dismay clenched her heart. Perhaps she was wrong. Perhaps he truly never wanted to see her again.

"You told me you didn't want to drag Caroline's name through the mud and make your tenants suffer the consequences of the broken engagement," she reasoned. Drawing in a shaky breath, striving to keep her voice even, she continued, pain shooting through her chest.

"Finding a woman to marry with enough money who would agree to a match will take you time—time you're not sure you have. Caroline's blasted fiancé could come back any day now."

Looking down at her feet, she hid welling tears. She hated the thought of him with another woman. She could not bear the thought of him laughing, or touching, or loving another. However, she wanted to see him happy. If giving him a loan and never speaking to him again meant he could have a chance to find another woman to love, she'd do it. But her heart would break.

"Just... please take it. In whatever form you wish."

"You seem rather eager to marry me off," he whispered. "Are you anxious to be rid of me?"

Danni snorted, swatting impatiently at the light rivulets brushing her cheeks. "Of course not. I just want you to be happy."

His eyes flickered. It was the only change in his rigid posture.

Taking a deep breath, she decided to take a chance. "I—I'm not engaged."

"I know. Your father told me when I was freed."

Danni felt her heart break, as any last bit of hope she had for them vanished. She ached to be as they were once, with laughter and easy smiles. With passion and love between them. She wished she could convince him they could have that again.

"Damn it, Marcus! Why won't you look at me?"

The air filled with heavy uncertainty. Finally, unable to bear his answer, she dropped her gaze to her slippered feet.

Suddenly, warmth washed over her, a ragged breath

fanned from the top of her hair and down along her neck. Startled, she snapped her head up to find Marcus not only looking at her, but towering close, very close, over her. She tilted her head back, refusing to back down. His face was shuttered, but his eyes were scorched with need and pain.

"Because, if I look at how lovely you are in that dress, I will not be able to say what I need to."

Danni found herself unable to breathe. As if unconsciously, he lifted his hand towards her cheek. Her heart skipped. But his arm dropped before he touched her. She bit back a disappointed cry.

"I don't deserve you, Danni. Your father wants me to prove I'm worthy of you, but I'm not. We both know that. And he knows that. You are like the sun and I am a new moon, not even worthy of your light's reflection. You deserve a man like Hemsworth. He doesn't have a past. He is not haunted. He is a good man and can give you the marriage and children you want. He can help your father politically."

He drew a shuddering breath, his eyes softening for the first time. His gaze swept over her, bringing heat to her cheeks. Danni opened her mouth to speak, but he wouldn't allow her to. "I'm happy to see you one more time. Happy you wore my gift." He smiled softly, sadly, revealing his dimple. "I love you, little one, but I can not be with you."

He turned away then, hurrying into the crush. He merged with the gaiety and laughter, attempting to lose himself among the partners dancing across the middle of the black-and-white-checkered tiles. Periodically, bodies would part, giving her a glimpse of his rigid back.

Standing at the threshold of the ballroom, she met two pairs of eyes peeking, shocked, through a plum tree. One set brown, belonging to Annabel, the other a light green. Caroline and Annabel had spied on them. Of course they would.

She looked back at the love of her life, fast disappearing from her forever. He was halfway across the ballroom before she fully understood what he had said.

And she lost her temper. She clenched her fists at her sides as white-hot anger seared her lungs. Oh, how she wanted to pull a Ginny and kick him. Instead, she settled for yelling.

"You bleedin' idiot!"

Heads snapped in her direction. Widened eyes fixed on her flushed face. Soft music screeched to a halt and dancers fell still. Marcus froze mid-step, his head whipping around to face her, his eyes open in obvious shock.

She ignored the titters of excitement as she stalked towards him, the crowd parting like the Red Sea. At the sight of her approach, Marcus's gaze widened and he stepped back. Danni stopped toe to toe, refusing to give him a chance to speak. "Must you *always* try my patience? Honestly, sometimes I can not fathom the thoughts in that head of yours."

His mouth parted, but no words emerged. His gaze flitted nervously about them. She knew the *ton* was riveted by the potential scandal and impending gossip. She didn't care. Because she had something to say.

She caught his hand in hers.

He jerked in surprise.

"I built up my parents' marriage into a standard for all love. I thought no one could be in love unless they were happy all the time. I believed that love and marriage were a fairy tale, glossing over the hard work of marriage. I convinced myself the only real marriage was one where the couple was always glowing with love and everything was perfect.

"Now I can see I did that to hide from the pain of losing my mother and father. Now I understand that loving someone does not mean I will never be angry or frustrated with him. Marriage can be just as beautiful with a flawed couple, working together, choosing to build a life together."

His eyes were riveted to her, vulnerability coloring them dark. He still did not speak. She took a deep breath and continued with her monologue. "Your demons are terrible things to bear. You've been marked more deeply than I could possibly imagine. When I first met you, I thought you were horrid. You manipulated and insulted me. And then I learned about you, and your past, and all the kindness and love you have firmly encaged in your heart. I admit, your troubles scared me. I was convinced you could never give me what I wanted. I could never have a perfect marriage with you. But I was looking at fairy tales all wrong."

His face clouded with confusion and he visibly gulped. His voice was soft when he spoke, his eyes glancing uneasily around them again. "I don't understand."

Squeezing his hand in hers, she smiled up at him. "You are not perfect, Marcus Bradley, but neither am I. You are rash, stubborn, overbearing, and refuse to see the good in yourself."

He snorted, filled with disbelief. "What good, Danielle?"

She brushed her lips across his knuckles. Audible gasps echoed around them, followed by a rustle of skirts as women quickly escorted young misses from the room.

Danni didn't care. She wanted the world to realize just how wonderful this man was. "You may think you don't deserve me, but every day, I wonder what I can do to deserve *you*—a man so kind, so fiercely loyal, and with so great a capacity for love."

Marcus remained speechless, frozen in place.

Amusement twitched her lips, and she paused, memorizing his handsome features, scars and all. "We may not be perfect, but our love is perfect for me. I love you, Marcus. If I could be so lucky as to have you by my side for the rest of my life, I would be the happiest woman in the world. I want us to write our own fairy tale, Marcus."

And then she kissed him. She kissed him with all the love in her heart and soul. With all her desire and with her fervent dream for a forever together.

He did not respond. His body was stiff and unyielding, and she felt a trickle of fear. Would he refuse? Would he decide she wasn't worth the trouble?

But then, his arms closed around her, pulling her close and deepening the kiss shamelessly. Danni sighed happily when they finally broke free. A huge smile split his face.

"I love you, Danni."

"I love you too, my beast."

Marcus's hands stroked her flaming cheeks. "You certainly know how to make a man listen, little one." His gaze flickered about them, his green gaze dancing with laughter. "Rather spectacularly so."

She scanned their audience, noting several collapsed

women being revived with bottles of smelling salts by their companions. Danni felt herself flush. "I do, don't I?"

"I have one question..."

"Anything."

"Was that a proposal?"

She shrugged. "If you'd like it to be. I'm improvising here."

He groaned with mock horror. "It will be a miracle if we reach the altar. Your last stint at improvising nearly killed me."

"As I seem to recall, that fiasco was all your fault."

"Mine?" He whispered furiously, "You're the one who runs a business for that sort of thing."

"Not for much longer. My father demands that I shut it down."

A discreet cough interrupted. The two turned simultaneously to find the baron, lips turned in a disapproving glare. Her heart halted for a moment, afraid he'd cause a scene objecting to her choice of husband. Then she noticed the glow of happiness lurking in his eyes. Her eyes burned. For the first time since her mother died, her father looked himself again.

"Seems as if I raised quite the eccentric young woman," he declared to the ballroom.

Marcus chuckled softly as Danni shot her father a murderous look. *So much for our sentimental moment.*

The baron took a small sip from his champagne glass. The movement was oddly proper, as if he was trying to erase the scandal her scene had no doubt caused.

She could only nod politely, hyperaware of all the eyes on them.

His gaze shifted from her to Marcus, assessing him

from head to foot. After a moment, his gaze returned to her. "Are you absolutely certain about this, Danielle?"

"Yes," she said without hesitation.

The Baron of Seaton sighed and muttered softly, "Best make the most of this, then."

Turning towards the scandalized crowd, he lifted his glass again. "It would seem I have an announcement. Three cheers to my daughter, the Honorable Miss Danielle Strafford, recently engaged to Marcus Bradley, Marquis of Fleetwood."

The room remained silent as he took a rather large sip.

Shock stiffened the faces of the *ton*, freezing them into complete silence. A small smile slipped across his features.

"I think I could get used to having a beast for a son-in-law."

Epilogue

༄

$\mathcal{M}$erriment from the wedding reception trickled in through the entrance to the study, but Caroline Bradley paid it no heed. She didn't hear anything other than the steady, growing thrum of her heart as icy hot anger surged through her veins.

"Why didn't you tell me about this before now?" she seethed, trying to keep her voice low so the guests only feet away wouldn't hear. She uneasily adjusted her elbow-length gloves in an effort to control her reaction to the news. "I knew you were hiding something when you explained how you ended up in jail, but this...!"

The scarred, blond giant seated behind the behemoth desk that had once belonged to their father seemed to flounder. "I wanted to protect you, Caro."

The woman massaged her temples. The weight of her long locks of golden hair, artfully piled atop her head, was starting to give her a headache. Why did everyone always think she needed protection? Her father had been a complete and utter ass—not that she'd *ever* say such a thing aloud—and, yes, he'd done things no father should even *contemplate*, but that didn't make her some wilting flower. In fact, she thought, pulling on her glove again, her childhood had only made her stronger, not weaker.

And, by God, she lived with the St. Leons! That loving but eccentric family had more drama than any group of people she had ever met. If she could remain in the collective presence of those five siblings for more than ten minutes without losing her sanity, she could certainly manage unexpected and unpleasant family complications of her own.

Learning about an unknown fiancé was certainly not going to break her. She would not allow it. The very idea she'd collapse into a sniveling heap on the Persian rug was highly offensive. Stiffening her spine, she cleared her face of all expression and gathered her thoughts.

No, Lady Caroline Bradley would not crumple.

Caroline Bradley was going to *do* something about it.

"Marcus"—she sighed, feeling the weight of the world on her shoulders—"I appreciate everything you've done for me so far—it's more than I could ever hope to repay in this lifetime—however, I'm a grown woman. I am perfectly capable of handling something like this."

Her brother sighed. "You've been through so much. I can't—"

"And you haven't?" she snapped.

"Caroline…"

Taking another deep breath to calm herself, erecting that perfect poise she'd become famous for over the years, she gestured to the door where voices trickled in. "Your happiness is waiting for you on the other side of that door. You've done more than enough for me by se-curing the necessary funds to break the betrothal contract. As I understand from what you've just told me, all that is left to end this unpleasant affair is to obtain the duke's agreement and signature. Is that correct?"

"Yes. Hopefully, it will be a simple matter."

"Well, then, I am asking you to allow me to handle it."

"But—"

Caro held up a gloved hand. "No. Your bride is waiting for you, Marcus. I refuse to let you delay your wedding trip to search out the duke. The man hasn't been around for years! I highly doubt he'll reappear within the next five minutes."

Jade eyes hardened a fraction, assessing, measuring. Caro steeled herself, straightening her shoulders and bracing her feet. He was obviously doubtful she could handle this, and she was determined to prove she could.

Even if she didn't have the slightest idea how to go about it. Solicitors would be useless. The blasted man had disappeared shortly after murdering his father.

She swallowed and adjusted her gloves for courage.

The silent tension in the room was suddenly broken with a grunt. Marcus's gaze softened and he leaned back in his chair. "If you insist..."

"I do. Very much so."

A small grin slipped across his features, lessening his scars and making him seem much younger. "All right. I'll leave Harwood's signature to you. Frankly, it is very un-likely that anything will happen while Danni and I are out of touch, and if anything *does*, Llywelyn will handle it until I return."

She sighed silently with frustration. Apparently, her

friend's eldest brother had been chosen to oversee her activities in Marcus's absence. Honestly, how could her brother agree to let her obtain the required signature in one sentence, and in the next, appoint another man to "handle it" for her. Once again, Marcus had assigned her a protector. She bit her lip to control her unladylike response.

Pushing that aside, she decided to seize the opportunity presented—a chance to prove to her brother she didn't need protection anymore. And once the Duke of Harwood signed the infernal papers and the money breaking her betrothal exchanged hands, she would finally be...

Free.

"Thank you, Marcus." She straightened her posture again and settled a complacent smile across her features. This was, after all, a very happy day. Marcus had finally found someone to love him and share the rest of his life with him. After the horrors their father had inflicted on their lives, Marcus deserved every second of happiness he could muster.

"Shall we rejoin the reception?"

The tall man grimaced. "No matter what Danni says, public appearances and parties never get easier."

Caro scoffed. "I don't believe you. I think someone is using that as an excuse to stick improperly close to his bride."

A devilish glint entered his eyes as he stood from the desk. "Possibly."

Fighting the unladylike urge to roll her eyes, she followed the blond giant from the room.

It was times like these, when she stood next to her

brother, that she was thankful for her height. She hated when someone looked down upon her, probably stemming from her father's favorite form of intimidation. That she could look most men in the eye was a great comfort. It made her feel an equal, as if she had control over their encounters, and to a point, she did. She easily intimidated most men, which was why she was going to die an old maid.

Very happily.

The pair stood in the large threshold, observing the crowd who'd come from the morning ceremony to the Fleetwoods' townhouse for a wedding breakfast. Marcus and Danni had tried to keep the event small, knowing full well how many gawkers were anxious to witness the Beast's marriage. Only their closest friends and, because of the bride's father's political position, the most important government officials, were invited to attend. But the dining room was filled with well-wishers.

"I see the earl has arrived." Caroline spotted the Earl of Hemsworth, Danielle's recently jilted suitor.

"Would that he hadn't," grumbled Marcus, a hint of jealousy in his tone.

Caro hid a smile as she commented, "He seems content with how events were resolved."

Marcus grunted, lifting his chin towards the small group of women surrounding the politically motivated man. "I bet he is. Seems women enjoy soothing his wounded heart in flocks."

She bit back a laugh at the caustic tone. Caro had to agree. She could not particularly understand the attraction of the Ton's Angel. He was rumored to be a kind and considerate man, but he seemed immensely boring.

"And how were some of the Foley-Foster sisters tempted to attend?" she asked as she shifted her gaze to the other side of the room. Four giggly, redheaded girls had their heads bowed, deep in conversation. Caro's heart softened at the sight of the third eldest, Miss Ginny "the Ninny" Foley-Foster. The girl had made certain Marcus was extricated from the legal repercussions of his actions, even though she had no real reasons for doing so. Without her forgiveness and understanding, Caro's idiot brother would still be in jail.

"According to Danni, Ginny threatened to marry the next person who offered and never come home again if the admiral didn't let them attend."

"Oh." She laughed. "Is she as naive as they say?"

"Thick as a brick, but I will never be able to repay her kindness."

The youngest of the family group, a girl of perhaps four years, suddenly turned, as if feeling their eyes on her. Her arms crossed angrily, and she stared unwavering at Marcus with what one could describe only as a "death" glare.

Marcus turned to view the wallpaper behind him, avoiding the child, and whispered in her ear, "But her sister there. I swear she will grow to be a murderess."

Caroline smothered a highly inappropriate, surprised snort of laughter.

"Marcus, that's terrible!"

He gave a one-shouldered shrug, his eyes resting onto his new bride in the center of the room. Following his gaze, a smile crept onto Caro's face. Danni, her new sister-in-law, was bidding farewell to the guests. She practically glowed in her pale pink dress decorated with embroidered red roses. Fresh, red roses were artfully placed in her dark hair. By her side stood the Baron of Seaton, her father.

"Danielle looks lovely," Caro murmured over the heads of the crowd.

"True," he whispered, before suddenly smirking. "And she's carrying my child."

Caroline stiffened, wide eyes snapping to her brother's scarred face. Amusement danced over his features.

"My lord, it's time to depart," Weller interrupted, suddenly appearing beside Marcus and flashing her a warm smile. Caroline could hardly acknowledge him, her mind so awhirl with this latest bit of information.

Marcus turned to her. "We'll be home in a week. Weller has our direction if needed." And with that, Marcus weaved through the crowd to settle by Danni's side, the valet at his heels.

"Did your brother just—"

At the words, Caro shifted her stunned gaze to the equally shocked expression on the face of her best friend, Althea St. Leon. Of course the woman would have overheard. She had a knack for being in the right place, at just the right time, to hear all the juicy tidbits the *ton* had to offer.

"I believe so," she finally replied, unable to keep her pale green gaze from Danni's middle. Her brother would soon be a father... and she was going to be an aunt!

"Oh, my," Thea murmured, flicking open her painted fan to send a cool breeze across her face.

"Agreed."

"Well," the blonde drawled, adopting a knowing expression. "I knew this was going to happen."

Caro bit back a snort. "And how exactly did you know?"

"Sixth sense. All St. Leons have it."

Caro gave in to the urge to roll her eyes this time. It was the only suitable response one could give when dealing with her friend's outlandish statements. If she didn't, she'd end up throwing a fit trying to reason with her.

"Your brother is looking remarkably well. I am so very thrilled for them both." Thea fluttered her fan, watching said man sweep his new wife out the door.

Caroline nodded at her friend. "Yes. And our relationship has been much better as of late as well. I can only thank Danielle for that."

"Does that mean you'll be moving back here?" The panic in her friend's voice was unmistakable.

Warmth spread through her chest, turning her proper half smile into a genuine one. She had lived with the St. Leons since she and Thea became fast friends while away at school. She was thankful to them for allowing her shelter during breaks to avoid returning to her father. She loved them all as if they were her own blood. And it felt wonderful to know they didn't want her to leave. "Of course not. Llywelyn Castle is my home."

Relief permeated Althea's posture—shoulders slumped forward, rapid fanning slowed. Happiness burst across her face. "Good. We wouldn't have it any other way."

Silence lapsed between them, before she suddenly sighed. "With this wedding complete, London will be such a bore. I long for a grand adventure."

Caro ignored her. The statement was nothing new. Her devilish friend was always concocting escapades for entertainment at the expense of the social elite. Trouble was, they often had a habit of going awry. It was why Caro was hesitant to tell Thea of her conversation with her brother yet. She would probably launch a plot so daring Caroline's carefully constructed and protected reputation would be in tatters within hours.

A sudden murmur in the crowd drew her gaze. Heads pivoted towards the dining room door in unison.

"What is causing such a stir?"

Thea tried to peer over the heads of the guests without appearing to do just that. Her perfectly coiffed honey locks bounced as she hopped from foot to foot. Caroline's own interest stirred as the face of the matron next to her turned dangerously pale, paler than the finest ivory.

Gnawing at her bottom lip, she mimicked Thea, straining on her tiptoes. She caught a glimpse of dark hair moving purposely through the guests, people gasping and parting to form a path, quickly side-stepping to distance themselves from the approaching figure.

"Someone's arrived rather late." It was clear they were not going to discover what was agitating the crowd. They would have to wait for the gossip to reach them. She tugged Thea to the proper standing position. "Be patient. We will find out eventually."

The blonde sniffed in annoyed agreement before turning on her heel and dragging Caro towards the refreshment table set up along the long wall of windows. Stopping at the punch bowl, Thea handed her a precious crystal glass and chose one for herself.

She grinned. "I cannot imagine what can be of such interest. The most exciting thing to happen in years was Sir Arthur's wig falling in the punch bowl at Lady Fairchild's ball."

"I seem to remember your oh-so-convenient stumble that caused the displacement of said hairpiece."

Thea cast her a dangerous look. "Said stumble would not have occurred if a certain close friend of mine had not dared me to see if said hairpiece was attached."

Caro laughed. "Safe to say it was not."

Suddenly, a shadow fell across the tabletop. Thea's grin transformed into a mask of surprised fear. Caro blinked at the sudden change.

"Lady Caroline Bradley?"

Caroline turned to face the source of Thea's shock, freezing at the dark voice. A little thrill of dread ran up her spine. Standing before her was Lucifer himself. Swathed entirely from head to toe in black, he towered over the room, his height close to that of her brother's. Where her brother was broad about the chest, this man was lean, his fit body suggesting a catlike agility. Dragging her gaze up from his heavily bearded chin, she met his tilted steel gray eyes. Shivers of something new filled her as he bowed his inky head. Her breath caught in her throat.

"So *you* are my fiancée."

Caroline couldn't help it.

She fainted.

Lady Caroline Bradley is horrified when she discovers she's been secretly betrothed to a duke suspected of murder. But the duke, Lord Roderick FitzHugh, has plans of his own and may give Caroline the happy ending she's always wanted...

Please see the next page
for a preview of

Once Upon a Duke

Chapter One

❧

Roderick FitzHugh, the Duke of Harwood, was not insane. Therefore, someone trying to legally declare him so left a bitter taste in his mouth. These next few moments would determine whether his title could be saved.

Giles was such an arse. He was doing this just because he could.

He sighed, irritated, as he hovered in the doorway of the Marquis of Fleetwood's townhouse. He knew he was about to cause an uproar by crashing the man's wedding reception, but frankly, he didn't care. Roderick had seen him leave already, and according to his sources, Fleetwood and his bride wouldn't return for two weeks. It was the opportune time to make his move.

Roderick threw open the door, surprising the butler, and stepped into the foyer without introduction. Ignoring the butler's offers of assistance, he strode purposefully down an immense hallway, following the hum of voices, and emerged into an open double doorway.

The instant a particular chubby lord spotted him, a curse of disbelief passed the man's pursed lips. The lady in his company turned to investigate and, in his opinion, gave a rather overly dramatic shriek of shock. There was a domino effect after that, as people turned in horror and scurried out of his path.

He was neither royalty nor a biblical figure, therefore, crowds parting for him was downright infuriating. One would think he'd killed someone.

Oh, right.

They did.

With complete distain, he pinned the vipers with a dark glare. He disliked his role as villain, but he'd learned he had no choice but to play along. At first, the grief at the loss of his father, and the subsequent rejection by the society he had been groomed to lead, had devastated him. His identity had been ripped from him by these very people. After a time, he'd learned to accept his fearsome reputation and actually found it *enjoyable*, liberating. Most of his childhood and teen years had been spent following the strict dictates that defined a perfect gentleman. And even now, after several years abroad, and despite his anxiety, he found he *enjoyed* the stunned expressions on his former peers, *enjoyed* being viewed as someone to be feared. It was a different, but very potent, power.

What had actually convinced him to come back to this?

Roderick knew the answer to that—his cousin, Matthew. Along with a healthy dose of curiosity and masochism. Independently, none were good, combined . . . well, they resulted in *this*.

His cousin's voice floated through his mind. *"Just make a good impression, Roderick."*

He scoffed. He hadn't worried about first impressions in ages. And he didn't really want to start now, but foiling Giles's plan depended upon it. There was no way he'd allow that man control of his fortune. Not when Giles was the one responsible for all the ills he had suffered since the day his father was murdered.

Roderick avoided eye contact with one of the more vicious gossips of the *ton*, whose face paled to a frightening white, and scanned the crowd. According to Matthew, the woman he was looking for was taller than most women and renowned for her poise. She always wore elbow-length gloves, and had astonishingly long, blond hair famously piled intricately atop her head. She was considered a paragon among the *ton*.

She, Matthew had insisted, was just what Roderick needed to prove he was not insane, but actually quite rational and fully competent to manage his title, despite years of absence from Society.

It also helped immensely that the woman in question, one Lady Caroline Bradley, was very conveniently his fiancée. Really, if he discounted Giles, he'd experienced a certain amount of luck of late.

He didn't trust it. At all.

Still, Roderick was relieved he didn't have to ferret out a suitable deb and attempt an undoubtedly nightmarish courtship. Much too much effort, especially when he had no intention of marrying the chit. He just needed an acceptable woman of Society to help clean up his reputation. How had Matthew worded it?

"You'll be considered sane by association."

He snorted. Yes, that sounded about right.

Moving deeper into the room, he used his height to advantage, peering over balding heads and sparkling turbans. However, he found it uncommonly difficult. Whenever his gaze settled on one person too long, the crowd would huddle close together, as if numbers would protect them. From what? According to one whispering woman, she feared a bloody killing spree.

Suddenly his confidence faltered. He had once moved among this group with pride, basking in their respect. He hated to admit that their behavior cut. Deeply.

Roderick bit back a frustrated sigh. He was a duke, damn it. How could he have been brought so low as to be forced to hide himself away in another *continent*? And, how could a piece of him still long to be part of this life? Roderick ran a hand through his inky locks, banishing the thoughts, and pierced a nearby gentleman with a sneer of contempt. *Where the bloody hell was this damn woman?*

Turning abruptly, he ignored the scattering vermin in favor of two pretty blondes moving about the outer wall of the room, their pace even and full of assurance, as if they had not a care in the world. Or an accused murderer in their midst. Instantly, he liked them. Even better, the taller of the two women...

Poise?

Check.

Gloves?

Check—Rick dimly realized the delicate lace was a bit...uh, stirring...

Copious blond locks?

Check. A double check for the sheer quantity of it. He

wondered how her neck—a rather long and graceful neck, primed for kisses—hadn't snapped under the weight.

A lazy smirk of satisfaction lifted the corners of his mouth. He'd found Lady Caroline. And if her backside was any indication, he'd at least have something pretty to look at while he kept her company.

If she allowed him to keep her company.

He anticipated one of three responses from his lovely bride-to-be. The first, but unfortunately the least likely of the scenarios, was that Lady Bradley would calmly agree to his proposal—instead of a monetary payout to him for breaking their betrothal, he'd take a few months of "happy" public courting. The second and far more likely situation would be the lady's refusal to help him in any way, shape, or form. However, with the contract in place, she would have a difficult time marrying another. The last, and most disagreeable and problematic option, involved a wailing, wilting flower, who refused to help him on principle, or–God forbid—obediently agreed to the marriage.

Roderick didn't like his odds for a peaceful outcome tonight.

He approached them in time to hear her laugh. It was surprisingly pleasant and carefree, not what he'd expected from a woman who was reportedly a slave to propriety. He'd assumed the woman would be a sourpuss, whose laugh—if she had one—would be contrived and shallow.

He only saw the slender curve of her back again, but up close, she was even more promising than from afar. He assessed her companion. He conceded the woman was just as lovely, but the light in her eyes, clearly displaying her mischievous nature, was not to his taste. Too trouble-some. Her hair was a shade darker, a more golden color, than his fiancée's light blonde. And when he met her gaze over her friend's shoulder, its golden hue reminded him of a cat. Her cheeks paled and her fingers tightened to a white-knuckle grip on her delicate blue fan. A soft snap reached his ears and he realized its delicate spines had cracked.

His reputation had preceded him. Again.

Halting steps from his quarry, he addressed her back, momentarily distracted by the long seam of tiny buttons trailing from her elegant neck to the pleasingly smooth curve of her rear. "Lady Caroline Bradley?"

She spun on her heel, her skirt ballooning with the rapid movement.

Beautiful.

He tensed, struck by the woman's appearance. Roderick thought his heart may have actually skipped a beat.

Green. Her eyes were a light shade of green. They widened at the sight of him, giving her an incredibly innocent air. Her face was narrow and nose slightly up-turned at the tip. Gently curved brows and smooth pink lips softened her striking features. White blond hair was artfully swept up in intricate braids and woven with small pearls and verdant ribbons. She held her tall, willowy form completely erect, the result, he knew, of years of strict schooling. Her subtle curves were outlined by the perfectly tailored, emerald-colored gown, its skirt slightly twisted from her spin. It brushed scandalously against his legs, so near he was to her. He leaned even closer, as if pulled by the clinging grasp of its soft fabric. She was heartbreakingly beautiful.

And disconcertingly familiar.

He felt his brow furrow as Lady Caroline's face began to rapidly pale. He'd met her before, at some point in their lives. He was certain of it. Roderick *never* forgot a face. Especially not one as striking as hers. But the question was—where? He'd visited many cities with friends and his father before his death. He'd visited an even wider array since leaving London. Nowhere in those recollections could he place her. She was also too young to have been out in Society before he left England.

An uncomfortable, nagging feeling that he was forgetting something very important gripped him. He realized what he felt was guilt. That same feeling he'd experienced every time his father had admonished him for not meeting obligations he'd made. And while Roderick no longer considered himself a gentleman, the thought that he had in some way failed this woman swamped him. He'd talked to her, once upon a time.

Who the hell was she?

Shaking himself of all these thoughts rattling about in his head, he managed to focus on the matter at hand— proving he wasn't insane.

"So *you* are my fiancé."

Confusion and frustration emerged as a growl that even he could hear in his voice. *So much for a good first impression.*

Gloved fingers rose to her lips, which had rounded to form a silent, shocked, "Oh." His heart clenched in sudden envy of that white lace. He found himself waiting, oddly breathless, for her response to his announcement. Since he'd arrived so unexpectedly, he'd anticipated possible reactions. She could pale or flinch.

She could cuss or scream. She could cut him or storm away. She could—

Faint.

He blinked. She could definitely faint, he mused, as the lithe woman crumpled to the floor at his feet in a pile of green silk.

Roderick cleared his throat. "Well, that was unexpected."

Truly, he knew his reputation was in tatters, but he hadn't thought it was *that* dastardly. Matthew had alluded to wild rumors about his behavior, but what on earth had people been saying about him while he had been in France?

Lady Bradley's companion gasped, dropped to her knees and began shaking her. "Caro!"

Roderick blinked, momentarily paralyzed by the scene.

He highly doubted someone who'd just fainted should be manhandled quite so roughly.

"Caroline!"

He turned at the panicked voice. A male version of Lady Caroline's friend dropped to the floor. He shot Rick a murderous glare before propping the fallen woman on his arm and joining the attempt to revive her. Roderick experienced two revelations. The first—her swoon did not bode well for Matthew's plan. While it was a good one, it hinged upon the female actually being conscious throughout his courtship.

The second, one he only reluctantly acknowledged, was that the chivalry instilled in him since childhood was not dead after all. Surprisingly, it roared to life and kicked him in the gut.

"Damnit," he grumbled.

Kneeling, he pushed the others aside and scooped her in his arms.

As if unfrozen from a magic spell, the elites burst into shocked titters and hushed whispers. His fiancée's friends gaped.

Ignoring them all, Roderick swept her from the room. He hadn't a clue where he was going, but he very much doubted any woman would want to wake to find herself fodder for the *ton*'s gossip mill.

Each step jostled Lady Caroline closer, pressing her form to his chest. He hated to admit it, but he was pleased by how well she fit against him. She smelt pleasantly of grass and sunshine, as if she'd spent the day in the park. Her hair, brushing his neck and jaw, was as soft as the finest down. Heat radiated from the slit of exposed skin at the top of her glove, seeming to burn his right hand. The silk gown slid sensually across his other palm, giving him a new appreciation for the stuff.

Suddenly aware of just what picture he was painting for the *ton*, he lengthened his stride, and held her tighter. He'd serve as a shield for her against Society, no matter how battered a shield he may be.

"Your Grace!"

Rick paused at the urgent whisper. He glanced back into the room to find his intended's companion racing to catch up to him. She assessed him briefly before nodding to herself, seeming to have made a decision.

"This way. There's a study."

Roderick grunted and followed.

The shorter woman led him into a neat little chamber whose walls were lined with gold-lettered, leather-bound books. He laid Lady Caroline gently on a couch and stepped back so her friend could tend her. His fiancée moaned.

The woman shot him a panicked expression, whispering furiously, "I think it best if you weren't here when she woke."

Roderick, seeing the wisdom in that assessment, nodded. "I'll wait outside. Please let me know when she is ready to talk."

"Of course," the woman muttered, already giving her friend her full attention. He hurriedly exited the room, literally bumping into his fiancée's male friend.

Seeing him now, Roderick realized just how young he was. His furious glare was little more than a puppy attempting to stare down his master. Roderick dismissed the lanky man, his attention turned to the real threat: yet another blond man, much older, who was taking confident, commanding strides in Roderick's direction.

The man barely dipped his head in acknowledgment when he arrived at the doors, "I am Alec St. Leon, Viscount Llywelyn. Is my charge in the study?"

Charge? Wasn't Lady Caroline a bit old for such treatment? She was hardly a greenling to Society at two and twenty. In fact, she was practically on the shelf. Weighing the significance of this information on his plans, he nodded. "Yes. A woman, whom I assume is your sister, is seeing to her."

The pup gave Roderick one more deadly glare and disappeared into the room, roughly pushing him aside. Roderick smirked at the silly attempt at intimidation, and thought he saw Lord Llywelyn's eyes roll. Another eerily similar male, this one around his own age, rushed from the direction of the drawing room. Exactly who were all these valiant guardians of his fiancée?

"Alec, where's Caroline?"

"Inside, with King and Thea. I must speak with Caro. I assume you can keep His Grace here entertained for a few moments, Gregory?"

A half-crazed look suddenly entered the suspicious eyes of the newcomer. "Of course. Just leave it to me."

Roderick had barely settled himself against the wall opposite the door Lord Llywelyn had snapped shut before he felt cold metal shoved painfully against his cheekbone. He blinked at the familiar barrel of a pistol and followed the arm holding it to stare into Gregory St. Leon's face.

His smile was dark. "Shall I test my newest model pistol on you, *Your Grace*?"

Roderick sighed. It was going to be a long wait.

Fall in Love with Forever Romance

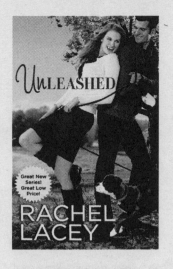

UNLEASHED
by Rachel Lacey

Cara has one rule: Don't get attached. It's served her well with the dogs she's fostered and the children she's nannied. But one smile from her sexy neighbor has her thinking some rules are made to be broken. Fans of Jill Shalvis will fall in love with this sassy, sexy debut!

MADE FOR YOU
by Lauren Layne

She's met her match...she just doesn't know it yet. Fans of Jennifer Probst and Rachel Van Dyken will fall head over heels for the second book in the Best Mistake series.

Fall in Love with Forever Romance

SCANDALOUS SUMMER NIGHTS
by Anne Barton

Fans of Tessa Dare, Julia Quinn, and Sarah MacLean will love this charming and wickedly witty new book in the Honeycote series about the passion—and peril—of falling in love with your brother's best friend.

HE'S NO PRINCE CHARMING
by Elle Daniels

A delightful retelling of the classic tale of *Beauty and the Beast* with a wonderful, sensual, and playful twist that fans of Elizabeth Hoyt won't want to miss!

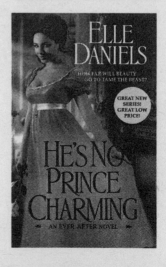

Fall in Love with Forever Romance

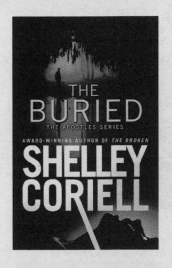

THE BURIED
by Shelley Coriell

"It's cold. And dark. I can't breathe."

Grace and "Hatch" thought they'd buried the past, but a killer on a grisly crime spree is about to unearth their deepest fears. Don't miss the next gripping thriller in the Apostles series.

SHOOTING SCARS
by Karina Halle

Ellie Watt has been kidnapped by her thuggish ex-boyfriend, leaving her current lover, Camden McQueen, to save the day. And there's nothing he won't do to rescue Ellie from this criminal and his entourage of killers in this fast-paced, sexy *USA Today* bestseller!

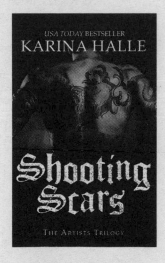

Fall in Love with Forever Romance

THE WICKED WAYS OF ALEXANDER KIDD
by Paula Quinn

The newest sinfully sexy Scottish romance in *New York Times* bestselling author Paula Quinn's Highland Heirs series, about the niece of a Highland chief who stows away on a pirate ship, desperate for adventure, and the pirate captain whose wicked ways inflame an irresistible desire...